Live to Ride

A Bicycle-Touring Novel

Bo Edwards

Pivo Publishing Corp.

What's brewing at the Pivo Pub?

Pivopub.com

Derek L. Jensen: *Mad Dogs and an Englishman*, 2007
Nonfiction.   An English cyclist gives a firsthand account of the historic Bikecentennial '76 bicycle tour across the United States, along with a tour through the Andes of South America and a ride from Vancouver to Anchorage by way of the Arctic Circle.

Bo Edwards: *Live to Ride*, 2008
A bicycle-touring novel.   Two American university students find romance, danger and much more on a bicycle tour in Great Britain one summer.

The Author Thanks...

(In no particular order) Helen & Derek • Jackie & Bill • Lorraine & Rob • Darlene & Dave • Terri, Doug & Kathryn • Patsy, Melissa, Heidi, Ephraim & Sasha • Shontell & Michael • Angela & family • Dinaz, Paula, Evedene, Charles, Jerry, Henry & Shirley, Bob, Pat and the rest of the AWN gang • The members, employees and benefactors of the International Youth Hostel Association and its affiliates.

In Memory Of...

Vince E. and Uncle Bob, two Puebloans who appreciated bicycles and witticisms. They left us way too soon.

Live to Ride

ISBN 978-0-9801345-0-6

What's brewing at the Pivo Pub? Find out at *http://www.pivopub.com/*.

ISBN: 978-0-9801345-0-6

9 780980 134506   90000

Pivo Publishing Corp.
Albany, OR, USA 97322-6372

Live to Ride

Table of Contents

Chapter I: *Prologue*

1.

E ric Fernandez and Roger Schmidt were training in the Wet Mountains of southern Colorado on their bicycles with an old friend of theirs from high school, George Fraser. Going east on State Highway 96 as they entered the Pueblo city limits, Eric led them into the intersection with State Highway 45. A teenage driver, under the influence of a caffé latte and a text message, made a sudden left turn in front of them. Roger and George avoided the collision, but Eric hit the front right fender of the car and sailed across the hood. He landed hard on the pavement, head first.

The English farmland looked like a patchwork quilt to the passengers in the airplane flying over it. Many of the passengers, among them Eric and Roger, were mesmerized by the view. It was not significantly different from the northeastern Colorado farmlands they had seen as they left Denver, except maybe the color. These two young Americans, like so many of the other passengers, were enjoying their first sight of Europe on a June afternoon. Eric thought about the bicycle crash of a year earlier while he looked out the airplane window.

"Are we there yet?"

"Not quite."

"Any crop circles down there?"

"None yet."

"Any mad cows?"

"Yes, and they're all mooing at us."

"Are we there now?"

Roger put down the crossword puzzle he had clipped from the previous Sunday's newspaper, and took in the view. Blackmore heroine, five letters, was one of the many clues that had him stumped. "Don't get discombobulated! We'll get there when we get there."

Jet lag, brief darkness during the flight, and cramped airplane seats all contributed to Eric and Roger's exhaustion, but the excitement of being in Europe for the first time kept them wide awake. They had seen only a few hours of darkness, mostly over the northeastern United States and neighboring Canada, during the thirteen-hour flight. The sky was nearly dark when the plane landed in Chicago for a brief layover. All they could see of the Great Lakes from above were some lights along the shorelines. Off-schedule meals worsened the jet lag. Upright airline seats prevented everyone, except a few small children, from sleeping comfortably.

Roger composed himself as the plane prepared to land at Heathrow Airport in southwestern London. "You look like hell, Chief." He wondered silently whether Eric was up to a long bicycle tour, even though he was in excellent shape.

"I feel like it, too. Pressure changes, lack of sleep..." Eric was disoriented and numb from the rapid altitude changes and deceleration of the plane. He had his doubts, too.

As they disembarked into Heathrow and proceeded onto the customs inspection area, Roger and Eric were still stunned by the atmosphere of Europe. It looked, sounded and smelled about the same as any other big-city airport, but somehow it just *felt* different. After clearing customs, they went to the luggage retrieval area to fetch sleeping bags, foam mattresses, panniers and the crates containing their disassembled bicycles. They already possessed their handlebar bags, which they had carried with them on the plane.

Roger did a double take as they walked past an eatery along the concourse. "Say! Wasn't that Jimi sitting there?"

"You mean the guy in the tie-dyed t-shirt, eating nachos with Sid Vicious?"

"Sid Vicious? I could've sworn that was Jerry Garcia!"

They continued walking.

"Whatever," Eric said. "My left eye is cloudy, and my right eye is out of focus."

"You know what's wrong with our generation? We don't have any *real* pop music legends."

"Like Jimi and Jerry and Sid?"

"Exactly! The idols of the Baby Boomers will still be famous long after ours have been forgotten."

"Dead celebrity sightings are so yesterday! Seen one, seen 'em all. Can't we come up with something original?"

"We could make a political statement, and pretend it's original."

"On second thought, let's stick with the dead celebrities. Even if they are a bit long in the tooth."

Eric brushed by someone who, at a glance, appeared to be talking to herself while she walked toward him. He had to look twice to notice the inconspicuous telephone headset she was wearing. "Did you bring your cell phone? Peter asked us to call him from the airport so he could estimate how long it would take us to get across London on the subway."

"What cell phone?"

"You don't have one either? I thought I was the last of our generation without his own cell phone."

"I plan to get one when I graduate, when I can afford it."

2

"I've been thinking along those lines too. I don't do enough talking to justify the expense of one right now. Would be nice to have sometimes, though."

"I wouldn't have brought it here even if I did have one. Too many things to carry on a bike, and we won't always have access to electricity."

Eric and Roger followed the signs to the Underground station. A ticket agent told them which train to ride, and pointed them to the correct platform. She was about their age, but she obviously had plenty of experience directing foreigners onto the Tube. They rode the blue Piccadilly Line eastward to South Kensington, then changed to the green District Line to Dagenham East. Trying not to interfere with anyone getting on or off, they put their bicycle crates in the aisle at the end of the last rail car. The other passengers represented a broad swath of humanity, including Asians and Africans as well as Europeans. They stopped in more than forty stations before they got off the train. A few of the station names sounded like places they had heard of, but most meant nothing to them. Away from central London, the train went above ground and gave them a view of urban England. Hundreds of people entered or left their car during the ride.

Only a few people remained in their car when the train stopped at Dagenham East. As they were gathering their equipment and stepping onto the platform, a friendly looking couple approached the train. The bespectacled man extended his hand and welcomed them in a thick cockney accent.

"'ello, lads! It's so good to see you both again!" He shook hands with them. "Welcome to England."

"A pleasure to see you again, too," Roger beamed.

Eric's appearance had already improved since the airport. "Peter, how have you been?"

The woman added an enthusiastic, "'ello!"

The man was Peter Evans, whom Eric and Roger had met on a group bicycle tour through the Rocky Mountains two summers earlier. Their plan this time was to tour the British Isles by bicycle, with Peter as their companion and guide. Peter introduced them to his wife, Inga, whom they had not met previously. Inga's smile and charm were overwhelming, and they could not have felt more welcome.

A cool, light rain began to fall as they loaded the bicycle crates on top of the Evans' car and the luggage inside. The two Americans both noticed the cool, humid climate, in contrast to the dry heat they had just left in Denver. Neither mentioned it. They both despised trivial weather discussions. London time was about 18:00 when the four started toward the Evans' home in Romford, Essex, on the eastern edge of greater London.

Peter and Inga, in their mid-thirties, were half a generation older than Roger and Eric. Peter was tall like Eric, and had the disproportionate build of an avid cyclist. A large bald spot radiated from the crown of reddish-brown hair on his head. His rough hands hinted that his work involved using wrenches more than shuffling papers. He was an equipment mechanic at a London factory. He had a gleam in his eye and a firm handshake that complemented his friendly demeanor very well. Inga was not as tall and slender as her husband, but her delightful countenance was easily a match for Peter's. Her blonde, wavy hair hung below her shoulders. A teacher, she wore a navy blue sweater, slacks and sensible shoes. Her own cockney accent, affected by the excitement of the moment, had a sing-song quality to it.

"You live a long way from the airport," Roger said. "London is even bigger than I'd imagined it would be."

"Quite a ways, yes," Inga said. "There's plenty more if you keep going east from here."

On the way to the Evans' house, Roger and Eric kept their attention toward the windows. Neither seemed to be able to take in enough of what they could see. They repeatedly asked Inga to identify things. She was pleased to see them so enthusiastic, despite their exhaustion. Peter stopped for petrol, and the Americans were surprised by the comparatively high price of it. That Peter thought nothing of paying so much for the gasoline to give them a ride further impressed upon them the generosity of the Evans.

Just outside of Romford, Peter stopped again at a small cluster of businesses. Eric and Roger followed him into a fish bar, where Peter purchased a takeout dinner. The aroma of fried fish was intoxicating to Roger when he was famished, as he was now. The strong scent even registered slightly with Eric's nearly dead sense of smell. The menu board had a number of things the Americans had never tasted, including donner kebabs and kidney pie.

The Evans' house was the end unit of a row of connected houses, just off the A12 highway and Ayr Way, between Rise Park and Bedfords Park. It looked like an apartment complex, but each resident owned her or his own section of the long building. The two-story house was compact, but very comfortable. The Evans knew how to use their limited space efficiently. Inga set the table and served the fish while Peter introduced their daughter Victoria to Eric and Roger.

"Vickie!" She clarifed her father's introduction of her. A pretty and somewhat precocious ten-year-old, Vickie had only a slight facial resemblance to her parents. Her mannerisms were very much like theirs, though, and she definitely had that Evans quality, that *je ne sais quoi.*

"Named for the queen, no doubt?" Roger said.

"Or the capital of British Columbia, maybe," Eric suggested.

"I thought we named you for that lake in Africa," Peter said. "Or was it the waterfall?"

"My grandmother, Victoria," Vickie insisted. "Right, Mum?"

Vickie had already eaten, but she sat at the table and told Roger and Eric about the British association football scene in great depth. Inga did not serve any beverage with the meal, and the Evans did not appear to think anything of it. Roger was trying to think of a polite, tactful way of asking for a glass of water.

"May I have a glass of water, please?" To hell with foreign protocol, Roger thought.

"Of course you may." Peter rose to go to the kitchen. "You too, Eric?"

"Yes, please."

"We forgot that Americans like a glass of water with their meals," Inga said. "I recall Peter telling about a stop he made in the mountains of Idaho two years ago. He had been in a chilling rain all day, and when he stopped in a little restaurant for lunch, the waitress brought him a glass of ice water without his even asking for it."

"What I really needed was a pot of hot coffee," Peter said when he entered the dining room. "I learned that Americans serve ice water in restaurants, no matter what."

The fried fish was delicious, but Eric was puzzled when he asked Peter what kind of fish it was. Eric thought he heard Peter say it was rock eel, but Eric was expecting some sort of cod. Eric realized that he was indeed eating an eel when he discovered the long spine inside the eel.

"My first eel," Roger said. "It tastes a lot better than a live one looks in the aquarium at the pet store."

"You should be careful what kind of seasoning you use on this. Thyme wounds all eels, you know," Eric said.

"I con-ger with that."

"But seriously, it reminds me of one of my grandmother's favorite songs, that one where Dean Martin identified an eel."

"What song is that?"

"*That's a Moray.*"

"I should've seen that one coming."

"You two are in for plenty of firsts and surprises," Inga said. "Haven't been out of America much, have you?"

"Not at all," Roger said.

"I've been to British Columbia a few times, and Mexico once," Eric said, "but never very far from the U.S. border."

"I have some good news and some bad news for you both," Peter announced. "I won't be able to accompany you on your tour. I had some

5

vacation time set aside, but one of the chaps who does my job when I'm on holiday retired three months earlier than he had said he would, and the other went in for open-heart surgery last week. I'm still training the apprentice for the retiree's old job."

"Sorry you can't join us then, and also about your friend with the bad heart," Roger said. "What's the good news?"

"That was the bad news, I hope," Eric said.

"That was the bad news, for me, anyway," Peter said. "The good news for you is that you will have to find the best parts of Great Britain all by yourselves."

"We'll miss having you with us to make a race out of it," Roger said. "I was looking forward to a rematch."

"I was too, but I'm quite confident in your abilities to find plenty of mischief to keep yourselves occupied for the next six weeks," Peter teased. "Plenty of young ladies, pubs, and wild scenery to satisfy your appetites for adventure."

"We came to look at museums!" Eric said. "The truth is, I'm sorry to hear you won't be available to guide us away from temptation."

"As you mentioned racing, I have some more good news," Peter added. "I took the liberty of entering both of you and me in some races this week. Are you game?"

"Not the Tour of Britain, or anything like that?"

"No, nothing like that," Peter paused. "I entered you in the Dauphiné Libéré." He said it with a straight face, and waited for a reaction from the Americans. "I'm joking, of course. I entered us in a criterium and a time trial. Expect about one hour of racing time in the criterium, and about half an hour in the time trial. All the competitors will be locals. Some of them are members of my club."

"I think we can handle that," Eric said.

Roger nodded, and he was pleased to hear Eric project that kind of confidence in himself.

"We do have a day set aside to show you around London," Inga said. "Would you like to see the landmarks in central London this week?"

"Definitely! That's why we're here."

Inga served a delicious hot apple crisp with a custard topping for dessert that she had prepared earlier in the day. Eric and Roger ate cautiously, observing the etiquette of their hosts. Roger, who would usually initiate and lead a mealtime conversation, held his tongue so that he would not come across as boorish. Eric also sat quietly, but that was normal for him.

After supper, everyone retired to the parlor to discuss Roger and Eric's journey and their family members. Roger's older brother Walter and one of Walter's friends had also been on the ride where they met Peter.

"How is your brother getting along, Roger," Peter asked, "and your two friends, George and Scott?"

"Walt finished his degree, got married and took a job with an electronics firm in Albuquerque, New Mexico, more than a year ago," Roger said. "He wanted to come with us, but he doesn't have much vacation time now. They took a nice honeymoon trip to Hawaii, so I don't feel too sorry for him not coming here."

"George would've come, but he was offered some high-level internship this summer at a research institute," Eric said. "He'll probably go on to graduate school. Smart, smart guy."

"I haven't seen much of Scotty since our ride with you, Peter," Roger continued. "He does some track racing, Walt tells me. They talk to each other every once in a while. I think he lives in Colorado Springs or Denver these days."

Inga poured a second cup of tea for everyone. The Evans drank their tea with whole milk and sugar, in typical British fashion, but the Americans drank it black, never having considered putting milk in tea. Vickie commented on their strange American tea-drinking habits. They were just beginning to discover the many dissimilarities between themselves and the British people.

"We brought you a book about the history of Colorado." Eric carefully removed the cellophane-wrapped book from the box containing his panniers.

"It has lots of full-color photos," Roger added. "You two can see some of the mountains we dragged Peter over."

"I certainly liked what I saw in your state," Peter said. "That pass we went over, across the Continental Divide, is still the highest I've ever been on a bicycle."

"Hoosier Pass?"

"Aye, that's the one."

"I've always visualized Colorado cities as looking like the sets in western movies and television shows," Inga said. "You know, places with Indians and cowboys and wooden sidewalks and dusty streets. I've never traveled out of Western Europe."

"A few towns in Colorado and the neighboring states actually do look like that," Roger said. "But very few."

Inga was pleased to learn that. The two Americans would soon learn that many other Europeans shared her misconceptions of modern Colorado and the other western states. Their hometown bore little resemblance to the setting of Louis L'Amour's *Milo Talon* at present, if it ever did.

Peter showed Roger and Eric to their bedroom in the upper level of the house. There were three bedrooms and a bathroom upstairs, and they were shown to the extra bedroom that the Evans used for storage. Peter had set up a cot next to the single bed, as the bed was only large enough for one person. They carried their luggage into their room, and Roger arranged his foam pad and sleeping bag on the cot. Their bicycle crates were in the garage behind the house. The absence of screens on the bedroom windows, flying insects and summer breeze seemed peculiar to them. Roger volunteered to sleep on the cot, because he could tell that Eric was more affected by jet lag than he was, and because Eric was taller.

Eric pondered his readiness for the long journey ahead. He fell asleep quickly, but Roger lay awake for nearly an hour. The tea and the excitement of being in Europe kept his mind buzzing. Not only were they in Europe for the first time in their lives, they were also about to begin a six-week vacation and bicycle tour unlike any they had ever taken. They were in the transition between adolescence and adulthood, and they wanted to make it one to remember with a trip to Europe. Already, Roger had much to say about Europe, especially to his fiancée, Marianne.

Marianne thought about Roger, too, as she reclined in first-class seating on a flight from Denver to her home in Honolulu. A glass of wine helped her relax, but not nearly enough. Roger had given her a ride to the airport a day before his flight to London. They exchanged a passionate good-bye kiss before she went through the airport security checkpoint. She would miss him for the six weeks he would be gone, but she hoped that would give her enough time to do what she had to do. Two of the biggest events in her life were coming up fast, and she barely had a clue what she was going to do about them.

A flight attendant cleared her tray table. "Can I get you anything else?"

"Another glass of white wine, please," Marianne said.

Chapter II: *Two Days at the Races*

2.

Peter awakened Eric and Roger in the morning with a cup of black tea and a digestive cracker for each of them. They were, once again, pleasantly surprised by the hospitality they were receiving. Neither was in the habit of being served in bed. They slowly roused themselves out of their beds, got dressed, and finished their eye-openers. Eric looked much livelier than he did the previous day.

Roger appeared to be only half awake as he lumbered down the stairs. This morning was no exception to his usual activity. His hair was not noticeably combed, his shoes were untied, and his eyes had a vacant look in them. When he arrived in the dining room, he exchanged a "good morning" with Inga and Vickie, and sank into the nearest chair.

Meanwhile, in the bathroom upstairs, Eric examined his face in the mirror. He had stopped shaving more than two months earlier. His beard was darker than Roger's, but not quite as uniform. He ran a comb through his nearly black hair. He opened his mouth underneath the cold water faucet, got a mouthful of water, and swallowed it with a Dilantin anticonvulsant capsule.

Even as Eric swallowed the capsule, he felt a surge of pain in his head and eyes, and a touch of vertigo. These painful, throbbing sensations were often accompanied by tremors throughout his body, especially in his jaw, hands and brow. Involuntary squinting, jaw-clenching and biting his tongue or cheek gums had become normal occurrences to him. The occasional, unintentional spoonerisms that marked his speech had become more frequent, and he had developed a slight stutter. He was conscious of all these symptoms of epilepsy. They had become a way of life for him ever since he had crashed on his bicycle in the training accident the previous August.

An ambulance delivered Eric to a local hospital, where he regained consciousness the next day. His bicycle needed a new front wheel. Eric was due for a week of hospitalization with a fractured skull, a concussion, a hearing loss, and massive road rash. He was restricted from riding his bicycle or driving a car for three weeks after his discharge.

Eric felt nearly normal when he returned to the University of Washington in September, except for some dizzy spells. A physician at the student health center examined him, found nothing wrong, and diagnosed him as a hypochondriac in so many words. Eric felt like a fool for his concern, so he ignored the recurring symptoms and went about his economic studies and extracurricular activities with abandon.

A grand mal seizure, or tonic-clonic in medical jargon, felled Eric in early November, and he suffered three more before that same physician examined him again. She tested him by electroencephalography, computerized axial tomography, and head x-rays. Ruling out the possibility of a brain tumor, she found evidence of scar tissue in his brain and diagnosed him as epileptic. Her examination, the prescribed treatment, and especially the disorder itself were all very harsh for him. The initial medicine made him listless and lethargic all day long. He had lost his senses of taste and smell. He was forced to withdraw from two of his required classes and curtail most of his extracurricular activities. He saw his career collapsing before it ever had a chance to begin, and he expected to be in college at least one more term than he had originally planned—if he could even stay in college.

As he was gradually learning to live with his limitations, Eric was also busy trying to rebuild himself during the winter and spring. His younger sister Mimi, then a senior in high school, wrote and called him regularly, encouraging him to keep at it. He credited her with saving him from dropping out of college, even though his grades had declined. With Mimi's help, and that of their older sister Marcia, he regained his confidence and felt secure enough to stay in school. He dated occasionally, but he did not have any steady girlfriends. He rode his bicycle as much as his busy schedule permitted.

In March, Roger and George proposed a bicycle tour of Europe. Eric's parents offered to buy him an airline ticket if he would pay for the rest of the vacation himself. Eric had enough money in his savings account from the previous summer's labor, and he was feeling reasonably fit, but he was less than certain he could do it. Mimi advised him to do his best in school, then spend the few weeks of summer prior to the proposed date of departure in June training and working. He took her advice and, as he thought back on it, was fortunate to have a sister who was so foresighted.

George received a lucrative summer job offer in late April that he could not refuse, so he balked at the European tour. Roger's parents paid for his round-trip ticket, and he and Eric decided on a six-week bicycle tour, starting and ending at Heathrow Airport, from late June to early August. Eric was able to pass all his subjects that semester, with tremendous effort, and he felt well prepared when they embarked on their tour.

Eric ignored the headache, knowing it would soon go away. He thought about Mimi and all the things he already wanted to tell her about Europe as he walked down the stairs and into the dining area. He would be writing a postcard to her, their older sister and their parents in the next few days to let them know that everything was all right so far. He would send them e-mail, too, from the Evans' computer just as soon as he could.

Over breakfast, Peter and the two Americans discussed the preliminaries of the tour. Peter explained the International Youth Hostel system, and recommended it to them. They were both in need of riding gloves and some other miscellaneous equipment, and they needed to convert their American traveler's checks, in dollars, to British traveler's cheques, in pounds. Roger wanted to visit a frame builder near Romford that Peter had mentioned to him in correspondence in the spring. Roger was convinced he could not go to Europe and return home without a custom-built bicycle frame for himself. In short, they needed to familiarize themselves with the United Kingdom. But before they could do any of these things, they needed to assemble their bicycles.

"Give me a shout if you need anything," Peter told them on the back porch.

"We came well equipped," Roger answered. "You can never carry too many tools."

"I hope we don't need most of them when we're on the road," Eric added.

Eric and Roger removed their Novara and Trek, respectively, from their crates and began assembly with the set of tools they were sharing. Each had provided and carried about half of the tools so that, together, they could make most any minor repair and many major ones as well. They were equipped to remove and replace virtually any part on their bicycles, with the exception of their headsets and bottom brackets. They had no reason to anticipate problems there. Roger was a bit preoccupied as he thought about the adventure they were planning during the next six weeks. Eric hummed a tune as they attached wheels, crank arms, chains, chain rings, rear derailleurs, handlebars, seat posts and luggage racks to their bicycle frames.

"Hand me that pedal wrench, please."

"Trade you for the hex keys."

Roger was 21 years young, and a few centimeters shorter than Eric. His hair, skin and beard were at least one shade of brown lighter than those of Eric. Roger was very outspoken and assertive and sometimes overly zealous about arguing trivial subjects, but he could initiate and maintain a conversation almost effortlessly with friends and strangers alike. Eric, like many of Roger's other friends, was quite envious of the latter characteristic. If Roger wanted to become friendly with an attractive woman at a social gathering, he could and did so without hesitation, and quite often, with great success. Roger's weathered face was not as striking as Eric's handsome, boyish features—one of the many reasons Roger kept a beard—but his

11

charming wit, impeccable manners and good-natured demeanor more than made up for any shortcomings in beauty. Except for his unruly hair, Roger always looked presentable. He usually attired his lean, athletic body in fashionable outdoor clothing.

"What's with you lately, Squire?" Eric tightened his pedals into the crank arms. "You've been very moody for someone who has everything going for him. Big vacation, graduating and getting married in a year."

Roger was reluctant to answer. It was a question he knew someone would ask, sooner or later. "Things aren't entirely good." He tightened the derailleur bolt very carefully before he continued. "I haven't told anyone, but I'm having serious doubts about the engagement."

"Really? Dare I ask why?" Eric was mildly surprised. "Not that it's any of my business."

"We're in love, I'm sure of that. The trouble is, I think we might be in love for the wrong reasons."

"That sounds corny enough. What wrong reasons?"

"It probably does sound very corny," Roger said, "but her family is filthy rich, and I sometimes think in terms of how much money I'm marrying."

"Money is a good thing to have these days. Besides, an aristocrat is as easy to love as a peasant, as they say. Are you saying you love the dowry more than the bride?"

"Maybe, quite possibly," Roger continued. "What's more is that she hasn't quite outgrown her teenage rebelliousness. I think her attraction to me has something to do with her need to defy her family, show them how independent she is. They probably want her to marry someone from their own social standing. An engineering student from a middle-class family is marginal, but a medical student from a wealthy family would be much better in their eyes, I'm guessing."

"Have they told you this, or are you jumping to conclusions?" Eric inserted his seat post into the frame, estimated a comfortable height, and tightened the bolt in the seat tube. "Have you even met them, her parents, I mean?"

"No, I haven't met them." Roger lifted his chain with a paper towel, then hooked the chain over two teeth in his larger chain ring. He turned the crank forward while lifting the rear wheel, to get the chain fully on the chain ring. "A few months ago, her dad was in Denver on a business trip. I think I told you some time ago they live in Honolulu, and he's on the board of directors of several large companies. This was shortly after we announced our engagement, and you'd think he'd want to meet his future son-in-law."

"Didn't he invite you to have dinner with him?" Eric sat on his saddle while balancing against the wall of the garage. A little too low, he decided.

He loosened the bolt, raised the saddle about a few millimeters, and tried it again.

"Maybe he did, but Marianne didn't tell me about his visit until after he left. She had some vague reason why she didn't arrange a meeting between her dad and me. It didn't have to be a dinner or anything formal. Just a brief introduction at the airport would've been adequate. I think she met him somewhere for dinner and told him I couldn't make it, so she wouldn't have to introduce me to him. I've introduced her to everyone in my immediate family, plus a few other relatives."

"It does sound a little strange, but you still might be assuming too much."

"I did meet her older brother's wife shortly before the engagement as she was passing through Denver," Roger continued. "Older brother's a junior executive in one of dad's companies, just a few years out of college. Sister-in-law's a real society woman in southern California, and she makes no secret of how much she likes to spend the family fortune on herself. I have nothing against people like that, I really don't, but the truth is, I'm not sure I want to be one of them. I'm *not* one of them."

"Get a grip, Squire! Money burns a hole in your pocket. Always has. Since when does the potential for great wealth make Roger Schmidt nervous?"

"I knew this would sound preposterous if I tried to put it into words. I just have this sneaky feeling, intuition or whatever, that something is amiss."

"Is she pregnant? Is there a little Roger on the way?"

"No, it's nothing like that." Roger inserted the stem into the headset and aligned the handlebar. "She's not pregnant. The root of the problem lies elsewhere."

"You would know better than anyone else. What's Marianne doing now? Are you planning a trip to Hawaii later on?"

"She went to Hawaii for a while, but she has a summer job at a bank in Denver. I haven't exactly been invited to Hawaii yet, and my travel budget is spent for at least a year with our journey here. I should admit, though, that Marianne encouraged me to come here. It wouldn't have taken much arm-twisting on her part to have gotten me to go with her to Hawaii instead of Europe with you, as you can imagine."

"I know she's good-looking because I've seen your pictures of her." Eric was satisfied with the height of his saddle. He dismounted, and tightened the seatpost bolt with a hex key. "She's smart, her family's got *beaucoup* bucks, and she lets you go to Europe with your friend when you could be sunning at Waikiki with her, and you want to let it all go because of some silly intuition. It's your future, so don't let me or anyone else make that big decision for you."

Like Eric, Roger had spent his first few weeks of summer working and training. He worked as an engineering laboratory assistant at the University of Colorado, for the benefit of graduate students who were preparing their dissertations. During the summer term, he performed mechanical testing and finite-element analyses, mostly for a postdoctoral fellow from Iran. He had earned nearly two thousand dollars from that and other jobs, and he felt well prepared for the journey in terms of money. He updated his equipment by buying new tires, cables and brake pads. He spent many of his off-hours riding in the foothills of northern Colorado, where he knew of several steep canyon highways in which he could condition himself. He spent evenings and weekends with Marianne Murakami, a debutante, sorority sister and student at the University of Denver. She had little regard for cycling, but they read the same kinds of literature, laughed at the same jokes, liked dancing together and enjoyed one another's company.

Peter guided Roger and Eric through Romford on his custom-built bicycle. The Americans were very disoriented by riding on the left side of the street. The sights of suburban London diverted their attention from the traffic on their drive from the railway station the previous evening, but this situation required their full attention. The drizzle, narrow roads, dense traffic and absence of stop signs increased their awkwardness. They both immediately noticed the smooth pavement, distinct lane-dividing stripes, broad shoulders, and good drainage characteristics of British roadways. They were dumbfounded as they followed Peter into their first roundabout, a traffic control device, not knowing what to expect around the bend.

"You should have stopped at that last intersection," Peter cautioned Eric. Peter pointed out the broken white stripes that represented stop signs, which appeared to be nothing more than crosswalks to the Americans. "I'm sorry I didn't tell you that earlier."

"I'll stop twice at the next one."

The first stop of the morning was at a local branch of Lloyd's Bank, one of the major banks in the U.K. Eric and Roger exchanged their traveler's cheques in American dollars for the same in British pounds. The bank seemed archaic to them, as the tellers worked behind thick glass windows in a room that was separate from where the customers stood, and moved currency and documents through a shallow depression in the counter at the base of the window. It was quite a contrast from the typical American bank where tellers and customers were separated only by a chest-high counter. The tellers also seemed somewhat reserved, in comparison to the smile-and-kind-word, "Have a nice day!" manner of most American bank employees.

A local bicycle dealer, where Peter bought tires and tubes and other incidental items, was the next stop. Roger and Eric looked at garments but did not find any to their liking. They each bought a Union Jack appliqué to sew on their handlebar bags. They were both looking for long-sleeve, Italian-made jerseys and leather riding gloves. Eric wanted two chamois-lined shorts. The few jerseys and shorts in this store were too similar to what the Americans could buy at home. Peter exchanged small talk with the employees, who knew him on a first-name basis, and then the trio left.

Peter again led the way, this time to a frame builder in an industrial district on the eastern edge of London proper. The two Americans were still having difficulty with the concept of riding in the wrong direction. Eric noticed, in many neighborhoods, that the motorists not only drove on the wrong side, but that many of the streets were concrete and the sidewalks asphalt. A truck driver carelessly backed his lorry into the street in front of Roger, and he went down in his attempt to avoid a collision.

"You all right?" Eric stopped to help Roger get up. Peter was ten or twenty meters ahead and had not noticed the incident.

"I'll live, but that bastard didn't even notice what happened." Roger was referring to the truck driver. His expression showed his frustration with negotiating British traffic. His Trek was uninjured, and he and Eric resumed riding. Peter had slowed and they soon caught up with him.

"Do those *Give Way* signs mean yield to oncoming traffic," Roger asked, "or do they mean for motorists to give way to their urge to bag as many cyclists as possible?"

"I'd say that British motorists are at least as aggressive and impatient as most American drivers," Eric said.

"We have every kind here," Peter agreed. "Always keep your eyes peeled in traffic. Some of the drivers make our drunken football fans seem like gentlemen."

The frame builder's workshop was little more than a one-car garage. The frame builder, a gray-haired, bespectacled man in his late 50s named Henry Smythe, seemed a little reserved about building a frame for an American customer. Like the bicycle dealer's employees, he and Peter knew each other by name. Smythe's shop was adorned with examples of his handiwork, including a tandem and several racing frames. His tools were modest in terms of quantity and modernity, but all were well maintained and of high quality. An oxyacetylene torch and several jigs and vises were among his collection of tools, parts and scraps. The shop appeared to be cluttered to Roger and Eric, but Smythe seemed to know the whereabouts of everything important.

Mr. Smythe did not label his finished, painted frames with his own name. Rather, he used an Italian name, which he explained was his mother-in-law's maiden name and sounded more exotic than Smythe for a great bicycle frame. Smythe had his own copyrighted logo and bottom bracket design, and his name appeared in fine print on the logo decals he used. His frames were painted by a nearby subcontractor.

Smythe eyed Roger and Eric carefully, as if unsure how far he should trust them. His demeanor was gruff at first. "Americans, are you? I think that's what Peter said."

"Yes. We met Peter on a bicycle tour in the western United States two years ago."

"I'll write up a contract when we decide how you want your frame to be. I expect half down, and the other half is due when the frame is complete. I prefer cash, but I'll accept a cheque if it's drawn on a local bank."

"I left my checkbook at home. I'll pay cash."

Smythe still seemed cautious, but he warmed up a little. He pulled out some manufacturer's literature and a thick 3-ring binder of his own making. The binder contained photographs of frames he had built, along with engineering drawings and detailed specifications for every aspect of frame design and construction. His frames had a "retro" look about them, as he preferred brazed lug joints to the more common butt welds used in most of the mass-produced frames. He showed the two Americans the advantages and disadvantages of titanium, aluminum and carbon fiber frames, and explained why he thought alloy steel from Europe's two largest tubing manufacturers was still the best value in frame construction. He even had some kind remarks for Roger's Trek frame, although he considered it inferior to his own.

Eric studied a framed photograph hanging on the wall of a racing team posing with a bicycle. "Did you build this one for this team?"

"Actually, I've built several for that team, including the one in the picture. That's the Lenoir-Whitcombe team. Lenoir is a French company, and Whitcombe is here in London. They've been jointly sponsoring a team for years."

"I've never heard of them. Any big-name racers?"

"They're pretty well known locally, but certainly not outside Europe. They compete in the Tour of Britain, Tour of Ireland, things like that. Mostly pro-am and the lesser-known professional races. A few have moved up to the teams that enter the Tour de France and the other big stage races."

Roger took a look at the photograph. "Sort of a farm team for the big leagues, then?"

"Yes, I suppose you could say that. Anyway, they've been some of my best word-of-mouth salesmen. I'm always proud to see one of them winning something on one of my creations."

Peter went back home to prepare for work while Smythe and Roger discussed the frame to be built. Peter was sure his guests could find their way back, since his home was only a few kilometers from Smythe's shop.

Eric rode to a nearby Chinese takeout restaurant and brought back lunch for himself and Roger. They returned to the Evans' home in the early afternoon after Smythe and Roger agreed upon the dimensions, materials, joining processes, brazed-on accessories, color and price of Roger's frame-to-be.

"I hope I'm doing the right thing here," Roger said while they rode back to Romford. "Mr. Smythe looked us over as if he was identifying a suspect in a police line-up."

"We're foreigners, remember. He probably wants to be sure he isn't going to get stuck with a custom frame that he can't sell, in case you decide to return to America without it."

"Probably so. But keep in mind, I'm risking more than 200 pounds myself. Not exactly small change for me."

"You still have time to back out of it."

Eric noted that Roger seemed unsure about many things these days, which was quite unusual for Roger. They continued riding, and found the Evans' house after only a few wrong turns. Long, straight streets were rare in England. Every street had at least one big curve, and changed names every few blocks.

"Have you decided where you want to go, dear?" Inga addressed nearly everyone as "dear."

"We're still working on it," Roger said, "but it looks like we'll be heading north from here."

"Everything will be new to us no matter where we go." Eric was looking at the titles in a bookcase in the Evans' parlor. A copy of *Tom Jones* was lying on top, and had a bookmark in its center. He opened the book to read the inside flaps of the dust jacket. "Are you reading this one?"

"Yes, I try to read a classic every once in a while," Inga said. "It's taken me two months to get that far. I'll be reading a little faster once the summer is in full swing."

"It's not unusual," Roger quipped, "to read Fielding's novel, I mean."

"I'll try to remember that."

"Fantastic!"

Eric thought a moment about what Roger had just said, then furrowed his brow. "We are not amused!" He continued his conversation with Inga. "Peter mentioned that you're a teacher at a school near here."

"I'm a kindergarten teacher," Inga explained. "It keeps me busy and I love being around the little ones."

"I've seen some students in uniforms at the bus stops," Eric said. "Aren't they on summer vacation yet?"

"They're in school until the end of June. We had about three weeks off at Easter." Inga went about her work. "Peter had so much to say about

17

Colorado when he returned from there. Tell me your version of how you met him."

Three years earlier, Peter had signed up for a two-week group tour of Wyoming and Colorado that mostly followed the TransAmerica Trail. He flew to Salt Lake City and rode from there to the start of the tour in Yellowstone National Park. Eric, George, Roger, Roger's older brother Walter, and a friend of Walter had taken their bicycles by bus to Yellowstone for the same tour. The five Americans noticed the gregarious Englishman a day or two into the ride and struck up a friendship with him. From there, the ride became a six-way race through the Rocky Mountains, as the Englishman and the Americans were all determined to demonstrate the superiority of their nationality. The contest ended in a draw, as the Americans returned home to Pueblo. Before parting, Peter gave each of them a standing invitation to tour Europe with him. Peter had made many acquaintances on his previous tours of the British Isles and the European mainland, but these Americans were the first who could maintain his pace day after day. He was intrigued by the prospect of touring with them again sometime. Peter stayed two days with his newfound friends in Pueblo, before he rode to Denver and flew home from there.

Inga prepared a delicious supper that evening, a casserole she called *toad in a hole*. Peter took his guests to Eastway Cycle Circuit in East London afterward. They were quite impressed with Eastway, a small park intended exclusively as a criterium course, complete with locker rooms, grandstands, a concession and a well designed 1.6-km course. The park also had some mountain bike trails outside the paved loop. The pavement was in good shape, and the course had several interesting curves and hills. The starting line was very wide, to accommodate a large field of racers. The grounds were nicely kept, with plenty of trees and grass, and there was a pedestrian tunnel beneath the track for spectators to walk into the center of the loop without interfering with the racers. Peter mentioned that Eastway, built in the 1970s, is the only criterium course of its kind in the United Kingdom. They rode their bicycles around the track several times, and then put their bicycles back into Peter's car as dusk fell.

Peter had arranged beforehand for them to enter an informal race. "This is where we'll be racing on Sunday afternoon," he said on the drive back to Romford. "It's nothing big, but the competition should be stiff enough to get you going."

3.

Peter parked his Triumph beside Saint James's Park, and he, Inga, Eric and Roger walked through the park toward a courtyard where a throng was converging. They were some 25 kilometers from Romford. Peter's employer was nearby, and Peter rode that distance on his bicycle to and from work four days a week. The two Americans knew they had seen only a small section of greater London along that distance, but they were determined to take in as much of this gigantic metropolis as they could.

The quartet found spaces to stand along the wrought iron fence of the courtyard, where guardsmen in ceremonial uniforms performed an impressive drill. The beefeaters, clad in fuzzy brown helmets called busbies, bright red jackets with brass buttons, navy blue trousers, and shiny black boots, moved with precision and made the routine look effortless. It had all the polish characteristic of a British military exercise.

Roger pulled out his camera and attempted to take a photograph of the guards, but a careening tourist jostled him and almost forced the camera out of his hands. Roger was miffed, but the tourist quickly disappeared into the crowd as if nothing had happened.

Inga and Peter did not seem overly impressed with the drill, as they had seen it many times. They wanted their young friends to experience London, and they were eager to return the hospitality Peter had enjoyed in Colorado a few years earlier. After a few minutes of drill, the Evans guided them toward other attractions.

"We have visitors year around from nearly every country in the world," Peter commented. "You can find every kind here."

Downtown London had no shortage of tourist attractions or, despite the cool air and threatening clouds, tourists. The attractions included numerous statues and other memorials, fountains, beefeaters, bridges, churches, government buildings and a large four-faced clock in a tower. The tourists came in every color, shape, and size; from every nation and ethnic group. Many of the tourists were, like Roger and Eric, on their own, while others were members of guided groups with chartered buses. Some of the tourists were themselves British, and many were from the United States, Canada, Australia and western Europe. They noticed some people dressed in traditional robes common to Arabic nations and the Indian subcontinent, and others dressed in bowling shirts, floral prints, polyester slacks and penny loafers so common to North Americans. They were as intrigued by the huge collage of world citizens as they were by the statues and buildings. Pigeons were as abundant as people near the fountains, where many tourists were feeding them. Roger posed for his own camera as if he were trying to stomp the pigeons.

Apart from the royal and historical attractions, London looked like most big cities in the United States. Vice entrepreneurs were not difficult to find—pornographic bookstores, strip shows, pubs and bookmakers.

"What, exactly, does pub mean?" Eric asked. "I know what a pub is, but I'm curious about the word."

"It's short for public house, or what you'd call tavern or bar in your country," Peter said. "Public houses are open to the public, and serve more than just the house brand of ale or whiskey. Private clubs are not called pubs."

"I see."

"Why do you have to be eighteen or older to go into the bookmaker's?" Roger wondered aloud, after he read the sign on a bookmaker's door.

"It's a betting parlor for horse racing and other such gambling events," Inga explained. "Illegal for children to gamble in this country."

"I thought it was a print shop where they bound books, or something like that."

"I did, too." Eric said. "Are we dense, or what?"

"You're not so daft," Inga said. "You just have to learn to speak English, that's all."

Except for the unusual diction and syntax on their signs and displays, none of the businesses were particularly noteworthy, although the gutters and sidewalks were remarkably clean and free of rubbish. They did not care much for window-shopping, but the Evans seemed to be leading them toward something more important than the boutiques they were passing.

Inga pointed toward a large church. "Here's a place that you've probably heard of."

"It makes the world news sometimes, and it's been in some movies," Peter added.

Saint Paul's Cathedral caught their fancy without any further prompting from the Evans. More than three hundred years old, it was beautifully maintained and big enough to hold three or four normal-size churches. The architecture, consisting of high pillars and broad arches, was magnificent, as were the many icons in the huge sanctuary. The floors and walls contained the tombs of many faithful Anglicans from centuries past. The Americans took pictures of the building and its grounds, as did many of the other tourists, and they wondered what the previous cathedral on this site, which was destroyed in the fire of 1666, looked like.

The next stop of the day was at the City of London Youth Hostel near St. Paul's and the Thames. Peter and Inga had stayed in youth hostels many times throughout Great Britain and elsewhere in Europe, and they wanted Roger and Eric to be able to take advantage of this low-cost and widely available form of lodging. The Americans paid the three-year membership fee and received Hostelling International membership cards that would admit them to any youth hostel in the world.

In the late afternoon, on their way back to the Evans' car, the four stopped at the Prime Minister's house at 10 Downing Street. A troop of Boy Scouts was admiring the building while Inga took pictures of Eric and Roger near the black door bearing the distinctive house number. The house looked much the same as it did when Winston Churchill posed in front of it for magazine and newspaper photographers in the early 1940s, except for some modern security features. As the four resumed their walk toward the Evans' car, the topic of conversation turned toward the prime minister.

"I find it interesting that one of your longest-serving prime ministers was a woman," Eric said to Inga and Peter. "We've never had a woman in the Oval Office, you know."

"You Yanks are behind the times," Peter said. "You'd be surprised what women can do."

"He always talks like that in front of me," Inga said. "I'm onto him."

Peter showed Eric and Roger to three bicycle dealers, but the first two did not have much of what they were seeking. The third was Peter's favorite shop, where he had bought his racing bike, and it had a good selection of clothing and accessories. Away from the high-rent district of central London, the third store was almost as large as the first two combined. The store smelled of new rubber tires. Long racks of bicycles, two-high in most places, extended along each wall and down the center. The new bicycles were mostly Raleighs and the house brand, with a few French, Italian, Japanese and American brands among them. Mountain bikes, titanium racing bikes, recumbents and even a few touring bikes were represented on the racks. Several mechanics wearing denim aprons hurried in and out of the repair area like waiters at a busy restaurant during lunch hour.

The two Americans admired some not-for-sale classic bicycles that were on display from the shop owner's private collection. A bright yellow, top-of-the-line Zeus 2000 Supercronos from the late 1970s, the frame and components all made by the same company in Eibar, Guipúzcoa, Spain, stood in one corner of the store. A placard in front of a Cinelli with Nuovo Record components from the 1960s proclaimed that the bike had once been ridden by Tom Simpson, the 1965 World Champion. A black-and-white photograph of Simpson straddling a Cinelli supported the claim, but the bike in the photo could have been most any Cinelli. The caption on the photo noted that Simpson is still considered Britain's greatest road racer, four decades after his tragic death on Mont Ventoux in the 1967 Tour de France. An early-1970s Lambert with its original cast aluminum fork represented England. Eric and Roger had heard of long-defunct Lambert, but it was the first time either had ever seen one. An old Schwinn Paramount tandem was the American contribution to the collection. A Gitane equipped with a discontinued Mavic gruppo had been used by one of the teams in the 1989 Tour de France. A photograph showed the store's smiling owner standing among the uniformed racing team members. An early Fuji built for its domestic market had labels and components bearing only Japanese characters. The frame on a 1950s single-speed bicycle from Argentina was bolted together at one of the joints, rather than welded or brazed. All the classic bicycles had been meticulously restored, and the owner was obviously proud of his museum pieces.

"Does your dad still have his Zeus?" Roger asked Eric.

"Still does. He even rides it once in a great while. It's not as fancy as that one. He bought it back in the seventies when he was in college. I think Zeus folded somewhere in the 1980s."

"I hope he hangs onto it. It's a collector's item now."

"I hadn't thought of that until you mentioned it. I'll tell him that when I get home."

In the clothing section, Roger selected a long-sleeved jersey bearing a yellow and black logo. Eric picked out a similar jersey and admired it. The fabric was a thick wool blend, ideal for cold-weather wear. The price was high and he immediately talked himself out of buying such an extravagance. He was about to put the jersey back on the rack when a clerk touched his shoulder from behind.

"Why don't you try it on?" She caught Eric's attention immediately when she made eye contact.

"Sure. Why not?" He could not resist her lovely smile for long, and he knew it. He handed his things to Inga and Peter, and pulled the jersey on over his T-shirt. An Italian size III, it was very tight for him and the sleeves did not quite cover his wrists.

The clerk stood facing Eric and gently put her hands on his shoulders, sizing him up. "It looks very good on you, but way too small. Which size do you have?"

"I think it's a three."

She reached around his neck, stood on her tiptoes, and pulled the collar out enough to read the tag. "Size three? Let's try a four. No, better yet, a five. You want to be able to peel it off easily." She flipped through the jerseys on the rack until she found one with a Size V tag, with eye-catching green and blue insignia. She removed the jersey from its hanger and handed it to Eric. "Try that one."

Eric removed the Size III jersey, and pulled on the Size V. The shoulder seams were just beyond the edges of his shoulders, and the cuffs of the sleeves went to his wrist bones. "That feels a little better. Not too tight, not

22

too loose." He very much liked all the attention she was giving him. He rarely got that kind of service in clothing stores.

The clerk stepped back to inspect him. "Hold up your arms. Very good. Arms at your sides now. Turn around, please. Let's have a look at you from the back." He did as she requested. She pinched and tugged the fabric in several places to be sure of the fit. She smoothed some wrinkles with her palms. "Yes, I'd say that's about right. It will shrink just a little the first time you wash it." She lightly pushed one of his shoulders and pulled the other to turn him toward her again. "You do look impressive! Very good indeed."

Eric looked her in the eye and smiled. He knew he was not going to leave without buying that handsome green and blue jersey. He removed the jersey and handed it to the clerk. "I like it, and I'll take it."

"Will that be everything?"

"No. I need some other things, too. Give me a few minutes."

Eric and Roger were immediately in love with their beautifully embroidered, Italian-made racing jerseys. Roger also bought a pair of riding gloves and Eric bought two Italian-made chamois shorts. Roger looked for a headset for his new frame, but the store did not have the model he wanted in stock.

Roger admired his newest jersey. "We'll be advertising brands nobody's ever heard of, when we get back home."

"I've often wondered why we pay some companies so much for the privilege of advertising their names on our clothing." Eric gently rubbed the fabric between his thumb and index finger, savoring the texture. It was the fanciest jersey he had ever owned.

"You'll never get a jersey if you wait for them to pay you," Peter said, "unless you're good enough to race professionally."

On the way back to Romford, Peter stopped at a theater in Essex and bought two tickets for a Monday night performance of the opera *The Who's Tommy* for his guests. They had driven by the theater on their way into London, and both Eric and Roger remarked that they had heard of it but never seen it. Inga and Peter mentioned they had seen the show a few weeks earlier and enjoyed it thoroughly.

"I don't mean to pry, but is your epilepsy going to cause problems for you?" Inga asked Eric over supper at a restaurant. "I really don't know anything about it. We just want you to be safe when you're riding."

"I wouldn't be here if I thought it would be a problem." Eric's confidence—or was it bravado?—sounded sincere. "Epilepsy is a hindrance, but it's one I've learned to live with, to control. Just a little scar tissue in my brain, that's all."

The Evans were aware of Eric's epilepsy, as he had described his crash and its aftermath in correspondence several months earlier. They were concerned that he might have difficulty with the proposed bicycle tour, although he looked far more fit than they had anticipated when they met him and Roger at the airport. He showed no signs of weakness or pessimism, and this raised their confidence in him. They did notice his peculiar squinting a few times.

"When is the big day?" Inga asked Roger. "Have you set a wedding date yet?"

"Next summer sometime." Roger's lack of enthusiasm was evident. "Haven't set a specific date yet. I want both of us to graduate from college first."

Peter noted the melancholy. "You seem a little overwhelmed by the idea. It's not as bad as you think. Is it, love?" Inga smiled at Peter and nuzzled him in response.

"Truth be known, I'm having some second thoughts." Roger hesitated a moment before he continued, unsure whether he should burden the Evans with his woes. He told them what he had told Eric while they were assembling their bicycles.

Peter assessed the situation for a moment. "Why don't you ring her up? Make a list of what you want to say, then give her a call straight away. The sound of her voice will bring you around."

"You can use our telephone if you want," Inga added. "Or you can use a public telephone if you want a little more privacy. It'll do you a lot of good. Marianne will be delighted to hear from you."

"That's an excellent suggestion. I'll think about what I want to say, and give her a call tomorrow afternoon. She might be back from Hawaii by now."

4.

Roger awoke, got dressed, and returned to the bedroom to awaken Eric just as Peter was bringing in their morning tea. The Evans were about to leave for their Anglican church, but Peter invited them to help themselves to the breakfast items Inga had left on the table for them. As the Evans left, Roger reminded himself of how lucky he and Eric were to be staying with them.

Eric was in his usual deep sleep until Roger yanked his covers off him and turned on the overhead light. Eric grumbled and slowly dragged himself out of bed and got dressed. Roger looked out the window, which did not have or need screens, and noticed the dense clouds and the cool air. He enjoyed not talking or even thinking about weather, but this contrast to the blistering, dry heat of Colorado shocked his senses. He tried to straighten his cowlicks with a comb, to little avail. He put the comb back in his pocket and walked down the stairs to the dining area.

Roger and Eric recapped their experiences thus far over breakfast. Both were thoroughly impressed, amazed and bewildered, all at the same time, but not disappointed.

Roger sipped some tea. "We were incredibly fortunate, meeting Peter the way we did. What are the odds of something like that?"

"I doubt that any amount of money could buy the hospitality we've received. They're almost too generous. I'm beginning to feel guilty and lazy for accepting it." Eric scored an orange with a paring knife and began to unwind the peel.

"I'm getting anxious, in spite of our pleasant stay here, to get our tour underway."

"I am too. Let's decide today what all we have to do around here and then leave while we're still welcome. Savvy?"

Roger spread some marmalade on a slice of toast. "Let's see...We have a criterium at Eastway and tea this afternoon; tomorrow we cruise downtown London and drink tea; Tuesday we drink tea, visit the frame builder, drink tea, and ride in the time-trial; and Wednesday, we drink tea and head north. That should give us plenty of time for preparation, which reminds me that I need to send some e-mail and a few postcards back home so they'll know we arrived safely. What'll I say? How about:

Dear Mum & Dad:
Having a wonderful time. Wish you were here.
The weather is great! Miss you.
Love,
Number Two Son"

Eric tried to speak, but stuttered the first syllable. He put his forehead in his hands, with his elbows on the table.

"Epilepsy bothering you this early?"

"My brain's throbbing a bit, but that's not unusual. I'll get over it sooner or later. Part of the problem is that I'm not 100% awake yet. I promise you, though, I won't let this ruin our fun."

"You're not handicapped. You told me that yourself not too long ago, and I still believe it."

Eric returned to what they were discussing. "Is that all you're going to write to your parents? And what about Marianne?"

"No, I'm just being my usual sarcastic self because I don't write formal letters very well. I never know what to say, if you can believe that. I'd rather talk than write. Marianne knows that, but she'll have a hissy fit if I don't send her something soon."

"Don't mention the weather."

"I never mention the weather!" Roger gave Eric a stern look. "And you never talk about your epilepsy. Inga and Peter mentioned their concern about it to me."

"What did you tell them?"

"I told them I don't know much about it, but that it hasn't stopped you from coming this far, like you said last night at dinner. You haven't told me much about it, either."

"The reason I don't say much about it is that I tend to get an overload of unwanted sympathy and bad advice when I do," Eric snapped. "I can do everything now that I was able to do before I had my first seizure." The subject annoyed Eric, so he changed it. "Don't forget to call Marianne."

"It's the middle of the night in Denver, remember. I'll call her this afternoon."

They were preparing their bicycles for the criterium when the Evans returned from church. Another family two doors away in the same building returned home just moments after the Evans. The two Americans both noticed the tall girl walking in behind her parents. Vickie waved to her, and she flashed a bright smile and waved back. A pretty pastel mini-dress nicely contrasted her dark skin and nearly waist-length dreadlocks.

"Your neighbor?" Roger asked Vickie.

"Yes. Her name's Melanie."

"Her parents came here from Jamaica when she was a baby," Inga said. "They have a green grocery in London. Her older brother is in the Royal Navy, studying to be an officer, they tell us."

"I think she's about nineteen," Vickie added. "Do you like her?"

"Let's just say she has a certain appeal. Be a dear and introduce us to her next time we see her, will you?"

The field of some forty riders in the criterium made Eric and Roger a bit nervous. Eric wore his comfortable new shorts and the jersey of his university cycling club. He looked like a seasoned racer even if he did not exactly feel like one. Roger wore his Boulder-area club jersey. They both felt a little out of place racing on their touring-equipped bicycles. Their competitors, including Peter, were all properly equipped for racing, with narrow tires, road pedals and high gear ratios. Several of the other racers were members of Peter's club, and their jerseys matched his. Peter exchanged small talk with them.

The first lap of the race was hectic as riders clicked their shoes into their pedals and adjusted their derailleurs for optimum cadence. With their hearts pounding and lungs heaving, Peter, Roger and Eric jockeyed for positions near the middle of the large pack, where they stayed for most of the race. Roger noticed one of Peter's teammates riding a bicycle that had been made by Henry Smythe.

Some stronger riders, all with shaved legs, broke away on the second lap, but Peter and the two Americans were among the more conservative riders who did not attempt to chase the leaders. Eric could not hear anyone around him gasping for breath as he was, but he maintained the pace. He knew the others had to be winded, too, by the agonizing expressions on their sweaty faces.

Eric coughed up some bile, which left a horrendously bitter taste in his mouth. He rinsed it with a quick sip from his water bottle, but the burning sensation in his throat remained. The *peloton* was slipping away from him as they rounded a curve. He sucked air deep into his lungs, stood up, and forced his way back into the cluster of racers. He was not going to be dropped on the second lap, especially when Roger and Peter were holding their own.

Eric maintained his place in the *peloton* in the third lap, beside Peter and about two bicycle lengths behind Roger. The Shaved Legs who were still in the *peloton* pushed the pace, while the Hairy Legs brought up the rear. The pace was right at Eric's upper limit, and he knew he was not strong enough to lead. He paid close attention to the rear wheel of the rider immediately in front of him, knowing all too well the consequences of overlapping wheels. Peter's racing style was conservative, like that of Eric. He preferred time-trials to criteriums. Roger shuffled positions with several other riders every two hundred meters or so. Roger even led the *peloton* briefly, but he, too, knew that several of his immediate competitors were stronger than he was. His best bet was to let the strongest riders, the Shaved Legs, lead the pace line, thereby doing most of the work.

About midway through the penultimate lap, five or six riders with shaved legs who had been leading the *peloton* started to pull away from the other twenty or so riders, including Peter, Eric and Roger. Eric glanced backward as he rounded a curve and noticed three particularly strong riders who had broken away from the others early in the race were gaining on the *peloton*. They had already lapped the stragglers. Eric did not want to be lapped, but he did not have the strength to chase down the nearer breakaway group. Roger and Peter were struggling to hold their positions alongside Eric as the *peloton* began to spread.

The leading three riders, all very strong and aggressive compared to the others, crossed the finish line just moments before they would have lapped

27

the *peloton* containing Peter, Eric, Roger and two of Peter's teammates. The *peloton* broke up into several smaller clusters of riders as they began the last lap of the race. Several racers drew their water bottles and took a quick drink along a flat stretch of the course. The final rise was coming up fast, and it was sure to separate the *peloton* even more.

One of the smooth-legged racers charged up the rise. He was trying to shake free of the others as they strained to get up the hill. The finish line was less than a minute away. Eric, Peter, Roger and three other pairs of Shaved Legs reeled in the surging leader just beyond the top of the rise. He did not have the power to leave them behind. Eric rested behind the others as they closed the gap. The rest of the *peloton* was fading. They rounded the final turn when Peter's teammate on the Smythe frame started to make his move. Eric at the rear was the first to notice the maneuver.

Eric stood up in his pedals and silently tapped Peter and Roger on the shoulder as he passed them. They knew immediately what Eric was doing, and they got in behind him. Eric poured all he had left into staying with Peter's teammate on the Smythe bicycle. Eric could almost taste the finish line in the distance. He knew exactly what he had to do.

5.

When Marianne arrived at home, she and her mother were glad to see each other, for about half an hour. Marianne knew she would not have to wait long for the interrogation and the lectures. Her mother could be such a busybody. You need to do this. You should have done that. Where have you been? Who were you with? What did you do there? Marianne was sure you-need-to were the three ugliest words in the English language. She made a habit of ignoring any sentence prefaced with that dreadful phrase.

"I'm meeting some friends in Kauai for a few days," Marianne announced after she had been home for a week that seemed like a month.

"Your father's returning from California late Friday, and we have a get-together at the club on Saturday. He'll want to see you, and there are some people I'd like you to meet at the party. Your brother and Leslie are coming next week for a few days."

Marianne loved her father, but his business interests always seemed to have priority over family matters and everything else. She really wanted to introduce Roger to him at the Denver airport a few months earlier, but Mr. Murakami met her briefly and then spent the rest of his layover in the airline's private lounge negotiating a real estate transaction by telephone, as she predicted he would. She did not want to subject Roger to that kind of indifference.

Mrs. Murakami liked to show Marianne off to friends at lavish social functions. Her mother's friends often made comments about her figure, her clothing and other superficial traits. They often had a son, grandson or nephew they just knew was perfect for her. They had no idea what was perfect for her, because they never considered her to be anything more than a potential trophy wife with a good pedigree. When Marianne was eighteen, the husband of one of them, more than a little intoxicated at the time, tried to grope her under the dining table at a debutante ball. Marianne, without saying a word, doused him with a full glass of red wine. His white shirt and tailored linen suit bore the stains of her wrath. The couple never spoke to her again, or to her parents. Those were just a few of the reasons she wanted to be with friends on the beach, rather than with the elite of Honolulu at the country club.

"I don't want to meet anyone! I have some things to discuss with Jenny and the other girls." Marianne wanted Roger right now. She needed him here. She thought about what Roger would think of her parents' social circle, and how he might fit into it. Deep down, she knew he could not possibly fit.

The original *peloton* stretched more than half a lap by the end of the race. Eric pulled Roger and Peter ahead of Peter's teammate on the Smythe frame, then got in front of the teammate. He faded in the final sprint. His epilepsy was bothering him, and he did not want to risk crashing in the sprint for the finish. Mostly, he was just too tired to contest the race at that point. Roger summoned all his remaining strength at the end and crossed the finish line in front of Peter. The teammate tried to challenge Roger and Peter in the sprint, but they used the sizable advantage Eric had given them to pull away from him as they approached the finish line. The teammate finished just in front of Eric, but a few seconds behind Peter and Roger.

They were not at all disappointed with their respective performances, and they were glad to have avoided crashing. Roger was especially pleased with Eric's gambit, and said so. Peter also used Eric's draft to finish better than he ever had in several previous races at Eastway.

Roger took some photographs of riders in the next race. Peter was greeted by Inga's sister and her husband, a Dutchman who worked for the Dutch government in London. Peter introduced Roger and Eric to Anne and Hans, who were also bicycling enthusiasts. Peter and Hans had ridden together in Europe.

"The lot of you rode a good race," Anne said.

"Thanks, but I've had better days," Eric said. "I'm really not much of a competitor at heart."

"You do well from my point of view." Hans' English was perfect. He spoke in a very mellifluous voice, his Dutch accent remarkably subtle. "Peter has told us of your tour in America. Perhaps some day we can all get together for a tour somewhere.

Eric managed a weak smile. "I'd like that."

"He's better than he admits," Roger said. "If you'll all excuse me for a moment, I need to make a telephone call to a certain someone in the United States. Did I see a phone around here somewhere, Peter?"

"You probably did. It's right over there." Peter gestured toward the grandstand, and Roger left in that direction. "Hans is quite right about you, Eric, he is. You're going to have a good tour. The nice thing about a tour is that you really have only yourself to compete against."

Roger returned a few minutes later, after Peter and Eric had loaded the bicycles into Peter's car. "No luck today. No one answered, and her answering machine must be turned off. She went home to Hawaii for a week, and she left before I did. I thought she'd be back by now. No response on her cell phone, either. She must be out of range, or else she turned it off."

"Maybe she stayed a few extra days," Eric said. "I'd spend a few extra days in Hawaii if I were there. I'd turn my cell phone off, too, if I had one, so no one could pester me with idle chit-chat."

"Try again in a few days," Peter said. "You'll catch her at home sooner or later, or with her cell phone on."

6.

Peter awakened Roger at 7:30 with a cup of tea and a digestive. After Peter left the room and closed the door, Roger turned on the overhead light, but Eric did not respond. The sound of a jet engine, a front-row seat at a pop concert, or an earthquake of magnitude less than 8.5 on the Richter scale could not have awakened Eric, or so it seemed to Roger. He pulled the covers off Eric, and the combination of cool morning air and bright light began to affect sleepy Eric.

"Earth to Eric. Wake up, Eric. Shine and rise."

"Bloody hell! A guy can't ever get any shut-eye around here!" Eric reached for the bedclothes, but Roger pulled the bedding onto the floor and seized Eric's pillow. "Cut the grab-ass!" Roger grabbed Eric's ankles and pulled him toward the foot of the bed. "All right, damn you! I'm getting up. Let go of me, numbnuts!"

"We have an audience with the Queen today, so we have to get an early start, wanker," Roger replied.

"What is a wanker, anyway?"

"One who wanks, probably. I read it somewhere a while back, and I heard one of the racers calling his teammate a wanker yesterday."

It was a typical wake-up routine for the two. Neither could understand, or had much empathy for, the other's sleeping and waking habits. Peter and Inga were due at their jobs and Vickie at her school that Monday morning. Eric and Roger were planning to visit downtown London again, but unaccompanied this time.

The Evans made suggestions during breakfast of what their guests should see and what they should avoid, and told them how to get to a subway station near their destination. They picked up a Tube Map at the airport station, but the system was immense and many of the stations had unusual names.

Roger and Eric walked several blocks to a bus stop. They rode the bus a kilometer or two to the same train station where they got off from the airport, and boarded a London-bound train. When the train entered London proper, it became a subway. The subway was still a novelty to both of them, but neither got very excited about it. They transferred to the Central Line at Mile End, and finally arrived at Tottenham Court Road more than an hour after they left Romford.

They were headed for the British Museum a few blocks from the underground station, but the traffic on the busy streets was so dense that they could barely see light between the vehicles. They were not sure which way to look for oncoming traffic, but they finally crossed the street safely after waiting quite awhile for a traffic signal to change. Crossing busy streets in the U.K., where everyone drives on the wrong side of the road, scared the daylights out of both of them, even with the "Look Right" signs painted on the asphalt.

They had a map, but the street names changed every few blocks. They circled around several blocks before they asked a newsagent for directions. They had no sense of direction in London. A crowd had already gathered outside the British Museum when they arrived. An older man in a wheelchair, a disabled veteran perhaps, wished everyone in the garden a pleasant day as he held out a cup.

"Good morning to you, me lads." The beggar approached Roger and Eric. "Lovely day, isn't it?"

Eric dropped a coin into the beggar's cup. "Don't spend it all in one place."

They walked to Regent's Park, northwest of the City Centre, after they had seen the Rosetta Stone and enough antiquities to satisfy their curiosity. The park, a sprawling garden of grass, trees, flowers and a canal, was a welcome relief from the noise, traffic, and dull gray buildings surrounding it. They sought a comfortable spot on the lush grass that was so much healthier than their sun-scorched, irrigated lawns in Colorado. Very few people were in the park, and no rotating sprinklers were threatening to soak anyone. Signs along the paved paths warned them: "Don't foul the footpath," "Kerb your dog," and "Keep Britain tidy." Indeed, Regent's Park was very clean and tidy. They parked themselves on the lawn near, but not quite underneath, some trees.

"If we were in, say, Denver City Park right now," Roger said, "we'd be wearing shorts and sandals and lying in the shade of one of these trees. Women of all colors, wearing tight shorts and bikini tops, would be within viewing distance. We'd flirt with the more attractive ones..."

Eric put the edge of his hand against his face to shield his voice from Roger and turned toward his imaginary television audience. "What he's trying not to say is that he's disappointed because he was expecting to find a scantily-clad, hedonistic society out enjoying the summer sun. But what a big surprise he got!" He turned back toward Roger. "Tough luck around here."

"Those schoolgirls in their outdated dresses are looking better all the time," Roger said. Vickie had told them the public schools were still in session, even in late June. The oldest students were about sixteen.

"You're too old for them now, Squire, not to mention, engaged. I must admit I have noticed some sweet young things in the Evans' neighborhood." Eric was thinking more about the tour than about the schoolgirls. "Maybe we ought to blow off England and Scotland and cruise on down to the Mediterranean coasts of Spain, France and Italy, since Peter won't be with us."

"How well do you understand Old World Spanish?" Roger asked.

"All the Spanish I know is from Mexican dialects. Don't know much Castilian," Eric answered. "I'm comfortable with the language here in England."

"Sod that idea, then. We'll stay in the U.K. as planned. We'll just have to appreciate the schoolgirls."

"Mimi will be surprised when I tell her about the people here. Little does she know how cool the air is and how modestly dressed most of the people are here in London." Eric leaned back, supported by his elbows.

"The women here probably think we're strange-looking." Roger sat with his knees up, and his arms wrapped around his knees. He gazed into the distance "Two rubes from another planet."

Unsure of what to do and where to go, they decided to walk southward toward the government buildings and the River Thames. Along the way, a series of busy streets, they saw quite a potpourri of international enterprise. The streets were lined with numerous small businesses, most of which were very specialized. They saw few supermarkets, shopping centers or indoor malls. Instead, there were tobacconists, newsagents, fruiterers, chemists, fish mongers and green grocers, among others. The advertisements on the billboards often puzzled the two Americans, as did some of the traffic signs. The sights and sounds and scents were unfamiliar, and the crowds and dense traffic unnerving at times, but they felt entirely secure in London. They were content to be there.

"What do you say we quaff an ale?" Roger was looking at a liquor store they were approaching.

Eric glanced at his digital watch. "A bit early, I'd say. It's only 11:14."

"Nonsense! Think of it as an aperitif."

"We'll look like riffraff, drinking out of paper bags."

"Then we won't use paper bags," Roger said. They bought one can each of an unchilled lager brewed somewhere near London, and discreetly drank it as they continued their stroll.

"It's a good idea to imbibe on an empty stomach, that way, you don't have to spend so much money to get buzzed. Takes less time, too." Roger felt the effects of the small amount of beer by the time the can was empty.

"Since you mention empty stomachs, let's get some grub. What do you say we stop at the next fruit market?" Eric's tolerance of alcohol had decreased markedly as a result of his epilepsy, or so it seemed, but he allowed himself an occasional beer or glass of wine.

By mid-afternoon, they had walked along the edge of a residential area and had arrived at a busy roundabout back in the business district. They sat on the edge of what appeared to be just another monument, in the center of the roundabout. Several other people, most of whom looked like vagrants or relics from the flower-power generation, sat around the statue of Eros. Eric and Roger sat, read the surrounding billboards and watched the traffic, wondering what to do and where to go next.

"Are we at Picadilly Circus or Trafalgar Square, or none of the above?" Roger asked.

"Yes, it's probably one of those three. You'd never know we were at a famous place by the looks of it, would you?" Eric noticed a number of unsavory characters milling about the fountain where a statue of Eros graced the top of a tall pedestal.

One of the more colorful people moved toward them and knelt down next to Roger. The man had long, unkempt hair and a scraggily mustache. His neat clothing, necktie included, belied his hairstyle. They tried to avoid making eye contact with him, but he was persistent.

"'ello!"

"Hello," they both answered.

"Would you, a, like to buy a joint?" the man said quietly, trying to be cautious and inconspicuous.

"A joint? You mean marijuana?" Roger spoke in an equally cautious voice, mimicking the stranger.

"Yeah, that's right, marijuana," the man said as Eric watched.

Roger looked at Eric, then back at the man. "No."

"It's good stuff, really good. I just need a few quid to get to Birmingham and…"

"Don't make me have to explain what *no* means!"

"Only five quid for…"

"He said no, mate," Eric said. "We're not buying."

"I can get you some pure cocaine straight away if…"

"He's not getting our point very well, Chief. We're going to have to hack off his gonads."

"You cut the left one and I'll get the right one." Eric gave no hint that he might be bluffing.

"This one?"

"No. His other left one."

"Really now, I just want to…excuse me!" The man bolted into the crowd when he saw them withdraw their Swiss Army knives from their pockets and open the longer blades. He reappeared a minute later on the other side of the circle and presented his spiel to another potential customer.

"Poor sod. I think we frightened him."

"I hate when that happens."

"Strange, but even the riffraff here have that characteristic British formality. Did you notice how polite he was?"

"We thought that stiff-upper-lip was just a cliché, but maybe not. I thought for a minute there, the bloke was going to ask us to join him for tea."

Roger and Eric consulted their map again, and decided to find the government buildings collectively known as Whitehall near where they had been on Saturday. When they found the government complex, a huge block of dull gray buildings, they joined a queue of camera-bearing tourists outside one of the building entrances. After twenty minutes of waiting, the line did not move even the slightest, so they left in search of something more fruitful.

"The River Thames is not too far away." Eric pronounced Thames as if it rhymed with shames. "Let's take a walk along it and look at the famous bridges."

"You mean the River Thames." Roger correctly pronounced Thames.

"That's what I said, Thames," Eric again deliberately mispronounced the word. "It ought to be spelled T-e-m-z. That would make more sense."

They approached the Thames near the Westminster Bridge and walked along its north bank. The first thing they noticed was the 130-meter Ferris wheel, the London Eye, across the river. They were impressed by the wide, clean, well maintained sidewalk, several meters above the water level, at the top of the Victoria Embankment. The view of London from the riverbank was good, even though it was at a lower elevation than the city. No available space in London went unused, they noted. The apartments, stores and offices were tightly packed, but they enjoyed the wide-open view from the riverbank. The Thames was a huge river by their standards, and the sight of large, commercial, ocean-going boats in a river was unfamiliar. The wall between the sidewalk and the building up above contained few graffiti except for a few political motifs.

Neither the Tate Gallery nor the London Bridge really struck their fancy. They walked and talked along the river until they happened upon a tourist attraction they did very much want to see, the Tower of London. Both had read and heard of the Tower, but what they actually saw from upriver was the magnificent Tower Bridge. They thought the Tower was one of the towers of the bridge, but they discovered the real Tower to be a castle near the north bridge tower. Unfortunately for them, they arrived at the Tower too late in the day, and it was closed. So much for the crown jewels, they decided. They walked around the Tower grounds and inspected the cannons and external walls of the medieval fortress.

The picturesque Tower Bridge was not closed, and its bright-colored details provided a much better backdrop for several photographs than the earthy walls of the Tower itself. Automobile traffic on the bridge was severe, but it had wide sidewalks on each side where Eric and Roger each posed in front of the north tower while the other took photographs. For each photo, the photographer had to stand quite a ways back from the subject in order to get a significant part of the bridge tower in the picture. They were thoroughly impressed by the Tower Bridge, so much that they took the time to walk all the way across it and back.

Not far from the bridge was a moored ship, albeit small, that had been used by Richard Byrd in Antarctica. The boat was not spectacular, but it evoked visions of Antarctica in them.

"Ever thought of taking a vacation in Antarctica?" Eric asked.

"I'd go in a New York minute." Roger looked at the boat for a moment, then continued walking.

"Same here."

They continued along the river until the walkway ended. They walked a few blocks into the city where they found the Whitechapel underground station. Before boarding the train, Eric perused their subway map again to be certain they were going in the right direction. They were spent from their long walk. A seat on the train felt good to both of them. They expected another hour before they would be at the Evans' home in Romford, but that would give them adequate time to unwind before supper.

Vickie and Inga were sitting on the Evans' front step talking to their neighbor Melanie when the two Americans arrived. Inga introduced Roger and Eric to Melanie, then went inside to prepare the evening meal. Melanie looked fetching in tight shorts and a V-neck T-shirt. She spoke in the same cockney dialect as the Evans, and seemed quite charmed to meet the two foreigners.

Roger liked her enough that he decided to take action. "We have an extra ticket for a performance tonight. Would you like to join us?"

7.

Peter changed into cycling attire at the end of his shift, and got on his bicycle for the ride home. He waved good-bye to several colleagues on his way out of the parking lot. Many of them took the Tube to get home, some rode a bus or carpooled, and a few drove their own car to work. They all seemed to admire Peter for commuting by bicycle year-around. He had been riding the same route, with only minor variations, daily for almost fifteen years. He thought about his two young American friends and their native country while he rode. They reminded him of himself a decade or more earlier. His Rocky Mountain tour was without a doubt one of the highlights of his life, but he did not envy the Americans. He liked their country thoroughly, but being an Englishman in England was just fine with him. He had everything he needed. The United Kingdom had plenty of room for improvement—politically, economically, culturally and otherwise—but he was entirely comfortable with his lot in life. He hoped Eric and Roger would find similar peace of mind.

"I'd love to, really, but I've already accepted a date with a boy named Rory. He's such a dream. I've been hoping for months he'd ask me out someday." Melanie had that far-away look in her eye, as if Rory were everything she could ever want, and then some. "And he finally did."

Roger took it all in stride. "Tough bananas for us, Chief."

Melanie batted her carefully decorated eyes, large and brown and slightly seductive, at Roger first and then Eric. "Maybe some other time."

They discussed their adventures with Inga, Peter and Vickie over supper. The Evans were amused by their guests' naïveté, as well as their method of handling pushers. Inga drove Eric and Roger to the Queen's Theatre, a very plush and modern theater complete with a pub beneath the lobby, to see a local performance of the opera *The Who's Tommy*, for which Peter had purchased tickets on Saturday.

Peter brought them back to Romford after the show, where the Evans discussed the performance with them, over late-night tea. "How was your night at the opera?" he asked.

"All very good!" Roger looked satisfied for a change, having temporarily forgotten his romantic difficulties.

"Not your usual Lerner and Lowe musical, was it?" Inga passed a plate of digestives around the dining table.

"Not at all," Roger agreed. "Not your usual Gilbert and Sullivan opera, either."

"I'll bet the chorus girls in Tommy's Holiday Camp caught your eye," Vickie suggested.

"Did they ever!" Eric's face lit up just a bit. "I'll be dancing with them in my dreams tonight." They all continued discussing the show while Inga poured another round of tea.

"Are you two ready for a time trial tomorrow evening?" Peter asked.

"As ready as we're going to be," Roger said, and Eric nodded in agreement.

"Mr. Smythe called whilst you were at the theatre," Inga said. "Said he had some concerns to iron out with you, Roger."

"Nothing wrong, I hope."

"He didn't say anything was amiss, but I was a little surprised he would call in the evening."

"Eric and I'll go see him in the morning. We'll be out of your hair the morning after the time trial, I promise."

8.

Roger purchased his Trek on clearance when he was in high school. It was already dated when he bought it, but the price was right and it was built for speed. He had used it for racing, touring and commuting, and he had spent many happy hours in its saddle. The mostly French-made components were gradually wearing out. Many had been discontinued and could not be replaced easily, even on the Internet auction sites. He hoped it would last until he was done with college. His plan was to spend his first paycheck on a new, top-of-the-line bicycle. Peter had mentioned an acquaintance, Henry Smythe, who had built frames for some of Peter's racing and touring friends. Roger could not resist the impulse to get a custom frame in Europe, even if it did stretch his budget. He would buy the frame first, and the components would have to wait a year or so.

37

Roger and Eric spent the morning and a good part of the afternoon unintentionally sight-seeing in Essex. They searched in vain for the frame builder's shop for more than half an hour, until some local cyclists guided them to it. They knew it was near a brewery, which they found easily, but the lack of building numbers and street directions put them in a tizzy as soon as they were beyond the Evans' neighborhood.

Urban Essex was interesting, not because of any tourist attractions, but because it provided a very representative cross-section of urban life in England. The county was named for its 11th century residents, the East Saxons. The Saxons were named for their weapon of choice, a short sword known as the *seax*. Essex residents saw few tourists, especially foreigners, in their locale, and thus did not put up a front for strangers. The passersby in Essex had every reason to assume Roger and Eric were also locals, and paid no attention to them. Being incognito, they had the opportunity to observe Britons who were not involved with the tourist industry.

The architecture of the houses, businesses, churches and factories in Essex was unremarkable, a collage of bricks, concrete, and slate. The newer houses looked much like the older ones, just a little glossier. Lush gardens, trees and grass complemented the structures greatly, and the residential neighborhoods in Essex were most appealing. The lupines in bloom were especially delightful.

Roger made final arrangements with Henry Smythe regarding the frame during the late morning while Eric transcribed some thoughts and sketched a crude road map of the area in his journal. Smythe's call to the Evans the previous evening was normal for him. He set his own schedule, and he was a bit of a perfectionist. The gruffness he displayed when they first met was almost nonexistent this time. Eric returned to the Chinese takeout, where he had been the previous Friday, to fetch some lunch for Roger and himself.

"What is it you do for a living?" Smythe asked as he looked over the contract.

"We're both college students. Eric's an economics major. I'm studying engineering."

"A good profession to be in. I was an aircraft mechanic when I was about your age, in the Royal Air Force. The engineers who designed the aeroplanes would sometimes ask our opinion about things. I'm not sure if they really cared what the enlisted men thought, or if they just wanted a pat on the back. Building frames doesn't pay as well, but I like what I do."

"Best kind of job to have."

"My daughter's a little older than you are, then. She just turned twenty-nine. My little girl's going to get married next month, finally."

"I intend to do that myself in about a year."

"She's been engaged twice before. The first one never showed up at the altar. I think she broke off the second one. He seemed like a fine young man, until she found out he was still legally married to someone else. This one's named Grahame Wright, so I tell her she finally found Mr. Right." Smythe was pleased with his joke, and Roger laughed with him.

"Third time's a charm, you hope."

Roger silently hoped that he was not destined for any broken engagements. Mr. Smythe seemed satisfied with his future son-in-law, and said so. Did Marianne's parents feel that way, too?

The frame was all but fabricated by mid-afternoon, and Roger had done as much as he could except make the final payment for it. Mr. Smythe and Roger both seemed much more at ease with one another than they had previously. The two Americans had considerably less difficulty finding their way back to the Evans' house than they had finding the frame-builder. They stopped at a post office for stamps along the way back to Romford.

"You did well in that criterium. I couldn't have beaten that guy in the sprint if you hadn't pulled Peter and me along when he started to break." Roger rode alongside Eric. "Are you still having any doubts about yourself?"

"I did all right in the race, but I paid for it afterward. My brain felt like hell, although I'm not sure it was a result of racing. I could have felt that way for most any reason."

"That's not what I want to hear from you."

"Maybe not, but it's the truth." Eric slowed for a broken white stripe at an intersection, looked both ways, and accelerated when he saw no cars coming.

"Peter already registered us for the time trial this evening. You could withdraw if you want."

"No, I need the training. I don't care if I finish last, as long as I finish. It'll do me good."

Schools were dismissed while Eric and Roger were riding, and again they noticed and discussed the lasses they saw walking home. Vickie had told them that students attended British public schools through age sixteen, roughly the equivalent of tenth grade in American high schools. Upon graduation, the options for students were about the same as in the U.S.: entry-level employment, prep school or college, military service, homemaker, or parent-sponge. A parent-sponge is one who lives with parents but does not contribute much to the family income or his own upkeep. Roger and Eric knew a few such sponges among their high school buddies.

The schoolgirls, though only sixteen or thereabouts, looked older in their uniforms, which were dresses made of thick, dark wool in layers. Some wore white nylons, which were not nearly as becoming as skin-colored nylons to the Americans' eyes. Even though the day was in late June, the uniforms, boys' and girls' alike, looked like they were designed for winter use. The overcast sky and cool atmosphere were hardly what they considered summer weather, as they themselves wore jeans and lined jackets, so perhaps the uniforms were not as uncomfortable as they had originally thought.

Peter, Roger and Eric rode to an informal, twenty-kilometer time trial near Brentwood after supper. The evening sky, because of London's high latitude, above 51° north, compared to Denver's 40° and Seattle's 48°, was suitably light for cycling at this time of year until about 22:00. The racecourse was a dual carriageway, starting at one interchange, turning around at the next one, and returning to the first one.

About twenty people, mostly men and members of Peter's cycling club, entered the race. Peter's brother-in-law, Hans, was among the competitors this time. The two Americans did not have high expectations for themselves, as the only significant riding they had done in the past two weeks was the criterium at Eastway. The race was a time trial, where racers start one at a time every thirty seconds, and ride the entire course individually. A slower rider might be caught by the person behind him, or a faster rider might catch up with person before him, but the difference in speed between the two in either case discourages any team tactics.

Roger was the first racer out of the starting gate. He found a comfortable pace, looked over his shoulder to make sure the next racer was not gaining on him, and brought his breathing into synchronization with his pedaling cadence. Somewhat distracted by thoughts of Marianne, he took a wrong turn at the top of the overpass near the end of the course and lost some time. He was rankled by his poor performance, but he forgot about it soon afterward.

Eric started four riders after Roger. He felt strong, energetic and surprisingly relaxed. The criterium at Eastway made him tense, but riding alone in a time trial did not have that effect on him. He did not feel the usual headache and vertigo, so he maintained a faster pace than usual. When he came to the overpass where the course turned around, he stood up in his pedals and sprinted up the ramp. Taking a sip from his water bottle on the downside of the ramp on the other side of the divided highway, he knew the tour would be great as long as he felt this good. The rider immediately behind him had not yet started up the overpass when Eric got to the bottom on the other side, but the rider in front of Eric was within his reach. Eric caught up with the rider in front of him just before the overpass near the end of the racecourse. He again sprinted up the overpass for a strong finish, almost catching the rider who started one minute before him.

Hans started three riders after Eric, and Peter started last. Peter knew the course well, and considered the time trial as his racing specialty. He rode full throttle the whole way, not wanting to be bested again by the younger Americans. His teammates considered him the best time-trialist in the club, and he was determined to live up to his reputation. He caught up with the rider immediately before him near the middle of the return leg of the course, and caught the rider before that one near the finish line. Roger, Eric, Hans and the others watched him cross the finish line and cheered him onward.

Anne met Hans, Peter, the two Americans and some of Peter's club mates at a pub near the racecourse after the race. Peter introduced Roger and Eric to his club mates, and ordered a pitcher of lager for everyone seated around the outdoor tables, which set everyone at ease. Roger was back to his voluble self, and quickly became the center of attention. Beer had the tendency to cause that in him. Although most of the cockney banter of Peter's friends slipped past him, Eric had no trouble making conversation with members of Peter's extended family, and he felt well accepted by them.

Hans approached the table a few minutes after the others had been seated. "Well done, Peter, you won the time trial once again." He held the timekeeper's log sheet and clipboard.

"Nobody beats the old man at his own game on his home turf!" Peter made no attempt to conceal his pride.

"I see you had a strong showing, too, Eric."

Neither Eric nor Roger had seen the time sheet.

"I felt good today, but as I said at the last race, I'm really not a competitor at heart." Eric was uncomfortable with compliments about his cycling abilities, especially since the big crash.

"I don't know about that," Hans said. "You finished second, four seconds behind Peter. Nearly half a minute ahead of Rob, who was third."

Rob was one of the other cyclists seated at the table, about the same age as Roger and Eric, maybe a little older. They had seen Rob in the criterium at Eastway. In fact, he was the rider whom Eric held in check while Roger and Peter sprinted across the finish line ahead of him. Rob let out a hearty laugh, and raised his mug toward Eric. "Good show, governor! Your team tactics were good, and so is your time trial. Another fine performance by Peter, too!"

Rob was also the rider in the criterium whom Roger had noticed riding on a Smythe frame. Roger was pleased to meet someone who could vouch for Mr. Smythe's handiwork. It was most reassuring. Roger seized the opportunity to discuss Smythe frames with Rob.

"I was riding to win," Peter admitted. "The timekeepers said you looked like you were enjoying the scenery."

"They exaggerate." Eric, like Peter, was proud of his performance, now that he knew the results. He was especially pleased with his time trial, as compared to what he considered a lackluster performance in the criterium. "I was busting my buns out there, just like everyone else."

"You're ready for tomorrow's tour," Roger said. "I knew you would be."

Peter finished his glass of ale. "How's Smythe coming along with your frame?"

"Mr. Smythe seems to know very well what he's doing. He hasn't actually started it yet, but I have complete confidence in him."

"No worries, then," Peter said.

"You'll be very pleased with any frame Mr. Smythe builds for you. I've had mine, what, four or five years now. Wouldn't trade it for anything," Rob said.

"I noticed your frame in the criterium. I'm looking forward to having one similar to it."

"Do you need a headset or bottom bracket or anything? I should've suggested it when we were at one of the bicycle shops," Peter said.

"That one store didn't have the headset I wanted, but I can get the whole *gruppo* back home, if I have any money left."

"There's an importer in a city called Harrogate up north. They're said to have very competitive prices. You might pop into it if you're going through Yorkshire."

"Do you have the name and address?"

"I'll look it up for you when we get home this evening. They advertise in the cycling magazine I read every month."

On the ride back to Romford, Roger and Eric noticed what they would later be told were "cat's eyes," small red reflectors along the dividing line of the road. The sun had already set and the sky was nearly dark, but most of the drivers were not using their headlights, only their parking lights. When the drivers would pass the cyclists, they would flash their bright lights. The roads were in good condition and the shoulders were adequately wide and free of debris, such that the cyclists had a safe place to ride. They had no complaints about the maintenance and design of British roads.

"Ten years ago, I placed fifth in the national time trial championships, less than two minutes behind the winner," Peter explained to Eric and Roger while they rode. "Two of the chaps who finished ahead of me later raced in the Olympics, one in the men's road race and both of them in the time trial. The winner turned pro a few months later, and he became one of Britain's top stage racers."

"Did you ever consider pursuing a racing career?" Roger asked.

"I thought about it for another year, until I crashed early in the following season and broke my wrist and dislocated my knee. I recovered but didn't race again that season. I also had Inga and a baby named Vickie to support." He smiled at the memory. "I might've had the time and money for a racing career if I'd stayed single, but I'm not sorry I chose a family over racing."

"Point well taken." Roger was riding to the right of Peter, almost shoulder to shoulder.

"A family has better long-term prospects than a racing career." Eric was riding nearest the curb, to Peter's left. "But a racing career could have its rewards, if you're that good."

"Yes, quite," Peter agreed. "But as I said, I made the best choice. No regrets whatsoever."

They discussed their itinerary with Inga when the men returned to Romford. In the morning, a Wednesday, Roger and Eric would finally be getting their bicycle tour underway. Their plans were by no means definite, but their intentions were to visit the North Sea coast, Sherwood Forest, York, the Yorkshire Dales, and the Scottish Highlands. They had no idea how long this would take, but they also wanted to spend some time in Southern England and, maybe, Wales. By Inga's suggestion, they decided to ride to Cambridge and spend the night there. She telephoned the hostel and booked a bed for each of them.

Upstairs, Eric began his preparation for the following morning. "Why did you tell Melanie we had an extra ticket to the opera yesterday? There were only two."

Roger smirked at the suggestion. "Thanks for not calling my bluff in front of her. We could've bought a third ticket, or else you could've taken her and I'd have thought of some reason I couldn't go at the last minute. Or we could have done rock-paper-scissors to decide who got to go with her. You have to think fast when you get a chance like that."

Eric was impressed with Roger's cleverness. He was also a little annoyed by Roger's matchmaking, even though a date with Melanie would have been great. The trouble was, he had no clue as to how to sustain a conversation with her. "You don't have to find a date for me. I can manage on my own, although I don't think the two of us combined would be half the man the incomparable Rory seems to be."

"If you want the girl, you have to be creative. And resourceful. Especially when you're competing with a he-man hunk studmuffin beefcake like Rory."

"I don't even try to compete with the Rorys of the world. I never win."

Roger packed his panniers. "A night at the opera, and a day—make that two days—at the races. Kind of like the Marx brothers. I'm ready for whatever lies ahead. I'm comfortable with the new frame, too, finally."

43

"Your frame's going to be fine," Eric said. "I'm starting to get comfortably familiar with the foreign country we're in, our bicycles are assembled, and we're official youth hostel members. We're ready for anything." He hoped he sounded more confident than he felt. His head was throbbing and his vision was blurry.

Chapter III: *Frontier Justice in Yorkshire*

9.

Eric had little trouble getting out of bed that Wednesday morning. He was ecstatic about finally getting the bicycle tour underway. He was annoyed by the delay of departure caused by Roger's custom frame, but he kept it to himself. Today, he and Roger would have the chance to explore new territory.

Roger and Eric ate breakfast with the Evans, bade farewell, and rode toward the outskirts of greater London. They had already memorized, with the help of the Evans and a map, the names and directions of the first several roads they would use. They had another map to guide them to Cambridgeshire via Saffron Walden.

They filled their water bottles in Romford, but drank very little in spite of the warm sunshine and head wind blowing on them all day. Trying to avoid the London traffic and the M11 motorway, they followed the A12 to Brentwood. From there, they turned north up the A128 toward Harlow and the A11. The air was much more humid here than it would have been in Colorado at the same temperature. The traffic was fierce, and the ride had a gentle upward slope out of the Thames valley. With their panniers, handlebar bags, sleeping bags and camping mattresses on their bicycles, they slowly rode northward. They were disappointed by their sluggishness, but they knew they would get faster after a few days on the road.

Saffron Walden, a town just south of the Cambridgeshire county line in Essex, was a convenient place for them to break for lunch. They stopped at a grocery store two blocks from the highway, where they purchased a block of cheese, some oranges and a loaf of what they assumed to be saffron bread for their midday meal.

"It feels good to be on the road, finally." Eric bit into his sandwich. "Seems like we're hardly getting anywhere, though."

"Things always look smaller on a map." Roger sliced some cheese and made himself a sandwich. "I'm sorry about the delay. My new frame has been a bit more complicated than I thought it would."

"Not a problem. Gave us a good excuse to spend some time in London. This cheese sandwich would be perfect if I had a microwave oven here to melt the cheese," Eric observed, "and maybe some Dijon mustard, too." Peter had introduced them to Cheshire cheese sandwiches the previous week, using wheat bread and some sort of relish unfamiliar to them, probably a type of chutney.

"One of the reasons I like cycling is that nearly everything tastes good, and I can eat as much as I want," Roger said. "Have some more bread." They did not buy any chutney, but their sandwiches were good anyway, and they devoured the whole loaf of bread.

Eric got on his bicycle and onto the road that would take him back onto the A130 to Cambridge. Roger looked for a receptacle near the grocery store to deposit their trash. A dark, older-model sedan hastily approaching from the opposite direction made a sudden right turn in front of Eric, taking his right of way and forcing him to make a skidding stop.

"*Pendejo!*" Eric shouted as he jabbed his index finger toward the car. The driver had not even signaled for a turn, and Eric would have become a hood ornament had he not been able to stop quickly.

A man in the back seat shouted an obscenity back at Eric, then hurled an empty glass bottle that narrowly missed him. The car disappeared in traffic down the road before he had a chance to see the license plate or recognize the make. The one thing he did notice was the broken lens of the left taillight.

Roger stood in his pedals to catch up with Eric. "What happened there?" He had barely noticed the car as it passed.

"Some jerk turned right in front of me, then threw that bottle at me!" Eric's face was red in anger, which was unusual because his feathers were not easily ruffled. "Almost hit me! Twice!"

They resumed their ride northward toward the A10 with no further incidents. They did not see the dark sedan again.

Cambridge, a city of some 100,000 people, was not particularly eye-catching, but the traffic and hills taxed the two Americans and they were glad to be somewhere. They knew little of Cambridge, other than its famous university. It was where Isaac Newton performed much of his research on gravity, calculus, motion and optics some three and a half centuries earlier. It was where a young Charles Darwin began his career as a naturalist around 1831. A local told them that Cambridge University was actually a group of small colleges, including Newton's Trinity College and Darwin's alma mater, Christ's College. Their plan was to spend the night in the youth hostel, and it took them awhile to find it. Neither had ever stayed in a youth hostel, but they had membership cards and they were prepared to use the Youth Hostel Association lodging system.

The youth hostel system originated in Germany circa 1909. Richard Schirmann, a young schoolteacher assigned to a mining town, sought low-cost lodging for urban students and others of modest means during nature explorations. The original hostels were classrooms that were vacant during the summer months. He established the first dedicated hostel in 1912 in a castle in Altena, North Rhine Westphalia, near Dortmund. Following the interruption by the Great War, the concept spread across Germany. France and the United Kingdom got their first youth hostels by 1930. Herr Schirmann's idea caught on around the world in due time, even in the United States. He died in 1961 at age 87.

The hostel, a typically British-looking Victorian building on Tenison Road southeast of the city centre, was teeming with travelers not unlike Roger and Eric. Some of the other guests were also cyclists. The building looked like a boarding school on the inside, and a man with the title of Warden registered them and assigned them to bunk beds in a third floor men's dormitory. The warden briefed all registrants on the subject of rules, which were also posted near the registration window. The bunks were small and did not have as much space underneath for luggage as the Americans would have liked. They stowed their gear beside the bed inside wooden lockers, and secured their bicycles in a storage room with a cable and combination lock. The door to their room was always locked, but they shared the room with six strangers. They wondered about the security of their gear, until they realized that all of the other guests faced the same dilemma.

The warden issued each of them a sheet sleeping bag. They made their own beds by unfolding the sheet bag on the bunk mattress, inserting the pillow at the head end, and covering it with a heavy blanket known by the French name duvet. By the time they were situated in the hostel, they were hungry for supper. The hostel had cooking facilities for its guests and an evening meal was available, as the hostel guidebook said it would, but they wanted to see the nearby restaurants first.

The found some interesting restaurants a short walk from the hostel, but nothing really caught their fancy. They intended to avoid eat-in restaurants as much as possible to keep their expenses down. They had already overloaded on Chinese food in London. They were not in the mood yet for anything deep-fried, and the pub fare would have to wait until another day. They walked back to the hostel and ate the evening meal served by the hostel staff. It was hardly gourmet, but the food and tea were plentiful and reasonably priced.

They took a stroll through the neighborhood after supper and stopped at a park where a cricket match was in progress. They watched for a while, but could not resist comment on the game.

"In U.S. cities that have no night life, we roll up the sidewalks at dusk and go home." Eric stood with his hands on his hips. "In the U.K., apparently, they play cricket. Don't these people recognize a boring game when they see one?"

"It is a little on the dull side," Roger said. "I'm surprised the outfielders don't bring camp stools to sit on while they're idle. I suppose these people have nothing better to do."

"Somebody probably says, 'Hey, everybody, let's put on a cricket match!' Still, from where I'm standing, it looks pointless."

"You'll notice, too, that the players are all wearing clean white uniforms. That clearly indicates to me that no one is doing anything significant. Hell, I've seen fresh hospital gowns that weren't as clean as what these cricketers are wearing."

"They should learn to play softball. A friend of mine at UW was on an intramural softball team. One of their players came down with a bad case of mononucleosis, so he asked me to be a stand-in for the last three games of the season. I had a great time with it."

"I don't think I've played softball or baseball since our little-league days."

"I hadn't either, but they talked me into playing, and I'm glad they did. I was rusty at first, but I hit a two-run double in my third at-bat. It's very satisfying to bat in some runs, or catch a deep fly."

Roger continued to watch the game in silence, and deep in thought. "What do you think of our first youth hostel?"

"They have too many rules and not enough privacy." Eric shifted his weight from his left leg to his right.

"I'm not so sure about those sheet sleeping bags, either," Roger added. "Just like everywhere else, you get what you pay for."

"I suppose, considering the size of the hostel here, that it gets visitors to the colleges year around," Eric said. "Some of these visitors do not take care of the premises as well as they could, so the warden has to act tough with everyone."

"Rowdy college students? Like us? Who'd have thought?"

"Do you think all the hostels will be like this one, or is this one just characteristic of a college town?"

"I'll be optimistic and say we have greener pastures ahead, as we get farther from London. We paid for membership even if we don't use it, and I want us to get our money's worth."

They returned to the hostel shortly before it closed at 22:00, and they were nearly too late for showers. They did not sweat as much as expected, but they showered anyway and went to bed without further ado. The North Sea lay ahead of them tomorrow.

10.

Roger awoke immediately at 7:30 when the daylight became sufficiently intense. Eight men slept in four double bunk beds in a room on the shady side of the building. Roger went through the usual ritual of rousing Eric out of the sack. Eric was on the bottom bunk, shaded from the light.

"Rise and shine, Chief. It's a beautiful day." Roger had little enthusiasm in his voice. He knew the rain outside, without even looking at it closely, was going to make the day's ride less than pleasant. Eric knew, too, but he arose with no more resistance than a grumble.

A man in the next bunk watched with amusement as Eric struggled to wake. Roger noticed that the man, probably a few years Roger's senior, had front and rear panniers among his equipment, and inferred correctly that he was also a cyclist.

"That's a big load of equipment you have there, just for one person."

"Yes, but I need all of it." The man had a Germanic-sounding accent. "I use everything here." They could see that his two pairs of panniers contained an abundance of clothing, tools, and cooking and camping equipment.

"Where are you from?" Roger asked.

"Amsterdam. And you?"

Eric finally got himself dressed, a few minutes after Roger and the Dutchman, and took the initiative. "I live at 213 Pine Street in Mayfield, right next door to the Cleavers." Eric pointed toward Roger. "He lives on Evergreen Terrace, across from the Simpsons." Years of cable television had given him a warped sense of humor.

"I do not understand where that is." The Dutchman was puzzled.

Eric got his retribution, since the Dutchman was amused by Eric's difficulty at getting out of bed. Eric was in a vindictive mood because he slept so poorly. "It was a joke. Actually, we're both from Colorado, in the western United States. I'm attending a university in Seattle, Washington. Have you been in the U.S.?"

"No, but I have heard of Colorado. It is often compared to Switzerland, and I have cycled there." The Dutchman's mention of cycling in Switzerland impressed them. "I know where Seattle is."

"Would you care to join us for breakfast in the dining room? I'm Roger Schmidt and he's Eric Fernandez, but you can call us Roger and Eric for short."

"Christian Meijer. Please call me Christian. I will be very happy to join you in the dining room. You must tell me about bicycle touring in the western United States."

"We know a little something about that!"

The men went downstairs to the dining room. Roger noticed that Christian's panniers and handlebar bag were of an older design, made in the United Kingdom. The panniers were no doubt sturdy, Roger thought, but he was convinced that his and Eric's panniers, made in the USA, were of better design. Roger concluded that, even though the American bicycle

49

manufacturing industry lagged behind Europe's and Japan's for decades, it was closing the gap in the 21st century. His career dream was to get hired in the bicycle industry and help raise the U.S. in the worldwide market. He wanted to start a company that could upstage the Italians, Japanese, French and the like. If that was not possible, he wanted to work for one of the foreign manufacturers.

At breakfast, the two Americans discussed politics, history, languages, geography and cycling with Christian, whose English was far better than their Dutch. Like Roger and Eric, Christian was bound for Scotland with no specific itinerary, and he intended to stay in hostels or camp where necessary. Christian was a graduate student enjoying his summer vacation in the best way he knew.

Breakfast at the hostel was the usual British fare of tea, dry toast, corn flakes, eggs and bacon. The two Americans both opted for the continental breakfast, with yogurt and a croissant instead of eggs and meat. Christian's appetite was moderate compared to those of Eric and Roger, who made sure the toast plate and tea pitcher were empty before they left the table. Each ate enough to satisfy his hunger and stifle his tongue. Afterward, they put their sheet sleeping bags in the laundry bin and folded their duvets on their bunks.

Roger and Eric loaded their gear onto their Trek and Novara, respectively, checked out of the hostel, and emerged onto the wet streets of Cambridge. The warden had booked beds for them at the hostel in King's Lynn. Christian took photos of the two Americans in front of the hostel with their cameras. The photos were the only souvenirs from Cambridge they would take with them.

They followed the A10 highway through the fields and farms of Cambridgeshire and Norfolk north toward The Wash. They wore rain suits, but their perspiration made them as damp on the inside as they were on the outside in a very short time. The temperature was comfortable for riding, but the high humidity left everything damp. The roads were built for efficient drainage, but passing cars generated a spray that soaked and soiled Eric and Roger even when the rain ceased intermittently. Gusty headwinds kept them off-balance all day long.

The traffic was dense along the entire route, and by lunchtime, they both wondered silently why they ever left the creature comforts of home. To compound their misery, neither slept well the previous night. The beds were uncomfortable and one of their roommates snored. This was the vacation of their lives, and they were presently miserable.

In a small town past Littleport in Norfolk County, more of a wide spot in the road, they stopped for lunch at a grocery store. Their hands were wet as they ate, even though they were not beneath the rain. The saturated air would not evaporate any more moisture. A shiny red Ferrari was parked at a petrol station, and they took pictures of it. This was quite a spectacle to an American tourist. They sat and contemplated their slow progress while they ate, but they remained optimistic. There would be better days ahead.

They were crossing a region of marshy lowlands known as The Fens. The grass grew very quickly on the fertile farmlands, sometimes overgrowing the road, fences and farm buildings. The roadside grass began immediately where the asphalt ended, so that the highway did not have a dirt shoulder. The sign on a pub along the route indicated, "No football coaches." The Americans took it to mean that team buses were not allowed in the parking lot. They smiled at the connotations the sign would have if it were on a tavern in their own country.

An intriguing landmark stood along the A10 between Cambridge and The Wash, a sign that acknowledged their presence in a town named Denver. They saw nothing in the vicinity that suggested a town, only farms and rural homesteads. Regardless, the sign warranted a rest stop and a photograph. The rain had stopped temporarily, but Roger's and Eric's clothes were damp.

"What's a city like Denver doing in a place like this," Eric scoffed, "and just exactly where is this alleged Denver, anyway?"

"I don't see the city anywhere, but it gives me a feeling of reassurance to know we're so close to home."

Eric took a drink from his water bottle. "I have an aunt and uncle in Denver. I'm sure they'd put us up for the night. Trouble is, I have no idea how to get to their house from here."

"A lot of help you are!" Roger unfolded a road map and studied it. "Let's see if we can get to King's Lynn before they roll up the sidewalks. It's on the North Sea coast."

"Or before a cricket match is initiated. I'd rather be almost anywhere else but here. Let's get moving."

A short distance up the road, another sign pointed them toward the Denver Windmill. They took the turn and found the actual town of Denver just west of the highway. The windmill, built in 1835, looked interesting and was worth a photograph, but they did not take the tour. Instead, they went straight for the bakery. A fresh cheese scone with butter helped them forget the weather outside for a few minutes. They followed signs through Downham Market back to the A10 toward King's Lynn.

Their tires slung water and road grit continuously while they rode. The spray from the front tire coated their down tubes, cranks and lower legs. The spray from the rear tire coated their seat tubes and front derailleurs. The plastic panel on their rear racks was all that protected their backsides from a cold, dirty spray. The grit clung to the lubricant on their chains and formed thick deposits between their rear sprockets. They would have paid any price for fenders on a day like this.

51

Finally, after nearly six long hours of slow riding, they were in King's Lynn on the North Sea coast. Their approach from the south took them through the newer sections of the city, past a modern shopping complex with a large home-improvement store, a supermarket and several franchise businesses. Once they crossed the railroad tracks, the town looked much like most of the other medieval towns they had been through—an aging mass of earth-colored bricks, stones, concrete and asphalt. Regardless, they were glad to be somewhere, except they had no idea where to go once they were in the town. An arch over the street drew them toward it, for some reason. The arch looked like a miniature version of the famous Arc de Triomphe in Paris, but they did not notice any inscription as they rode through it. They did not really care much about the arch, they just wanted to locate the hostel.

A sign near the city centre directed Roger and Eric to turn left off the A10 to get to the youth hostel in Old Town. The street wound around the ancient buildings and took them to the Great Ouse River, pronounced "ooze." They followed the riverside College Lane to a hostel sign pointing to Thoresby College. The front door of the college was locked, so they walked around the building to a narrow alley where they found the hostel entrance. It was not the sort of place they would have found had they not been looking for it. They parked their bicycles in the narrow cobblestone-lined alley while they registered.

"This is a college?" Eric wondered aloud as he and Roger walked their bicycles to the storage room on the river side of the building.

"I get the impression the British definition of a college is somewhat different from ours. This looks more like a boarding school to me. The guidebook says it's 500 years old."

"Doesn't look a day over 400." Eric unlocked the door and wheeled his bicycle inside. He had already carried his other gear to a dormitory on the upper floor.

Roger lifted his bicycle two or three centimeters off the ground and dropped it to shake some of the water and grime off of it. He repeated the action twice. "I hope everything dries off overnight. We really got soaked today."

They jogged back to the side-door entrance through the light rain. Upstairs, they removed their damp cycling clothes and put on jeans and T-shirts that were not entirely dry. They took their wettest clothing to the drying room and hung it up. They draped their other items around their bed frames and over some plastic stacking chairs in their room. Most of the other guests were also using the drying room, and it was filled to capacity. An evening meal was not available at the King's Lynn Youth Hostel, so the two Americans put their raincoats on and walked into the business district a few blocks from the hostel.

"What're you in the mood for tonight?"

"I don't know. Nothing that I've seen so far."

"Seen a grocery store anywhere? We could self-cater our dinner. I think self-cater means cook it yourself." Roger noticed the term "self-catering" on the signs at the hostel registration window.

"Only the big-box store where we entered the city, and I'm in no mood to ride back there in the rain. Let's look at all our options before we choose something neither of us wants."

They looked at several eat-in restaurants, but did not find any take-outs. They found a small grocery store but it did not have much in the way of items they could use to make a meal. They settled on an Indian restaurant. They liked Indian food, but what they really needed after a day in the rain was comfort food, which was not available. They both ate in silence and hardly looked at each other throughout the meal. They went back to the small grocery for apple juice for dessert before they returned to the hostel for the night.

Eric got undressed in the dormitory and pulled on the flannel boxer shorts he wore for sleeping. He found his shaving kit in one pannier, and grabbed his towel from the back of a chair. "Do you think we maybe should have toured the Mediterranean coast instead of this jungle?"

"It was miserable today." Roger did not really answer the question. "But we came physically prepared for this, and I suppose it's just a matter of preparing ourselves mentally for bad weather. Tomorrow will be better. The rain can't fall forever."

"That's what Noah's neighbors said before they went camping." Eric looked at a map. "Anyway, how about if we aim for Nottinghamshire tomorrow? I want to see Sherwood Forest while we're here. Maybe we can see Robin Hood's old haunts."

"Actually, I was hoping to spend some time at the Norfolk Coast, Chief, but I guess there's not much interesting about a cold, rain-swept ocean." Roger pulled back the blanket and got into his bed. He showered earlier while Eric was writing in his journal. "No girls in thong bathing suits, no Roger in whatever he wears on the beach. Is there a hostel in Nottingham or somewhere nearby? Not that I want to fight more big-city traffic."

"The Sheriff of Nottingham might not take kindly to us strangers," Eric said. "Might think we're Merry Men."

"If tomorrow is like today has been, then no matter how well I sleep tonight, I won't be feeling merry."

Eric opened the guidebook to the North West Cities and Peak District section. "Let's see. The nearest one is called Sherwood Forest. It's in Nottinghamshire, but it's a ways north of Nottingham. The rest are to the west of Sheffield. Sound good?"

"Let's do it."

Eric showered, and sat in the common room afterward. He wrote more in his journal, studied his map again, glanced at the reading material provided by the hostel, and exchanged small talk with other hostel guests. By 22:00, he was ready for bed. He and Roger both slept soundly as a result of the punishment they received from the day's ride. In the morning, they would be on their way to the mythical Sherwood Forest of Nottinghamshire, via Lincolnshire.

11.

The first thing Eric did at 7:00 was open a curtain and look out the window. For some strange reason, he got up before Roger did, and he felt great after a good night's sleep—until he noticed the rain was still falling. Even though they had packed their gear in plastic and coated nylon bags inside their panniers, everything seemed damp, and they knew everything would get more damp before anything would be dry. Eric's cheerful demeanor quickly changed for the worse.

Roger was not moving as quickly as usual, and he looked weary. The day had all the potential of a river flowing out of the Dead Sea.

"I was thinking yesterday that things could only get better." Roger slowly got out of bed and reached for his clothes. "You know how much it hurts me to talk about weather, even mention it just in passing, but this stinking rain reminds me of what the citizens of Sodom and Gomorrah must have felt like when God smote them with fire and brimstone. I admit I've committed a few minor sins in my time, but I didn't think the punishment would be this. When is it going to end? It's spoiling our vacation!"

"You know I feel the same way, but there isn't a thing we can do about it. Pardon my optimism, but I can't imagine Nottinghamshire being any worse than this. It'll probably be just as bad, but not worse."

They reluctantly swallowed the last of their breakfast and returned to their room for their gear. The time was nearly 9:00 when they were ready to leave the hostel, as was the case the previous day, and they resigned themselves to getting a late start. They knew they had at least twelve hours of daylight ahead of them, and so their late start was of no consequence. The warden booked beds for them at the Sherwood Forest Youth Hostel in Edwinstowe, Nottinghamshire, when they handed in their room keys. They bade her farewell, and cast themselves adrift on the rain-swept streets of King's Lynn, Norfolk.

Before leaving King's Lynn, they stopped at the superstore and bought lunch ingredients. The interior of the store looked about the same as any

American supermarket, except that the cookies and crackers were in the Biscuits aisle. They were surprised to see precooked pancakes for sale in the bakery section. They saw a sign for crumpets, but could not find anything labeled as such. Was "crumpets" a collective term, like biscuits and cakes? Everything seemed so familiar, yet so foreign. They noticed bottled water at a good price, which reminded them the tap water in their bicycle bottles had a metallic flavor. They added a pair of two-liter bottles to their grocery cart.

Roger and Eric followed the A17 along The Wash coast and across The Fens into Lincolnshire County. The "A" highways were midway between the controlled-access motorways and the rural "B" highways. To their displeasure, lorries and cars were using those same highways, but neither the traffic nor the rain was as bad as on the previous day. They admired the healthy-looking trees and grass on the roadside farms in sparsely-populated southern Lincolnshire. The area was densely populated in comparison to most of the western U.S., but they noticed the gradual decrease in civilization and increase in wilderness all the way from London.

Using their lower gears, they tried to maintain a steady pace. Dirt and sand slung by their tires accumulated quickly on their bodies, bicycles and luggage. Their brakes were slow to respond to their grip. They did nearly all their training in dry weather, but they were beginning to think they should have done more in the worst conditions to prepare themselves for this. As before, fenders would have helped.

The differences between British and American farms were striking. Most of the fields they could see from the highway showed few signs of activity. Few farmers were farming, livestock grazing, or crops growing. The properties were distinctly separated by knee-high stone fences that looked like they had been built eons ago. Barbed wire and shoulder-high fences were scarce, as were wooden, wire and chain-link fencing. The rolling hills and grids superimposed upon them by the stone fences reminded the two Americans of a huge patchwork quilt, as they had seen from their airplane on its approach to London. They did not see many farm animals, so they assumed the farms in the region grew food crops.

A section of the A17 was closed for road maintenance near Holbeach. They were detoured onto the A151 toward Spalding. The A16 toward Boston eventually put them back on the A17 to Sleaford after adding 11 kilometers to their journey.

By early afternoon, the rain stopped and the pavement dried even though the sky was still very cloudy. Roger and Eric and their equipment were damp and dirty, but the respite from the rain was most welcome. They stopped for lunch near Sleaford.

"Lunch tastes just a little better when it's dry." Eric chewed his sandwich savagely. He always had a big appetite, but riding made him that much hungrier.

"Nothing tastes very good to me right now."

"What's ailing you, anyway?"

"I ache all over, but I'm not sure why. I feel very weak, too." Roger's expression agreed with his words. "I'm getting saddle sores already."

"The saddle sores must be contagious," Eric said. "I almost feel like I've been straddling a belt sander. It's amazing how we forget the agony of long-distance cycling from one summer to the next."

"I have some diaper-rash ointment for the saddle sores. You'll have to try it this evening."

"Where did you learn about that?"

"One of my brother's cycling friends became a father last year. It worked on his baby, so he tried it on himself. He raved about it to Walter, and Walt told me about it."

"I'll try it. Can you make it to Sherwood Forest, or should we hole up here for the night?"

"I'd rather move onward. I'm not that sick. Considering the possibility of rain, we need a B&B or a hostel. We're not equipped to camp in this." They did not bring a tent, and thus were not prepared to camp under inclement weather.

"Have a little faith. We'll get through this part soon enough." Eric started on a second sandwich.

Roger ate more slowly. He did not have his usual big appetite. "The kind of faith I have in Santa Claus, the tooth fairy and the Easter Bunny?"

"It's all in accordance with the prophecies. *Capisce?*"

"If you say so, doc. All I know is, my resources are dwindling."

Eric and Roger crossed the county line into Nottinghamshire in the mid-afternoon and arrived in Newark shortly thereafter. They caught a glimpse of the sun through a gap in the cloud cover, and they were thrilled to be riding into a town with dry streets. They had covered 120 kilometers since King's Lynn.

"How are you doing?" Eric already knew the answer by the sluggish way Roger was riding.

"Terrible!" Roger said in a weak voice.

"You want to stop here for the night?"

"No, I don't, but we probably should. I'm coming down with something."

They had no idea where to look for a bed-and-breakfast, a small guesthouse better known as a "B&B." They arbitrarily chose a street radiating from the city centre of Newark, a city of some 25,000 people, and looked for a B&B or hotel. Newark looked about like all the cities they had visited so far, with its concrete and brick fences and houses, the modern and the medieval. The ruins of an ancient castle in the center of town were under renovation. They were content, for the moment, to be riding slowly and looking around, instead of just passing through and not noticing the subtleties of British life. Roger was especially glad to be riding slowly. He felt as bad as he looked.

Eric stopped at one of the brick and concrete buildings, leaned his bicycle against the building, and went inside. Roger slowly followed him into the discreetly marked B&B. Eric was already making arrangements with the owners, a middle-aged single woman and her nubile daughter, by the time Roger dragged himself through the door. The ground floor of the B&B was a lounge, with a supply of liquor locked in a cabinet behind a bar, and the guests' rooms were on the upper floor. The women invited them to stow their bicycles in a shed behind the building.

Eric took the bicycles around the building to the shed while Roger carried their equipment up to their room. Their comfortable, quiet room, and the attractive younger woman who showed them to it, were worth the pain and suffering they had gone through to get there. They changed from their riding clothes into jeans, sneakers and long-sleeve shirts. Roger just sat on his bed and looked glum. His eyes were bloodshot. He drank from his water bottle in a futile attempt to quell the fever and fatigue.

"I'm getting hungry again. You?"

"Not really, but I need to eat something. Got to keep my strength up. Would you mind bringing me back a little something?"

"Some drugs?"

"I have ibuprofen if I need it. A sandwich, small fish and chips, kebab, egg roll, whatever you can get for under three quid. You know by now what I like and dislike." Roger removed a £5 note from his wallet and handed it to Eric.

Roger undressed and drew a hot bath after Eric left. The bathroom was exactly that—a room with a tub but no sink, toilet or shower. The toilet room and bathroom were common to all guests at the B&B, and each bedroom had a sink. Roger savored the pleasure of lying in a tub of warm water after a day of riding through cool rain. He still felt horrible, but the bath helped.

Eric walked into the business district a few blocks away in search of an eatery and a pay phone. He called the hostel in Edwinstowe to change his reservation. The hostel was already booked full for the following night, but the warden said to try again later, as several others were likely to alter their bookings. Eric looked at every food outlet in the neighborhood before settling on anything. He read the menus in the front windows of a fish bar, two pubs, a Chinese take-out, a Thai restaurant and a Pakistani take-out. He did not miss the usual fast-food franchises back home.

Eric arrived at the B&B with his evening meal in a plastic bag. Roger had just gotten out of the bath and was getting dressed.

Eric handed Roger some change, all in coins. "I got us one kebab and one egg roll each, and one serving of fish and chips. I can get more if we need more."

"Turkish, Chinese and British, all in one meal. Probably more than enough for me." Roger felt a little better after the bath, but his fever was still raging. He ate the kebab and egg roll very slowly. It took a whole lot of effort for him to eat anything. Eric wolfed down his food, including all the fish and chips.

"I did something this evening that I don't ever recall doing," Eric said after his bath. "I made a ring in the bathtub. I didn't realize how filthy I was."

"So did I," Roger admitted, "and I had a lot of trouble cleaning my ring off the tub. I'm talking Dirt with a capital D."

"A Fruit & Nut is calling my name from a store about two blocks from here. You want one?"

"Not now, but get me one anyway. It'll get eaten."

Eric walked to the small grocery for chocolate bars, while Roger just lay on his bed under a blanket. When Eric returned to the B&B, the younger woman was serving some guests in the bar. She smiled at Eric and acknowledged his presence.

"When would you like me to knock you up?" she asked Eric.

The question took him aback, as the woman's expression looked much more innocent and sincere than her words sounded in American lingo. "I'm game anytime. Knock me up at your convenience."

"How about seven o'clock?" She was puzzled by Eric's strange response to a perfectly normal question.

"In the morning?" Eric was still not sure what sort of knocking up he would be receiving. He glanced at his watch and noticed that seven o'clock in the evening had already passed.

"Yes, of course, in the morning." She was growing impatient.

"Fine. Knock me up at seven in the morning."

Eric went back upstairs where Roger was contemplating his journal from his bed. They discussed the day's events while they wrote in their journals.

Eric's journal was eloquently written, in a style combining journalistic objectivity with sarcastic opinions. Eric's words were mostly prosaic, but he also recorded rhymes, limericks and British idioms when they came to mind. Eric and Roger enjoyed writing and reciting obscene limericks, and they would occasionally attempt to add melodies to their rhymes, although they rarely wrote an entire song. Roger's journal was mostly a record of expenditures and names and locations of places where they had been. Roger did not have Eric's gift for writing, but Roger developed the habit of noting his observations and opinions when he saw how much Eric was absorbed by it.

"The clerk is going to knock me up at seven in the morning. Would you mind giving us a few minutes of privacy?"

"Knock you up, did you say?" Roger said in a croaky voice. "I suppose you think she'll show up here in a teddy, ready to shag you."

"Isn't that what you do when you knock someone up?" Eric now sounded a little disappointed. "I didn't make any moves on her, she just offered, sweet and innocent as could be."

"I hate to throw a wet blanket on your plans, but I think she meant she's going to knock on the door at seven to wake us up," Roger said. "A wake up call for hotels that don't have telephones in the rooms."

"Well, dip me in a vat of raw sewage! I was really looking forward to getting knocked up tomorrow."

"How could someone as swarthy as you be so…so blond?"

"I was a ditzy blonde with big hair and manicured nails in one of my previous incarnations."

Roger was shivering, and his aches were worse than earlier in the day. He went to bed wearing his long-sleeved, wool-blend cycling clothes, while the sky was still light.

"Are you going to sleep in your elf suit?"

"I have the ch-ch-chills." Roger's teeth chattered as he spoke.

"Anything I can get you?" Eric set down his journal and pen.

"Just let me sleep, and hope that I'm better tomorrow." Roger barely paid attention to Eric as he thought about calling Marianne again. He would call or send e-mail when he felt better.

"Get some serious shut-eye, then. I'll be doing the same pretty soon, after I finish describing the day in my journal and see where we're going tomorrow." Eric took another look at the map before he folded it and put it away. "Tomorrow, better things will happen. We'll meet some babes, maybe. Put any other thoughts out of your mind tonight." Eric hoped they would be able to go somewhere tomorrow. He also hoped he did not get whatever was ailing Roger.

12.

For the second consecutive day, Eric was out of bed before Roger. A knock on the door promptly at 7:00 gave him a jolt. Roger rose slowly, but he looked much better than he did before he fell asleep the previous night. He was uncomfortably warm and sweaty now because of his woolens. The fever broken, he no longer felt chilled. His aches and pains had not entirely disappeared, but he had no trouble getting dressed and walking downstairs to the dining room for breakfast. They were both relieved to know that Roger felt strong enough for another day's ride.

"The toast is so dry," Roger said, "that it makes the silica gel in a desiccator seem saturated."

"The toast is so dry," Eric argued, "it makes Bordeaux's best clarets, even the Lafites and Latours, drool with envy."

"It makes the Atacama desert look like a rain forest." Roger spread some marmalade on a slice of toast and took a bite.

"It makes the counties of Utah and Kansas feel like the counties of Nevada and Colorado," Eric insisted.

"It makes your parents look sober. So there!"

"It makes your witticisms sound humorous." Eric poured another cup of tea for himself. "No, on second thought, your dry wit makes the toast seem like soggy bread."

"You always have to get the last word in."

"I do not," Eric said. "Go ahead, have the last word. But I get the penultimate word."

"You're starting to sound like an Englishman," Roger said.

"Balderdash!"

"We ought to remove ourselves from here, ASAP. You can see that the sky is threatening to unload on us again." Roger gestured toward a window, where dark clouds were visible across the horizon.

"I've been told that Little John and Triar...I mean Friar Tuck, don't sign autographs after 11:30." Eric tilted his head back to get the last drop out of his teacup. "We'd better hurry to Sherwood Forest so we can get a picture of them shaking hands with us."

"I've been pining for the forest."

"That's a terrible pun."

"Maybe we'll find a Robin Hood museum somewhere. My mother pestered me for a month before departure to look in every museum we see." Roger finished his toast. His appetite was nearly back to normal. He washed the toast down with tea. "Did you study the map last night?"

"Yes, and I think we should aim toward York, if you're up to it. If not, we can try the Sherwood Forest hostel again," Eric said. "It's in a town called Edwinstowe somewhere northwest of here. It's not on the map. Must be very small. If it's too close, we can keep going into the Peak District. The warden couldn't book us for tonight, but she thought somebody might cancel and we could have their beds. I called on my way to get our supper yesterday."

"York might be too far for one day. Let's take a look at Sherwood Forest, and decide what to do from there." Roger wiped his lips with a napkin. "I'm feeling all right now. Way better than I felt yesterday. Don't know what hit me, but I think it's gone now."

They were mildly surprised when the clerk charged them an additional fifty pence each for storing their bicycles in the shed. They took a last admiring glance at the clerk before they left. They appreciated their first rainless morning since they left Essex, and their enthusiasm for cycling was returning. A roundabout in Newark put them on the A616 toward Ollerton. They encountered numerous hamlets, and they stopped at a bakery in one for a second breakfast of scones. They were not worried at all about overindulgence. They knew they were getting plenty of exercise from riding. Each hamlet had a roadside pub, often with a colorful name.

The forest had a tranquilizing effect on them. Its tall trees and rolling hills captured their imagination much more than the flat farmlands did. Traffic on the lesser highways was moderate, and the absence of rain allowed them to wear short racing pants and short-sleeve jerseys. They took several pictures of each other from their bicycles while in motion, and the effect made for some of their best photography on the entire journey. They both realized that they had finally discovered the type of touring they were seeking. The forest and the quaint villages of Nottinghamshire had all the charm of any place they had ever been. They were so enthralled by the beauty and serenity of the region that they let their attention wander from their most immediate environs.

They were not far from the Yorkshire counties—North, South and West, and East Riding of Yorkshire. North Yorkshire, by far the largest in area and smallest in population of the four, was definitely on their itinerary. They were mildly familiar with Yorkshire, its cattle and sheep farms and its Dales, from literature and television.

More than an hour after they left Newark, Eric slowed and moved toward the edge of the road somewhere after a wide spot in the road named Kneesall. "Ride slowly. I'll catch up with you in a minute. Got to use the loo."

"I've heard the pro racers can do that without getting off their bikes."

"Maybe so, but they aren't carrying panniers and a sleeping bag."

"I hope they move to the rear of the *peloton* before they try that maneuver."

Eric stopped, dismounted, and signaled Roger to continue. Roger slackened his pace and studied the map beneath the plastic window in the top of his handlebar bag while he waited for Eric. Roger paid no attention to the automobile approaching from behind.

The dark green car swerved too close to Roger, forcing him off the pavement. He tried to regain control of the awkward bicycle in the grass and gravel alongside the road, but he went down before the car would allow him back on the asphalt. The car stopped while he lay in a damp, grassy gully beneath his bicycle.

He expected the driver to apologize and help him get back upright, something to the effect of, "Sorry about that, old man! Can I give you a lift?" He intended to admonish the driver about allowing enough room while passing and staying within his own lane. Instead, two passengers jumped out. One of them knocked the wind out of the cyclist with a soccer-style kick to the back from a heavy boot. The assailant added a fist to the side of Roger's head. The other quickly ransacked his panniers, and added another direct free kick to Roger's chest. They found little of value to them except his wallet, passport, Swiss Army knife and the digital watch they removed from his wrist. They returned to the car and disappeared over the horizon before Eric was even close enough to see what had happened, let alone identify the car.

Eric was carrying his bicycle back onto the highway when he noticed something peculiar happening several hundred meters ahead. He intuitively sprinted as fast as he could to the scene where the car stopped ever so briefly, right about where he expected to find Roger, whom he could not see. The car was long gone when Eric arrived.

Eric shouted a string of biblical names when he arrived at the gully where Roger lay dazed. Eric dismounted again, set his bicycle aside, and moved quickly to Roger's side. "Are you all right? Say something!" Roger did not respond immediately.

Roger coughed as Eric pulled him ever so gently from the trickling water. Roger caught his breath, and then babbled with his eyes closed while Eric loosened Roger's helmet strap and twisted his shoes out of their pedals. Eric lifted the bicycle off Roger very carefully while Roger writhed in agony. Eric pinned him on dry ground to prevent him from further injuring himself. Within a few minutes, Roger regained full consciousness and his normal breathing and pulse rates. Roger's first coherent words were mostly obscene epithets.

"Tell me what happened!" Eric tried to remain calm in the face of calamity. "Did you get a good look at them?"

"It was a one-armed man!" Roger did not spare the sarcasm. His chest hurt front and back, and he coughed painfully when he tried to talk or take a deep breath. "No, I didn't get more than about one or two seconds of glance at them." He gradually recalled what details he knew of the incident and described them to Eric, who wisely recorded them in his journal. No bones appeared to be broken, but he was certainly not unscathed. His panniers and other gear were wet and dirty, but did not appear to be irreparably damaged. His Trek was scratched and scuffed and the front wheel was bent enough to be in need of truing. His wristwatch, a gift of his late grandparents for his high school graduation, had been stolen, along with his passport and the cash in his wallet.

Eric's precautionary arrest of Roger's spine proved unnecessary, but Roger had plenty of scrapes and bruises everywhere. His left shoulder was lacerated and bruised, and his jersey was torn at that spot, too. His left forearm, hip and knee had scrapes and contusions, and his back, head and neck were sore as a result of the impact against the ground. His ribs on one side ached with each breath. His helmet absorbed some of the punch to his head, but his cheek was bruised and swollen. The blows he received enhanced all the other injuries. He had rolled down an embankment of soft grass and loose soil instead of crashing on pavement, and he was wearing a helmet and gloves, all of which probably prevented him from sustaining much more serious injuries.

The front wheel of the Trek was bent and two spokes were broken. The left brake lever was twisted from its standard position on the handlebar. The handlebar was not noticeably bent, but the tape on its left side was shredded from the brake lever to the end plug. The tape was no great loss—it was already worn and due for replacement. The cage of the left pedal was scarred, but the spindle was not bent. The remainder of the bicycle and equipment did not appear to be damaged. Eric applied a bandage to Roger's shoulder, and then went to work on the front wheel while Roger cleaned and dried himself as best he could with the supplies at hand, and then rested on his camping mattress.

The incident occurred in less than a minute, and Roger was completely taken by surprise. He could not provide much information. He recognized the car as a two-door, dark green, older-model Citröen, a name he was not even sure how to pronounce. The image of the ugly face of the front passenger, the one who led the assault, was deeply imbedded in Roger's memory, although he barely glimpsed the other two thugs. It was something he would not soon forget.

An hour after the incident, they finished replacing the broken spokes, truing the front wheel, repositioning the brake lever, and straightening the fork as well as they could. Roger knew that the fork and rim were permanently deformed, but they could be replaced. His psyche was also injured, but it could not be replaced for any amount of money.

Roger's anger and Eric's alarum were slow to subside, but the ride toward Ollerton helped them vent their emotions constructively. They stayed close to each other, wary of traffic. A strong feeling of cynicism overcame their earlier enjoyment of the countryside and the picturesque villages. The vacation that should have been the time of their lives was rapidly becoming the disaster of their lives. Still, Roger's strong suit was confidence, and already he was determined to make the best of the situation.

Ollerton was farther from the scene of the crime than it looked on the map. They had not gotten very far from Newark, but a feeling of desperation made everything seem farther and steeper than it was. A roundabout in Ollerton put them onto the A6075 west toward Edwinstowe. Eric hoped they could find accommodations at the hostel, or somewhere, in Edwinstowe. They were in no shape to go much farther after the vicious attack on Roger.

Edwinstowe was such a small town that it did not even show on their map, but it certainly looked inviting. At first, they overshot the turnoff to the hostel in the center of town. They turned around when they saw the back of the hostel sign for the opposite direction. They turned on Forest Corner and climbed a hill toward a sizable forest park. They turned again just before the park to get to the youth hostel. The town made quite a big deal of its Robin Hood heritage, as did the thoroughly modern hostel. The building and its setting in the forest were most attractive. The two Americans were preoccupied, and they hardly noticed the bucolic charm.

"Mr. Fernandez?" The warden repeated the name Eric had given her as he inquired about beds. She pushed her bifocals up so she could read her reservation book. "Yes, I took your call yesterday. Looks like I don't have any beds available tonight. So sorry! The Lincoln and Matlock hostels are both about 30 miles from here. Or you might be able to get into one of the B&Bs in town. But hurry, they fill up fast." The telephone at her desk rang and she turned to answer it. "Excuse me."

Eric and Roger nodded and turned toward the front door of the hostel. The place looked so inviting, but Murphy's Law was in full force at the moment. Roger's color was better than it was the previous day, almost back to normal, but he looked awful with road rash and a torn jersey. His mood was even worse than his appearance. Nothing was going their way. They had planned this vacation for nearly a year, and it was falling apart in every way in just a few days. They noticed several no-vacancy signs on the inns as they rode into Edwinstowe. They were trying to avoid the pricier accommodations, but even the better hotels were full. The nearest hostels seemed very far for Roger's condition, even though they had not ridden very far from Newark. They pushed open the hostel door and got back on their bicycles.

"Now what? Look for a B&B, or keep going?"

"I need to make a report to the police. Let's meet back here in an hour. If you can't find anything, we're not too far from several larger cities. Just stay in the city limits. I think we're safe in the town."

Eric rode west along the A6075 to the edge of town, but did not see any hotels or B&Bs with rooms available. A sixth sense pushed him beyond the city limits until he came to a crossing of the National Cycle Route. He checked his watch and took a look at the light traffic in both directions. He expected Roger's assailants to be long gone from the area, but he kept his eyes peeled anyway. He turned south onto the paved bicycle path and followed it into the forest. He was unfamiliar with the Route, but it certainly captured his interest. The path became gravel about half a kilometer away from the highway, and passed some residential properties. Intrigued, Eric turned around, went back to the highway, and returned to Edwinstowe. In the town, he turned onto a one-way loop opposite the road to the hostel. The loop took him into the business district, which was populated mostly by eateries. He stopped at a small grocery store for two bananas and two peaches, lunch for Roger and himself. He continued around the loop but did not find a place to stay overnight. The loop took him back to the highway, and he returned to the hostel with only some food and an awareness of a network of bicycle trails.

Roger rode back to Ollerton, where he found the local law-enforcement office and filed a complaint. He wondered if he was talking to the modern-day Sheriff of Nottingham, but he was in no mood for chitchat. The officer in residence was unable to offer anything more than an admonition to be careful. The methamphetamine addicts would do whatever they had to do to get their fix, even steal from tourists. Drug-dealing gangs from the larger cities in the Midlands were a vicious lot, but they were rarely a problem in the rural areas. The officer did know of a few other instances of cyclists getting shaken down in Nottinghamshire and neighboring counties, but none of the victims had been able provide enough information to arrest any suspects. Roger got the impression the police considered it a petty crime, and were not overly concerned about it. He felt like he had wasted his time, but what else could he do? He looked for accommodations on his way back to the hostel, but found nothing. He mulled over his options as he rode.

"Find anything?" Roger was waiting outside the hostel when Eric returned a few minutes after his own arrival. Roger liked the town and the hostel setting, but they were not nearly enough to offset his anger and disappointment.

"Nothing in this town, but I got us some lunch." Eric handed a banana and a peach to Roger, and began peeling the other banana for himself. "I found a bike path, too. Wish I had a map for it."

"Thanks." Roger had not been thinking about food, but he was actually quite hungry. The fruit tempered his rage briefly.

They ate in silence and focused on faraway objects in the forest. The sky was overcast but the dry weather held. Roger looked at the map and decided to shoot for Worksop up the B6034. They were trying to use the less-traveled roads to avoid the hazards of traffic, but they had not expected the hazards of not enough traffic. They went inside the hostel to use the loo, a Britishism from the French *lieu d'aisance*. The warden pointed them down the hall. They got back on their bicycles and were about to continue north up the road of the hostel's address

The warden came out the front door and waved to get their attention as they were leaving. "I just had a cancellation from a party of three. Would you like their beds?"

Roger and Eric registered for the night and put their gear in the Robin Hood room. All the rooms had a similar theme. They were silently relieved to know where they would be spending the night, and they were out of harm's way for the moment. Their room had three other bunks, and all six beds had someone's gear on them. A sink and shower were in an attached room. The toilet was behind the nearest door in the hallway. The warden asked about Roger's injuries. She had heard rumors of roving gangs in the Midlands, but had not seen any direct evidence of it until now. She thought the illicit drug trade might be involved. Only not in rural areas like Edwinstowe.

Once they settled into the hostel, they fine-tuned their earlier maintenance on Roger's bicycle outside the bicycle shed. The damage was superficial and would not stop Roger from continuing the ride. The concrete pad in front of the hostel made for a much better place to work on a bicycle than the dense grass beside the highway. He still had his traveler's cheques to buy food and lodging. Peace of mind was the biggest loss, the worst damage, inflicted by the highwaymen.

As the hostel had cooking facilities, they decided to buy groceries and prepare their supper themselves. At the market Eric found earlier, they were able to round up some cheese, fruit, vegetables, bread, tea bags, orange juice, skim milk and müesli. They were set for supper and breakfast. A block up the loop from the market, they bought some pineapple fritters at a fish bar.

Roger and Eric had hardly spoken to each other since the mugging. They were both angry and upset, but neither was mad at the other. The tranquillity of Edwinstowe had a calming effect on both of them. They prepared their supper, ate and washed their dishes without saying much of anything to anyone in the busy kitchen and dining room. Eric sensed Roger had more on his mind than he was willing to admit. Roger stepped out the side door of the warm dining room into the cooler evening air outside after they finished cleaning. Eric followed him out, dreading what he was about to hear when they were out of earshot of the other guests.

"This vacation is ruined! I felt better this morning, and then those bastards jumped me! Considering how well I defended myself, I might just as well have been comatose!"

"You can't blame yourself for what they did to you. Shit happens! You know that."

"That's beside the point. It's the most humiliating thing that's ever happened to me!"

"What can we do about it, besides nothing? We've spent a lot of time and money on this. Get a grip!"

"I'm quitting! I've had enough!"

13.

Eric arose from a fitful sleep at 6:30. He just sat with his legs over the edge of the bunk for several minutes, thinking about the many things he should have done and what little he could still do to save the day. He had tried, pleaded, with Roger to reconsider his decision to abandon the tour, but to no avail. Roger had been plagued by romantic troubles, highwaymen, foul weather and illness, and he was ready to throw in the towel. It was over for Roger, and Eric was not looking forward to either continuing on his own, or returning to Colorado with his fair-weather friend.

"It's not at all like you to be a quitter," Eric had argued after the previous night's supper. They had stir-fried some vegetables, but even a tasty meal did not mollify Roger.

"I'm cutting my losses, and spare me the pep talk. It's too late for that." Roger would not be dissuaded.

"Well, I'm not quitting! I'm staying for the next four weeks, like we originally planned. Things will start looking up. I know they will."

"I'm sure things will look up. For you. I should've just gone to Hawaii with Marianne in the first place. The longer I stay here, the worse things get!"

"Thanks for leaving me on my own! I was counting on you. It'll be just great if your muggers find me all by myself on some lonely highway!"

"You have plenty of options, not the least of which is to return to London with me and ride in some other part of Europe where there are no muggers."

"How are you going to leave, anyway? They took your passport."

"I'll figure out something when I get to London." Roger had ended the discussion with that, but Eric was far from satisfied.

Eric had played all his best cards in this standoff, and he was still losing. He tried one more maneuver over breakfast. "How about, give it one more day. Let's ride to York. We'll both have all day to think about it, to cool off. Maybe we can get you a new passport in York. This is one hell of a way for us to part company. You'll probably have to go to York anyway to get a train to London."

"I can get one in Sheffield or Nottingham. They're both closer than York, and they might even have an consulate where I can get a passport."

"Suit yourself then." Eric resigned himself to having lost the battle.

Roger contemplated what Eric had said for a few minutes. He did not much like the idea of leaving Eric by himself, even under ideal circumstances. "All right. One more day. Maybe we'll even spot them, so we can turn them over to the police, or something like that. But only one day. I've got big problems, and they get bigger every day."

"Our luck will change, if we stay together and look out for each other."

Roger nodded in agreement. Teamwork was more critical now than ever. "Thanks for fixing my bike yesterday."

"*De nada, amigo.*"

Roger thought about Marianne, but he was in no mood for what he had to discuss with her. He would have loved to hear her soothing, comforting voice, but it would have to wait for a more opportune time. Perhaps the ride to York would clear his head long enough for some rational thought. They finished their breakfast and prepared to leave the hostel.

The two Americans retrieved their bicycles from the bicycle shed and loaded up their equipment. An English family that had also spent the night at the hostel was setting out for a walking tour on one of the many trails through Sherwood Forest. A little girl of about 8 or 9 years was wearing a green Robin Hood hat.

"Where are you going?" the girl asked Roger. She smiled at him in a way that he could not resist smiling back.

"York. And you?"

"We're going to explore the forest and find the band of Merry Men!" She had no lack of enthusiasm for her much-anticipated adventure among knights and archers and fair maidens.

"You're certainly dressed for the occasion. Have a good walk."

"All the best!"

The two Americans rode north up the B6034 past the Sherwood Forest Park, over a ridge, through a roundabout and into Worksop. The forest ended there. Navigating the streets of Worksop, they found the A60 into the farmlands south of Doncaster. Larger than most of the cities they had seen since London, Doncaster had heavy traffic and a variety of wrong turns for them to avoid. They found a bakery-café before they left Doncaster, and stopped for a fresh scone sliced in half with whipped cream and berry jam in the middle. Satisfied with their pre-lunch snack, they continued on to the A19 to Selby and more flat farmland.

"Keep your eyes peeled." Roger's slightly bent fork increased his awkwardness, and his wounds slowed him down just a bit. They gradually built up momentum. The heavy luggage on their bicycles precluded sprint starts.

"I wrote down your vague description of the car, Squire. I also memorized it. Let's make sure we don't get separated today." Eric felt strong, but all of their recent troubles had taken an emotional toll on him. Roger's slower-than-usual pace was just right, under the circumstances.

They stayed close together all the way, and they both paid close attention to automobile traffic in both directions. Roger was still sore from the assault, but not too sore to ride. He was content to be riding right there and then, in spite of everything that had happened, but his conscience was still divided between enthusiasm and doubt. The doubt had a lead on the enthusiasm, and he knew it. He vowed to himself not to let his anger and paranoia overcome Eric's perseverance at any cost. The pavement was dry, and that alone improved his outlook. They kept their eyes open for anything that looked like the car used by Roger's assailants, but they did not see any that looked suspicious. The ride was pleasant enough under warm, dry weather that even Roger thought at times about other things than what happened to him the previous day. The sky was overcast as usual, but the rain was waiting for another time to fall.

The A19 took them across a motorway that went to Leeds, and through several hamlets. Their bicycles were functioning well and they kept up a healthy pace all the way to Selby. They admired a huge castle restoration project in the city centre before stopping for a lunch of fruit at a co-op grocery. They wasted a few minutes trying to follow the signs to the public toilet. When they finally found it, it was closed for maintenance. A second loo required a 20-pence coin for entry. Both had spent their last coins of that size at the grocery. They would have to suffer for a while.

A bridge over the River Ouse took them from Selby to Barlby, where a sign pointed them to the National Cycle Route. Eric was excited to give it a try, and Roger' interest was piqued. They were both a bit disappointed to find a dirt path along a berm parallel to the river. A paved bicycle path apart from the highway was highly desirable, but a dirt path offered no real advantages. They continued along the A19 out of Barlby until they came to another point of access to National Cycle Route 65 where it was paved. They looked at the heavy traffic on the A19 and chose the bike path.

The bike path gradually deviated from the A19, and became hard-packed dirt again a few kilometers from Selby. The Americans looked for a side path back to the pavement of the A19 but did not find one. They had a choice of backtracking or continuing ahead on the dirt. They opted for the dirt, and their patience was rewarded a few kilometers later where the path was paved again. The path was lined with trees, tall grass and bushes, shielding it from the highway and the farms. They passed several pedestrians and cyclist in both directions, including a woman and her young daughter out for a ride.

"Excuse me, does this path take us into York?" Eric asked the woman. He could not see the highway any longer, and he was not sure whether he was still moving parallel to it.

"Yes, it'll get you to York. You have a ways to go yet. Have you noticed the planets?" The woman was referring to some markers along the path that showed the relative positions of the nine planets with respect to the sun.

"No, I hadn't really noticed. Is it a scale model of the solar system?"

"Yes, that's what it is. We're rather proud of our path and our educational project."

"We'll have to stop at the next planet monument and take a look. Thanks for pointing it out."

"All the best!" The woman and her daughter let the faster riders pass them.

Eric and Roger paid attention to the planet markers and stopped at the next one briefly to read the plaque and get a drink from their water bottles. The path did not intersect any of the small towns along the A19, but it did cross a very large horse racing track on the outskirts of York. As they entered a residential neighborhood at the south end of town, the path became a city street and delivered them to another path along the River Ouse.

York, a city of just over 100,000 people about 110 kilometers north of Edwinstowe, was not nearly as big or as well known as the New World city that was named for it, but "Old" York was rich in historical and cultural significance nonetheless. The Evans and several stateside people had urged Roger and Eric to spend some time looking through York's numerous museums and excavated ruins. Romans, Vikings, Saxons and Normans, among other tribes, all occupied York at some time, and all left at least a few relics behind for the archaeologists.

The Americans quickly noticed what a busy place York could be, especially during the summer tourist season. The streets were crowded with pedestrians, cars and bicycles. They left the riverside path and followed a series of busy streets near the river, hoping to spot a youth hostel sign somewhere. They did see some signs for the railway station. They had no idea where to find the hostel, but they were drawn toward the spires of a large building they could see from a distance. They rode through the city centre toward the spires. A steep slope took them up a short rise from the river amid dense traffic and narrow streets. The gigantic medieval building was the York Minster, a name they recognized from their hostel guide. They thought they knew how to get to the hostel from the Minster. Like all the British cities they had been in, the streets of York were anything but straight, and changed names every few blocks.

They circled around the York Minster to get their bearings. They were awed by the size of the church, some ten stories high with a footprint of about three square blocks. Mega-churches were neither a recent invention, nor an American one! They followed the A19 to the northwest for quite a ways out of the city centre. Quite unsure whether they were in the right part of town or headed in the right direction, they surprised themselves when they found Clifton Green and Water End. They were even more surprised to find the hostel only a block or so from the riverbank and its paved path where they had been.

The 150-bed York Youth Hostel was originally a Victorian mansion. Eric and Roger rode into the courtyard of the attached white buildings and leaned their bicycles against a wall just outside the self-catering kitchen and the bicycle storage room. They were assigned to a room on the upper level, and they carried their panniers upstairs. They chose a bunk away from the door that gave them a view of the garden and the trees that stood between the riverside escarpment and the hostel property. Some roommates extended a friendly welcome to the two newcomers. Two German backpackers, a Japanese backpacker and a 40-something American cyclist shared their room. The Germans and the Japanese all spoke very good English.

"Luck o' the Spanish," Eric said. "We got here safely, and we found it without too much trouble. I'm glad we booked our beds here before we left Edwinstowe."

"We might be luckier than I think we are," Roger agreed. "Let's see if York's all it's cracked up to be. I want to find the railway station and check on trains to London."

Eric groaned in silence at that comment, but he had run out of arguments to the contrary. He did all he could to talk Roger into continuing on the tour, yet he was not even sure he wanted to continue at this point. They had not seen any dark green sedans that day, but they knew it was prowling around somewhere. They stowed their gear in their bedside lockers and under the bottom bunk, and rode along the river toward the city centre. They had seen a bicycle store at the south end, a few blocks from the Castle Museum. They rode in circles trying to find the store, wasting fifteen precious minutes while they did. They finally found it with nearly 20 minutes to spare before closing time. Eric selected a can of aerosol dog repellent, nicely spiced with cayenne pepper. Roger did not buy the pepper spray, figuring he would be on a train back to London in the morning, but he did get some spare spokes.

Upon leaving the bicycle store, they got back on the riverside path in the direction of the hostel. When they came to the ancient wall that once surrounded the oldest parts of the city, they crossed the river on a busy bridge that took them to the railway station a few blocks from the river.

The York Railway Station, adjacent to the National Railway Museum and the appropriately named Royal York Hotel, was a huge transportation center. They expected something more modest for no particular reason. The building appeared much larger and busier than any train station they had seen in the USA. Several city and chartered buses were idling under the large canopy over the front entrance, as were several taxis. Hundreds of pedestrians were walking in every direction, and the street in front was very busy. They were reminded that Europeans use trains much more than Americans in the western states do. The crowds, the traffic and the size of the building were just a little intimidating to Roger. Was he losing his nerve? They rode under the canopy and parked their bicycles along the front wall.

"I'll wait out here with the bikes while you buy your ticket." Eric made no attempt at all to hide the disappointment in his voice.

In the ambiance of York, Roger had briefly forgotten all about his plan to abandon the tour. He had felt so certain about it this morning. Now, he was having doubts. He continued to think about it. No, he could not go back on his latest plan. He hated to be indecisive. Eric would be fine without him, maybe even better off without all of Roger's recent troubles to slow him down. He reached for the door into the railway station.

14.

A tall man in his mid-20s sat at the kitchen table in a rundown apartment in Leeds, counting a wad of paper money. Death was the sobriquet he had tattooed on himself in several places, and it seemed to inspire a certain amount of fear in people who met him. Death and his two unkempt associates had made several deliveries today, and the payoff was sweet. He had well over one thousand pounds, plus about three hundred euros. One of his best customers made frequent trips onto the Continent and often paid him in euros, which was just fine. Exchanging currencies was no big deal, as long as it was in cash.

A cloud of cigarette smoke filled the room where the two associates, Zed and Skin, sat on the sofa with Death's girlfriend and watched a football match on television. They had already drained several bottles of ale. The gang leader hardly trusted either one of them, but they were very useful, and they had never been disloyal. They could intimidate just about anyone with their sinister looks alone, and they could be very brutal enforcers with anyone who needed a little persuasion. Zed was virtually illiterate, having been in and out of foster homes and juvenile detention all his life. Skin, an ex-con, was rarely sober enough to read anything. Death counted out each one's share of the day's haul and put them in separate piles.

Death did not give much thought to this line of work anymore. He had been distributing pills, weapons, cocaine, methamphetamine and heroin for nearly a decade. He made a decent living, and he did not have to pay any income taxes. In addition to the two associates, his live-in girlfriend, his dear old mum and his girlfriend here in Leeds would always provide him with an alibi if he needed it. He gave his widowed mother enough cash every month to pay her rent, bet on horses and buy groceries. His girlfriend in Leeds did not complain as long as he supplied her cocaine habit regularly. His live-in girlfriend was smart enough to keep her nose out of his business transactions. He provided her with ample cash, and left her free to do whatever she wanted most of the time.

Skin had once been a promising rugby player, but a drug habit and a string of deliberate fouls ended that. He had a reputation for instigating fights after professional football matches, and was no stranger to the Manchester police for it. He followed the European teams religiously, and he had once stabbed a man after a match in Brussels. The Belgian police never caught up with him, and he liked to brag about it in pubs while discussing football with friends. He had met Zed in jail, and they were both introduced to Death by an employer who specialized in drug trafficking.

Their employer had a rival whom they knew only as the Duke of Salford, after a suburb of Manchester that was one of the Duke's strongholds. The Duke's gang had muscled in on their distribution territory in central England very successfully. The Duke ran a tight ship, keeping everyone's identity and methods in his organization secret. Death's syndicate was losing profits and steady customers to the Duke. A rumor had been circulating that the Duke occasionally used teenagers on bicycles as couriers. Death and his two friends were on the lookout for cyclists who might be working for the Duke.

Zed and Skin had recently taken to supplementing their income whenever the mood struck. Summertime was tourist season, and they had shaken down several foreign tourists. They both intensely disliked foreigners. Bicyclists riding solo on rural highways were easy targets, even if they were not working for the Duke. The passports they had stolen from the tourists would fetch a high price from a friend who specialized in identity theft and forged documents. Death considered a US passport for himself. He had heard from his primary contact, a shadowy character somewhere in Leeds, that the action in the big cities of the United States, Australia and Canada could be very lucrative for someone like himself. Someone willing to take a few risks. The American cyclist in one passport photo wore a beard. How difficult could it be to impersonate him?

Death helped himself to another bottle of ale. "Your money's on the table."

Zed acknowledged with a grunt, which was about the limit of his articulation. Skin looked up briefly and nodded, his pupils darting side to side as they always did.

"We're going to Bradford in the morning. Got to make a few deliveries there. Nottingham in the afternoon."

"Yeah."

"I've got a little job to do after that. The Man has a score to settle with the Duke. Meet me in the usual spot tomorrow evening, after you collect those debts."

Death's contact offered him a bonus for taking action against a suspected member of the Duke's gang who was using his legitimate employer's warehouse as a front for narcotics and fencing. The timing had to be precise, but neither of his two associates had any sense of time. Death wanted to handle this one by himself.

15.

"Eric! Roger!" someone shouted from across the bus apron in front of the busy railway station.

"Who the...?" Roger paused at the door and turned. It was none other than Christian Meijer, the Dutch cyclist they had met in Cambridge.

"Christian! Fancy meeting you here!" Eric was surprised and delighted to see him. Most anything would have made an improvement over his glum situation.

"I was hoping I would find you two at another hostel or somewhere. I wanted to warn you."

The comment intrigued Eric. "What's up?"

Christian dismounted his bicycle and leaned it against the wall near Eric and Roger's bicycles. He unstrapped his helmet, took off his sunglasses, and held them in his hands before he spoke. "Two days ago, I believe it was Friday, some men in a car tried to force me off the highway. They succeeded in that, but another motorist approached and they drove away quickly. A farm hand gave me a ride into the nearest village in his lorry, but he could not read the license plate on the car that harassed me."

"Whereabouts did this happen?" Roger was now very interested in Christian's story.

"Somewhere in rural Humberside, or East Riding of Yorkshire, or whatever that county is called now. It was not near any large cities."

"How badly were you hurt?" Eric asked.

"No serious injuries to me or my bicycle," Christian said, "but I was cut and bruised, and I landed in mud. I'm quite certain those men intended to steal my valuables, and they could have very easily had that farm hand not been close by. I spent nearly two hours that evening straightening my wheels and making other repairs on my bicycle. I wasn't badly hurt, but I was certainly shaken by what happened. I've been warning all the cyclists I've seen lately. A Dutch woman I met yesterday told me she had been robbed by some young men she described to me. I think she was talking about the same people. She saw them drive away in what she thought was an old Citröen."

Eric and Roger told Christian their story, and all three concluded that they were talking about the same highwaymen.

"Do you have any plans this evening, Christian? We'd like to have you join us for an evening meal," Eric said.

"You look like you're about to go somewhere by train. I hope I'm not keeping you."

Eric looked at Roger and waited. Roger was on the spot for an explanation, and he knew it. He drew in a deep breath and exhaled before he spoke. Christian's question was an innocent one. He had no way of knowing why Roger was about to enter the railway station, and Roger was in no mood to rehash his other woes.

"No, we're not going anywhere by train," Roger offered. "We're just here to…a…use the loo." He avoided making eye contact with Eric, because he knew Eric had won this argument and was very self-satisfied for it.

"Don't let me keep you from it, then. Actually, I'm trying to find the York Youth Hostel. Do you know where it is?"

The Americans led Christian back to the hostel, where he had booked a bed from his previous overnight stop. He was assigned to a different room. After he stowed his gear and his bicycle, they met in the hostel cafeteria for their 3-course evening meal. They carried their food on trays out to the patio, where they discussed their misadventures. The Americans were amazed at how much Christian's story was like their own.

Two hours later, after tea and dessert and plenty of lively conversation, they went up to their rooms. Roger and Eric were both very content, having enjoyed the kind of evening they had come for—an impromptu, informal supper and conversation with someone about their age from another nation in a pleasant setting. The conversation could have continued for hours if not for nightfall. Christian was very knowledgeable about many interesting subjects, not the least of which was bicycling.

Roger took a shower while Eric threw a load of his and Roger's dirty clothes in the wash. After the shower, Roger put the clothes in the dryer, and sat down at one of the computers in the common room to make use of the coin-operated Internet service. He drank a pint of ale from the in-hostel pub while he surfed and sent e-mail. He sent a memo to his older brother and his friend George about the mugging and related events. He sent memos to his parents and Marianne, too, but he kept those messages upbeat. He did not want to cause undue alarm.

Eric felt sated after eating a little too much, so he took a walk along the river path until the bloated feeling subsided. He also needed a little time to himself to think about some recent events. He was delighted to have Roger back on the tour, even though he wondered what other trouble might find them.

As he walked back along Water End toward the hostel, Eric's daydream was interrupted by the sound of a noisy car approaching from behind. The muffler was definitely in need of replacement, and an engine tune-up would not have hurt, either. He turned and looked, and saw a dark-colored car, but it was not yet close enough for him to identify it. It looked more like a Renault or MG than a Citröen, and it appeared to be black. False alarm, Eric said to himself.

Eric ignored the car as it came closer to him. The car was less than twenty meters behind Eric when he heard the engine slow down considerably. Reflexively, he snatched the dog repellent can from his pocket with his right hand, and looked over his right shoulder. Beside him was the noisy car, a dark blue, old but well kept Citröen.

A chill ran up Eric's spine as the car approached him. He quickly moved away from the curb. He tried to make eye contact with the two men in the car, but they wore glasses and paid only scant attention to him. They appeared to be Indians or Middle Easterners, neatly groomed and wearing clean ironed Madras shirts. Roger was sure his assailants were white, had tattoos and dressed more like a motorcycle gang. The driver punched the accelerator pedal after the car passed Eric. The car disappeared in the distance and left Eric a little unnerved but also unscathed.

The incident, all five seconds of it, rattled Eric, but he was highly doubtful the car he had just seen was the one that had forced Roger off the highway. He regretted not getting the full license plate number, but there was no way he could have gotten it. The two occupants of the car hardly looked culpable, and Eric thought about how many similar-looking cars, probably upwards of one hundred, he had seen since his arrival in England. He hurried back to the hostel, where he told Roger about the dark Citröen.

"We're getting paranoid, I think. That car could have been our buddies, but I doubt it. Your description of them doesn't sound like the jokers who jumped me."

"Probably wasn't them, then. I am being paranoid. Still, I'm glad Christian talked you into staying. I have a feeling our luck will change for the better very soon."

"I hope so. We need it. Christian's timing was perfect."

They both hated the thought that three people out of hundreds of thousands in this part of England were keeping them very much on edge.

16.

The morning sun was shining brightly through the bedroom curtains, but Roger was none too eager to rise. He slept well, and he felt good. He had endured continuous rain, illness and even a brutal assault, but all that seemed like it was in the distant past. He had all but dismissed his plan to abandon the tour, although he knew he had to secure a new passport somehow, and soon. He pulled himself out of his bed and got dressed, happy to be right there in York. He paused in silent meditation while he gazed out the window. He rattled Eric and reminded him of the morning's agenda.

"Out of bed, morning-breath. It's time to rock and roll."

"Shut your putrid gob!" Eric was not at all reluctant to use some of the British colloquialisms he had absorbed from literature, television and movies. "I'm coming."

Eric and Roger discussed their plans while they ate breakfast with Christian and some other guests in the dining room. The warden granted them permission to leave their gear at the hostel while they visited the Minster. Nearby Harrogate, where Roger intended to shop for a headset for his new frame, would be their destination following the sites of York.

The Castle Museum was even better than they expected. They were easily able to guide themselves among the displays, and they did not have a queue to wait in before entering. One section of the museum was a replica of a mid-nineteenth century English neighborhood, including a hansom, a cobblestone street, gas-fired street lamps and building façades reminiscent of the architectural style of that time. Eric bought a postcard featuring the hansom and its horse and driver mannequins in front of a brick mansion. The museum had an abundance of artifacts and authentic-looking replicas, all providing a detailed visualization of the Yorkshires' colorful history.

Another building was a preserved grain mill of some sort. A rivulet drove a wooden waterwheel on one wall of the gray stone building. The prism-shaped stones were probably forerunners of modern-day mortar block.

The ambiance of the museum made the two Americans feel as though they were taking a walk through England a century or two in the past. They briefly forgot their troubles.

Clifford's Tower, a Norman fortress originally built in A.D. 1068 atop a steep hill by William the Conqueror's soldiers and modified in 1245, was spectacular. A long flight of uneven steps led to the entrance, an archway characteristic of Norman architecture. Roger was inspired by the soundness of the structure, in spite of its age and weathered appearance. As an engineering student, he admired the handiwork of the forebears of his profession. Eric recalled mention of the fortress in Sir Walter Scott's *Ivanhoe*, and he visualized that story again from his present perspective. Another wall stood behind the outer wall to form the turrets and walkways along the perimeter of the fort. One walkway, supported by the inner and outer walls, was at mid-height, and a second walkway was almost at the top of the walls. The view of York from the upper walkway certainly deserved a photograph. They were duly impressed by the nine hundred year-old fort that was so well preserved even with the tourists climbing on it.

When they had their fill of the museum and tower, they moved on toward the business district in search of lunch. A bakery and a fruit market had what they needed. They mounted their bicycles and rode at a leisurely pace until they arrived in a park where more Roman and Norman ruins were on display. They sat down on a park bench to eat.

One of the ruins was the foundation and walls of an ancient infirmary known as Saint Leonard's Hospital. By comparison, they noticed how far hospitals have evolved in the last millennium or two. Saint Leonard's appeared to have its operating and waiting rooms; pre-op, post-op, maternity, psychiatric, and intensive care wards; administrative and physicians' offices; broom closet; and cafeteria all crowded into a few small rooms. They assumed that an emergency room was out of the question.

Roger's attention was distracted from the ruins by some seedy-looking punks. The ruffians were sitting on another park bench, arrogantly heckling tourists. Roger scrutinized the punks for a moment before Eric realized what was happening.

"Are they...?" Eric seized Roger's elbow, as if to prevent him from attacking.

"No, they're not the bastards who jumped me." Roger jerked his arm from Eric's grasp. "But I had to be certain."

Eric led Roger back toward the ruins, away from the punks. "Let's not pick a fight with some arrogant jerks on an impulse."

"Chill, Chief." Roger's expression returned to normal. "I had to check out the hoodlums on the bench. They looked a lot like my assailants."

"Are you sure you could identify them if you did see them? They might not be easy to find if they're not in their car."

"I don't know," Roger said. "But I would recognize my watch if one of them was wearing it."

"What would you do if you did spot them?"

"Hell if I know! If we do see them, I just hope it's on our terms and not theirs, as was the case last time. I hope we see them before they see us."

York Minster cathedral was awe-inspiring, a nice complement to Castle Museum and Clifford's Tower, and easily a rival of Saint Paul's Cathedral in London. The 13th century church was as much an art museum as a house of worship. Lancet arches supporting the ceiling appeared to be more than fifteen meters high, and the nave and choir area were at least fifty meters on a side. The tourists were dwarfed by the pillars that formed the arches. Huge, elaborate stained-glass windows adorned the walls on each side of the sanctuary, as did larger-than-life marble statues of royalty and religious figures. Finely crafted icons and inscribed marble were abundant throughout the huge building.

Eric and Roger took several photographs of the interior of the church, including the pulpit, pews and a row of statues of exalted men wearing crowns and curly mustaches standing on pedestals against a wall. From there, they climbed a long, narrow, helical staircase of stone to the top of one of the towers.

The two front corners of York Minster had high towers, which served little purpose other than to provide a nice view of York from the roof. The other tower was closed to the public, but it was identical to the one they climbed. The roof of the abbey and its towers were decorated by numerous spires. Roger took some photographs of the panoramic view from the roof of the tower, and then sat down with Eric to appreciate their presence in the church that was unlike any they knew of anywhere in the United States.

"Old Saint What's-Her-Name's has nothing on this house of the Lord. Right, Chief?" Roger was referring to a church across the street from their high school. The church had also been the site of their Boy Scout meetings a decade earlier.

Eric added, "If you were to set the pews against the walls, there'd be enough room for a basketball court. Makes me wonder why so many American churches have gymnasiums these days. The British build theirs big enough to be gymnasiums or concert halls."

"It amazes me that this grandiose structure was built for and by people whose own homes were very, very humble compared to this," Roger said. "I suppose it was built in a time when the abbey was, without question, the most important building in town."

Eric admired the bird's-eye view of York from the tower. "I don't regret living in an age when my house is more important to me than the church or the feudal lord's manor."

"Feels good to breathe the clean, crisp air up here." Roger took a deep breath, held it for a moment, and exhaled. "I'm going to miss York. This is by far the best place we've seen so far. We ought to get moving, though. Can't enjoy this forever."

"Is there anything in Harrogate besides that bicycle dealer, whatever its name is?"

"Nothing much that I know of," Roger replied. "Inga mentioned some gardens there. Probably just another average town like Cambridge, King's Lynn, *et cetera*. I don't need to see any gardens. We don't have to go that way, if you'd rather not."

"Might as well. You said you wanted to buy a headset for your new frame. Let's get it done while we're here. I'd like to see this bicycle store myself." Eric took some photographs of the city before turning toward the door to the helical staircase.

Roger and Eric rode back to the hostel for their panniers and sleeping bags. They circled around York in the mid-afternoon to get to the A59. They rode across mostly flat country to Harrogate, a town of 65,000 people, about 40 kilometers west of York on the other side of the A1 motorway.

The sheep and the stone fences were all a part of the scenery between York and Harrogate. The vegetation was much more green than that growing on the Great Plains of the U.S. The highway was reasonably well kept, and the scenery provided for a comfortable if unremarkable ride. They kept a close watch on the fairly heavy traffic that passed them, but they saw nothing that looked like a suspicious, dark green Citröen. Roger felt better than he did the previous day, and he was able to ride just a little faster.

They rolled into Harrogate in the late afternoon, and searched in vain for nearly an hour for their bicycle importer. Roger downloaded a map to the store at the hostel in York, but they had trouble following it. They reluctantly asked a pedestrian where they could find it. When they did find the dealership, it was closed for the day. They found a grocery store and bought ingredients for a cold supper. They had no hostel or B&B to stay in, but the pleasantly warm evening air encouraged them to camp in a park within the city.

The park was a sprawling, nearly flat area of grass with a few trees in clusters. Several blocks long and wide, the park might have made a good golf course. They were the only people in the park, and they ate their supper on one of the few picnic tables. Although the park offered little shelter other than darkness after nightfall, they felt safe camping there, largely because of its abandonment by the locals.

A man walking his boxer strolled by their dining area and started a conversation with them just in passing. The man lit a cigarette for himself and offered one to Eric and Roger, which they politely declined. The man asked them about their destination and where they started. They asked him about life in Harrogate and England. The casual conversation lasted nearly an hour, touching a wide variety of subjects, and the man seemed especially interested in the Americans' opinions regarding world politics. The man wished them a successful journey and continued his walk with his dog.

Feeling restless, they changed clothes, mounted their bicycles and rode away in an arbitrary direction. They turned right at the Empress Roundabout. Their destination was the nearest pub, and they were not too discriminative in their choice of watering holes, as one was like any other to them. They rode a few blocks until they came upon two pubs half a block apart on opposite sides of the street. They rode toward the closer pub, but something caught Eric's eye in the parking lot at the other pub.

"Let's check out that Jaguar over there."

"I was hoping we'd find one of those somewhere."

They rode to the second pub, where a shiny yellow Jaguar XKE from the 1960s was parked. An impressive car, it would have made quite a chick magnet back home. They were about to go in when Eric noticed another car two slots away from the Jaguar. The sight of an older, dark green Citröen in front of them made their hearts pound. The left tail light lens was broken! The adrenaline rush that Eric felt told him that Roger's assailants were the very same people he had cursed at near Saffron Walden after one of them threw a bottle at him. They nearly killed Roger for my indiscretion, Eric thought. His whole body trembled with the notion of what was about to unfold.

They parked their bicycles on the side of the row of buildings behind some bushes, and locked them to a railing. The bicycles were concealed from the front door of the pub and the parking area. Clad in jeans and long-sleeve shirts, they walked into the pub and sat down at a table near the door. They were as nervous as underage schoolboys trying to get served in a bar for the first time.

They discreetly scrutinized the clientele while a waitress brought each of them a pint of lager. Two trashy-looking thugs came out of the men's room and resumed their places at the counter where they were drinking ale and flirting with another waitress. They did not notice Eric and Roger across the room, nor did they appear interested in any of the other twenty or so customers. The two Americans studied them for a moment, then turned to each other.

"Remember the bottle-throwing incident on our way to Cambridge the other day?" Eric spoke quietly, but without whispering. "I'm pretty sure that's the same car. The left tail light was broken."

"So we've met them twice before. Trouble always comes in threes."

"But are we sure it's them?"

"I'm not absolutely certain, but I think so. I really do. I didn't get a very good look the first time, but that might be my watch on that one's wrist, and that car... But where's the third one?" Roger tried to keep his excitement from being overheard.

"Maybe he got arrested," Eric said. "I'm convinced that we've found the right people, but what do we do now?"

Roger thought a moment before he spoke. "First, find a piece of paper or take a napkin, and write down the car license number twice. Put one in your pocket and the other in your luggage. Tear a third piece and write it for me. Then, look in one of the rear pockets of my handlebar bag. I have a valve stem remover in there somewhere. If you can do it without being noticed, loosen their valve stems slightly. I want to keep an eye on them. If they start toward the door, I'll walk out in front of them. If you see me, act innocent and pretend you don't know me. Are you with me?"

"Don't try anything by yourself. Two against one isn't very good odds."

"I don't intend to."

"Why in the hell do you just happen to have a valve stem remover handy?" Eric wondered aloud. "Your bicycle has Presta valves."

"I carry it on my mountain bike sometimes. Schraeder valves, you know. But I didn't bother to remove the tool for this trip. Now go."

Eric took a deep breath and another swallow of his lager before he walked out the door as inconspicuously as he could. He did not think the hoodlums were likely to recognize Roger. He copied the license number, and meditated for a moment before searching for the valve stem remover. The sun had set but the sky was not yet dark. The Jaguar had departed while he and Roger were inside quaffing ale. He knelt down by a back wheel of the car and inserted the tool. He loosened the valve stem slightly, releasing a barely audible hiss of air. A voice from behind nearly startled him to death.

"Anything wrong?" a passerby said. Eric had not seen or heard the man approaching, and his response was one of alarm.

"No, no, nothing really." Eric was nervous, and it showed. "Just a...checking the air pressure. Thought I had a puncture."

"I didn't mean to startle you like that, lad. I'd be glad to help."

"No, thank you, I'm fine." Eric hid the tool in the palm of his hand. "I'm a very capable mechanic. It's very kind of you to offer your assistance, sir."

"Not at all," the man said. "I was just taking a walk. Goodnight to you."

"Thank you again, and goodnight."

The man walked away and Eric waited until he was out of sight before continuing what he was doing. The surprise nearly made him hemorrhage, but he collected himself and continued.

"Chill out, Eric," he said to himself after a few deep breaths. "Don't get discombobulated."

He was not sure why he was draining the car tires. It seemed very juvenile, like something he might have tried in middle school. He reassured himself that the car's owners tried, and succeeded to a considerable degree, to hurt Roger and him. Revenge was justified, no matter how petty the act. At least the hoodlums would not be able to chase or harass anyone with their car for a while.

Eric crept over near the bushes and watched the door after he had loosened all four valve stems. The sound of the leaking air was quiet enough, but it was also very slow. Eric waited in the shadows for several minutes, but no one entered or left the pub. A wave of daring overcame him, and he completely removed a rear-wheel valve stem and discarded it in a large trash bin. He noticed a flattened foil roaster pan in the trash bin, which he removed and unfolded. He hid in the shadows again while the air hissed from the tire, but again, no one noticed. The foil pan did not appear to be cracked anywhere, so he took the pan and one of his wrenches under the car and drained the oil. He discarded the oil plug in the trash bin, and wiped his hands clean on the napkin he had brought from the pub. During the next few minutes, Eric cautiously removed the remaining three valve stems and discarded them in the trash bin. He waited again, and audaciously opened the car door to turn on the headlights. A second thought told him to leave the lights off, so the car would not attract undue attention. He wanted the driver to attempt to start the engine without any oil in it. Something on the floor of the car caught his attention, and he grabbed it before he went back inside the pub. The car had four very flat tires now. He regretted not having any engine coolant with which to spike the gasoline.

In the meantime, while Eric was tuning the car, Roger sat and observed. He was aware of how he had been barking orders at Eric, who ordinarily would have told him to eat a bucket of excrement. He made a mental note to apologize for his surliness later. He kept his face toward the table and watched the hoodlums out of the corner of his eye. He had difficulty withholding his rage when he saw one of them proudly showing his wristwatch to the waitress. The hoodlums did not seem to be in any hurry to leave, and the tension in Roger's mind increased exponentially with time. Their delay gave him plenty of time to plan his and Eric's next move, but he could not think of anything feasible or sensible.

A woman in her mid-thirties, probably a blue-collar worker at the end of her shift if her jeans and chambray shirt meant anything, sidled up to Roger and sat down next to him. Moderately attractive, and already three sheets to the wind, she looked him over while waiting for him to make the next move.

"Haven't seen you in here before, lad." Her breath was scented with ale and gin.

"No, probably not. Lass." Under any other circumstances, he would have flirted with her. He knew what she wanted, but he was not interested in leaving with her right now.

As if her Yorkshire accent were not already difficult enough for him to understand, her drunken slur made her almost incomprehensible. "You could buy me another one, handsome."

"You're a thirsty critter tonight, love." He pretended to be uninterested in her. He thought she might make good cover for whatever he was going to do about the hoodlums, or else she might interfere in a big way. He hated to be kept waiting for anything, especially the unknown.

Eric walked back into the pub through a side door adjoining a dining area. Roger ordered a second round for himself and the woman, and he was more relaxed than when he entered the pub. Eric slowly finished his first stein even though he knew it would probably give him a headache. He, too, watched the hoodlums out the corner of his eye, and told Roger what he had done outside when the woman left to use the ladies' room.

Nearly an hour later, the situation was almost the same as it had been. A few customers came and went, but nothing else changed. Roger excused himself for a moment to inspect the bicycles, and they were fine. Roger was pleased with what Eric had done. If nothing else, it would prevent the hoodlums from following them before late the next day. Roger and Eric would be long gone from Harrogate by that time. Inspired, Roger unscrewed the rear license plate and threw it in the trash bin. That should get the attention of the police somewhere. Roger returned to his table where still nothing significant had happened. The woman was putting the same moves on Eric that had left Roger unfazed.

Another half hour went by, and Eric was about to suggest that he and Roger leave when another customer entered the pub through the front door. The tall, shabby newcomer joined the other two at the counter, and Roger recognized the third one as the front passenger in the car when it struck him. Their long, scraggly hair had not been washed or trimmed any time recently. All three had several ugly tattoos, and looked like they could be members of a motorcycle gang.

The woman bummed a cigarette from another customer and sat down again with the two Americans. While she turned her attention to Roger, Eric took his dog repellent from his pocket and sprayed some on the rim of her stein and into the ale. She gagged when she took another drink, and spat a mouthful of ale back into the glass.

"Christ, what'd they do to my ale!" The foam from her lips was dripping onto her shirt.

"You should ask the bartender for another glass. Mine has that off-taste, too," Eric said. When she stood up and stumbled toward the bar, Eric extinguished her cigarette in her ale. "I was barely tolerating her. Then she lit that cigarette and…"

The three thugs went into the men's room that was located behind the back wall of the barroom. "Let's go!" Roger muttered as he tapped Eric's shoulder with his outstretched fingers. He and Eric stood up and walked toward the men's room a moment after the hoodlums went into it. They moved on instinct. They did not waste a second considering what was about to happen. Their inebriated friend was trying to get the bartender's attention and did not notice what they were doing.

Roger paused for a second outside the men's room door, then he swiftly pushed it open and stepped in, with Eric right behind him. The three hoodlums looked up with surprise at the two strangers who were glaring at them.

"What you want?" the tall one, snarled. He looked even huskier and more menacing up close than he did from across the room. He wore tattered jeans, a black leather vest and steel-capped work boots. A small scar decorated his cheek, and he wore a much larger one on his forearm. A tattoo on his shoulder was indistinguishable, except for the word "Death" in big letters at the bottom of it.

He was evidently the leader of the three. Zed, the barrel-chested one nearest Eric, and Skin, the tall medium-build in the center, were just as menacing. They all reeked of sweat, smoke and liquor. Eric's opposite was about his same height, but probably weighed half again as much as Eric. He had dark tattoos on both arms and a misshapen nose that had been in at least one brawl. Skin's eyes wandered in different directions, unable to focus on anything. He swayed as he stood, his fingers fidgeting at mid-chest. Roger and Eric were outnumbered and out-muscled by a considerable margin.

Unintimidated, Roger spoke in a low, firm voice, *a la* Clint Eastwood. "I want my watch and my knife back, and my money, too."

The three hoodlums looked at each other incredulously, as if they could not believe his audacity. "Fuck off, foreigner," the leader said. They all looked at each other again and laughed ever so slightly. Death reached into his pocket, drew a large switchblade, and waved it toward Roger as a warning. They looked at Roger and Eric again, challenging the Americans to make the next move. Zed moved a little closer to the door, as if to block the two Americans from leaving.

Roger looked at the switchblade, drew away from it, and turned toward Eric. Roger motioned with a nod toward the door, as if to tell Eric that they should leave immediately.   The arm holding the switchblade relaxed momentarily. A shiny, stolen wristwatch briefly reflected the light from the ceiling into Roger's eye.   Roger suddenly turned back toward the big hoodlum, grabbed and yanked the wrist of the hand wielding the switchblade with his right hand, and followed through with a hard left jab to his adversary's wide-open throat. Death yelped in pain and reeled backwards until he collided with the steel post that supported the toilet enclosure. He glanced off the post and slumped to the floor, gasping for air. The knife skidded across the tile floor into a corner, well out of anyone's immediate reach.

The foray began in earnest, two against two now.   Eric was not aggressive by nature and did not consider himself much of a fighter, but he rose to the occasion without hesitation. A punch grazed his nose and cheek, and he deflected another with his forearm. He countered with an uppercut to the solar plexus, a jab to the face, and a kick that missed the groin but struck the inside of Zed's thigh on his femoral artery. They got into a clinch, with elements of wrestling, shoving, jabbing and even dancing. Eric split Zed's lip with a solid punch and drove him back a step.   The burly hoodlum grunted painfully, then hurled his bulk against Eric. Unable to avoid the thrust, Eric was slammed against the wall behind him.   The light switch gouged him between the shoulder blades. The sharp pain would have made him scream, but the air had already been forced from his lungs. Zed reared back to deliver the knockout punch. Eric saw it coming and twisted to dodge the punch aimed at his face. The fist hit the masonry wall instead, and left a mark. Zed might have finished Eric off right then and there, but for his aching knuckles.

Zed backed away and tried to shake the sting out of his broken hand. The action came to a halt for a few seconds as each man stopped to catch his breath and deal with his pain. Roger yelped as a punch staggered him. Eric reflexively tried to assist Roger, but Zed shoved Eric against the wall once more and reached into his vest for a weapon with his good hand.

Eric knew he had only one or two seconds left before he would be disemboweled, and he barely had enough strength to remain standing. The pepper spray! Desperately, Eric groped for the small canister in his pocket. He directed a stream of cayenne pepper into the eyes just as Zed's fingers found the knife. He fumbled the knife and tried to shield his eyes. Eric turned the spray toward the nostrils and gaping mouth. He landed a kick to Zed's knee and nearly toppled him. He smashed the canister against the sore hand, drove a knee into Zed's mid-section, and put all his remaining strength into an elbow strike to the face. Skin was using his longer reach to choke

Roger against a wall. The burly hoodlum's head whiplashed backward as he stumbled over the outstretched leg of Death on the floor, and took Skin down with him. It gave Eric and Roger the respite they needed to gain the upper hand.

Skin and Zed, without their leader, were no match for the two frenzied Americans beyond that point. The fight ended barely more than a minute after it started. Eric and Roger stuffed three unconscious pulps into the toilet stall. Neither uttered a single word.

Roger pulled his watch off the wrist of Skin, then broke the arm with a powerful blow against the back of his opponent's elbow. He reached for two back pockets and simultaneously yanked them off of the tattered jeans. A wallet fell out of one, and he picked it up, along with his monogrammed Swiss Army knife. Eric ripped open another pair of pockets. Some loose cash fell out of one, about fifty pounds worth. A sandwich bag containing some pills and a vial of white powder came out of the other. Eric angrily crushed the vial with his shoe, and stomped on Zed's swollen hand to make sure it would not be used against him anytime soon.

Eric spotted a key on the floor and picked it up, along with the cash that had fallen. Roger used the sink to quickly rinse some blood off his hands and the corner of his mouth, while Eric hastily closed the door on the stall. Roger pushed open a sash window above the sink, stepped up onto a sling Eric made with his fingers, and climbed out of the building into its backyard. Eric followed, assisted by a pull from Roger. Eric pulled the window shut behind him. They were in a small courtyard, enclosed by a high wall with glass shards embedded in the top edge to discourage intruders. Roger reached for the wrought iron gate, the only way out of the courtyard other than through the kitchen, but it was locked. They were trapped!

17.

Roger shook the gate, almost in a state of panic, but it did not budge. They both looked around to see if there was any alternative exit, anything that could help them escape without being noticed. The wall was too high to scale easily, and the broken glass would have shredded their flesh as they went over, even if they had a ladder or something to boost them. They were not about to try to climb back in the men's room window. They had no choice but to use the screen door into the kitchen, which would undoubtedly draw the attention of the employees.

Eric heard footsteps coming toward the back door of the building from inside. He grabbed Roger and pulled him away from the gate. They stood in the shadows with their backs against the back wall of the building while a kitchen worker carried some trash out through the back door. They had to hold their breath to prevent their panting from being heard. They watched in silence as the employee unlocked the gate with his key, and carried the trash out to a bin to the right. Eric and Roger quickly dashed through the open gate and fled to the left. The employee turned to see what the noise was at the gate behind him, but they were already around the side of the building before he could see them.

The two Americans crept down a narrow alley around to where their bikes were parked. They unlocked their bicycles, and sprinted into the darkness in the direction from whence they came earlier in the evening. Their bodies trembled as they rode, but they did not dare look back at the pub. They arrived back at the park in about one-third the time they spent riding to the pub, and both were breathless upon stopping. The traffic in Harrogate was light at that hour, a good thing as they did not have any lights. They dismounted near where they had eaten supper, laid their bicycles down, and parked themselves on the grass next to their bikes. They stared at the stars, worried, for quite a while before either could muster any words.

"God, I'm scared, Eric." Roger spoke in a weak voice, still trying to catch his breath. "I saw my watch, and I just got carried away, and then..."

"...went ape! Bloody hell! How did we ever get involved in this? Why us?" Eric fumbled for a tissue in his handlebar bag to absorb the blood trickling from his nose.

"This is one hell of a night," Roger said in what was definitely an understatement. "They'll come after us again, if the police don't get us first!"

"We won't get another chance!" Eric spoke as if he were soliloquizing. "We could be in worse shape than we were before that second incident."

"Keep your pepper spray in one hand, and your S.A. knife in the other. Open the awl and hold it between your middle finger and your ring finger when you make a fist. Hold the larger blade downward with the sharp edge away from your body. That way, if someone tries to kick it out of your hand, he gets stabbed in the foot."

"Just make sure it isn't me before you slash somebody!"

The two quietly discussed their strategy for several minutes, then silence fell again. They lay on the cool grass, watching and listening to everything around them, waiting for something to happen. An hour later, they were quite alone in the park and the darkened city was quiet. No police cars or ambulances rushed by the park, no sirens were heard, and no gangs ransacked the neighborhood in search of them. The night was quiet, and traffic on the streets bordering the park was infrequent. That what they had done was of little importance to anyone else slowly dawned on them. Nearly two hours after they left the pub, the inevitable as they imagined it had not yet happened, and perhaps never would.

"We really punched their lights out!" Roger sounded just a little smug. "You know, they couldn't possibly come after us tonight. Even if we hadn't fought, their car will remain immobile at least until tomorrow."

"But did that last guy come in a separate car?"

"I don't know. Maybe they do have another car. The more I try to analyze what happened, the worse it sounds for us."

"One of them must have lost his car key." Eric suddenly remembered it was in his pocket. "I picked it and some cash up after the brawl."

"How did you get it out of him?"

"I think my fist was in his eye. Must have jarred the key right out of his hand. What do you suppose was in that sandwich bag?"

"Meth, heroin, cocaine, bleached flour, confectioners' sugar," Roger said. "Who knows? I just hope someone finds it before they wake up."

"Someone probably already found them, and that someone called the police by now. I would call the cops if I found three unconscious bodies in a restroom."

"It occurred to me that the police might not make a big deal out of three hoodlums who lost a fight, unless one of them died."

"Don't even think of it!" Eric said. "We have enough problems right now without worrying about whether we sent some creep to the Promised Land. What'd you do with that guy's wallet?"

"I still have it, now that you mention it. I've never robbed anybody before. We're in deep shit, Chief. I'm a felon!" Roger took deep breaths and exhaled slowly. "I'm sorry I dragged you into this."

"We're still in this together, Squire. We had no choice but to fight our way out of there. I saw it coming when my adversary moved in front of the door. What do we do now?"

"Let's worry about our own survival. Picking fights isn't a habit of mine. I don't want to spend the rest of our vacation in jail. How do they spell it, g-a-o-l? And I especially don't want to stand trial. I doubt very seriously Scotland Yard would take kindly to us foreigners and our frontier style of justice."

"Let's be sure we're wearing something different tomorrow. I don't think anyone in that pub would have noticed a hippopotamus if we'd brought one in, but I'd still rather not be remembered by anyone here. I hope our lady friend has a nasty hangover tomorrow and doesn't remember anything."

"She was drunk off her ass. Don't worry about her."

Eric rose to his knees and hands and crawled to his gear, where he put his water bottle, Dilantin, and toothbrush to use. He remarked that the night would be their first night of camping. The sensation of feeling, instead of seeing, his equipment prompted the thought. Both would have been quite content to be camping with only the night sky above them, if only the present circumstances were different. They unfolded their mattresses to lie down but slept in their clothes in case of emergency.

"I suppose we should thank our lucky stars that we're here, alive and well." Eric made a pillow out of one of his stuff sacks. "In better shape than our enemies, anyway."

"I don't feel very lucky, really, but I know that it could have been a lot worse for us. I'll see you in the morning." Roger was about to lie down, when he sprang up suddenly. "Oh my god! My passport! They still have it!"

18.

A dark-featured man with a receding hairline sat in his car across the street from the pub where his quarry had gone inside. A Royal Marines veteran who had served in Iraq, he looked and behaved like an ordinary gentleman. He got out of his car, adjusted his tan sports coat, and surveyed the neighborhood. He was about to execute his plan when he saw two figures excitedly bolt from the alley, hop on bicycles, and flee into the darkness. Whoever they were, they did not look at all like the type of people the police would normally be chasing. He wondered what they were up to as he ducked into the shadow of a tall tree. The man waited cautiously, but no one followed the two cyclists after several minutes. An anonymous client in Manchester was paying him a tidy sum to tail some associates of a rival, and inflict collateral damage to remind them to stay off his turf and leave his young couriers alone. The enforcers had gotten a little complacent of late— they bragged to strangers in pubs and showed off their distinctive tattoos. Their guard was down, and it was time to cut this Death bloke and his mates down to size.

"They still have my passport!"

"No, they don't! I found it on the floor in their car, and put it deep in your handlebar bag. I meant to tell you, but with all the excitement, I completely forgot about it. Sorry about that."

"Damn! I nearly had a coronary! We just might survive this town."

"We just might. Let's get some shut-eye, if we can."

Exhaustion quickly overcame anxiety, frustration, fear and Eric's very noticeable aura, and they fell asleep. The rest of Harrogate was already asleep.

The morning sun was just barely over the horizon, but it was a dog making its morning rounds only three meters from Roger and Eric's camp that awakened them with a jolt. The dog's owner, not the same man they had conversed with the previous evening, stood several meters away with the unattached leash in one hand. The man called for his dog, and wished them a good morning.

"Of all the places in this park," Roger said, "that Airedale had to choose the tree nearest us."

Eric looked around cautiously, as if an attack might be imminent. "Nothing else happened last night. No one found us, if anyone was looking."

"We're still alive and healthy. Let's not push our luck by loitering around here any longer." Roger rolled his mattress and stuffed his sleeping bag, and attached them to his rack.

"You don't look so healthy, Squire. You have a bruise over your left eye."

Roger felt his left brow with his fingers. "A bit sore and swollen, but no big deal. Strange that I didn't feel it last night. My lip is still swollen and my left hand aches, too. I must've punched someone harder than I thought. Looks like you have some dried blood in your whiskers."

"I probably do. I'm sore all over. That other monster beat the hell out of me. I'm still not sure how we made it out of there alive. The pepper spray saved me twice yesterday."

"You're telling me! I've been beaten up twice already. I crushed that gangly dude's nose with my best punch, and he came right back at me like nothing happened. He had me by the throat until you threw the big bruiser on top of him."

"Shifty-eyes was probably high on angel dust or something. Anyway, we're alive and we're not in jail. Ready to hit the road?"

"Maybe we should forget about the bicycle dealer, and just get out of Dodge as fast as we can."

"After what we've been through? Let's get your headset, and act as innocent as we can. The police might be interested in us if we look like we're in a hurry to leave."

They stayed in civilian clothes, albeit not the same clothes they wore in the pub the previous evening. They loaded their bicycles and rode toward the bicycle importer's store across town. They stopped at a bakery along the way for a breakfast of scones, which they ate while sitting in the parking lot of the importer, waiting for it to open. A man arrived a few minutes later and opened the store.

The store was nothing more than a sales counter and a warehouse, but it did have all its merchandise on display in catalogs. The warehouse was apparently well stocked, and the clerk quickly found the headset Roger wanted for his new frame-to-be. He paid cash, not wanting to leave a paper trail in Harrogate.

With some catalogs seldom seen back home and a few new components in their possession, they rode to the edge of Harrogate. They found a thicket and changed into their riding attire. They had no particular destination in mind yet. They just wanted to get far away from Harrogate as quickly as they could.

One of the pillars of Eric and Roger's friendship was their tendency to think alike, as was happening as they rode north on the A61 toward Ripon. Both were pondering the many dreadful possibilities of what three hoodlums in a dark green sedan might be doing. Could the thugs, by some rare chance, be on the same highway that they were on, going in the same direction? It was highly unlikely, in consideration of all the highways out of Harrogate. Would the hoodlums be roaming the region, attacking every cyclist in sight, in hopes of getting revenge on the ones who took them by surprise in that pub? Could their car have been fixed already? That was unlikely, too, but far from impossible. Were they able to walk away from the fight scene? Did anyone find them unconscious? Did anyone find the questionable substances they dropped? Did they recognize Roger as someone they had encountered previously? Were the police looking for two cyclists? These were among the many questions, few possible answers, and even fewer definite answers that they contemplated in silence as they pedaled.

They rode just as cautiously and attentively as they had since Saturday. They scrutinized the sparse traffic, and Eric kept his pepper spray can where he could quickly use it. The sky became progressively darker, and rain threatened by lunchtime. The verdant rolling hills, stone fences, sheep farms and occasional castle ruins still managed to capture a sizable portion of their interest, even though the scenery was already quite familiar and their thoughts were concentrated on a recent incident that happened in a pub not far away.

Eric noticed a sign near Killinghall pointing to a turn-off to a town named Hampsthwaite. That name caught his fancy. He tried to think of another word with six consecutive consonants, making five distinct sounds. He could not think of any. His mind drifted toward some of the colorful names of towns he had seen. His favorite thus far had been Saracen's Head in Lincolnshire. He assumed that name dated back to the Crusades, although the connection was not obvious.

They stopped for a bite in Ripon and checked their map and their hostel guidebook. Over bananas from a fruiterer, they considered their options and weighed the odds of encountering their enemies again.

"There are several hostels in the region, Lovesome Hill, Brompton, Richmond."

"Some of those are camping barns. I don't mind camping, but a place with a shower would be nice tonight."

"Yes, it would, and we don't *have* to stay in a hostel."

"They're cheaper than B&Bs. We should use them as much as possible."

"I see we're not very far from Thirsk. Do you mind if we go to Thirsk?"

"What's so special about Thirsk?"

"My mom read a series of books by an author who lived there, a veterinarian, I think. She suggested I check it out if I got the chance. This is our chance."

"There's a hostel west of Richmond called Grinton Lodge. The shortest way there is up the A6108 from here in Ripon. Thirsk is kind of out of the way for that."

"It is, but that remote highway makes me a little nervous."

"Not only that, but if they don't have any beds, we might have trouble finding alternative lodging nearby."

"How about if we ride to Thirsk and decide where to spend the night when we get there. If the rain comes, we stay in Thirsk. If not, we can call the hostel from there and book beds for the night."

"Sounds like a plan."

The threatening weather and the need to get away from Harrogate pushed them onward. The A61 was hilly, but not especially steep anywhere. They had a tailwind when they crossed the motorway, and it helped them maintain a steady pace. They felt comfortably far from Harrogate, and the numerous highway junctions along the way virtually assured them of no more chance meetings with the hoodlums, or did it? They could not be certain of their safety yet.

The hair on Eric's neck stood up when a patrol car passed them in the opposite direction. They could not tell whether the car was highway patrol or county sheriff, but it was definitely law enforcement, and the driver did notice them. The uniformed officer was driving slower than the speed limit, and he studied the two cyclists for a moment. Roger felt his heart skip a beat. The car disappeared behind them without further ado a few seconds later.

Eric and Roger stopped at a superstore in Thirsk for bottled water, a second lunch and some other needed supplies. They decided to take their chances with the weather, and called the Grinton Lodge Youth Hostel from a pay phone inside the store. The hostel still had a few beds available. A man outside the store asked about their journey, and advised them to use a roundabout at the north end of Northallerton to get to Richmond. The route was not shown on their folding map, and they had to avoid the motorway. The man wished them well as they set forth into Thirsk.

The town centre of Thirsk was bustling with tourists and locals alike. They asked a woman to take a picture of them in front of the clocktower. The town could hardly have been more quaint. They followed signs to an old house in a row of old houses about two blocks from the clocktower, where they found the James Herriott Museum. Herriott was a Depression-era veterinarian whose *All Creatures Great and Small* series of memoirs brought him international fame in the 1970s.

"Do we have time to take the tour?" Eric asked when they went inside the museum store.

"Why not? We're here."

They took a quick tour of the Herriott Museum and the real Skeldale House next door. The museum depicted life in Yorkshire in the 1930s, a bleak time that affected Europe just as much as the United States. The house still bore the shiny brass nameplates of Herriott and his business partner. Inside was their veterinary surgery restored to how it looked in Herriott's earlier books. The Americans were inspired to explore the Yorkshire Dales, and they added Herriott's name to their reading lists.

From Thirsk, they rode north up the A168 to Northallerton. The traffic was lighter than it had been on the A61. They were starting to see more animals on the roadside farms than they did closer to London, or maybe their perception had been suddenly warped by the veterinary museum in Thirsk. They found the roundabout right where the man at the grocery store said it would be. They turned west onto the B6271 and followed the Swale River toward Richmond against a headwind in the late afternoon.

The B6271 took a somewhat tortuous route toward the northwest, but it eventually brought them back to the motorway. The Americans kept their eyes open for signs pointing the way to Richmond, the nearest town to Grinton that appeared on their folding map. They crossed over the motorway near Brompton-on-Swale and began the arduous climb up the Swaledale toward Richmond. Everything looked so close on their map, but the headwind and the steady climb kept them moving slowly all the way. The injuries they suffered in the brawl slowed them even more. They checked their map on several occasions just to make sure they had not taken a wrong turn somewhere.

They felt a glimmer of hope when they came to Richmond. They assumed Grinton was just a few kilometers beyond Richmond. They felt a few sprinkles of rain every so often as one dark cloud after another blew over them. Richmond was an attractive and charming hillside town that they would have explored further if they had the time, but they were trying to get to the hostel in time for the evening meal. The only map they had showing

Grinton was inside their hostel guidebook, and it made Grinton look very remote indeed. They were not sure where else they might find supper if they were too late for it at the hostel.

The climbing did not ease up in the least beyond Richmond, nor did the wind. Roger and Eric both made a mental note of the sign just before Richmond that indicated their entrance into the Yorkshire Dales National Park, their first national park in a foreign country. They pushed on along the B6270 another 16 kilometers until they finally found Grinton in the early evening. They were tired and famished and even a little cold and damp when they stopped to check directions. They were in Grinton, but the hostel was up a long, steep moor to the south. The town itself was nothing more than a scenic wide spot in the road. Their watches indicated a quarter past seven, and they assumed they had missed the evening meal, as most hostels served at 18:00. They were not looking forward to riding back down the windy moor in search of a pub or restaurant.

They shifted into their lowest gears and began the ascent toward Leyburn past some sheep farms. The hostel, converted from an 18th-century hunting lodge, was farther up the moor than they hoped it would be, and seemed almost unreachable until they finally spotted the sign bearing the YHA logo. They parked their bicycles in the courtyard, out of the wind, and walked in the main door. They were out of breath from the long climb, and it was 19:30 when they entered the hostel.

"I was wondering when you two would arrive! Get to the dining room quickly whilst they still have some food left," the warden exhorted them as they registered for the night.

"I thought we'd missed it," Roger said. "Don't you serve at six?"

"No, at seven. We start a little later than most of the other hostels. Because of our remote location, many of our guests arrive after six."

"Our lucky day! We'll be there in a New York minute."

The hostel seemed quiet at the warden's desk, but was quite lively in the dining area. A large group of teenagers from a college prep school in Carlisle occupied most of the seats and had just finished their supper. Some adults invited the two newcomers to sit at their table. An assistant warden brought each of them a steaming bowl of potato soup and bread, followed by vegetable pizza, a baked potato, peas and maize. A fresh pot of tea with milk and sugar was on the table to complement the eclectic courses. Dessert was sponge cake with warm custard. They discussed their day's ride, certain details omitted, with a woman cyclist from Manchester. The food was most appetizing and in the right amounts. Even Roger showed some satisfaction after several difficult days on the road.

After supper, Eric and Roger stowed their bicycles in the storage room. They were full but not sated, and their thoughts had been on cycling and scenery for most of the afternoon. They had not seen any sign of their tormentors all day.

"We made it, and we're a good distance from Harrogate," Eric said in the courtyard, well out of earshot of anyone but Roger. "Are we safe yet?"

"I don't know. We manage to find those creeps where we least expect them. I'd say we're safe here for the night, but who knows what we'll encounter next?"

"Today was a rough day, but I feel like we're doing what we came here to do. That was a good ride, especially from about Richmond."

"It was, and what a view from here!" Roger surveyed the moors surrounding the hostel property in the dim evening light. "I think we came to the right place."

"Harrogate was a nice town, but if I ever see it again, it'll be way too soon!"

They carried their panniers up the stairs to their dormitory. Some of the teenagers were watching England in a professional soccer match on a television in the common room. The television reception was terrible in the dales. Others were playing billiards in the game room. The two Americans showered and watched some of the soccer match while they described the day's events in their journals.

Eric sent an e-mail to George Fraser from a coin-operated computer in the hostel. He included a description of his and Roger's encounters with the hoodlums, the driving license inside the wallet Roger confiscated, and the license number of the Citröen. Eric instructed George to keep the information to himself and not worry about it unless something happened to them, and provide authorities with it if anything did happen. His in-box contained only a travel promotion, an offer for prescription drugs, and a solicitation for his bank account number from a Nigerian dissident with ten million dollars to share. He deleted them all before quitting his session. Roger sent a note to Marianne that he wanted to speak to her, but he did not mention the Harrogate incident to her. He also sent a brief note to everyone in his address book about where he and Eric had been, and where they were going.

Eric and Roger got up to return to their room shortly after 22:00. The hostel was winding down for the night, and some of the guests had already gone to bed. Two guests, both English, were having a friendly chat with the warden at the registration desk.

"Cyclists, are you?" one of the women asked of Eric and Roger. "Where've you been so far?"

"We're on our way to Scotland," Roger said. He wanted to deflect any suspicion.

"We stayed in Thirsk last night," Eric added. He changed the subject, in hopes that no one would ask for details about places where they had not actually been. He asked about the Yorkshire Dales, and the three Britons had plenty to say about that. He and Roger said goodnight and turned toward the stairwell to the dormitories.

"That was quite an affair in Harrogate the other night, was it?" the other woman said to the warden.

"Aye, 'twas indeed," the warden agreed.

Roger and Eric overheard the comment as they started up the stairs. They looked at each other, but slowly continued up the stairs in silence. The women bade the warden a good night and said nothing more about Harrogate.

19.

Eric and Roger were understandably reluctant to rise and shine. They were comfortable and secure in the hostel, and they had to make up for the sleep they missed in the park in Harrogate. They sat with a woman with an unusual accent in the dining room. She told them she was from Malta. The cyclist from Manchester joined them. Many of the teenagers sat at adjacent tables, with the girls clustered at one end and the boys at the other. The Americans were glad they were past the age where mixing socially with the opposite sex was the ultimate challenge.

As Scotland was still too far for one day's ride, they decided to aim for Alston, Cumbria, where they could stay in a youth hostel. Alston, a small mountain town on the South Tyne River, lay near Cross Fell in the Cumbrian Mountains. They expected the moors and dales between Grinton and Alston to be even longer and steeper than what they had encountered already. The warden booked accommodations for them in Alston.

The two Americans loaded their panniers onto their bicycles in the hostel courtyard after a continental breakfast that was about the same as what they had at previous hostels. They admired the vista across the field where two horses were grazing and swishing flies with their long tails. They rode down the dale to Grinton where they had to stop at an intersection at the bottom. With a left turn, they resumed riding westward on the B6270 up the Swaledale.

The weather was friendlier than it had been the previous day. The sky was mostly sunny and the wind had abated. The air was pleasantly cool, yet warm enough that the two cyclists wore short sleeves. The road seemed a little steeper and it was a steady climb for nearly 30 kilometers. They passed through several picturesque villages and crossed the Swale River a few times.

Some of the towns and bridges made excellent backdrops for photographs. The density of trees gradually declined as they gained elevation. Sheep pastures and walking trails were abundant. The national park, unlike most in the United States, was almost entirely on privately owned land, but tourists in cars, on bicycles and on foot were everywhere.

The roadside scenery was the best they had seen yet. Tall, dense, green grass covered the ground everywhere except where the sheep were grazing upon it. The sheep appeared to outnumber the people in this region and were abundant on both sides of the road. The docile sheep went well with the tranquil ambiance. The Americans raced each other up the dale at times, often making use of the innermost part of their handlebars.

Eric, in the lead, stopped near a waterfall for a respite and a photograph. Roger, right behind, stopped beside Eric. Roger rolled his bicycle forward about half a wheel revolution, then scooted his front tire from side to side across the pavement.

"You can only dodge the sheep dip so many times."

Eric looked at the horizon. "I like the view here, spectacular in an unusual way. It fills the senses in a way that's different from any place I've been. Very refreshing, and not what most Americans expect when they think of England. It just feels a little different here."

Roger sniffed the air. "Smells different, too."

"I wouldn't know that." Eric took a whiff but detected nothing.

"You're probably lucky if you can't smell the sheep manure. Otherwise, I'd say you're missing twenty percent of the whole picture."

"Maybe forty percent," Eric said. "I lost my sense of taste, too, for all intents and purposes. Even the four basic flavor sensations are weak on my tongue. I identify food mostly by texture. Good thing I don't have to wear glasses."

"Is that a cyclist I see way up ahead?"

"Looks like it. Maybe two or more. Think we can catch them?"

"Let's find out."

They took off in pursuit of the distant figures that appeared to be cyclists. They were far enough away that the figures could have been pedestrians, horses or even mailboxes. Eric and Roger exchanged turns at the front several times, each trying to maintain a hectic pace. Between Gunnerside and Thwaite, they gradually closed the gap until they could distinctly see three cyclists ahead of them on two bicycles. One rider was on a recumbent, and the other two on a tandem. The three riders opened the gap somewhat on a short downhill, but Roger and Eric used their advantage on the long uphill that followed, and finally caught the three.

Eric was out of breath as he spoke to the man on the front of the tandem and the woman in the rear seat. "You're not easy to catch on this dale!"

The matching multicolored jerseys with multiple trademarks hinted the two might be Americans or Canadians. "We have an advantage on the flats and the down-hills on a tandem, but you can probably beat us going uphill," the man said. The couple appeared to be in their late forties. They had front and rear panniers.

"How long have you been chasing us?" the woman asked. Her long salt-and-pepper hair fluttered in the breeze.

"About half an hour, I think," Roger said. "As he said, you're not easy to catch, even going uphill."

"Blame my brother-in-law!" The tandem pilot gestured toward the man on the recumbent whom Eric and Roger were about to pass. "He sets the pace. He's a very strong rider. We're just trying to keep up with him."

The two younger Americans exchanged friendly greetings with the man on the recumbent as they passed him. His bicycle, too, was heavily loaded with touring gear. He looked very comfortable as he leaned back in his chair, his arms by his side to control the low steering mechanism. Neither Roger nor Eric had ever ridden a tandem or a recumbent. They both wondered what it would be like to be riding one or the other right now. They looked ahead and saw a few more cyclists to pursue, and quickly forgot about the friendly people they had just passed.

At Thwaite, they turned north toward Keld where they passed another remote youth hostel. They had climbed more than 20 kilometers and the summit was in sight, but it did not seem to be getting any closer. The concentration of sheep, trees, towns and tourists was diminishing with the altitude, and the Swale River was getting narrower and shallower. They used their lowest gears frequently, but they were determined to find the top of the seemingly endless Swaledale.

In the distance was a pair of signs, one on each side of the road. They were approaching what appeared to be a saddle in the vast ridge they had been climbing for more than two hours. They could not see the road rising any beyond the signs. Excited to have reached some landmark, they quickened their pace until a post with alternating red and white stripes came into view. The sign on the left side of the narrow highway welcomed them to Cumbria County. They took the post to indicate the summit of Swaledale. The sign on the right side, facing the opposite direction, indicated the North Yorkshire county line and the entrance to Yorkshire Dales National Park. Nothing indicated the elevation of the pass over what amounted to Great Britain's continental divide.

"They don't make a big deal about the altitude of strategic high points like this one," Roger noted. "In the U.S., this pass would have a name and an altitude sign."

"I'm guessing 500 or 600 meters. That sound about right to you?"

"Yes, in that ballpark."

An English family had parked their car in a layby at the summit. The Americans stopped to admire the view of the long valley they had ascended. They asked the family to take pictures of them with their cameras as they rode past the two signs. The wife and husband were delighted to help, and they were impressed that anyone would attempt to climb the dales on a bicycle. The grassy, treeless, windswept summit looked unlike any other landscape they had seen in England. They expected the photos would be among the best of the entire tour. Roger thought about how he nearly made the decision to miss all this, and what a loss it would have been.

"Most of the tourists from your country never see this part of England," the man remarked.

The woman added, "They don't know what they're missing."

"Bad for them, good for us," Roger replied. He greatly appreciated the quiet solitude of the English highlands. He felt safe from his enemies here. He felt alive.

The English family got back in their car and drove down the Swaledale. Roger and Eric continued westward down another long dale to Kirkby Stephen, 17 kilometers away. The descent was fast and the cool breeze dried the sweat they had worked up while climbing the Swaledale. They arrived in Kirkby Stephen in time for lunch, and the town offered several choices.

From the end of the B6270, they turned north onto the A685, which was also the main street of Kirkby Stephen. Everything looked good—a fish bar, a bakery, two cafés, a green grocer and a sweets shop. They had worked up quite an appetite while climbing the dales. They chose the fish bar. A foot patrolman was walking along the street in front of the fish bar when Roger and Eric were about to enter it. Once again, the two Americans were apprehensive.

"Afternoon," the constable said to them, as a matter of courtesy.

"Afternoon," they replied, not quite in unison. They continued walking with their bicycles, as if all was well. They felt as if Scotland Yard was on their tail, preparing to arrest them the moment they assumed they had gotten away scot-free.

Roger and Eric carried their food outside, as all the seats in the fish bar were occupied, and they sat on the edge of a planter box to eat. As before, they covered their food with malt vinegar and HP sauce.

"Katherine Bates must have been eating fish and chips when she wrote *America the Beautiful*."

"Fish and chips on Pikes Peak back then? Not likely! Why do you say that?"

"Cod shad his grease on thee…"

"Ugh!" Roger stuffed three chips in his mouth. "Who would've ever thought we'd be celebrating Independence Day like this?" he asked rhetorically. "I don't think anyone in this town realizes today is a national holiday."

"I didn't realize it, either, until you mentioned it. My concept of time has been waning since we left Denver. July fourth is upon us already, and my internal calendar is still on the June page." Eric wolfed down a fish fillet, famished as he was from the morning's ride.

"We're a healthy distance from Harrogate now," Roger said, "and we've crossed quite a number of highways leading elsewhere. The road we took was only one of several out of Harrogate. From a probability viewpoint, I'd say those scumbags are unlikely to be driving this way. But I'm bothered…"

"You engineers and your probability predictions! Count me among the twenty percent who don't believe in statistics. As you were saying?"

"I'm bothered to know what happened at that pub after we left, and I'd like to be much more certain than I am that we won't meet them again, ever."

"I'm wondering if the long arm of the law is reaching out for us." Eric's expression turned very serious. "We might be safely far from our hoodlum friends, but the police can find us anywhere on this island if they're looking for us. They've already found us twice since Harrogate."

"In any case, there's not a whole lot we can do, except keep our wits about us when we ride, and not say anything that might incriminate us."

"We'll just have to wait and see. No use fretting about it now."

They finished the meal with a pastry from the bakery. On their way through Kirkby Stephen, they noticed yet another hostel. They rode north on the A685 through the lowlands of the Pennine Range toward Brough. They crossed under a dual carriageway and began climbing the moors on the B6276. They were no longer inside the national park, but the terrain was essentially the same as the Yorkshire Dales. As with Swaledale, they used their lowest gears frequently.

The broad ridge crest was also the Durham county line. They followed the Lune River past a reservoir down to Middleton-in-Teesdale. They could count on one hand the number of cars they saw on the B6276, and they did not see any other cyclists. The roads, the weather and everything else were hardly perfect, but very agreeable. It was a great day for cycling.

From Middleton, the two Americans turned north up the Teesdale on the B6277. They had 20 kilometers of steady climbing ahead of them. This highway was just as lonely as the previous one, and that was just fine with them. They passed a remote youth hostel at Langdon Beck, the third one they had seen since Grinton. They kept their eyes open for a certain sedan, but they paid much more attention to the broad vistas surrounding them.

They saw plenty of sheep, stone fences and public trails, but few people. It looked like a great place for hiking, if they had the time and equipment.

They were exhausted by the climbing and slight head wind. They made a point of catching and passing some other cyclists who were carrying less gear than they. They did it mostly to satisfy their egos, but it added to their fatigue. The stone bridges over the brooks and the river looked like ideal fishing spots, although neither of them cared much for fresh-water fish. They settled for photographs of the bridges and brooks, instead.

Eric and Roger reached the summit of Teesdale in the late afternoon, only to find it unmarked by anything more substantial than a surveyor's pole and the county line. They stopped to stretch, catch their breath and get a drink of water. The sky was partly sunny, but rain did not appear to be a threat. The breeze dried the sweat they had worked up during the long ascent. The Tees River seemed to disappear into the moor.

"Would that summit over there be Cross Fell?" Roger pointed toward the mound on the western horizon.

"It must be. I wish we had time to hike over there. I'd like to see it up close. I wonder why we haven't seen more cyclists and hikers up here. People don't know what they're missing."

"This isn't the England you see on calendars and in the tour guides, but I'm glad we found it. I've used just about every gear ratio I have today."

Eric took a glance at his map. "Alston isn't very far now, and it looks like downhill most of the way. We're just east of the Lake District. I'll add that to the list of places I'd like to see in the future."

Roger and Eric rolled into Alston at 18:30. Their hostel guidebook told them to look for The Firs at the south end of town. They did not see any YHA signs from the B6277, which approached from the south. The main street through Alston was steep, with a grade of as much as fourteen percent. They reluctantly rode down the hill to the intersection with the A686. Still not finding the hostel, they turned around and struggled back up the steep hillside to where the road became nearly level. A good-looking employee of a restaurant-pub was sweeping the front steps of the business ahead of them. Roger knew just what to ask her, and Eric was right behind him. The young lady smiled at the cyclists as they approached.

"Excuse me, where can I find the youth hostel?"

"Ute hosto?" She had a strong foreign accent, and the phrase was apparently unfamiliar to her.

"Yes, the Alston Youth Hostel. Do you know where it is?"

"Wait, I ask." She called to a co-worker inside the restaurant.

A young man came out, and gave her an affectionate squeeze to her delight. "'ello, what can I do for you?" He seemed defensive, as if afraid the two strangers were putting the moves on his girl.

"We're looking for the youth hostel. Do you know where it is?"

"We have three hostels. You want The Firs?"

"Yes, that's it, The Firs. Our guidebook says it's on the south end of Alston, but we came from the south," Roger pointed toward the Teesdale summit, "and we didn't see any signs."

"That's not the south end. Keep going down this hill and turn left on the A686. You can't miss it."

Eric had missed many things he had been told he "couldn't miss." Still, it sounded easy enough, and he did not want to look like a fool in front of the girl with the sexy smile. "We seem to have lost our sense of direction. Thanks."

Eric and Roger took the man's advice and rode back down the hill toward the South Tyne River. The whole town of Alston looked like it might slide down the mountainside into the river on a moment's notice, but they were not worried. They did not intend to stay in Alston more than one night. The main drag itself was of interest to them, a steep brick street. They found the hostel about where he said it would be.

The modern interior of the hostel changed their minds about the antiquity of Alston. The warden was a friendly chap, probably in his mid-thirties, who graciously received all the guests. Eric and Roger assumed a bunk bed in one of the men's dormitories upstairs. The duvet on each bed was almost as thick as the mattress. The small blue building was not filled to capacity, and it seemed quiet and remote. They knew they had found a good place to spend the night.

A newspaper that someone had left behind was lying on a chair in the dormitory. Eric was about to pick it up when a better idea came to mind. "Ready to rustle up some grub?" He looked at his watch as if to see if it really was meal time.

"I could use a shower first. I got soaked with sweat today." Roger glanced at his watch, too. He was glad to have it back, and the thought brought a smile to his lips. The smile faded with his next thought, which had to do with the possibility of the police and a certain gang looking for him and Eric.

"I get nasty headaches when I'm hungry," Eric said. "I don't know what the connection is, but I'm less likely to have a seizure on a full stomach."

"Take a shower first, if you can suffer a few minutes longer, and then I'd like to find a nice restaurant." Roger pulled his shaving kit from his panniers. "Something other than fish and chips."

"A warm shower, a good meal in a relaxing place," Eric thought aloud. "For that, I can suffer a few more minutes." He set the newspaper aside without reading any of it.

"Let's splurge then. I saw a nice-looking hotel restaurant that we passed near the T-intersection." Roger removed his cycling clothes, and changed into shorts and a T-shirt. "I wouldn't mind that place where we asked for directions to the hostel, but I think that guy was jealously guarding his girl. He didn't like the way we looked at her."

"Maybe he didn't like the way she was looking at us. She was definitely cute."

They showered and walked into the town in the cool evening air in search of the restaurant Roger had seen. Roger wore a rugby shirt from New Zealand. Eric donned his plaid flannel shirt.

At the hotel, Roger and Eric ate roast lamb, mashed potatoes and Yorkshire pudding served on fine China by a teenage waitress whose manners and grace suggested many years of experience. The waitress kept their teacups full throughout dinner, although she seemed surprised when they each requested a glass of water. With her expert assistance, they enjoyed the most comfortable and relaxing meal they had eaten since they left Romford. A glass of Beaujolais Villages red wine helped set them at ease, too.

"What's up with you?" Roger asked Eric, who was squinting.

Eric paused while eating to rest his forehead in his palm, his elbow supported by the table. He did not answer immediately. "Mild seizure." He mumbled his response, as he lifted his head and took his elbow off the table. "I've had a few in recent days. I feel like I'm on a merry-go-round when I close my eyes."

They both wondered silently, once again, when their combined difficulties would bring their tour to a complete halt. They were getting hammered from all sides. A coherent look returned to Eric's eyes and he resumed eating as if all was normal.

"I'm slowly, very gradually, beginning to feel at ease," Roger said. "We've been so tense for the past few days. I hope I'm not letting my guard down too soon."

"I'm beginning to feel a little better, too." Eric sprinkled some pepper on his potatoes. He had taken to using pepper and other spices liberally since his crash, because they left a mild flavor sensation on his tongue. "I still haven't heard any more about—how did that woman put it?—the affair in Harrogate."

"I don't know what she meant. Best that we don't discuss it here, though."

"Let's forget about it for now. There's nothing we can do. I'd prefer to concentrate my thoughts on my dinner."

"This sheep is great." Roger took a bite. "I haven't eaten a roast lamb in ages."

"This does seem like the sort of place where you'd expect to eat well-prepared lamb. It sounded better to me than steak and kidney pie, or anything else on the menu," Eric said. "Do you think the waitress would accept a date with me tonight?"

"I doubt it. The drive-in movie is closed and the high school dance is scheduled for the weekend. What else is there to do with a date? Besides all that, she probably thinks you're a twit."

"Is twit what the British call us socially challenged people?" Eric took a bite of the Yorkshire pudding, something he had never eaten until now. It was not something he would recommend to his vegetarian or diet-conscious friends.

When they finished, the waitress took their plates. Smiling pleasantly but coyly, she made eye contact with each of them as she went about her work at their table. Her gaze soothed their torment, comforted them after what they had been through recently. They sat transfixed as they watched her carry their plates into the kitchen. She was a few years their junior, but her patient and gentle treatment of them came when they needed it most. Her youth only added to the pleasant ambiance.

"Would you like some dessert now?" the waitress asked.

"What do you recommend?" Roger made eye contact and turned on his usual charming smile.

"Tonight, we have..." The girl momentarily forgot what she meant to say. She noticed their flirtatious gaze on her for the first time. "We have fresh strawberries and cream, spotted dick and bread pudding. I recommend them all."

"I'd like some bread pudding, and he'll have the spotted dick," Eric deadpanned.

Roger nearly choked on the tea he was sipping. He set the cup down hurriedly, clumsily wiped his mouth with his napkin, and coughed a few times before he could speak. "Strawberries and cream sounds good to me." He tried to suppress embarrassment, more coughing and a smirk all at the same time. "I'm not in the mood for spotted dick this evening."

"I'll return with your desserts and some more tea in a moment." The waitress hesitantly turned away.

"What the hell is spotted dick, anyway?" Roger asked Eric after the waitress left. "It sounds like some sort of venereal disease."

"I don't know! I just wanted to see if I could get a rise out of either of you. As if I could resist making a joke about something called spotted dick?"

"Actually, it might be pretty good. Maybe I'll be brave enough to try it next time, if I know what it is first. I've liked just about all the sweets we've had in this country."

They sipped tea in silence, until the waitress returned with the desserts. She cleared the other dishes from their table. They admired her form as she worked her way around the table.

"You've taken such good care of us this evening," Roger commented.

"It's been a pleasure, really." The girl tried not to look or sound embarrassed. "Are both of you Americans?"

"Yes, from Colorado," Roger said. "On the other side of the planet."

"Are you a native of Cumbria?" Eric forced himself to make eye contact with her, even though it was against his nature to do so. To his pleasant surprise, she returned a look that was almost seductive.

"I was born at a hospital in Carlisle, but I've lived all my life near Alston."

"All seventeen years of it?" Roger hoped he had not underestimated her age.

"All sixteen years." She seemed flattered by Roger's suggestion.

"Do you see many Americans around these parts?"

"A few every summer. Are you staying here long?"

"Not long enough, I'm sure," Roger said. "There's so much to see, and so little time."

"We expect to be in Scotland tomorrow," Eric said, "but we'll mention you in our travel logs."

On their way out of the restaurant, they bade the waitress goodnight, and thanked her again for serving them so well. She thanked them for their patronage and smiled as she watched them leave.

"A lovely girl, that one," Eric mused. "Maybe I should have asked her for that date. I think she liked us."

"I guess we'll never know, will we?" Roger led the way as they walked along a side street in the twilight. They walked through a residential neighborhood to get back to the hostel.

A few blocks from the hotel, they came across a soccer pitch carved into the rugged terrain. The field, like most of the town, was deserted. They walked across the field toward the river. Eric dribbled an imaginary soccer ball down one touchline, feinted to the outside, spun around toward the penalty box, and took a wide-angle shot at the goal. He clenched his fists over his head, as if he had just scored the go-ahead goal.

"The sweeper would have blocked your shot. That is, if he's not playing cricket instead."

"Just shows to go you how small this town really is. They're not even out here playing cricket tonight."

"I could get bored here quickly, but it does have that small-town splendor."

"I noticed on the restaurant menu and in the hostel guidebook that Alston is the highest market town in England. What do you suppose they mean by market town?"

"I saw that, too. I think they mean it's a real town, incorporated, as opposed to a cluster of buildings with collective name, like Grinton."

"Sort of like Leadville, as opposed to Alma, in our native state?"

"Probably. What I haven't seen anywhere yet is the elevation. You'd think they'd want to quantify their bragging rights."

They walked back toward the hostel as they carried on their pointless discussion of small towns. A trail called the Pennine Way passed alongside the hostel property. The trail looked most inviting, and instantly fired their imaginations. Neither had given any thought to their ongoing predicament since before dinner, and both were in good moods when they arrived at the hostel.

"What is this Pennine Way, and where does it start and end?" Eric asked the warden at the registration desk.

The warden pointed at a map of Great Britain on the wall. "It's a 443-kilometer footpath from the Peak District National Park in Edale, Derbyshire, to Kirk Yetholm, Borders, in southeastern Scotland. I walked the length of it a few years ago, I did. Took me about three weeks. Does it look like something you'd like to do?"

"Definitely! But it will have to be another time. We're only equipped for cycling, not hiking."

"It's an adventure. It's not for everyone, but you'd probably like it."

They made a note to consider hiking all or part of the Pennine Way on their next visit to England. They prepared to wind down for the night, starting with describing the day's events in their journals as they sat in the common room. Neither noticed the tall figure as he walked into the room a few minutes after they did, but his familiar voice caught their attention immediately.

"I was hoping I would see you two again." Christian Meijer had a very serious look on his face. "I heard some news that might be of interest to you."

"Christian! Pull up a chair and join us," Eric said.

Christian's remark could not have had a more sobering effect on them. Without a moment's hesitation, they knew what he was talking about. Their pulse rates accelerated as they waited for him to continue. He sat down with them at the table.

"A Dutch woman, a cyclist I mentioned to you in York, found me yesterday as I was leaving the York hostel. She said she had been in Harrogate on Tuesday, looking for a certain bicycle importer. She noticed a car that had been set on fire. Next to it was the car that she thought was used by the three who robbed her. She went inside and asked the innkeeper to contact the police." Christian appeared relaxed but still serious.

The Americans perspired in anticipation of what they were about to hear.

"The innkeeper told her they had already been arrested," Christian continued. "They had been seriously injured in the water closet, somehow. I don't know much more than that, but apparently it is part of a gang war, you know? Anyway, I'm sure they were the same three who harassed me. And you, too, probably."

"Anything else?" Roger asked eagerly. The most important part was coming.

"As far as I know, they are still in jail. Charged with a number of crimes. My Dutch friend made a statement to the police, although I doubt she will be able to testify against these people." Christian's expression turned from very serious into a broad smile.

Roger smiled, too. "They got what they had coming."

"We can start enjoying our vacation again," Eric said. "This calls for a drink."

"Would you like to find a pub tonight?"

Roger and Eric looked at each other for an answer. "Sure! We have a little time before the hostel closes for the night. And we know just the place."

They walked into town via the residential shortcut the two Americans had discovered a little earlier. They went in the pub where their attractive friend with the foreign accent was waiting tables. She brought them a round of ale and made small talk with them in her charming broken English. Her protector was nowhere to be seen. She was just as friendly and tempting as she had been earlier. They continued to discuss the current state of affairs over ale. Both Eric and Roger had to go to a lot of trouble to restrain themselves from admitting, or even hinting, that they were involved. The temptation to boast of it was strong, but they managed to stifle themselves. Knowing that neither the police nor the hoodlums were looking for them lifted a tremendous burden from their consciences, just what they needed. They wondered if Christian knew any more than what he had told them, or if he suspected them of anything. Whether he suspected anything was irrelevant, they concluded. He was as relieved as they were to be free of further menace.

"My journey has improved very much since I was told what happened," Christian said as they walked back to the hostel in the dark. "I think we will not see the likes of these people any more."

The hostel was not so easy to find in the dark, even though they knew where to find it. That part of Alston had few street lights or porch lights to guide them. Most of the guests were already in bed when they returned.

Christian went off to bed in high spirits. The newspaper, a local one from the previous day that Eric had seen earlier in the dormitory, was now on the counter of the warden's registration desk. Eric picked it up to read the headlines. At the bottom of the front page was an article about an explosion and a fire in a warehouse near Harrogate. No one had been injured, but the loss was estimated at well over one hundred thousand pounds. The disaster had occurred the same night Roger and Eric were in Harrogate, and the authorities suspected arson.

Eric pointed the article out to Roger. "The big affair in Harrogate, maybe?"

"That's a safe bet."

"Probably, but let's not talk about it here and now. I want to think about the rest of our vacation for a change."

Roger and Eric looked at a map in their dormitory room. Their next destination was a hostel near Selkirk, Borders, in southern Scotland. They expected to see more of the rugged terrain they had been traversing. The Cheviot Hills lay between Alston and Selkirk.

"With all the excitement lately, I'd kind of forgotten about Marianne. But, I'll call her again as soon as I can. I need to hear her voice. I should be sending her more e-mail than I have been." Roger started undressing in preparation for bedtime. "I've been a fool, Chief. If I were married to Marianne, we could afford to travel in style, securely. But no, Roger the Honorable, man of lofty principles, has to question everyone else's motives, as if he has the moral high ground on everyone. What happened to us lately could have happened anyway, but it doesn't have to happen again. I'm going to marry her as soon as I can, before she finds somebody else who's not such a nitwit."

Chapter IV: *A Bonnie Lass in Highland*

20.

When Roger and Eric awoke, they were still elated with their newfound peace of mind, although Roger was now almost as aware of Eric's condition as Eric was. They slept well, in spite of the single thick, heavy duvets that made them too warm during the night. They got cold when they set the blanket aside, so they were left with the choice of temperature extremes. The duvets helped them imagine the experience of sleeping beneath a cow. They felt fortunate that no one in the room snored, as had not been the case at most of the previous hostels.

The Americans used the computer in the common room to examine their options. They noticed a large gap between the hostels of northern England and the few in southern Scotland. Edinburgh was too far for one day's ride, especially with the moors and dales they expected to climb. The weather was doubtful, too. They asked the warden to book beds for them at the Broadmeadows Youth Hostel in Yarrowford, Borders. Yarrowford was too small to appear on their map, but the hostel web site put it about 8 kilometers west of Selkirk on the A708. The guidebook described Broadmeadows as the first youth hostel in Scotland, in a building made for that purpose in 1930.

Christian said farewell and turned right on the A686 toward Hexham to the northeast. Roger and Eric took a last look at the hostel, and went left on the A686. Just across the river, they turned right on the A689 and followed the river and the Pennine Way to the north. A mist enveloped Alston during the night, and it turned into an intermittent light rain once they crossed the county line from Cumbria into Northumberland.

From Alston northward into Northumberland National Park, the roads and countryside had all the elements that made the previous few days' riding so pleasant, except the rain. Forested hills surrounded them. Although they missed Scafell Pike in western Cumbria, and Cross Fell was behind them, they were still among England's highest mountains. The population in this area was sparse, Northumberland being England's least populous county. They were quite content to see more sheep than people. The scenery was gorgeous, and they did not have to share it with much of anyone.

They followed the South Tyne River at a moderate pace to the A69 near Greenhead. The mist dried up, but they wore long sleeves and leg warmers all morning. They stopped for lunch in Gilsland, a wide spot along Hadrian's Wall and the B6318. They purchased some Cornish pastries and bananas, and sat on the Roman fort ruins to eat. Hadrian's Wall, named for the Roman emperor who ordered its construction in the second century A.D., was nothing spectacular, but it was a landmark well known to locals from Solway Firth to Newcastle-upon-Tyne. The wall marked the northern boundary of Roman-occupied England, built to protect Roman colonists from the Picts and other tribes from the north. Stones had been removed from the wall to build houses and other structures over the centuries, but it was still in good shape.

"Why didn't you tell me about the car you set on fire?"

"Me? I thought you did that! Maybe there *is* something to this gang war we've been hearing about. We were probably caught in the cross-fire!"

"I can only guess the burned car was the Vauxhall. I wanted to ask Christian if it was, but he would not have known a detail like that, and I didn't want to draw any suspicion on us by asking."

"I wonder if somebody followed the guy with the Death tattoos, and set his car on fire after we left. Or maybe the burned car had nothing to do with us, although I'd be surprised if it didn't."

"I just hope we're far enough away from the action and nobody cares about us anymore!"

They ate in silence for a while, and contemplated the various scenarios of what happened after they left the pub in Harrogate. They felt safe now, but they were also well aware of England's notorious underworld.

"Why does everyone around here make such a big deal out of Hadrian's Wall?" Roger asked. "This wall is shoulder-high at best."

"You can be sure no barbarians leading hordes of alligators ever attacked the Romans behind this wall," Eric said.

"I suppose the big deal is that it's still standing after nineteen centuries."

About the time they finished eating, rain began to fall from the clouds that had been accumulating all morning. They took shelter in a nearby walkway tunnel beneath railroad tracks, where they used the time to chronicle their exploits in their journals and write some postcards to their families. They bought postcards at a Tourist Information Centre that had photographs and diagrams of the wall. They changed into short sleeves, as the day had gotten warmer.

They resumed their journey when the rain stopped, even though the pavement was still wet. They wore their rain suits, but their perspiration condensed inside the waterproof, breathable fabric and made them nearly as wet inside the garments as they would have been without the rain suits. They removed their rain suits when their clothes were saturated. Synthetic fabrics kept them as comfortable as possible under the circumstances.

The occasionally winding highways took them through forests of both conifers and hardwoods, over small rivers, and through the occasional roundabout. They dodged roadkill that mostly consisted of rabbits, unlike

Colorado where it was squirrels and Washington where it was raccoons and nutria. They climbed and descended several moors as they approached the English-Scottish border. The forests did not go very high on the moors. The trees were replaced on the higher ground by fields of heather with miniature deep-purple flowers.

In the mid-afternoon, somewhere along the seldom-used B6318, they noticed a change in their environs. They were not sure what had changed—it could have been the grass, shrubbery, foliage or pavement—but they knew they had crossed into Scotland. The border between the two states was entirely arbitrary. It did not appear to coincide with a river, mountain range or any other geological barrier. The earlier rains deposited some of the leaves from roadside trees on the pavement, and the mat of damp leaves formed a slippery surface on the otherwise coarse asphalt.

Roger pointed at a grove of conifers when they stopped briefly to check a map. "Can I assume these are Scotch pines?"

"I don't know a pine from a fir from a spruce, but I've been looking for the Scotch broom. We have that all over the Northwest. I assume it originated here."

On one sharp downhill curve, Roger felt his bicycle slide sideways. He slowed to prevent further slipping. The eerie sensation of almost falling made him cautious. Eric rode into the turn slightly faster than Roger did, but by the time Eric could feel his bicycle sliding sideways, his brake pads were too wet to allow him to slow down in time to steady himself. His wheels locked in the grip of his brakes, but his bicycle slid across the wet leaves into a guard cable on the outside of the curve. He flipped over the cable into a cushion of more wet leaves beside the road.

Roger stopped as quickly as he could, turned around, and rode back up the hill to the spot where Eric lay cursing and groaning. With Roger's help, Eric picked himself up and peeled the wet leaves off his clothes and bicycle. Eric was sore and dazed, but he had no obvious injuries other than a laceration on the bridge of his nose where his sunglasses had been forced against his face upon impact. His front wheel and frame were bent, and his rear brake lever was broken.

"Did you overestimate the curve, or what?" Roger scolded.

"I probably did." Eric spoke in a weak voice that sounded as if he thought he had been somewhere else when the crash occurred.

"Eric! What the hell? Your brain was adrift in another galaxy when you entered the turn, wasn't it?"

Eric sounded genuinely apologetic. "I don't usually have any problems when I'm riding, or doing anything physically strenuous."

"If you're ready to quit, we can probably catch a train or a bus back to London somewhere around here!"

"I overestimated the curve, that's all." Eric was insistent, even though the doubt in his words was clearly evident. "I'll be all right in a few minutes, and then we'll continue on to Selkirk. Let's have a look at my bike."

Another cyclist, a woman about the same age as Eric and Roger, rode up to the crash scene. They had not seen any other cyclists in the area until she appeared. She looked over Eric while he picked himself up, and shook her head.

"You'll have to ride better than that around here, you will. Scotland's no place for beginners like yourself, lad." Her accent was unmistakably Scottish. She shook her head side to side as she spoke, as if scolding a child.

Eric had not noticed her until she spoke to him. "Beg your pardon?" He had heard what she said, and his tone of voice indicated his irritation with the insult. Beg-your-pardon was his cordial way of saying what he really meant, shut the fuck up.

"I said, you'll have to ride…"

"I heard you the first time!" Eric's blood was near boiling with rage. "Are you here to offer your help, or did you just come for a laugh?"

"Now don't get your knickers in a bunch, mate!"

Eric glared at her.

Straddling the frame of her Raleigh, the woman shrugged her shoulders, then smiled at Roger. He could not see her eyes behind her stylish sunglasses, but he smiled back and winked. She was nearly as tall as Roger, and slender. Tight Lycra cycling shorts and a crop-top covered a well-tanned, shapely figure. A fading surgical scar on her left knee was the only blemish on her long, smooth legs. All that showed of her reddish-brown hair was a long ponytail hanging below her helmet. The brass ring in her pierced navel spoke for itself. Her luggage was two compact panniers over her rear wheel. She carried a small handlebar bag, but no front panniers, sleeping bag or tent. Her bicycle was remarkably clean, as if she had not been in the rain much lately. She turned her bicycle, and resumed her ride northward, the same direction as the two Americans were going.

"Who the hell was that…that…?" Eric stood up and began rearranging himself. Only his gentlemanly nature kept him from finishing the question with a sexist slur.

"I don't know, but she must've been following us." Roger watched her disappear in the distance. "Nice looking critter. I wonder if she rides as well as she talks."

"She had a lot of nerve telling me that! Must think she's really something." Eric was seething, her condescending words still ringing in his ears.

"She looks to be going our way, so maybe we'll catch her once we get moving again. I wouldn't mind seeing more of her." Roger took a drink from his water bottle before getting down to business.

Using the fork as a makeshift truing stand, Roger replaced the broken spokes and straightened the wheel well enough that it could be used again. Eric would have to wait for a new brake lever until he could get one in Edinburgh. The slight bend in the downtube would have to wait until they returned to Romford, where Henry Smythe could straighten it. Eric was angry with himself for overestimating the curve, but Roger said nothing more and tried to be pleasant about the matter. To Roger, the situation was reminiscent of his own mishap in Nottinghamshire, except that this one did not involve an assailant. Roger felt like he was returning a favor to Eric by repairing Eric's bicycle, and it gave him some satisfaction in the midst of the disaster.

Slowed by Eric's crash, they rode the short distance through the forest into Langholm in Dumfries and Galloway County. A slight but steady headwind resisted their progress all the way. They climbed a dale to the Borders county line in the late afternoon along the A7. Somewhere across the county line they entered the Teviot drainage and descended into Hawick, 38 kilometers from Langholm. They had seen few people and automobiles during the day, neither of which they missed. They did not see the Scottish cyclist again, much as Eric wanted to catch her and prove a point about his cycling abilities. The Cheviot Hills near the English-Scottish border were not quite as high or steep as what they had been climbing in Yorkshire and Cumbria, but plenty challenging just the same.

Hawick was the largest town they had seen all day, and they did not have to think twice about stopping at a superstore for groceries. The hostel was strictly self-catering, and it was a ways out of Selkirk. Eric and Roger did not expect to find a superstore in Selkirk, and were not sure it would be open when they arrived even if they did find one. They locked their bicycles to a railing near several other bicycles on one side of the store.

"We've been eating fish and chips morning, noon and night." Eric wanted some vegetables for a change, something not deep-fried. "Grab a couple of good-size potatoes. I'll get an onion and bell pepper."

Roger reached into a bin of potatoes, then looked up. "Our friend had the same idea. See her over there?"

"I'm trying not to."

The Scottish woman went on her way without noticing the two Americans. They also bought some mushrooms, Leicester cheese, peaches, tea bags, Fruit & Nut bars, oranges, yogurt and apple juice. They were all set for supper and breakfast. They still had 26 kilometers of rounded plateaus to climb on the way to Broadmeadows. They continued along the A7, where the traffic increased somewhat and they saw a few cyclists.

They were very tired as they entered Selkirk. They had been thinking about Selkirk all day long and it gave them a short-lived euphoric feeling, until they realized they had at least another 8 kilometers to go beyond Selkirk. They passed a brightly illuminated fish bar in Selkirk they had seen advertised on the web site they looked at in Alston. Just beyond the fish bar, they turned onto the A708 toward Yarrow.

Traffic was virtually nonexistent west of Selkirk. The mostly cloudy sky was getting dimmer, but they still had a few hours of daylight. They hoped they were on the right road, because they did not have much time or energy for backtracking. An occasional sign indicated they were heading toward Yarrow. They watched their odometers carefully, silently counting down the distance to where they expected to find the hostel. The Yarrow Valley had a gentle slope, but it seemed very difficult after all the climbing they had done, and Eric's crash.

A YHA sign at one turn-off indicated a footpath to the hostel. They were tempted to use it until they checked their guidebook, which told them to look for a telephone booth. A few hundred meters farther around a bend brought them to a red telephone box, where another YHA sign pointed to a fairly steep gravel road to the right. They turned up the damp track and struggled with the slope. The hostel driveway was much longer than they expected, and the dampness from earlier rains made it seem that much worse. Water dripped on them from the tall trees that obscured the houses and B&Bs in the vicinity.

"Damn! We made it." Eric was relieved to finally be at the end of their day's journey. For him, it had been the most difficult day thus far.

"I'm tired, I'm starved and I'm filthy. Let's not waste any time out here."

The warden had been expecting them. Several tents were pitched in the front yard, where a large group of English teenagers was camping. The hostel was entirely on one level, and smaller than most of the hostels they had seen. It was not the sort of place they would have found had they not been looking for it. It was way off the beaten path. They parked their bicycles in the storage shed and carried their gear into the men's dormitory. They needed a drying room for the clothes they were wearing and a few items in their panniers, but this was their first hostel that did not have one. The warden suggested they spread their damp clothing near the heating units or the fireplace in the common room. The hostel had plenty of empty bunks, giving the few indoor guests a choice of places to sleep. Roger and Eric selected their bunks and changed into dry clothing.

They took their groceries into the kitchen to begin preparing their evening meal and to refrigerate their breakfast items. Roger sliced the potatoes and put a pot of water on the stove to boil, while Eric chopped the vegetables.

"Got back on the road again, I see." A familiar, feminine voice with a very Scottish accent surprised Eric and Roger in the kitchen. "I'm surprised you made it this far."

A slender young woman with reddish-brown hair stood in the doorway of the kitchen. She was wearing black stretch pants, sandals and a zippered sweatshirt. The two Americans noticed a radiant face, soft blue eyes and a seductive smile that were obscured by sunglasses and a cycling helmet earlier in the day. The stretch pant, the kind women wear for aerobic exercising, accentuated every curve and every well-toned muscle from her waist to her ankles. The sweatshirt was unzipped enough to attract their attention.

"Yes, of course we did," was Eric's curt reply. He did not return the smile, but Roger did. "We're big boys, and we know how to take care of ourselves." He was on the defensive. Their first introduction of the day was not a good one.

Roger ignored Eric's sarcasm, and took the initiative. "We're starting to think about tonight's supper. What's a good thing to cook when you're in Scotland?"

"You could make a pot of haggis." The woman kept Roger transfixed in her gaze. He was not sure if she was undressing him with her eyes, or loathing him.

"Did you bring the recipé?" Roger asked.

The woman broke her noncommittal expression for the first time with a short laugh. "No, and I couldn't prepare it if my life depended on it. Would you settle on fish and chips?"

The condescending tone had evaporated, and the woman was starting to come across as marginally likable to Eric. He did not let down his guard, though. She set some food items on the counter in the kitchen and looked underneath for a suitable pot to begin cooking.

"Would you care to join us for supper?" Roger took his chances inviting her, knowing she could easily respond with ridicule.

She hesitated, shrugged and proceeded into the kitchen with a grocery sack in one hand. "I don't mind if I do." She had not really made eye contact with Eric except at the first glance, and now he was miffed because she ignored him. She introduced herself as Nancy MacLane, a triathlete in the summer and ski bum in the winter, from Aberdeen. Her triathlon days were probably over, she explained, due to some recurring knee problems, but the cycling segment was her favorite and she liked to ride even when not competing.

The Americans ate their peaches while they cooked. The peaches were at just about optimum ripeness—sweet, juicy and moderately firm. A cup of tea further brightened their spirits. They sautéed the diced onion, mushrooms and peppers with boiled potato slices, and melted shredded cheese on top of the vegetable mixture. Roger sliced Nancy's potato and added it to his pot while she prepared her other vegetables. Their other food went into the common refrigerator. They used a felt-tip pen to write their names and their departure date on the plastic sack from the superstore in Hawick before they refrigerated it. Two other guests were also in the kitchen, just finishing their cooking.

"Have your injuries gotten any worse since this afternoon?" Roger sat down with Eric and Nancy at the dining table to eat.

"No, I'm fine, physically," Eric said. "But I'm still pissed because it damaged my bicycle. I should've been more careful."

Roger scooped up some food with his spoon. "Can you make it to Edinburgh tomorrow?"

"I can, and I hope my brake and wheel can, too," Eric said. "I guess each of us now knows how the other felt in Sherwood Forest last week, more or less."

"More or less." Roger was not too eager to discuss the Harrogate incident in mixed company yet.

"Did you crash in Sherwood Forest, Roger?"

Nancy seemed all too ready to make an issue of the Americans' shortcomings, it seemed to Eric. He was barely on speaking terms with her, even though she and Roger had apparently become very friendly.

"A car forced me off the road." Roger hoped the subject would change if he did not elaborate.

"Is that how you got that bruise above your eye?" Nancy was as hungry as the men, and she ate as ravenously as they did. She seemed mildly pleased that they had helped her with the cooking.

"No, that came later. We got into a fight with the people in the car. We were afraid they might be out looking for us, but it's been several days and several hundred kilometers since we last saw them." Roger continued eating the potatoes until they were all gone. He usually ate one course at a time, finishing it before moving on to the next course.

"They brought a lot of misery on us, but I think we're safe from them now. I feel like we can daydream when we ride instead of looking for enemies." Eric stabbed a potato slice with his fork. He turned the fork over, British style, before inserting the potato into his mouth. "They got what they deserved, and we got away, I hope." He felt a bit awkward using his fork the British way, but he had been consciously practicing it at mealtimes lately.

117

"I thought you two were English when I saw you lying in the grass beside the road today. You talk like Americans, but you carry on like Englishmen after a football match, crashing and fighting and God knows what else." Nancy had a chip on her shoulder about something.

"Is it men, the English, or specifically English men that you don't like?" Eric looked Nancy in the eye when he spoke. He wanted to find a weak spot in that huge ego she wore on her sleeve. She ignored the question.

"Many lessons to be learned from that incident," Roger said. "We got our revenge, but we risked way too much."

Eric felt as if his previous statement had put Nancy in her place, if only temporarily. "We risked getting killed, injured, arrested, incarcerated, sued and deported all for a wristwatch, a passport and a little frontier justice. I've been in a few scuffles at school, but no one ever pulled a knife on me before."

"On top of that, my bicycle is still damaged. Our heroics didn't really get us much restitution." Roger had opened up to the subject, but he was careful not to say anything incriminating in front of Nancy. He had, in fact, recovered enough cash from the three hoodlums to cover the cost of his custom frame. He did not want to think about the sources of that cash.

"We never followed or searched for them. Karma or destiny or whatever put us in contact with them each time." Eric finished his glass of water. He got up for a refill.

"Do you think Christian suspected anything?" Roger asked. "I had a strong urge to tell him our side of the story."

"Was a friend of yours involved?" Nancy was a little nonplused when she saw that Eric could be just as caustic as she, but she was quick to bounce back.

"A Dutch cyclist we'd met had also been harassed by these hoodlums." Eric noticed just a slight, very slight, thawing of the ice between himself and Nancy. "I had that same urge, but we were smart to keep everything to ourselves. I don't think Christian suspected anything of us, and if he did, I'm sure our secret's safe with him."

"Until just recently, I thought violent crime like what happened to us could only happen in the U.S. Christian said he might have expected it in Amsterdam, but not here. We foreigners have a lot to learn about your country," Roger said. Eric nodded in agreement.

"You foreigners are being naïve," Nancy said. "Jack the Ripper was British, you know. English, in fact. You'll be safe in the Scottish countryside."

"George will be envious when we tell him we were in Scotland." Roger briefly described George Fraser to Nancy. She showed some interest in their Scottish-surnamed friend.

"Maybe we should console him with an authentic tartan memento," Eric said. "Let's start looking for a kilt or bagpipe in his color."

"You foreigners think we all play the pipes and wear kilts, don't you?" Nancy's sarcastic style was never very far beneath the surface, Eric noted. She had a way of making the most innocent statement sound like a cutting remark.

"And drink scotch, too," Eric added. "Don't forget the scotch. Our whole notion of Scottish people comes from a character on *The Simpsons*."

"Willy the groundskeeper?" Nancy rolled her eyes. She knew very well what Eric was talking about.

"That's the one."

"You'll have much to learn about Scotland, then."

"I'm sure somebody in Edinburgh sells those sorts of things to gullible tourists like ourselves," Roger surmised. "How far into Scotland should we go?"

"We should spend a week or so here. We have plenty of time, so why rush it?" Eric said. "I do want to see the Highlands, but I'm not sure how long it will take us to get there."

"At your speed, it might take you a week. If you can stay on the road." The real Nancy, in Eric's mind, had returned.

"We can get there just as fast as you can. Probably faster." Eric considered Nancy's last comment a challenge, and he accepted it.

"To the Highlands, then!" Roger was almost oblivious to the developing rivalry. "That'll be our goal. Where are you headed?"

"Wherever my imagination takes me," Nancy said. "I don't need an itinerary in Scotland."

They washed their dishes and cleaned the kitchen after supper. The Americans fetched their journals and stationery, and went in the dining room to write. Nancy parked in front of the fireplace in the common room next to the dining room, and chatted with some of the guests. One wall of the common room had a small clan map of Scotland on it.

Roger stopped to look at the map before he sat down. "I doubt there's any need to ask where the Frasers come from." He noticed the predominance of the Fraser clans on the map. "Strange, but I don't think Fraser is the most common Scottish name in the U.S. What say you, Chief?"

"I'd say Campbell and Gordon and several names that begin with 'Mc' are more common than Fraser there. I'd also say that Frazier is a more common spelling than Fraser, if they have the same origin."

"How do you pronounce Edinburgh?" Roger asked the warden, who was standing nearby. Roger pronounced it as four syllables, "ed-in-burro."

"It's ed-n-bur-r-r-ra." The warden, in his Scottish brogue, pronounced it as three syllables, with emphasis on the first and third. His tongue fluttered over the 'r' sound.

"Does the pronunciation depend what part of Scotland you're from?"

"Aye, a little. I come from Glasgow. We have our way of saying it. The Highlanders, the southerners and the English all have a slightly different way of saying it. You'll find fifty dialects between here and York."

The two Americans were becoming more and more aware of the differences between regional British accents, and especially between English and Scottish dialects, as they listened to Nancy and the warden. He explained that the suffix "-burgh" means city in Gaelic.

"Is there anything worth seeing in Edinburgh, or is it just another big city?"

"It's probably the best place in Scotland for tourists, it is. The Scottish Parliament meets there, the royal family has a residence. Birthplace and hometown of many famous Scots. Very historic. Great shopping on Princes Street. If you'll be staying at a youth hostel, I'll book it for you right now. They fill up fast this time of year. You might want to stay two nights if you can."

"In that case, please do."

The warden used his computer to check the availability of beds at the Edinburgh hostels. "I've got you down for two beds at the Eglinton hostel. The Bruntsfield hostel is already full."

Later, as Eric and Roger were about to retire for the evening, they discussed with Nancy their plan to ride to Edinburgh in the morning. She had not decided where she would be going. In the men's dormitory, they exchanged some additional thoughts about where they had been and where they were going.

"Scotland the Brave, and an unusual place to spend our first night in it!" Roger was in a good mood, thanks in part to his chance encounter with Nancy. "I liked northern England, but I'm so happy it's behind us now. What do you think of Nancy?"

"She's a tomboy with a Texas-size ego. If she wants to make a race of it tomorrow, she's going to have to earn bragging rights." Eric removed his T-shirt and laid it over his panniers so it would air out overnight. He turned his cycling shorts inside out for the same reason.

"I think she's kind of cute—big ego, acid tongue and all. Maybe she's that bonnie lass you've been hoping to meet, Chief." Roger squirmed his way into his sheet sleeping bag. "I'm looking forward to Edinburgh tomorrow."

"I am, too." Eric let the first comment go without rebuttal. "I'll see you there tomorrow, Squire."

21.

Roger and Eric got their earliest start yet, and Nancy joined them in the dining room at 7:15. The warden was up, but all the other guests were still in bed. The oranges, cherry yogurt, apple juice and tea they bought in Hawick got them going. Nancy washed some fruit and a croissant down with tea before she said farewell and left. The Americans were impressed with how efficiently she moved in the early morning, and how lightly she packed for traveling.

They intended to go back to Selkirk and take the A7 from Galashiels into Edinburgh, but the warden suggested a scenic back road that would avoid much of the traffic. The alternate route was not shown on their map. He drew a map of the Yarrow Valley and directed them through Innerleithen. They packed up their gear, loaded their bicycles, and walked 1.5 kilometers down the dirt track to the A708. Light rain had fallen intermittently during the night, and the morning was overcast and misty. A few of the campers on the front lawn were beginning to stir.

Once on the A708, they rode west up the secluded, forested valley toward Yarrow. The pavement was wet and they felt the occasional light drizzle. They came to a hotel near Mountbenger where the warden had told them to look for a turn-off to Innerleithen. They turned north up the B709 and began climbing the moors that bordered the Yarrow Valley. Traffic was rare on both highways. The sun started to poke through the clouds as the riders crested the broad ridge that separated the Yarrow and Tweed Valleys.

Roger's Trek sustained a punctured rear tire descending into Innerleithen. He hated to have to remove the back wheel because it required three hands to do it in the absence of a jig. Eric made himself useful and held the frame while Roger manipulated the chain, derailleur and wheel. Roger needed only a few minutes and his tire levers to remove the tire, replace the punctured tube with a spare, and remount the tire. He folded the punctured tube, secured it with rubber bands, and inserted it into his pannier. He would patch it later. They got underway again, but found a bakery in Innerleithen and had to stop for a fruit scone and a map check.

Eric wolfed down his scone. "I'm disappointed. I wanted to see how well our friend Nancy rides."

"She really put a burr under your saddle, didn't she?" Roger practically swallowed his scone whole.

"She got me fired up, all right. She thinks her shit don't stink."

"You meet all kinds on a bike tour. Maybe we'll see her again somewhere. If she said where she's going today, I didn't catch it."

"Me, neither. Not that I care."

They continued north on the B709 over the Moorfoot Hills. The road took them right through the fairway of a golf course in a narrow valley. Some of the golfers gave them a sidelong glance, as if they were intruding on private property. The pavement gradually dried up. They felt as if they had the forest and the moors all to themselves. The moors were not as tall or as steep as what they had been climbing between Grinton and Alston, but adequately challenging just the same. They emerged from the wilderness at Heriot near the Midlothian county line. The B709 ended there, and they turned left onto the A7 for a straight shot into Edinburgh.

The traffic increased substantially on the A7. Rolling hills replaced the moors as they neared the Firth of Forth coast. They stopped for a nature break at the Scottish Mining Museum in the suburb of Newtongrange. Public restrooms always seemed to be in short supply when the Americans were most in need. They walked by the cafeteria of the museum and noticed haggis on the menu. Was it just Roger's imagination, or did the Scottish eatery have a slightly different aroma from the English eateries he had been in lately? The mining museum looked interesting, especially to Roger, but they did not want to leave all their gear outside, unattended.

Just beyond Newtongrange was Dalkeith, and the A7 became Dalkeith Road. They stopped at a park for a few minutes to watch a soccer team practice. The players were of a much higher caliber than Eric and Roger. Semi-professional, perhaps? They continued on past the University of Edinburgh medical school, which at a glance looked more like a microelectronics factory than a hospital. They stopped at a superstore near the Edinburgh city limits to purchase what they needed for lunch and supper. They ate the lunch items at one of the in-store cafeteria tables. The pavement was nearly dry but the sky was still overcast. They followed the signs to the city centre, on the assumption that the hostel ought to be somewhere near the downtown area.

Dalkeith Road became Clerk Street, then Nicolson Street. It brought the two cyclists to the edge of a deep valley filled with tall buildings, parks, castles, traffic, pedestrians and railroad yards. The large city centre of Edinburgh was spread out before them, and they had no idea where to go. They were in Scotland's capital and second-largest city, home to nearly half a million people. They stayed on Nicolson across South Bridge. Across High Street, also known as the Royal Mile, they were on North Bridge. North Bridge ended three blocks later at Princes Street, just past the sprawling roofs over the Waverly Railroad Station. The warden at Broadmeadows had said the Eglinton hostel was not far from Princes Street. They turned west onto Princes Street amid the crowds and the heavy traffic.

They rode the length of Princes Street, and turned south on Lothian Road. They came upon a bus stop that had a map of the city centre. The neighborhoods were color-coded, but they could not find Eglinton Crescent anywhere on the map. They checked their hostel guide pamphlet again.

"It says the hostel is in New Town."

"That's up the hill, on the other side of Princes Street, according to the map."

"The pink zone. Let's cruise up the hill and look for a hostel sign."

In the mid-afternoon, the Americans rode up the opposite side of the city centre valley from which they came. They rode the length of George Street, which took them past a statue of a historical figure at each intersection, but they did not find what they sought. They tried Queen Street, York Place and several other streets, where they found every kind of business and plenty of apartments, but no hint of a hostel. They were convinced the hostel was not to be found in New Town.

Once again on Princes Street, they stopped at a black-stained sandstone spire to figure out where they wanted to go. They were surprised to find themselves at the Walter Scott Monument, built in 1844 to a height of 61 meters, with a statue of Sir Walter in the center. Walking their bicycles through the crowds on the sidewalk was no easy task, but they managed it and took a few photographs. Next to the Scott Monument was a much smaller monument to nineteenth-century Scottish missionary David Livingstone, best known for his exploration of southern Africa. Roger and Eric admired the Livingstone Monument for a moment.

"Schmidt, I presume?" An unexpected yet familiar voice came from behind.

"Nancy!"

"Good show, lads. You made it here in spite of yourselves."

"Is that how you Scots say, 'Welcome to Edinburgh?'"

"Nay, that would be, '*Failte du Dùn Èideann.*'"

"Whatever!" Eric said. The Gaelic phrase sounded like gibberish to him. "You shouldn't have left Broadmeadows in such a hurry this morning. We could have made it a race to Edinburgh."

"I had things to do whilst you two were gadding about."

"Maybe so, but it looks like we got here before you did."

Nancy ignored the remark. She spoke mostly to Roger. "Are you looking for the Eglinton Youth Hostel? I might know where it is." She wore tight cycling shorts and a bright yellow jersey bearing a glut of French corporate logos.

"We've been searching for it the last half hour."

"I think it's near the Haymarket Railway Station."

123

"This one down here?" Eric pointed southeast toward the bridge they had crossed coming into the city centre.

"No, that's the Waverly Station." Nancy pointed west toward the near side of the Edinburgh Castle. "I think it's that way. Come on, then!"

Eric and Roger followed Nancy several blocks west on Princes Street to a T-intersection. The Americans were once again confused by the frequent street name changes. A sign at the intersection pointed toward the Haymarket Station. They rode past the station, saw the hostel sign, turned right up the hill, and found a set of arced streets. A few turns later, they were on Eglinton Crescent. The quiet street was lined with a long row of identical, three-story, contiguous buildings on one side and a private park on the other. The hostel was in the middle of the block. The neighbors included B&Bs, offices and private residences.

"Do you know your way around this city, or did you just get lucky finding this place?" Eric asked. He had only a vague idea where they were in relation to Princes Street.

"I've been here before, but it's been a few years. We rode a few extra blocks, but it's all coming back to me. Things are starting to look familiar."

"I wouldn't have found this all by myself," Eric said. Roger nodded in agreement.

"You just have to think like a Scot."

Nancy and Roger buzzed the warden from the locked front door, while Eric stayed outside with the bicycles. The warden unlocked the door with a remote control. The registration desk was about two rooms removed from the front door. Several people had been turned away for lack of a reservation, and were on their way out of the hostel. A pair of common rooms were just beyond the warden's office, the self-catering kitchen was in the basement, and all the dormitories were upstairs.

"You did book a bed from Broadmeadows, I hope?" Roger asked.

"Yes, after I overheard you asking the warden there to do it. Good thing we did, eh?"

"Did you stop at the superstore, or are you planning to get take-out food?"

"Self-catering," Nancy said. "I'm not new at this, like you two are."

Roger and Eric were assigned to Room 3 up one level, overlooking the front of the building, while Nancy was assigned to a women's dormitory on the same floor. The rooms were secured by magnetic-strip cards rather than metal keys, unlike the previous hostels. They all deposited their gear on their bunks, and locked their bicycles in a storage room beneath the front sidewalk.

The self-catering kitchen in the basement was hot, humid and crowded. A large Swedish family was making tacos for their evening meal. English,

Scottish, German, Chinese and Dutch guests were also using the kitchen. Eric boiled the potatoes this time and made the tea, while Roger filled whole-grain baguettes with green pepper and mushroom that he sliced. He shredded a block of Glocester cheese onto the sandwiches, and melted the cheese under a broiler. Nancy joined them with salad ingredients and a potato.

Nancy excused herself after supper to wash some laundry, while Eric and Roger contemplated the showers. They promptly went upstairs to the men's shower room to bathe.

"This is the best shower I've had since we arrived in this nation. Feels good on my weary bones." Roger's back, neck, shoulders, and thighs were tired and sore from riding, as was every other part of his body, even though he felt quite fit. He still ached in places from the punishment he received in Yorkshire. "It would feel even better if Nancy came in and scrubbed my back. I'd scrub hers, too, if she wanted."

"She'd say that her back is more sore and more tired than yours, because she rode farther and faster than you did."

"You might yet get your chance to race her through Scotland, Chief." Roger just stood under the hot water, as if to absorb it like a sponge.

"I've been thinking about an ex-girlfriend lately, although I'm not sure *girlfriend* is the right word. We only dated briefly, just a couple of months is all, but it had its moments."

"Do you miss her?"

"Yes and no." Eric lathered his hair with shampoo. "She wasn't really my type, and I wasn't exactly hers, either. She's a journalism major, but she's planning on a career in broadcasting. Wants to be a news anchorwoman on television. Likes to talk, especially about herself. A little like Nancy, in a way. She reminded me one time too many that I don't say very much. I told her that she talked enough for both us, and then some. That was the beginning of the end of our relationship, I think. It wasn't meant to be."

"No sense brooding over it, then." Roger went to work with a bar of soap. "She probably has a new boyfriend by now, anyway. All you have is your bicycle, your camping equipment and your self-respect to keep you warm at night."

"How bloody decent of you to remind me of that, Squire. I shouldn't let Nancy get to me the way she has, but she reminds me of that, too."

"You'll thank me some day for preventing you from taking yourself too seriously, Chief. You're a grown man now, and I don't feel sorry for you."

"I'm not so sure about having my self-respect or being a grown man," Eric said, "but I probably do take people like Nancy much too seriously."

Eric had also been thinking about Sylvia Trujillo, the girl he had taken to the prom when they were seniors in high school. The prom was only their second or third real date, but they went steady all through the summer after graduation. They had attended a graduation party together after the ceremony. The following evening, she invited him to go with her to take care of her older cousin's pets while the cousin was out of town for the weekend. They made love, the first time for either of them, on the screen-enclosed patio after dark. They enjoyed a number of similar intimate moments together throughout the summer. College in the autumn sent them in different directions, permanently. She went to one of the in-state colleges and, the last he had heard, was living with someone. It was the first and last time, to date, he had ever really been in love. He attended the University of Washington on a scholarship, and now he was beginning to wonder if the almighty college degree was all it was cracked up to be—it had already cost him dearly.

"I miss Marianne right now," Roger said. "I'll be glad to get back to her. I think I've had a case of the proverbial cold feet that some people get just before their wedding."

"I envy you," Eric started to say.

"A lot of guys do," Roger interrupted, "but I'm not really *that* well endowed. It's just an urban legend."

"I was referring to your engagement to Marianne, smart-ass!" Eric rinsed the shampoo out of his hair. "I envy you for having her, for being engaged to her. You could do worse, much worse."

"It is a good position to be in," Roger agreed, "especially when you consider that none of my friends from high school or college is married or even engaged yet."

Eric and Roger had dried themselves and dressed, and were on their way out of the shower room just as Nancy and two other women were on their way into the women's shower room along the same corridor. The women were engaged in conversation, but Nancy and Roger subtly acknowledged each other. Eric, watching the women behind him, nearly walked into a wall instead of the door Roger had opened.

"Earth to Eric! Come in, Eric!"

"Too much eye candy there. Bad for my health."

Hungry again after their showers, they took a walk with Nancy to a small grocery store across from the Haymarket Station for a Fruit & Nut bar. The evening air was quite cool, and the thought occurred to them that back home, people were wearing as little clothing as their modesty would allow, enjoying or perhaps cursing the July heat. The brisk walk made them briefly forget their sorrows.

In the evening, they repaired to the common room on the main floor. They exchanged small talk with the other hostelers in the room, most of who were watching the television. They used the computers to read and send e-mail. They discussed their plans for the following day before writing in their journals.

Roger and Eric decided to spend another day in Edinburgh, instead of riding northward to another town. They had been told of several tourist attractions in the city, and the city centre and surrounding hills looked like they might be worthy of an investigation. They booked another night at the Eglinton hostel, as did Nancy. The warden handed them free copies of a Welcome to Edinburgh guide booklet with a color-coded map of the city.

The sentences Eric wrote in his journal looked like a page of *non-sequiturs*. He transcribed his thoughts and recollections as they came to him, in no particular order. His loosely linked passages combined sincerity with nonsense, to wit:

> "Very few people here wear kilts. I suspect that kilts are reserved for ceremonial events, and not usually worn informally. I tried to look under one Scotsman's kilt to see what he was wearing underneath it. I was shocked when the angry bloke took a swing at me. I tried to be nice about the whole affair, but he would not tell me, so I never did find out. My epilepsy has bothered me some, especially during and shortly after our incident in Harrogate. I feel remarkably good not having the pressures of college with me here, but that altercation did me no good whatsoever. I have trouble remembering the day and date. Mimi will be surprised that we have not really painted any towns red thus far. She thinks all beautiful women are attracted to me. In my dreams! I have never dated a foreign woman, so I should have no reason to assume foreign women think the way American women do. Roger and I will be touring the city tomorrow. We might find something interesting. I have mixed emotions about our journey so far, but for the most part, I like it. I am especially enjoying our devil-may-care style of travel, in which we have no itinerary, schedules or other restrictions. Met a Scottish girl named Nancy yesterday. Still trying to decide whether I like her at all, and whether she likes me. She and Roger get along fabulously. She and I mix like oil and water."

"What do you want to do tomorrow?" Roger interrupted.

127

"I need to find a bicycle store, so I can buy a new brake lever and a few other things," Eric said. "New Town and Old Town should be good places to look for George's bagpipe."

"Let's check out Edinburgh Castle, like good little tourists." Roger closed his log and left it in his lap. "I think I'd like to climb that ridge near Holyrood Park, too. I bet the view up there is great."

"Sounds good enough for me and the girls I go with, Squire." Eric was paying more attention to his journal than to Roger.

"The view up there is quite panoramic. I assume you're talking about the Salisbury Crags." An Englishman sitting near Roger overheard their conversation. "It's well worth your trouble."

"Have you been up there?" Roger asked the man.

"Yes, I was there earlier today," the man said. "I've done quite a lot of hiking in Scotland recently. Are you both from America?"

"We're both from Colorado, in the southwestern United States, but Eric's been attending a university in Washington state, in the Northwest. Can you tell by my drawl?"

"People from your part of the world do tend to say things that no self-respecting Briton or Australian would say, like *y'all, you betcha* or *howdy*," the man said. "Some of your countrymen take much longer to articulate a sentence than we do, but I like your style of speech. No reason why you should use ours."

"You should hear us conjugate verbs like *mosey* and *hornswoggle*," Eric said.

"We manage to get our messages across to each other, surprisingly," Roger said. "I doubt we'll get to do much hiking here, but we're still thinking about the Highlands. What do you recommend there for cyclists?"

"Lovely country," the Englishman said. "Not very many people, but there are some highways north of here that you will probably find very challenging. Quite different from the rot in London most of your countrymen come to see. The Grampian Mountains are not as big as what you have in the western United States, but the roads are often steep and narrow. Loch Ness is quite scenic, too. I'd recommend the Cairngorms if you were on foot. As you're on bicycles, try to take in Loch Ness if you have the time."

22.

Eric and Roger made breakfast from the groceries they had purchased the previous day. They packed what they needed for the day into their handlebar bags, and registered for another night in the hostel. Nancy met them just as they were about to leave the hostel, and asked them where they were going. Roger invited her to guide them around the city. She grabbed a few items from her room upstairs, and joined them. She did not know Edinburgh well, but she had some local acquaintances and had been in the city many times. The major landmarks were all familiar to her. They withdrew their bicycles from the storage room and cast themselves adrift in the streets of Edinburgh.

A bicycle dealer that had been suggested by Nancy was the first stop of the day. Equipped with the map, they had little trouble navigating the larger-than-usual city. The store had a good stock of parts, including Eric's brake lever. They considered buying some extra parts, but the owner would not accept a traveler's cheque, so they bought only the brake lever, a spare tube and a few other necessities.

Riding comfortably beneath the warm morning sunshine, they rode up the Royal Mile to the Edinburgh Castle, a hilltop fortress begun as early as 900 A.D. They locked their bicycles near the foot of the stone bridge leading from the esplanade to the front entrance of the castle. They paid their admission, and crossed the bridge over the gap into the castle. The castle grounds were littered with camera-bearing tourists from around the world, but the panoramic view from the upper walls was superb.

Roger took several photographs from the upper walls where fourteenth-century cannons lay waiting for would-be invaders. He could see much of the city, the Firth of Forth, the North Sea and the industrial districts from this vantage point. The six-hundred-year-old cannons were well preserved, and durable enough that children were allowed to climb on them. Roger thought about how interested he would be to see the ironworks where the barrels and other parts were cast and forged. He wondered how long workers lasted in foundries of that time, before the advent of motorized cranes, hoists, conveyors, forklifts, protective clothing, and induction furnaces. The cannons, like Hadrian's Wall, represented yet another stage in the history of what is now known as defense contracting. The more he thought about the cannon factories, the more he appreciated being a twenty-first-century engineer instead of a fourteenth-century armorer.

"Check that out." Roger pointed toward an exhibit of long, two-hand swords. "The swords are as tall as the knights."

"I wonder how any swashbuckler could wield something like that," Eric said. "You couldn't behead heretics very easily with such a cumbersome sword."

"True, but you have to admire the handiwork of the blacksmiths who forged those things," Roger said.

Nancy revealed her patriotic feelings. "The blacksmiths were Scottish. What else would you expect?"

129

A number of people were gathered around a block of sandstone in one room of the castle. The stone had been beneath the Queen's throne until 1996, and had great symbolic meaning to the royal family and the Scots. The Stone of Destiny looked to the two Americans like something they would use to build a campfire ring or a garden border. Nancy admired the Stone, also known as the Stone of Scone, with great reverence.

"What's so great about the Stone of Scone?" Eric pronounced Scone as if it rhymed with cone.

Nancy corrected his mispronunciation, such that Scone rhymed with spoon. "It's the Stone of 'Skoon!'"

"All right, so what's the big deal with the Stone of 'Skoon?'" Eric exaggerated the last word.

"Think of it like your Liberty Bell, only much, much older and more sacred."

"That certainly explains everything!" He did not ask any more questions about the Stone.

Having had enough of the castle, they found an exit, and walked past a kilt-clad, expressionless sentry as they left. The sentry was the first person the Americans had seen wearing a kilt, knee-high tartan sox, tam-o'-shanter and sporran. Impressive looking in his traditional Scottish dress uniform, the sentry's purpose seemed to be more a photographic prop for the tourists than to actually guard the premises.

About two blocks down the Royal Mile from the castle, they stopped at St. Giles Cathedral, the original Presbyterian church. To the British, it was the Church of Scotland. The medieval stone building suffered the same black stains from coal smoke as many of the other older buildings in Edinburgh. A church elder smoking his pipe on the front steps pointed to a place where they could lock their bicycles, and welcomed them inside. The dark stone interior seemed like a cave inside, but for the large stained-glass mural windows. Nancy took a picture of Eric and Roger flanking a life-size statue of John Knox, the 16th-century Protestant Reformer who founded the church. They stopped for a quick peak inside Knox's Tudor-style house, another three blocks down the Royal Mile.

The three cyclists rode the rest of the way down the Royal Mile, Nancy leading the way. The Palace of Holyroodhouse, as they soon discovered, was temporarily closed to tourists. The royal family was due to arrive in a matter of days for a few weeks of whatever royal families do in Scotland. There was nothing outside and around the palace that caught their fancy, so they decided to try some window shopping along Princes Street.

Some of the downtown streets of Edinburgh had brick surfaces, akin to cobblestone, and as such were hardly suitable for bicycles. With their bicycles vibrating wildly on the brick streets, the two men had to stand on their pedals for the sake of masculine comfort and protection. Nancy hardly noticed the bricks. Eric observed that she easily rode as fast as he and Roger did, and she handled her bicycle just as well in the busy streets. He was duly impressed with her cycling abilities, but he was not about to tell her that.

The Edinburgh city centre looked somewhat like a scaled-down version of downtown London. The traffic was not as bad as London, but two cars collided in an intersection just a few seconds after Roger, Nancy and Eric rode through it. No one was injured, and the damage was superficial to both cars, but the sound of the impact was particularly unnerving to Eric. He immediately thought of his own bicycle crash the previous summer. He took a few deep breaths and tried to purge his mind of the thought.

A boutique that caught their fancy was a tartan specialties store. They were greeted by the proprietor dressed in a clan uniform similar to the one worn by the sentry at the castle. The store sold plaid flannel fabric in a variety of tartan patterns, including Fraser, Campbell, MacDonald, Sutherland and others. A long wall held racks of kilts, Argyle socks, ties, cashmere sweaters and other garments in those same patterns as well as neutral colors. Other racks displayed blankets, teacups, books and similar bric-a-brac. The bagpipes were in a display case in the center. The least expensive bagpipe in the store cost several hundred pounds, but all appeared to be top-quality instruments. Nancy proudly showed them her own clan's colors.

"You should get a jersey in your tartan," Eric suggested. "Do they have any cycling gear here?"

"A plaid jersey? Not likely!"

"What do you think George would like in the way of a memento of the tour he opted against?" Roger said.

"You don't think he'd want a necktie with the family tartan on it, do you?" Eric examined a tie rack. Nancy showed them the Fraser tie.

"He can get a tie at home. You know that," Roger said. "We can't afford a bagpipe. If we could, I'd want it for myself, so I could punish my roommates with it when they crank up their rap and hip-hop."

"A bagpipe could be an interesting thing to own," Eric said. "It would certainly make a unique conversation piece. You could serenade the sorority girls."

"What about plaid boxer shorts?"

"That must be what Scotsmen wear under their kilt!"

"A clan book? A mug decorated with Scottish icons?"

"How about a pair of those crazy lace-up shoes?"

"He'd hate us, but a West Highlands terrier sure would be cute."

"I don't know, but no hurry. We'll know it when we see it."

They looked at everything in the store, but could not agree on what Fraser plaid to buy for their friend George. The Americans bought a few mementos for themselves, but they were just a little annoyed for not being able to reach a consensus on what to buy.

Eric snapped his fingers, as if suddenly remembering something. "I meant to ask the man in the kilt something."

"What was that?" Nancy asked.

"I was wondering if he had any McFernandez or MacSchmidt plaids," Eric said. "I suppose those clans are somewhat obscure."

"About as likely as a MacLane clan in Mexico." Nancy spoke directly to Eric, to his surprise. "Now that we're here, I've never been inside the Scott Monument. Do you fancy it?"

"Inside?"

"Yes, it has steps inside. I'd like to see the city from the tower."

"Lead the way!"

Nancy guided her two American friends toward the dark-stained tower on the other side of Princes Street. It was a monument to lawyer and historical novelist Sir Walter Scott, an Edinburgh native. They walked up the 287 helical steps, stopping at each level for a look. The stairs got narrower from bottom to top, and the men had to turn sideways to get their shoulders through the uppermost threshold. At the top, they squeezed their way around a small viewing area for some photos and a panoramic view of the whole city. The shale tower opened in 1844, twelve years after Scott's death.

They mounted their bicycles again and rode back toward the royal palace and Holyrood Park. They continued until they reached a grassy ridge on the edge of the city, where they locked their bicycles together at the base of the Salisbury Crags and hiked upward. A pair of young lovers sat in the distance on the hillside, kissing each other with great passion and whispering sweet nothings.

Roger looked at the lovers, then at Nancy. "Some of your compatriots know how to live." He gave her a look that she found irresistible. Eric, a few steps away, surveyed the city below and paid no attention to his two companions.

"I thought you were getting married next year. That's what you told me, was it?" Nancy returned the seductive look, and moved her face closer to Roger's. Her bright blue eyes were brimming with passion, in a way that Roger had not seen previously. Their lips met for only a second, then separated. Roger looked very satisfied, while Nancy looked a little embarrassed.

"I am, but that was for your benefit only. I'm not allowed to get any pleasure out of it." Roger paused while he licked his lips. He drew the conclusion that Nancy was inexperienced at this sort of thing—truly the jock she said she was. "Well, not too much pleasure, at any rate."

Eric turned his attention back to Nancy and Roger. "He's full of horse manure, Nancy. Don't believe a word of what he tells you." He was surprised to hear himself address Nancy like that.

The seductive look returned to replace her momentary embarrassment. She flashed the look at Eric, but he failed to notice. He found nothing romantic about her.

"I knew it was a mistake coming with you! You're corrupting me, you are! My granddad thinks Americans are the most corrupt people on Earth, even worse than the English, the French and the Irish." Nancy's satisfied smile belied her words. She followed Eric up the hill, and Roger was right behind her.

"Your granddad sounds like the prototype of a certain cartoon character we've been discussing." Eric continued to lead them up the ridge.

"It feels good to be hiking, for some reason." Roger was still very pleased with himself. "Could it be that I miss the Rocky Mountains?"

"Could be," Eric said. "I haven't climbed anything significant for a year. I imagine some areas in the Highlands would make worthwhile climbing and camping."

"Maybe next time we're here, we'll come prepared to climb Ben Nevis, Scafell Pike, Mont Blanc or something," Roger said. "That would be just as good as cycling." They continued hiking to the top of the ridge.

"You're better athletes than I thought you were the first time I saw you." Nancy sat down in the wild grass along the ridgeline. "Come along with me to Aberdeen, Roger. You can come, too, Eric, if you want."

Roger sat down on one side of her, Eric on the other. "It sounds tempting. We'll consider it. Don't you have to get back to work at some point?"

Nancy tossed her head back in a gesture of nonchalance. She adjusted the elastic band on her ponytail. "I'll get back to work when I run out of money. I have friends and relatives all over Scotland. Sometimes I work for them, live with them for a while. I've waited tables, worked in factories, taught skiing. My parents are well known in Aberdeen. Through them, I can always get someone to put me up or find me a job. I've never stayed in one place very long, since I finished school. You can't get very far in sports if you tie yourself down with a career and a family."

"No, I suppose not, but there are advantages to careers and families. Our friends Peter and Inga in London explained that to us. Depends what you consider most important in life, I guess." Roger was paying more attention to the panoramic view than to what Nancy was saying. Eric noticed how easily he tuned her out without really showing it. "What do you think of our journey so far, Chief?"

"Overall, it's been good, except for a few problems." Eric decided to try being extra nice to Nancy, no matter what she said. It was her country, not his. "What I really like about Europe is that my ethnic membership here has only one name, American. In the U.S., people with Spanish names get called all kinds of epithets, some polite…"

"Hispanic, Latino, Chicano, Mexican," Roger explained.

"…and some downright rude…"

"I won't name 'em," Roger added. "Not polite conversation in our country."

"Nobody in England or Scotland gives a rat's ass what ethnic group I belong to. I like that. I'm just another American." Eric leaned back on his elbows and admired the view.

"We have ethnic groups here, too, but Spanish isn't really one of them."

"What's your impression, Squire, aside from the obvious?"

"I've learned a few lessons, the kinds of things you won't find in any college textbooks. We aren't as smart as we thought we were." Roger made eye contact with Nancy again, and his smile had a strangely domesticating effect on her.

"Do either of you play football at home?"

"We played soccer, the game you call football, up through high school, but not much any more. A little American football. No rugby." Roger was admiring Nancy's muscles. She did not have the physique of a body builder, but maybe that of a figure skater or gymnast.

"I miss it, although our caliber of play is probably way below what you'd see in Europe or South America. You?" Eric suspected he would be sorry for asking.

"My school won the Scottish girls' title a few years ago, my last year there. We defeated an all-girls private school here in Edinburgh for the championship. That was the last time I was in Edinburgh overnight. I scored the game-winning goal, and had two assists, I did." Nancy was obviously proud of her accomplishment.

"So you're quite the footballer, I see." Footballer, as opposed to football player, was a funny word to Roger. He had heard Vickie use the term in casual conversation.

"I was the leading scorer in all of Scotland that year. We could've beaten most of the boys' teams, too, had we been allowed to play them." Mere pride was far too modest a word to describe Nancy's recollection of her football heroics. "My best friend was the goalkeeper. Now she coaches at a school in a seaside hamlet north of Aberdeen. I might stop there for a short visit this trip. She'd love to meet you."

134

Roger looked at Eric with a sly smile, and raised his eyebrows twice in rapid succession. "Like I said, we're considering it."

Eric just rolled his eyeballs in response. He would ride with Nancy to Aberdeen, but he was not going to let her assume he was that easy to persuade.

Nancy, Eric and Roger stayed on the crags, walking, talking and observing, for an hour. When the time came to leave, they hiked down the hill, mounted their bicycles, and rode at a leisurely pace back toward the hostel. They stopped at a compact grocery store on Hanover Street to buy groceries for their supper.

"May I see your identification?" a cashier at the market requested of Eric, when he presented a traveler's cheque.

"I'm Prince William, but don't tell anyone I was here." Eric presented his passport.

The woman looked at the passport photograph, then at Eric. "You'd look like the person in the photograph if you'd comb your hair," she said, straight face and all. She gave him change and thanked him for his patronage.

"We've been in the wind today," Eric apologized. "Haven't seen a mirror since early morning." He detected just a hint of a smile from her as they left.

"Reaffirms my faith in Scottish retailers," Eric said outside the store, "after that surly bloke at the bicycle shop this morning."

"We're not all like him. Only the shopkeepers are. The rest of us are friendly."

Eric and Roger prepared a vegetable soufflé in the hostel kitchen. Nancy set the table and made tea. They used up some stale bread slices and created a dish that was surprisingly tasty. Their table was next to a tea towel hanging on the dining room wall printed with recipés for cock-a-leekie soup, haggis and other Scottish specialties.

Nancy hinted that she liked it. "What do you call this?"

"Poor man's haggis," Roger answered. "We made a stomach out of bangers, as we couldn't find any sheep's entrails in the fridge."

"And we filled it with leftover porridge and baked beans," Eric added. "Just like the way Grandma used to make it."

"I added a few Bueno tablets, or whatever they're called, so you don't get you-know-what."

"You told me the Bueno gave it flavor, you liar!"

"It can serve more than one purpose!"

"Not bad, coming from two Americans."

"It's even better than that lutefisk we concocted last year. We marinated fish-shaped Gardenburgers, and we washed them down with Yoo-Hoo mimosas."

"That sounds bizarre!"

"It was either Gardenburgers or Tofurkey! Which would you have chosen?"

Nancy held her plate in front of her with both hands, in her best Oliver Twist impression. "May I have more?"

Roger helped Eric install the brake lever, after they finished eating and washing their dishes. In the common room, Roger, Nancy and some other hostel guests watched television, while Eric looked at an Edinburgh newspaper. The television show was uninterrupted by advertising or network promotional trailers, much to the satisfaction of the few Americans in the audience.

The television show was some sort of variety show, but it was not the same as American variety. This was no *Tonight Show*. The actors had no shortages of the word "piss." The tone of the show brought to Eric's mind the daily tabloids he had seen in London, where a bare-breasted female was posing on Page 3. There was no nudity in the show, but the *double entendres* made it nearly as risqué as the tabloids.

In one sketch, a woman was interviewing a job applicant:

"We're looking for someone who can drill holes," the woman said.

"Sounds like a boring job," the applicant answered. Even British television added a laugh track, in case the audience failed to get the joke.

"Do you ever have a negative attitude?"

"No, never."

"Do you have a large vocabulary?"

"What do you mean by vocabulary?"

"Do you have a long attention span?" she asked.

He did not answer immediately. "Beg your pardon," he finally said. "Did you say something?"

"Can you make decisions quickly?"

"Yes...no...I think so, but I'm not sure. Maybe." The sketch ended with more canned laughter followed by applause. The host resumed center stage and introduced the next act.

"Anything interesting in the news today?" Roger asked Eric during a quiet moment in the show.

"Just the baseball scores in the Utah state tournament." Eric set the paper aside.

"What about Utah baseball?"

"The Ogden Nashes beat the Roy Rogers, six to four, in ten innings," Eric said, "and the Price Index defeated the Provo Loany, seven to three, in semifinal action."

"My money is on the Nashes in the finals." Roger turned his attention back to the television.

Later, after a movie, Roger invited Eric and Nancy to join him at a neighborhood pub. Nancy accepted, but Eric declined. He felt dulled by all that he had eaten for supper, and he wanted some time to himself. The other two left, while Eric retrieved his journal and threw a load of his and Roger's laundry into the washer in the basement.

As he wrote, Eric felt like he was in better spirits than he had been a day ago. The day was eventful, and he had plenty of subjects to cover in his journal, not the least of which was Nancy. He wished he had his acoustic guitar with him. He had a melody in mind, and he was eager to hear it from his guitar.

In a pub near the Haymarket Station, Roger studied a paper placemat that listed all the monarchs of England since William the Conqueror, while he and Nancy waited for their beverages.

"No point letting your trousers slip half way," Nancy said.

"Come again?" The remark took Roger by surprise.

"That's how I remember the royal houses."

"I'm missing something here. What on earth are you talking about?"

"Norman, Plantagenet, Lancaster, York, Tudor, Stuart, Hanover and Windsor, in that order. The first letter of each house is in the phrase, no point letting your trousers slip half-way."

"Very clever! For a moment there, I thought you were making a pass at me."

"In your wildest dreams!"

"You're no fun! You could at least humor me. I'll go out on a limb and assume the House of Stuart is your favorite."

"You catch on quickly, for an American."

The waitress brought a shot of scotch and a mug of ale.

Roger held his shot of single-malt scotch at eye-level over the center of the table where he and Nancy were seated. "Cheers," was the only toast that came to mind.

"*Slainte mhath*." Nancy pronounced it *slan-ja-va*. She tapped her mug of ale against his glass.

"Meaning?"

"My dad says it's Gaelic for, 'to your good health,' or something along those lines."

"You're not drinking scotch. What happened to your patriotic spirit?"

"I don't care much for scotch, or any kind of whisky. But my ale was brewed in Glasgow."

"Bock beer rots out your guts but vodka goes well."

"Sorry?"

"It's one way to decode the color bands on an electrical resistor. There are other versions of that mnemonic, including one I made up myself. Let's see, Bradford boys rudely offend Yorkshire girls, begetting vicious, greedy women. Black is zero, brown is one, red, orange, yellow and so forth. I'd have to think a minute to remember the rest. I won't remember the royal houses tomorrow, either."

"I still don't know what you mean, but don't explain it. Just drink your scotch. Do you like it?"

"Actually, I'm not all that crazy about whisky, either, but I have to drink scotch at least once while I'm in Scotland."

"Don't overdo it, then. I'll not be wanting to roll you back to the hostel."

"Now, when someone asks about my ethnicity, I can say I'm mostly German, but I have a little scotch in me."

Nancy smirked at the quip. "English comedians have been using that line since God was a boy!"

"I never claimed to be original."

She took another sip of her ale, set her glass down and wiped her lips with a napkin. "Tell me something about Eric..."

23.

Roger awoke to his wristwatch alarm at 6:45, and he awakened Eric immediately thereafter. They ate the usual continental breakfast served by the hostel staff, while most of the other hostelers were in the process of waking and dressing, including Nancy. They packed their panniers and loaded them onto their racks. This was the earliest start they had gotten thus far, and they were proud of themselves for it. They booked beds at the hostel in Braemar. Nancy hurriedly packed her gear and joined them in front of the hostel.

"I feel great today!" Roger's smile reinforced his words. "Are you kids ready for some serious cycling?"

"Damn right I am!" Eric sounded genuinely enthusiastic. "Let's find the Highlands today, maybe one of the places that Englishman mentioned the other night. Nancy?"

"I'm game!" Once again, Nancy looked tantalizing in her Lycra racing attire. Her jersey was light blue with a large Saltire, the Scottish flag, on the front. The flag had the white diagonal cross of Saint Andrew on a medium blue rectangular background. "Let's see what you lads can do!"

The warm, sunny day, with negligible breezes, was perfect for cycling, and they intended to make the most of it. From the hostel, they crossed a creek called the Water of Leith and passed through several suburbs on their way out of Edinburgh. They rode quite a ways westward along Queensferry Road to the Firth of Forth coast, through lush forested areas and urban sprawl. Amid dense traffic on a dual carriageway, they came to the largest bridge Roger had ever seen.

The Forth Road Bridge, about three kilometers from edge to edge, connected South Queensferry to North Queensferry across a narrow section of the firth near Inverkeithing. The suspension bridge was four car lanes and one bicycle-and-pedestrian lane wide. Motorists were assessed a toll for crossing, but cyclists and pedestrians could cross for free. Nancy, Eric and Roger were the only people using the bicycle lane. The two Americans were impressed by every aspect of the bridge.

They stopped at the center of the bridge and parked their bicycles against the steel railing separating the traffic lanes from the bicycle lane. They looked down at the murky green water far below them. As the two Americans had grown up in Colorado, far from any ocean coast, large bridges and waterways never failed to amaze them, especially Roger. Eric still admired large bridges, even after three years of living in Seattle. They both spat into the water before they took some photographs.

"Why do men always have to spit off a bridge? That's exactly what my brother would do if he were here." Nancy was hardly the epitome of femininity, but the practice still offended her sensibilities.

"Guys will be guys." Eric had not forgotten his manners, but he was not about to let a woman's presence prevent him from partaking in certain masculine rituals. "Try it. You might like it."

Nancy gave it a try. She reluctantly admitted spitting off a high bridge was not such a bad thing.

Finding the road to Perth was challenging for them. The motorway was off-limits, but the "bicycles permissible" route was obscured by a maze of highways that even Nancy could barely navigate. They began with the B981 to Cowdenbeath, after a policeman in a squad car gestured them toward the first exit ramp after the Forth Bridge. The sun shone brightly on central Scotland that fine Sunday morning in July. For the first time in days, the Americans were sweating and even tanning their now-bare backs in the summer heat. They stopped briefly, where Nancy stripped down to tight shorts and a crop top. Eric could not withhold a smile when Roger tossed him the bottle of sunscreen and suggested that he apply some to the exposed portions of Nancy's back. She applied sunscreen to their backs, too.

The B917, Old Perth Road, put them back on the motorway at one point. The B996 kept them going north through Kinross, but only about halfway to Perth. They backtracked, and took their chances on some unsigned rural roads that crossed over or under the motorway a time or two. The wind was nil, and once they found the A912 to Perth, they rode a fast pace all the way through the county and the Ochil Hills to Perth, Perthshire.

Eric felt a little uneasy as he assumed a position with his front wheel less than half a meter behind Roger's rear wheel, as tight of a paceline as Eric could tolerate. Five years earlier, he took down several cyclists in a peloton when his front wheel made contact with the rear wheel of the rider ahead of him. He did not want to make a fool of himself in front of Nancy again. He took his hands off the drop bars and wrapped his thumbs and index fingers around his brake lever housings, and shifted into a comfortable 52:16 gear ratio. Roger set the pace for quite a distance while Eric held on, all the while concentrating on the rear wheel he was following. Nancy remained behind Eric most of the way. An occasional drop of sweat would form on the tip of Eric's nose, then fall when it got too heavy and splash against the top tube of his frame. Except for a lapse every so often, he kept his breathing synchronized with his pedaling cadence, and his confidence increased.

Tired of pulling, Roger veered toward the center of the highway and motioned Eric to take the lead. Eric worked to take the lead and maintain the pace Roger had set. Roger, meanwhile, stood up in his pedals, stretched his quadriceps, and pulled the cuffs of his shorts down to a more comfortable level on his thighs. He moved in behind Nancy, then took each hand off his handlebar and shook it until some sensation returned to his fingers and wrists. He withdrew his water bottle from its cage, and squeezed a mouthful of water between his lips. He squirted some water on his face and beard, too. Although Eric had not pushed the pace anywhere since they left Romford, Roger was fully confident that Eric could hold his own on the A912 or any other highway. They traded places several times in regular intervals, one pulling with the other drafting, throughout the morning. Nancy maintained the pace, but did not take the lead when either of them offered it to her.

In Perth, a city of some 43,000 people on the Tay River near the Firth of Tay, they found a superstore beside the A912 at the south end of town. Their immediate need was lunch, but they also selected some groceries for their evening meal, not knowing what to expect in Braemar or when they would arrive.

In the bakery section of the store, Eric looked with curiosity at stacks of pancakes in plastic bags. "This is bizarre. Do people really buy pre-cooked pancakes?"

Nancy shot him a look of indignity. "Yes, really! And what's wrong with that?"

"We do have frozen pancakes in the US, I think, but most people make them fresh. It doesn't take much time or skill to make pancakes."

"You Americans think you know the best way to do everything!"

"Enough, already! You don't have to chew my ass off about it!"

"Chew your arse? Is that what they say in your country? So uncivilized!"

Eric was slowly learning not to think out loud in front of Nancy. He kept his mouth shut as he examined other products that were not usually available in American grocery stores.

Roger, looking at canned foods across the aisle, was reminded of his choice of desserts in Alston. "Tell me, what is spotted dick? I saw it on a menu in a small town in northern England."

"It's a steamed suet pudding with currants or raisins in it. My mum makes it sometimes, usually on holidays."

"Do you like it?"

"Not as much as pre-cooked hotcakes." Nancy gave Eric the eye as she said it. "Actually, it's pretty good. You should try it some time. It's better than it sounds."

They devoured the scones and fruit they bought outside the store for lunch. An English cyclist on his way into the store asked where they had been and where they were going. He rode a 1970s bicycle, and said he could carry ten days' worth of provisions. His front and rear racks were piled high with panniers and camping equipment. The Americans realized they were by no means the most eccentric riders on the road. Pleased with their rate of travel thus far, they perused their road map during lunch and considered their options.

The A85 led westward toward Fort William and Ben Nevis, near the southwest end of Loch Ness. The A9, a major thoroughfare, led directly to Inverness at the northeast end of Loch Ness, or to Fort William via the A86. The A93 traversed some of the higher Grampian Mountains and a number of small towns. Finally, the A94 led to Dundee and Aberdeen, Scotland's fourth and third largest cities, respectively. Wishing to avoid traffic and people, they chose to stick with the A93 as they had planned. Their goal for the day was the hostel in Braemar, beyond something called the Spittal of Glenshee. They were still a long way from Braemar.

"What is the Spittal of Glenshee? A town?" Roger asked Nancy.

"You'll see when we get there. I don't want to ruin the surprise for you."

"You're looking good, Chief." Roger took a bite out of a scone. "How do you feel?"

"Even better than I look." Eric drank some water. "You?"

141

"I'm still feeling good." Roger had not lost one bit of the enthusiasm he had in the early morning. "Let's continue the pace we've been doing this morning."

"I intend to. What about you, Nancy?"

"Aye. You haven't finished me off yet."

Nancy was showing signs of strain, much to Eric's satisfaction. He was tired too, but far from exhausted, and he fully intended to punish her for her earlier arrogance. He felt as though he was making headway toward that self-serving goal. He thought himself just a little fiendish for thinking that way, but he reminded himself that it was she who instigated this contest.

Nancy, Roger and Eric rode through the city centre and resumed a furious pace northward on the A93 over the rolling hills of Perthshire County. Again, they alternated places with one pulling while the other sucked wind in the slipstream, and their upper gears got plenty of use. Nancy took the lead a few times, but only for very brief intervals. Something in the air, perhaps the warm sunshine or even the fresh air itself, gave the Americans ardor that was a welcome change from the lethargy that had often plagued them during adverse conditions. Traffic was sparse, the highway in good condition, and the weather ideal. A mild tailwind helped. The day was intended by heavenly decree for cycling. They passed several other cyclists in each direction.

North of Perth, somewhere near Meikleour, they encountered an unusual attraction. As they rode along the narrow highway, they found themselves in a canyon of trees. A particularly high wall of foliage stood on the west side of the road. A sign midway along the wall declared it the Meikleour Beech Hedge Preservation, the tallest hedge in the world. They were not normally awed by hedges, as they had plenty of mundane hedges in their own neighborhoods, but the dimensions of this one made it just a little extraordinary. Not only that, but it was planted in 1745. The men photographed Nancy in front of the hedge from far enough away to demonstrate its size, and resumed their ride with their Scottish counterpart.

They drank some water at the hedge, and refilled their bottles from a two-liter bottle of water they bought in Perth. Refreshed, they continued riding. A border collie behind a fence in a yard beside the highway barked at them as they passed. A sign farther ahead pointed to a park and the Stone of Scone.

"I thought we saw the Stone of Scone in Edinburgh Castle," Eric commented. "What's up with this?"

"Maybe the Stone of Scone and the Stone of Destiny are two different rocks," Roger said.

"No, this is the Palace of Scone, I think. I've never been in it. The Stone of Scone was here at one time," Nancy said. "They probably have a replica of the Stone of Scone here now. You've already seen the real one. Do you want to stop and take a look?"

"I would, but we still have a long way to go. Some other time, maybe?"

Passing motorists were usually kind to them, but not always. Eric attempted to pass a slow-moving automobile over a bridge. The driver, inexplicably incensed, suddenly accelerated, passed Eric and cursed at him. Another motorist turned onto the highway from a side street only a few meters in front of Roger. He narrowly avoided a collision by promptly using his brakes and skidding. Roger shouted at the driver, who either ignored him or did not notice that anything had happened. Drivers' disregard for cyclists, they noted, was not limited to the United States.

They stopped at a store in the twin towns of Blairgowrie and Rattray for a breather and a Fruit & Nut bar. The upward slope of the highway increased toward the Grampian Mountains while the concentration of trees decreased. Heather and sheep were the only things remaining to hold the rocks in place. The pavement surface became coarser, probably to increase traction on the wintertime ice, although it also resisted bicycles more than smooth asphalt. Narrow streams cascaded down the hillsides into a creek that the highway followed for some twenty-five kilometers. They spotted and photographed a deer grazing among the sheep across the creek, two hundred meters away on the other side of the glen. Other than the highway, signs of civilization were few.

Roger moved himself right beside Nancy where she could hear him. "We call this road surface asphalt or Chip-Seal in America. Do you call it macadamising here?"

"I think we do. That's not a word I use in conversation, though. I would just call it highway. You university blokes use too many big words!"

"You're looking a little tired. Do you feel all right?"

"I *am* bloody tired!"

"So am I, but we have some hills to climb before we're done for the day."

"I thought I was the only one who's tired!" Eric shouted from the front. "Glad to hear the rest of you are feeling the burn."

They downshifted several times as they began their ascent of Glen Shee in the late afternoon. The sun was still high, but the air was cool enough that they wore their jerseys. They stopped near the Spittal of Glenshee, where a creek flowed beneath the highway, for a brief rest period. Nancy had fallen a few minutes behind, but Eric and Roger waited for her. A small sign warned them to "beware of adders," although they saw none. They rinsed the sweat off their faces in the cool water from the stream, and filled their water bottles once again from the bottled water they bought at the grocery store. The color of the heather and other wild grasses, they noticed, ranged from very light to very dark green. Much of the heather bloomed with dark purple flowers. The evergreen forest gradually disappeared with the elevation. The combination of colors against the horizon, along with the solitude of the region, gave it an air of mystery. The slight eeriness tempted them subconsciously to continue forward, in spite of their tense leg muscles and tired arms and backs.

Glen Shee, in no uncertain terms, was a son of a bitch, as Eric and Roger painfully discovered. From the bend where they could see the summit, it was about two kilometers up a 12% grade to the Devil's Elbow. They had ridden far, in the heat of the day with a full load of equipment attached to their bicycles, and were already taxed by the time they started really climbing. The pass was one of the steepest paved roads they had ever seen, or so they thought, and it was a long way to the top. Their gears were sized more for racing than touring, so they needed all their strength to climb the hill. The heavy loads of equipment on their bicycles, and the annoying flies buzzing around their heads added to their burdens. They moved at a walking pace in their lowest gear ratios, but they were moving. Nancy was far enough back that Roger and Eric could barely see her in the distance as they started up the pass. She was using the inner chain ring of her triple chain wheel, but even that was little help against Glen Shee.

At about two-thirds of the distance to the summit, Roger took a wild, frustrated swing at the flies with one hand. He lost his balance and fell over sideways. Eric, a few meters behind, stopped when he came to the place where Roger lay swearing and cursing at the persistent flies, the road and himself. Uninjured, Roger picked himself up and got back on his bike. They both struggled to click their second shoe into the pedal while staying upright. They used all the strength they had, until the slope lessened and they could see the ski area at the summit.

"My new bike is going to have a triple chain ring," Roger said. "I could have used a granny gear on this climb."

The summit of Glen Shee was marked by a pair of signs, one indicating the county line and the other entry into Cairngorms National Park. The Glenshee ski area stood idle not far from the highway. A few cars passed them in each direction while they snapped some photographs of the summit and the horrendous slope they had just climbed. They mounted their bicycles and began the long, fast descent down Glen Clunie.

The most difficult part of the day's ride was behind them, but they were not through all of the obstacles in their path. As they crossed the county line from Perthshire and Kinross to Aberdeenshire, they knew they still had fifteen kilometers between the summit and Braemar. They both dreaded the possibility they would have trouble finding the hostel in Braemar, as they did in York, Alston and Edinburgh. Locating the hostel was more important at the moment than waiting for Nancy to climb the pass, so they pressed on toward Braemar.

Thoroughly exhausted, Eric and Roger rode into Braemar just before 19:00, nearly eleven hours since Edinburgh, using every gear ratio they had along the way. The hostel, another Victorian hunting lodge, was right alongside the A93, just inside the city limits. They found it without really looking for it. They had no reason to think Nancy would fail to notice the SYHA sign, and they hoped she had not faltered somewhere along the way. The warden registered them, and sent them to a shed down behind the hostel for bicycle storage.

The two Americans selected bunks in one of the upstairs dormitories, and deposited their gear nearby. The building was unmistakably Victorian on the inside as well as outside, and reminded them of some of the more stately homes in the older neighborhoods of their hometown. They took the groceries they had bought in Perth downstairs to the kitchen, and began preparing their supper. Nancy had still not arrived.

"I hope Nancy didn't crash, or something bad happen," Eric said as he put two large russet potatoes in a sauce pan full of water on the gas stove.

Roger sliced two whole-wheat baguettes, and spread Nutella lavishly on each piece. "You're starting to sound like you care. I knew she'd get to you sooner or later."

"I look out for my cycling buddies, even the ones who get on my nerves like she does. In fact, to show what a good sport I am, I'm going to have a cup of tea waiting for her when she arrives."

"We really cleaned her clock today. I don't think she'll diss us again."

"That's one reason why I'll sleep well tonight."

The beleaguered Nancy crept into Braemar nearly an hour after Roger and Eric had arrived. She spotted the hostel and rode up the driveway. She looked thoroughly drained, her hands shaky and her knees barely able to support her while standing. Roger and Eric had already eaten their chocolate sandwiches while they waited for their potatoes to boil. They discussed world events with three Polish women about their age at the dining table. The women all spoke excellent English. Roger took Nancy's bicycle to the shed, and Eric carried her panniers up the stairs. He took her groceries to the kitchen and added her potato to the boiling water.

"Have a spot of tea," Eric said when Nancy entered the kitchen. He handed her a steaming mug, which brought a look of surprise and a weak smile to her face. "That was a Century Ride today, and we made it all the way."

"Thanks. You're more civilized than I thought." She sipped the tea, and it revitalized her a little. "I hope I have enough left in me for cooking."

Roger and Eric looked at each other, and Roger said, "Leave the cooking to us. Have a seat at the dining table and tell our Polish friends about your day."

"Leave the cooking to men? To American men? You're asking a lot!"

"You liked our cooking last night, no? You just relax. You've earned it."

Eric drained the potatoes, sliced them on plates, and covered them with butter, shredded Leicester cheese and black pepper. Roger used Nancy's bread to make her a Welsh rarebit, American style, to go with her potato. When they served her and sat down to eat, they noticed how easily she had engaged the Polish women and another Scottish woman in conversation. The Scottish woman had an extra Danish pastry she offered to Nancy.

Nancy took a shower after the two men. She came out of the bathroom wearing only a nightshirt, and passed Roger in the hallway. Bare except for the boxer shorts he slept in, he was on his way into the bathroom to brush his teeth. She smelled good from the soap as they passed, and her smooth skin had a clean shine to it. She managed half a smile as her face passed by his naked chest, but she could not make eye contact. Roger disappeared into the bathroom. Eric noticed Nancy slowly walking down the hall.

"Good ride today. Best one Roger and I've had since we've been in Europe." Eric, too, was bare except for shorts. He was starting to feel some sympathy for a vanquished opponent.

Nancy nodded in agreement. "You're as good as Roger said you are." She was too weak for any speech other than a whisper. "Good night, Eric." She looked at him with weary, withdrawn eyes as she passed, and lightly brushed his shoulder with her hand. She retired to her room, and he returned to his.

"I don't think I have it in me to ride tomorrow as far as we did today, Chief," Roger admitted, while he and Eric were about to get into their respective beds. "My body has taken too much abuse today. Where's the next youth hostel between here and Loch Ness?"

"It's in..." Eric flipped through the hostel guidebook. "...Tomintoul, not too far up the road from here, on the A939."

"Is it too close for a full day's ride?"

"It's fairly close, but there are some frisky-looking mountains between here and there. It probably won't be an easy ride. If we get to Tomintoul too early in the day, then we can try for, let's see, Grantown-on-Spey, or even Nairn."

146

"We'll see when we get there. In the meantime, I'm due for some serious shut-eye. I was going to try to call Marianne, but I'm too tired to talk."

"I thought of something we ought to buy first thing tomorrow, as soon as the stores in Braemar open. We might need it tomorrow."

"What's that?" Roger spoke from inside his bed. His eyes were already closed.

"A fly swatter," Eric teased.

"You have no name!" Roger was too tired to argue any further.

All their roommates appeared to be settled in their beds. Eric turned the light off and lay down in his bed. He and Roger were sound asleep mere moments later.

24.

The first light of morning awakened Eric, if only because of its contrast to the pitch-black night. The hall lights were left on all night, but the hostel grounds could not have been darker, due to the absence of any street lamps or porch lights. A restful night in the Cairngorms was what he needed, even though he awoke with an epileptic headache. He was out of bed by 6:45.

Roger was congested, but the steam from a mug of tea at breakfast helped him breathe. He was a little sore and sluggish getting up, but he was not about to admit it. He and Eric ate bananas and shredded wheat for breakfast. Nancy joined them a few minutes later for tea and digestive biscuits. The tea helped quell Eric's headache. They all booked beds at the hostel in Tomintoul. Wanting to call on an old friend in Ballater, Nancy left Braemar while the men were still packing and stripping their beds. She said she would meet them in Tomintoul.

The Americans toured Braemar for an hour, where they browsed in a tartan specialties store and purchased a few knickknacks to take home. They found little else of interest to them in Braemar, but they appreciated its mountain-town atmosphere. The town reminded them somewhat of Colorado's mountain towns where time was virtually static before and after ski season. They noted on their road map that Braemar lay on the 57th parallel, south of Juneau, Alaska, but north of Edmonton, Alberta. Situated along the upper Dee River, it was farther north than either had ever been. The Dee originated on nearby Ben Macdui, the second highest mountain in Scotland.

They stopped for some pictures of the Braemar Castle on their way out of town. The castle opened later, but they did not have time to wait. The scenery north of Braemar on the A93 was similar to the south side, hilly and forested. Traffic was again sparse, mostly tourists, and the sunny sky allowed them to ride comfortably in short-sleeve jerseys. Their pace was moderate, compared to the previous day's alacrity, but they were in no particular hurry.

At Balmoral Castle, they turned up the driveway to have a look. The castle itself was shrouded by dense evergreens, and barely visible from outside the fence. A sentry stopped them at the gate—some royal family members were in residence. Her majesty did not want to have a spot of tea or a shot of scotch with two American cyclists, he explained. He suggested a visitor center souvenir store just down the valley from the turn-off.

Roger and Eric stopped at the visitor center near Crathie. They looked at T-shirts bearing the Scottish flag, books about the mountains of Scotland and postcards before leaving. They came to the B976, what appeared to be a shortcut to Tomintoul, but they were not sure if the road was paved all the way. They stayed on the A93 to the Bridge of Gairn, where they turned north onto the A939 and followed the Glen of Gairn.

The ride from Braemar was nearly 30 kilometers downhill toward Ballater, but they began climbing the occasionally steep moors once they got on the A939 to Colnabaichin. They used gear ratios as low as 39:26 at times, and they silently cursed the pain they felt throughout their bodies, especially in their knees, as they climbed one hill after another.

Since the beginning of their tour, they had not been especially impressed with their speed, but they overtook many a cyclist along the way. The only cyclists who passed them did so near Richmond, and those two riders, both young men, were not carrying panniers or any other gear. They were surprised to find that European bicycle tourists were not as relatively fast as their racing counterparts.

"Hold it!" Roger's front tire sustained a blowout east of Brown Cow Hill, a peak along the ridge that divided the Dee and Don valleys. Eric was one bicycle length ahead.

Eric turned around and rode to where Roger had stopped. "Flat? Or should I ask, puncture?"

"Worse than that!" The wheel was not damaged, but the tube, which had not been patched previously, had an eight-centimeter long rip in it and could not be repaired.

"I hate it when that happens!"

"I wish I had my floor pump at times like this." Roger had a replacement tube in his seat bag, but he was disappointed that a sharp-edged piece of steel on the pavement destroyed a perfectly good tube. Even the green gelatinous tire liners he had installed could not prevent this puncture. He changed tubes while Eric assisted, and they resumed their ride within ten minutes of the incident.

Heat, flies, sheep and steep climbs plagued them early. Heat and exertion made them sweat profusely, and the flies had an affinity for perspiration. The numerous ascents slowed them enough that the flies could easily buzz around their heads. The timid sheep had trouble deciding which way to run when vehicles, such as Roger and Eric on their bicycles, approached. The persistent flies only added to Eric's headache discomfort and disorientation, but he did his best to tolerate a situation he was unable improve.

Roger passed some errant sheep. "They need a sign that says, 'No ewe turns.'"

"No, they need a sign that says, 'No bad puns,' or maybe just a 'Dip' sign. Plenty of that on the highway. Damn sheep."

"Damn rams," Roger said, mostly to himself. "Damn rams and lambs. A damn ram and lamb scam, that's what I call it."

"Say what?" Eric said over his shoulder.

"Pam and Sam Hamm's damn ram and lamb scam. I'm working on a headline for a newspaper article that hasn't been written."

The highway was narrow most of the way between Braemar and Tomintoul, but that feature did not seem to deter lorries and tour buses. The roads were only one lane wide with no center stripe in many places, and the passing buses full of gawking tourists made them appear even narrower. Bicyclists, conversely, were much less abundant than they had been between Edinburgh and Perth. They did not see any bicyclists beyond Balmoral Castle, not even Nancy.

Mountains along the A939 were very much like Glen Shee. Scotland's second, third and fourth highest mountains lay just west of the highway, less than thirty kilometers from Braemar. Roger and Eric crept up the moors, some having slopes as steep as twenty percent. The relief was not quite as great as Glen Shee anywhere, but it was close in some places. Lower gear ratios would have helped. They both knew that their hub cones were just tight enough and their brakes were centered around their rims, yet they felt like something was dragging, holding them back. They looked at their brakes from time to time for reassurance as they climbed.

A long, fast descent took them into Colnabaichin, where they turned west toward Cock Bridge. They followed the Don River up a deep, verdant valley about five kilometers. Once across the river at Cock Bridge, they began climbing up a high, steep moor. The weather was great, but the slope was relentless with few switchbacks to make the climb easier. The last big ridge brought them to the Lecht ski area at 610 meters above sea level. The ski slopes spanned the boundary between Aberdeenshire and Moray counties.

They stopped alongside the ski lodge for a respite. Roger sat on a low wall and checked the cleats of his shoes. One side was loose. He took out a hex key and tightened both cleats. He did not have any replacement screws in the event one should come loose and fall out. Eric checked his, too, just in case. They drank some water and took some pictures before they began the long descent into Tomintoul.

After thinking and even shouting obscenities at insects, sheep, buses and mountains for several hours, they arrived in Tomintoul. With three hundred or so citizens, Tomintoul was Scotland's highest town at 354 meters. They did not expect a rush on the hostel as had been the case in Edinburgh, so they stopped at a grocery store first instead of immediately going to the hostel. They leaned their bicycles against a wall along the A939, Main Street, in front of the grocery store. They noticed the fine road dirt that had accumulated on their brakes, forks, seat tubes and panniers. They hoped the hostel might have bike-washing facilities available, but they did not expect any.

"Tomintoul kinda sorta resembles the mountain towns in the western U.S.," Roger said. "Even more so than Braemar."

"It's exactly the same...only different." Eric took off his helmet and hooked the chin strap over his top tube. He took off his open-finger gloves and stowed them in the helmet. "I imagine Tomintoul as what Silverton, Colorado, would look like had it been built by Scottish pioneers."

"Let's hurry up with the mid-afternoon grocery shopping, or else our bicycles will be lost when they roll up the sidewalks here in the evening."

"No big hurry, Squire. Evening lasts until about midnight at this time of year here in the north."

They bought bananas, peanuts and oat cakes for lunch and the next day's breakfast. The store also offered whisky ice cream cones, which they could not resist. The ice cream was delicious. The oat cakes were bland, just ordinary crackers, but something the Americans had to try. They also bought noodles, mushrooms, a bell pepper and a jar of spaghetti sauce for their evening meal.

The hostel was a refurbished school about two blocks from the store. They rode the wrong way on Main Street in search of the hostel. The pleasant-looking town was only two or three blocks wide, and maybe ten blocks long. Main Street was lined with two-story stone houses, all lacking a front yard. They rode past the Town Square at the center of town before they turned around and found the hostel at the other end. The hostel was not at all crowded, and Nancy had not registered yet. As in Braemar, they had a choice of bunks.

"The day is still young. Do you want to tour a distillery?"

"Might as well. I think there's one north of town."

Roger and Eric left word with the warden where they were going, and asked him to pass it along to Nancy. Their bicycles felt incredibly light without the luggage, and they hurried off to find the scotch distillery. They rode down the Strath Avon on the B9136, and followed signs to a cluster of buildings. They were surrounded by the Glen Livet estate, home to several distilleries. An employee told them he was not conducting tours except by appointment. Just as they were about to leave, he had a change of heart and asked them to come inside. He hated to turn away potential customers, especially foreigners. He explained the process of roasting malted barley over a peat fire, fermenting the wort, distilling, aging, blending and bottling. It was similar to beer-brewing in many ways, except that the aging was in years instead of weeks, and the alcohol content of scotch was much higher. The visitor center had a series of framed posters that illustrated the production process, the company history and the characteristics that distinguish scotch whisky from all other kinds of whiskey. The tour guide proudly told them that whisky is derived from a Gaelic term, *uisge beatha*, meaning water of life. He added that Scots usually spell whisky without an *e*. They had a shot of the good stuff, thanked their host for accommodating them, and rode back to Tomintoul.

"That was interesting. I might want to consider working in a brewery, winery or distillery when I graduate. I can already see plenty of need for engineering expertise in a place like that," Roger said as they rode.

"It would probably be steady work, too. People don't stop buying liquor during a recession," Eric said. "Do you think we'll find Nancy at the hostel, or did she blow us off and return to Aberdeen?"

"I think she'll be there, even though she has plenty of reasons for deserting us. We punished her yesterday."

"I can think of several reasons why she deserved it. Still, she looked so pathetic when she finally made it to the hostel, I actually felt sorry for her. I kind of overdid the competitive thing. I'm trying to be nicer to her now."

"I'm tempted to buy a bottle of scotch when we get into town, but at twenty quid or more a bottle, I can wait until we get home. It's not cheap, even here at the source."

They returned to Tomintoul by 17:00 and went straight to the hostel, but Nancy still had not arrived. The late lunch discouraged them from an early supper, and they wanted to wait for Nancy anyway. They ventured into Tomintoul on foot. Clad in shorts and T-shirts, they walked along Tomnabat Lane toward the Town Square, but to no particular destination.

"It feels like summer here, finally," Eric said. He and Roger were clad in shorts and T-shirts. "I've been waiting nearly three weeks to wear shorts and a T-shirt outside. The locals probably don't know the pleasure of scantily-clad people mingling around a swimming pool or on a beach in the summertime."

151

Roger put his hands in his pockets. "I've almost forgotten that pleasure myself. It's been awhile. I did bring a bathing suit, though."

"So did I, but I doubt we'll find a swimming pool or a suitable beach around here." Eric continued walking, looking at everything in general, nothing in particular. "What did you tell Nancy about me the other night in Edinburgh? She made a comment last night that surprised me. 'You're as good as Roger said you are.'"

"I told her you were a nationally ranked road racer, before your accident. I got tired of her always having a better story to tell than I do. Whatever I've done, she did it first and she did it better than I did, or else she knows someone who did. I had to come up with something good." Roger had a satisfied smirk on his face. "I said it with a straight face, too, and that wasn't easy."

"For crying out loud! What do you think this is? Your birthday? You are such a heap of white trash! Why did you have to use me to fabricate a big lie?"

"It had more credibility that way. Besides, I also told her you were in a coma for a month after your crash. She seemed very awed by the whole story. She didn't attempt to out-brag that one. You lived up to it very well yesterday, without even knowing how big your reputation was."

"We're still racing, as far as she and I are concerned, all the way to Aberdeen." Eric wondered why he still managed to be surprised by Roger's audacity. He had never known anyone to outwit Roger.

"I thought you felt sorry for her. Which is it, fierce competition or pity?"

"A little of each. I'm ambivalent about her. What more can I say? Women do that to me sometimes! I guess I'm a sucker for a pretty face."

"That's one of my weaknesses, too." Roger checked his watch. "It shouldn't have taken her this long to ride from Braemar. I'm starting to think she abandoned us."

"Or maybe something happened to her. She tends to throw caution to the wind, even more than we do."

Roger changed the subject, now that Nancy had been humbled. He genuinely admired her cycling ability, as did Eric. They did not want to alienate her. "I like the atmosphere up north here. My occasional need for solitude is being fulfilled. I need to get away from the masses every once in a while."

"It's so much easier to think in a place like this," Eric agreed. "This would be a good place, I think, for an author or composer to set up a studio."

"I've long thought that about south-central Colorado," Roger said. "I get that same feeling of solitude here that I get when, say, I'm hiking in the Sangre de Cristo mountains. The two places look nothing like each other, and the locals are entirely different...I can't put my finger on any analogy."

"Many of the places where we've been have reminded me of places back home, even though there was no obvious similarity. How do you explain that?"

"What really puzzles me," Roger said, "is that I've dreamed we went home briefly and were coming back here. I've had that same weird dream twice now. I wonder if it means anything."

"I've had a similar dream, where we flew home to fetch something, then we were coming back. It made no sense at all."

They paid their respects at a fountain in the Town Square. A small statue of a woman stood in the center of the fountain. They assumed the figure represented the goddess of scotch, the Celtic equivalent of Bacchus, or something like that.

"Seen a pay phone anywhere?" Roger asked.

"Just one, but it looked so old that you'd probably have trouble making a connection to North America with it," Eric said. "Can you wait until Inverness?"

"I can wait." Roger's tone indicated his lack of enthusiasm on the subject.

"You don't really want to make that call, do you?"

"Not really. But I feel like I have to, now. I'm damned if I do, and damned if I don't. She hadn't responded to my e-mail, last time I checked. I've been having a good time lately, riding, competing with Nancy. Marianne and I have lots of things in common, but cycling and hiking are not among them. Are my priorities all screwed up?"

"Don't tell me you want to dump Marianne for Nancy!"

"No, and I don't mean Nancy specifically. What I do mean is, would I be happier with someone *like* Nancy, someone who likes to ride and hike as much as I do?"

"I'd say, concentrate on what you do have in common with Marianne, not on your differences."

"You're probably right, but I don't want to go through life wondering what might've been. I want to make the right decision the first time."

"I'm not the only one here who's ambivalent about certain women."

"Like you said, they do that to me sometimes."

They turned to begin their walk back to the hostel, when Nancy suddenly came to a stop before them. She looked dazzling as usual, and much more vivacious than she did when she arrived in Braemar.

"There you two are!"

"There you are! We thought you'd gotten lost or something." Eric was surprised by how glad he was to see her.

"Me, lost in Scotland? What have you been smoking? I registered at the hostel and dropped my things there. The warden said you took a walk into town. I thought I'd find you somewhere near here."

"We're getting hungry for supper. Hope you didn't eat already."

"No, and I'm famished! I haven't been to the grocer yet."

"We probably have enough for three, if you like spaghetti."

"Splendid! Did you get chocolate bars, too?"

"No, we must've forgotten."

"I'll get some, then. See you back at the hostel." Nancy gave them an inviting smile before she rode away toward the hostel.

When they arrived back at the hostel, the first thing Eric noticed was that some new guests had arrived while he and Roger were inspecting the town. A nice-looking woman with an English accent had registered and was carrying her gear into the women's dormitory. Roger did not notice her as he went into the men's dormitory for the supper ingredients.

Roger boiled the noodles and warmed the sauce while Eric chopped the vegetables. Nancy buttered slices of bread. She thought the Americans were peculiar for wanting their bread toasted for their evening meal. For her, toast was served only at breakfast. Garlic on the bread was out of the question in Tomintoul. She surprised them with three bottles of Scottish ale she had stored in the refrigerator, one for each of them.

"I know you Yanks like your beer cold," Nancy said. "They haven't been chilled long."

"It'll do just fine. Beer and spaghetti, only in Scotland," Eric said. He raised his bottle toward Nancy and added, "cheers," before he took a drink. "Mmmm! Nectar of the gods!"

"Cold enough," Roger agreed, and took a drink. "Ah! Mother's milk!"

"It's just ale! Nothing to get excited about, that."

"It's just ale," Eric quoted. "Only a woman would say something that ridiculous. I bet the men in your family wouldn't say it's just ale."

They sat with an Australian motorcyclist and a Scottish cyclist in the dining room. Both were a generation older than Nancy and the two Americans. The Australian, a colorful storyteller, led the conversation with tales of interesting people he had met in youth hostels in Europe, Australia and elsewhere. He was very articulate, and impressed them with the way he could speak of himself without sounding conceited or boastful. Meanwhile, the Scotsman, a quiet man, listened to the Australian but had little to say. As at Broadmeadows, Nancy had as healthy an appetite as the men.

After dinner, they washed their dishes and cleaned up the self-catering kitchen. They had finished off the entire package of noodles, the jar of sauce and the loaf of bread. They were all too full for tea and chocolate so soon after the meal. They used the time to make beds and take showers. Eric went into the kitchen to start boiling the water for tea, while Roger searched their luggage for tea bags. They assumed Nancy would provide the chocolate whenever she was done in her dormitory. The English woman entered the kitchen and said "hi" to Eric. Eric felt a little stiff as filled the kettle. It seemed like an eternity before Roger returned with the tea bags and sugar. Eric wanted to start a conversation with the woman, but he felt socially awkward. He was reminded of how he felt several years earlier, the first time he had asked a girl for a date. The woman looked at him, made eye contact briefly, and smiled at him in a friendly way.

"Did you put the water on to boil?" Roger was still not paying any attention to the woman.

"Yes, it's cooking." Eric looked at the kettle again to be sure he had turned on the flame under it.

Roger casually sat down at the dining table across from the woman, just as if he had known her for quite some time. "Good evening."

"Good evening," the woman said to him. She seemed to take an immediate interest in him, or at least his friendly manner.

"We're about to drink our evening tea," Roger said. "May I pour you a cup?"

"We'd be delighted," the woman said. Roger raised an eyebrow when he heard her say, "we." A man emerged from the men's room and sat down next to her.

"Join us for tea, dear?"

"If you're sure it won't be any trouble," the man said.

"No trouble at all," Roger said. "Bring two more cups out, will you, Chief?" The British attention to manners always impressed him.

Eric brought two more cups from the kitchen and poured the boiling water over the tea bags into a pot. He envied Roger for being able to make strangers into friends so quickly and easily. The presence of the man meant that Eric did not have to turn on the romantic charm, which seemed so difficult for him and so easy for Roger. It also meant that she was unavailable in case he did feel like turning on the charm.

"My name is Lisa," the woman said, "from London. And my husband, Trevor."

"Roger, the fourth earl of Pueblo. And my analyst, Doctor Fernandez."

"Eric, to my friends. Roger had a lobotomy on his birthday last year. That's why I'm here, to make sure he stays in therapy. He's wacko, you know. His inner child is a juvenile delinquent." Eric was actually better at conversation than he realized. He just needed someone to get him started, to break the ice.

155

Nancy entered the dining area and sat down. Eric pushed the tea kettle toward her. She swirled the tea bags a few times, added sugar and milk to her cup, and poured the tea.

"Our sidekick, Nancy, from Aberdeen. Nancy, meet Lisa and Trevor from London."

"I thought you were the sidekick," Nancy said. "I'm pleased to meet you both."

"How do you do?" Trevor said.

"You two aren't Scottish or English," Lisa said. "Americans?"

"Yes, from Colorado, in the southwestern part of the United States." Eric did his best to carry on the conversation while Roger sliced three Fruit & Nut chocolate bars into several sections. "I've been attending a university in Seattle, Washington, in the Northwest. You?"

"I'm actually Welsh myself, but I've been in London a several years now. Lisa was born and raised in St. John's Wood, London."

"Is that unusual in this country? I mean, English and Welsh people getting married?"

"We don't know any other English-Welsh couples, but it must be more common than we think it is. Jones is a Welsh name, and it's also one of the more common surnames in England. Meanwhile, Smith is an English name, but you see it all over Scotland. And there are plenty of Irish names in northern England, especially around Liverpool," Lisa said.

Eric looked at Nancy to see if she had any response to the mention of English blood among the Scottish people. She did not show any. "Interesting, maybe, but not really surprising. Neighboring populations tend to diffuse across the borders over a long period of time. To Americans, English and Welsh are pretty much the same."

"Similar, but not exactly alike. Are those your bicycles we saw as we came in?" Trevor asked.

Roger offered everyone some chocolate. "Two of them are. The two dirtiest ones, probably."

"Mine is cleaner than theirs," Nancy added. "We Scots have to keep up appearances."

"Are you hitchhiking or using public transportation, like trains?" Eric inquired."

"Some of everything," Trevor said, "but mostly trains. They're safe and reliable. Where have you been, and where are you going?"

Roger took the lead, without the slightest hesitation. "Eric and I spent a week in London, visiting some friends. We've been moving northward from there, slowly."

"We choose our next day's destination every evening," Eric added. "Someone recommended Loch Ness to us, so I expect that's where we're going tomorrow."

"We don't like to plan too far in advance," Roger said. "We'll all ride on to Aberdeen after Loch Ness."

"Have you three been traveling together since London?" Lisa mixed the sugar and milk into her tea very delicately, as if she were handling fine china. Roger and Eric both noticed that most of the Europeans they had met handled their tea very tenderly.

"No, we met in southern Scotland, not far from Hadrian's Wall," Eric said. He did not really want to rehash that story. He spoke first in hopes that Nancy would not embarrass him by describing his crash.

Nancy looked at Eric but did not refute what he said. "We were all going in the same direction, so we've been riding together. I've been learning the American way of cycling in Europe." She did not intend to make a fool of Eric as long as he did not brag about leaving her far behind on the ride over Glen Shee.

"We came by way of Loch Ness and Aviemore. We're on our way south now, but we've been in northern Scotland. Such lovely country around Loch Ness! Good walking in the Cairngorms." Lisa had a look of satisfaction as she sipped her tea that said she approved of the way Eric and Roger had prepared it. They both felt gratified.

"You must love this country, Nancy," Trevor said. "So many things to do, so much to see."

"I do," Nancy agreed. "I've never even been in London. Everything I need is here in Scotland."

"You have a nasty bruise under your eyebrow." Lisa studied Roger's face. "Did you crash somewhere?"

"Not exactly." Roger was once again reluctant to say much about his and Eric's fateful encounters in England, but he felt secure enough now to tell them an abridged version of what had happened.

"Dreadful!" Lisa was genuinely sorry to hear their story. "I do hope you're not disappointed with our country because of what happened to you. We're not all like those people who hurt you, thank goodness."

"I know you're not all like that," Roger said with a smile, "and we're not disappointed."

"The hoodlums notwithstanding," Eric said, "we've met a number of great people here. Nearly everyone has made us feel welcome."

"I work at Gatwick Airport," Trevor said. "I get upset anytime I hear of someone mistreating travelers, because we're both in the travel business and it's one of Great Britain's more important industries."

157

"I admire your courage for the way you confronted your assailants," Lisa said. "I would never be that brave."

"Courage and bravery didn't enter into it," Eric said. "We were foolish, that's all."

"We seem to be magnets for trouble," Roger said. "Nancy has kept us on the up and up since we've been in Scotland."

"I'm surprised I've stayed out of trouble since you've been in Scotland!" Nancy said. "I'm off to bed now. Can't keep my eyes open much longer. Goodnight, everyone." She took her mug into the kitchen and washed it quickly before she retired.

Something about Nancy drew Eric in, although he did not have a clue why. "Enough about our misfortunes." He changed the subject. Every time the altercation came up in conversation, he wanted to talk about something else. "Tell us about yourselves."

"We got married in December," Lisa said. "We weren't able to take the honeymoon we wanted straight away, so we took a long weekend in Normandy right after the wedding. We really wanted to see the Highlands in the summer, and here we are."

"Congratulations," Eric said. "We're both students, but it sounds as though you have real jobs."

"We work for the same company. That's how we met. I'm training to be a pilot. She's in the personnel department."

"We're saving as much as we can to buy a house. We'll probably have a baby after Trevor gets his pilot's license."

"I hope my future looks as rosy as yours when I graduate from college— if I graduate. Seems like it takes forever."

"It does take a long time, but stay with it," Trevor said. "You'll be glad you did."

Roger finished his chocolate bar. "Actually, we're doing all right for ourselves. We snapped at the only chance we're likely to get to travel to Europe."

"You did the right thing," Lisa said. "I would certainly jump at the chance to go to America or Canada."

"Are either of you married?" Trevor asked.

"I'm engaged," Roger said. "Our wedding will probably be in about a year. I want to finish college first, and I want Marianne to finish, too. It's very reassuring for me to meet newlyweds who tell me how happy they are with each other."

Trevor said, "Congratulations to you, too, then. It's the right thing to do."

"Sounds like you're doing everything right," Lisa added. "You'll make a good husband for her. What about you, Eric? Married?"

"No, I'm happy." Eric could not resist his stock response to that question, however inappropriate it was. His expression changed to a broad grin to show that he was only joking. "Sorry. I say that to draw attention away from my romantic ineptitude. I'm not much of a lady's man, in spite of my efforts."

Lisa looked at Trevor, and stifled a giggle. "I'm not so sure. I saw the way your Scottish friend was looking at you this evening."

25.

The hostel was remarkably cold at 7:00 on that July morning. The building was neither significantly heated nor insulated, and the hostelers could see their breath condensing in the cool air. Lisa and Trevor looked eager to greet the day, while Eric and Roger looked and felt like they had been trying to sleep on a roller coaster ride. Nancy sat down with them in the common room but hardly spoke. The Australian and the Scottish cyclist were at one end of the table.

Trevor and Lisa invited Nancy, Roger and Eric to join them for a breakfast of toast and tea. The Americans could not resist the impulse to cheer up and enjoy their last moments with this friendly couple who made their stay in Tomintoul remarkably pleasant. Nancy was coy, even a little defensive around the Englishwoman.

"You're not going to wear your jersey like that, are you?" Lisa said to Roger.

"Like what?" Roger had nearly forgotten the torn shoulder on his jersey, which seemed inconsequential compared to all the other things that had happened to him since he had been attacked.

"That big rip near your shoulder. Here, let me darn it for you."

"It's not that big of a deal. Don't go to any trouble over me."

"No trouble at all. That's why I carry this mending kit in my purse. Be a dear and spread some butter and marmalade on the toast, please." Lisa mended Roger's jersey, and within five minutes, it looked almost as it did before the highway incident.

Eric and Roger checked out of the hostel, loaded their gear onto their bicycles in the yard in front of the hostel, and waited for their friends. The sky was partly cloudy, but the air was still cool enough for them to wear their long-sleeve jerseys and leg warmers.

"Before you go, I want to give you something." Lisa took a cosmetic kit from her backpack and removed a bottle of foundation. "Hold still." She painted just enough of it around Roger's eyebrow to cover what remained of the unsightly bruise. "Now, you don't have to explain that to anyone else today."

"Much obliged. Don't tell anyone I'm wearing eye shadow."

"It's not eye shadow, silly, and your secret's safe with us."

"It was a pleasure meeting all of you," Trevor said. "All the best!"

Roger took out his camera and snapped a photograph of the English couple with their packs on their backs. They walked southward down the road toward the square while Nancy, Eric and Roger rode north. Trevor took a picture of them, too, with his camera. They all waved good-bye to each other, then turned and did not look back.

Nancy, Roger and Eric rode northwestward on the A939. Their goal for the day was Nairn, Highland, on the North Sea coast at Moray Firth. From Tomintoul, they descended into the Strath Avon and followed the Avon River briefly. They climbed over a minor ridge and dropped down into a deep valley that was also the border between Moray and Highland counties. Once across the Bridge of Brown, they immediately began climbing a tall, steep moor with a 20% grade. They needed all their strength and their lowest gears before they surmounted the Hills of Cromdale. The Americans waited for Nancy at the top. They were expecting a long, fast descent into Grantown-on-Spey. Their knees and feet needed the rest that would come from a downhill ride, but the wear would be transferred to their shoulder blades and hands.

Even with his riding gloves, Roger still had numbness in the two smaller fingers of his left hand, and he had trouble gripping a pencil or similar objects in his right hand. The physicians called it ulnar neuropathy. He adjusted his hand position often on the handlebar to ease the numbness, but to little avail. He could still grip his brake levers easily and change gears as necessary, but retrieving coins from his pocket was a difficult matter. His old leather saddle had long since taken the shape of his buttocks, but after several days of riding, he was keenly aware of the contours of the saddle. The grime on his chain and cluster bothered him in principle, but Eric also had plenty of dirt there, so they were on even terms. Nancy's chain was still disgustingly clean and shiny.

Dodging sheep for many a kilometer, they rested on the descent into the Spey valley, and arrived in Grantown-on-Spey in time for lunch. Their sixth sense led them to a fish bar for a satisfying lunch and an ice cream parlor in the same block for dessert.

Grantown-on-Spey, a pleasant-looking town of some 1600 citizens, like many towns and even some larger cities in the U.K., included in its moniker the name of a nearby geographical feature. This made sense to the two Americans, as Grantown lay along the banks of the Spey River. What puzzled them, though, was that the nomenclature did not appreciably follow

British colonists to the U.S., Australia, Canada and elsewhere. No one in the U.S. would conceive Denver-on-South Platte, Colorado Springs-next-the-Mountain or Seattle-by-the-Sound. Such names would be superfluous, yet the British did not seem to mind. Nancy had no explanation, and remarked that she had never given it a thought until the Americans mentioned it.

A tailwind helped propel them the remaining 40 kilometers to Nairn, a city of nearly 5900 people on the North Sea coast. It was as far north as they intended to go. Neither Eric nor Nancy tried to make a race of it, to Roger's mild surprise. Nancy did not try very much to compete for their attention with the Englishwoman, but he halfway expected her to compete in her more natural arena of cyclotouring.

Eric had a mild headache as usual, even though he was taking his medicine as scheduled. He suffered occasional instances of blurred vision and muscle spasms, but he had no disinclination to continue the ride. His Novara was dirty on the outside, but all of its bearings were rolling in clean lithium grease, and he knew all of its cups and cones were properly tightened. He, Roger and Nancy rode through Nairn until they were in a seaside park.

Wind blowing across the flat, grassy park kept a few kites airborne, but it was cold enough to force Roger and Eric to wear jeans and long-sleeve shirts over their cycling clothes. Nancy pulled on jeans and a thick sweater over hers. They parked their bicycles on the grass and strolled along the narrow strip of sand that was the beach. The seawater was even colder than the wind. This was no place for swimming or sunbathing, even in July. They found a comfortable grassy spot and sat down on it.

"You must've found something exciting in Ballater yesterday. We hardly saw you until late in the day." Roger was not overly concerned then or now, but he wanted to see what kind of reaction Nancy would have. Was she really interested in Eric, as Lisa had insinuated?

"An old friend lives near Ballater, a ski instructor at Lecht in the winter. He was surprised to see me. Invited me to stay for lunch." Nancy looked at Eric, then at Roger, to see what kind of reaction they would have. Roger showed some interest, while Eric just grunted an acknowledgment. "I saw you made friends with that English woman, Lisa."

"You meet all sorts of people on a bicycle tour. Sometimes English. Sometimes women." Roger did not wish to make an issue of it with Nancy. Eric remained silent, just watching the clouds and the waves.

"She certainly made a fuss over you, now, did she?"

"Her husband twisted my arm. I had to accept the favor." Roger rolled to one side and supported his head with his palm. "I think they were impressed last night that we made tea for them and shared our chocolate bars. They wanted to do something nice for us this morning. Sort of like the way that Scottish woman fed you when you showed up in Braemar the other evening." He could take the interrogation, and he could give it right back, too.

"We Scots look out for one another. She knew what I needed."

Tired out after a lack of sleep the previous night, they decided to test the park for "sleepability" before committing themselves to spend the night there. Few people were in the park and, except for the cold wind, it was a nice place to take a nap. The view of the sea from the park was interesting to Roger, for he had lived all his life in Colorado, far from any seacoast. Eric still liked to look at seascapes, even though he was attending college near a coast. The Puget Sound was a familiar sight to him, but he rarely saw the Pacific Ocean. Nancy had lived most of her life on this seacoast.

About two hours later, the wind diminished and they slowly arose from their naps. Roger, still congested, was especially sluggish, but the thought of supper prompted him. They mounted their bicycles and rode into the business district where they found an Indian restaurant.

They washed down several standard Indian courses with a pot of Scottish tea. The restaurant was actually a combination of Indian and British cuisine and decor. It was unlike the Indian restaurants in the U.S., which had much less British influence.

Roger finished his cup of British-style tea, not green tea. "Where do we go after Loch Ness tomorrow?"

"Is your invitation to Aberdeen still open?" Eric was sure that the ride from Edinburgh to Braemar convinced Nancy of his competitiveness. Was there anything else worth pursuing with her?

"Aye, of course it is. We can get there in two days from here."

"I'm game if you are, Squire. What do you say?"

Roger was noncommittal for his own sake, but he did not want Eric and Nancy to miss their big opportunity, now that they were beginning to like each other. "Why not? Let's do it."

"Any hostels between here and Aberdeen?"

"Aberdeen has one, but none in between. There are plenty of inns and B&Bs along the way. You won't have to stay at the hostel in Aberdeen. I know a better place."

They walked through the business district of Nairn after supper. Most stores were closed, but gentlemen wearing caps and neckties and ladies clad in skirts were abound, riding bicycles or walking dogs. Many passersby exchanged friendly greetings. Eric and Roger were impressed by the urbanities.

Nancy spotted a B&B, inquired within, and checked into a room for the night. Having no sleeping bag or pad, she did not fancy camping in the park with Roger and Eric. She tried to convince them to stay at the inn, but they were looking forward to a night on the beach, and declined. She agreed to meet them in the morning in the park where they had spent part of the afternoon.

On their way back toward the beach, they purchased a bottle of claret to celebrate the halfway mark of their journey. They sat on the grass, drank the claret, and watched the sun set, while they discussed their plans for the next three weeks. They wondered what changes, if any, would be awaiting them back home.

Urban camping was not entirely new to them, but neither had ever slept beside an ocean. The park was now deserted, and the only sounds came from the waves rolling in and out across the narrow beach. They finished writing in their journals in the twilight, and unrolled their mattress pads and sleeping bags. Roger did not see a telephone anywhere nearby, so he decided to save his call to Marianne for the following day.

"Since we have grass beneath us," Roger said, "am I safe in assuming the high tide does not come up this far?"

"I hope so," Eric said, "because my sleeping bag isn't guaranteed to float."

"What if you have a wet dream in it?"

"Voids the warranty. If you don't see me here in the morning, you can assume I had one and drifted away in it."

"You actually sounded enthusiastic about riding to Aberdeen with Nancy."

"I am, I guess. Nancy is one of those people who can give you ulcers and mesmerize you at the same time. If we didn't go with her to Aberdeen, I'd spend the rest of my life wondering what we missed. Plus, it might be interesting to see how a Scottish family lives."

For only the second time in three weeks, they felt unconfined by small rooms and small beds. In Nairn, like Harrogate, they had all the space they needed, but this time they were able to relax. The sound of the waves lulled them to sleep.

26.

"Lazy yanks! Get out of bed now, you two, or I'm coming in after you!"

Roger still had his eyes closed. "Mmmm! A warm Scottish babe in my sleeping bag. This is the best dream I've had in years!"

"It's not a dream, and I'm not here to warm you in your bag."

Nancy, kneeling between them, was the first thing Roger and Eric noticed when they awoke from a restful sleep into a cool morning. Neither one had drifted away in his sleep. Nancy awakened Eric by putting her cold hands on his bare neck and down his T-shirt. He was not nearly as surly as when Roger tried to roust him out of bed. The men dressed themselves discreetly in their sleeping bags, arose and broke camp. They loaded their gear onto their bicycles and followed Nancy out of the park.

On their way out of Nairn at 8:00, Nancy, Eric and Roger quickly devoured a loaf of brown bread together. They pulled their warm jackets over their long-sleeve racing tights and continued their ride. Avoiding the A96, they rode southwestward toward Inverness on the parallel B9091, a less-busy highway.

The pace was not especially fast. The air was inhibitively cold, and they were in no great hurry to get anywhere. The two Americans slept well in the park, but both were somewhat congested, and they both looked forward to a night on a real mattress. They knew they were not likely to find a truly comfortable bed in the next three weeks, but neither complained.

By midmorning, they were in Inverness, a city of 36,000 people, where the Ness River empties into Moray Firth. At a diner in the downtown area, they drank several cups of tea each to wash some food down and to uplift their spirits with caffeine. The waitress who served them spoke in an accent that almost could have passed as an American one, its Scottish overtones barely discernible. The two Americans had become well aware that not all Scottish people talk like American actors portraying Scottish characters with exaggerated accents, a la *Brigadoon*.

"How was your night on the beach?" Nancy poured tea from a large pot on top of whole milk and sugar in her cup, but did not lick the spoon after stirring it, as the Americans usually did.

"Not bad at all." Eric poured the tea first, but he did not lick the spoon this time. "And yours?"

"I persuaded the innkeepers to let me stay the night for free in exchange for some labor. I washed the dinner dishes and baked some scones for them. I often travel that way."

"Haven't you heard? People who live in guest houses shouldn't roll scones!" Eric said.

Nancy smiled at his silly witticism. "That was lame."

"Then try this on for size. What style of car should you drive if you want to overthrow Henry VIII?"

"Pray tell."

"A two-door coupe. For a Tudor coup."

"That was even worse."

"Ask him how he makes a living," Roger advised Nancy.

"Aye, then, how do you earn money?"

"I tighten loose women!"

Roger was pleased to hear some civil discourse between them, however inane it was. He wanted to keep it going. "I was under the impression that you didn't cook. You let us do all the cooking in Selkirk and Edinburgh."

Nancy laughed. "I said I didn't make haggis, but I didn't say I couldn't cook anything. Football and skiing aren't the only things I do well. And when we get to Aberdeen, I'll show you how to make scones and tea properly. The Scottish way."

Nancy, Roger and Eric followed an extremely narrow highway, the B862, toward the village of Dores along the southern shore of Loch Ness. They were pleasantly surprised to see farms and forests along the Ness River and lake shore instead of "See the Loch Ness Monster" entrepreneurs capitalizing on gullible tourists. They saw a few people and cars, but no boat rides to see the monster, no on-shore viewing devices at ten pence per look, and no curio shops. It was a far cry from Mammoth Cave, Niagara Falls or the Black Hills of South Dakota.

They continued southwestward beyond Dores until they found a spot where the road was very close to the shore, and separated from it only by a rocky clearing of public property. They stopped, leaned their bicycles against some boulders and looked out across the calm, murky water and the hazy air above it that added so much to the lake's mystique.

Loch Ness, about 38 kilometers long, 3 kilometers wide and as much as 130 meters deep, looked like a good setting for a mystery, but not necessarily one involving a serpent. Lying serenely in the Great Glen Fault between the Firth of Lorne and Moray Firth, adjacent to Loch Oich and Loch Lochy, the lake gave no hints of anything unusual.

The ambient temperature had risen considerably since the beginning of the day. They had removed their jackets in Inverness, but now they were comfortable enough to exchange longs for shorts, which they did in the privacy and seclusion of the forest. Nancy changed, behind a boulder, into the racing shorts and that crop-top that Roger and Eric had noticed the first time they saw her.

"I don't see any bleeding monster out there," Roger scoffed as he scrutinized the water and the opposite shore. "It's all a hoax, I say. Probably fabricated by the Highland tourist authority."

"It very well could be," Nancy agreed, "but then again, maybe not."

"She knows something about it that I don't know." Roger spoke to his imaginary audience out there in television land.

"Monster reports supposedly date back to the sixth century A.D., when Saint Columba prevented a river monster from eating a Pict." Nancy spoke very matter-of-factly.

"Who or what is a Pict?"

165

"The Picts were a non-Celtic tribe who occupied parts of this island in the first millennium. Famous for their tattoos. I think they became Gaels a few centuries after the Saint Columba incident, but that's another subject. Anyway, another monster allegedly pulled Columba's boat across this lake in return for perpetual freedom from Loch Ness, he did." Nancy looked very pleased with herself for knowing something about which her two college-bound friends knew nothing.

Neither Roger nor Eric had seen the scholarly Nancy until now. Roger said, "That story could be taken with a grain of salt, but it's interesting that people witnessed the monster long before tourism and mass media were invented."

"I've read more strange stories that are also somewhat less than believable. Further tales have it that Gaelic water horses appeared in the guise of Shetland ponies and carried children into the lake on their backs. This happened not only at Loch Ness, but also at several other Scottish lakes and even in Ireland and Norway."

"If I see a stray horse around here, I'll make damn sure I avoid it," Eric said. "I've heard the lake is quite deep, and could have underwater caverns and sea passages. Did your sources mention that?"

"The lake is more than 100 meters deep in some places. The water is darkened by peat sediments deposited by tributaries. Witnesses have described Nessie as looking like a giant slug or eel, with a mane on its neck and a head shaped like that of a seal or snail."

The alluring navel ring was still there, distracting them both from what she was saying.

"There is a slight difference between a seal's head and a snail's head," Roger said. "I suspect at least a few of the alleged sightings were actually of logs or something like that, and some of the witnesses had their perception distorted by that strong ale or scotch."

"Aye, no doubt. Skeptics say that the sightings could be logs or other vegetation, otters swimming as a group or even a German dirigible from the Great War."

Roger was impressed by her knowledge of Loch Ness, although he knew how well she could embellish her stories. "I would believe the logs or otters explanation, but I'm very skeptical myself of the dirigible story. Doesn't hold much water."

"Sounds a bit far-fetched, I agree," Eric said, "but not necessarily any more so than the monster story itself."

"Has anyone tried to classify the monster?" Roger asked.

"The books I've read did mention something about that. The consensus is that the monsters are probably not reptiles, as the water's too cold. Reptiles are air breathers, anyway. If they've gone ashore, then that disqualifies most species of fish. That still leaves amphibians and invertebrates, but the monsters are much larger than any known amphibian or invertebrate."

"We're overlooking only a small portion of the surface of the lake during the day. I seriously doubt we have any chance of proving or disproving the existence of Loch Ness monsters." Roger spoke as if he were genuinely disappointed. "Maybe some other time we can come back with a canoe, some sonar equipment and maybe a harpoon. Those suckers can't hide forever, if they're there."

Eric, too, was aware of Nancy's tendency toward hyperbole. "How do you know so much about the Loch Ness Monster, anyway? Or, does everyone in Scotland know what you just told us?"

Nancy gave them both a very firm look in the eyes. "Nay, nay. I had to write a lengthy report, and give a speech to my classmates, before I was permitted to graduate from school when I was sixteen. For my topic, I chose Celtic mythology and its place in modern Scotland." She pronounced Celtic with a *k* sound at the beginning, unlike the athletic teams in the U.S. who use that name. "The Loch Ness monster is an important part of Scottish folklore. I used it in my report."

Eric expected no harm if he gave her another chance to brag. "No doubt you passed the assignment with flying colors."

"Highest score in the class. My folks were very proud of me for it." Nancy looked smug, but this time she provided some evidence to corroborate her claim. Eric and Roger were still unsure whether she was a very persuasive huckster or a very accomplished young woman. They had long since given her the benefit of the doubt.

They contemplated the lake and discussed Gaelic folklore and other subjects until lunchtime. They rode back to Dores where they spotted a mobile grocery store, little more than a vegetable truck, and parked themselves on the roadside grass to eat fresh fruit for lunch.

A troop of Boy Scouts from Belgium approached on the footpath where they were sitting. As former Boy Scouts themselves, and Eagle Scouts at that, Roger and Eric felt compelled to inquire about the Belgian Boy Scout program. The Belgians, who had been camping somewhere in the region, had obviously been influenced by American television, as indicated by their style of English. Roger photographed the troop while its members struck a pose reminiscent of some famous television personalities.

"Have you ever noticed that television broadcasting is, by far, America's most effective instrument of foreign policy?" Eric finished a second banana and deposited the peel in a nearby trash bin.

Roger checked the zippers on his panniers in preparation for departure. "Is everyone ready to leave? I guess we'll want to ride back to Inverness the way we came, then turn southeast. Nancy?"

"I know the route from Inverness." Nancy mounted her Raleigh and sprinted off in the direction of Inverness. The men did not expect her to leave in such a hurry. They jumped on their own bicycles and worked to catch her, more than a kilometer from the lunch stop.

The fresh fruit gave them all a burst of energy, especially Nancy. They formed a paceline of sorts, and Nancy took the lead as often and for as much time as Eric and Roger did. She proved very aggressive on a bicycle, and any doubts they had regarding her strength and stamina, in comparison to her boastfulness, quickly disappeared. She rode like the racers they had competed against at Eastway and in the time-trial, all the way into Inverness. They were genuinely proud of her, and hoped she would continue to pace them like this all the way to Aberdeen.

Just outside the Inverness city limits, the road the three cyclists were on merged with another highway. The oncoming traffic was obscured by a forested ridge. Nancy was in the lead, with Eric and Roger close behind her. The men extended their fingers to reach their brake levers, not knowing what to expect around the ridge. Nancy bolted into the intersection, with less than one second of margin between safe passage and becoming a motorist's hood ornament. The driver braked and honked, the men yielded, and Nancy emerged safely in the far-left lane of the new highway.

Eric sprinted again to catch up with her. "You damn near bought it, fool! Take it easy, will you?"

Nancy glanced over her shoulder. Roger had passed Eric and was right beside her. "I ride like you do!" She continued the fast pace through the city, and the Americans stayed with her.

A traffic signal on the other side of town turned yellow when Eric and Roger were less than twenty meters away from the intersection. The mid-afternoon traffic was fairly dense, so they decided to stop, knowing they could catch her again. Nancy was a few meters ahead, and she kept going. Gripping his brakes, Eric cringed when he saw a car in the center lane start to make a right turn. As he anticipated, the car clipped Nancy's rear wheel and threw her to the pavement.

The driver, a fashionably dressed woman in her forties, screeched her brakes and jumped out of the car, horrified. Roger and Eric got off their bicycles and hastily propped them against a utility pole beside the road. Eric was hyperventilating, Nancy was shrieking in pain, and the driver was hysterical. Only Roger was left to do something heroic, and he was clueless. He looked to Eric for a cue. His heart was pounding the way it did during the wild escape in Harrogate. Two more motorists stopped to offer their assistance—one parked his car so as to shield Nancy from traffic in the lane where she lay.

"Nancy!" Roger knelt down beside her and gently released her feet from her pedals.

She tried to respond, but no sound came from her quivering lips. Eric was on the verge of a seizure, maybe, but he managed to lift the bicycle off of her. She was conscious, her head protected by a first-rate helmet, but she had plenty of road rash on her left knee, elbow and shoulder. She was able to move a little on her own, and Roger loosened her helmet and helped her assume a less painful position on her back. He held her hand and encouraged her to try to speak and remain conscious.

Eric came to Nancy's side a few seconds after Roger did, once he had regained his own composure. Watching the collision was very painful for him, and left him light-headed. He noticed that something about her shoulders was out of place, aside from the road rash. Her left collarbone was swollen and misshapen. He spoke soothingly to her while he gently examined the broken collarbone and stroked her hair. The brass ring was still in place in her firm abdomen, but he had not seen the soccer-ball tattoo below her shoulder until now.

Roger and Eric and the two motorists stayed with Nancy until an ambulance took her to a local clinic. Not critically injured, she was able to sit up and make a semi-coherent statement to a constable who arrived at the scene just moments before the ambulance. Roger asked the constable for the name of the clinic, then watched the ambulance speed away with Nancy inside. Eric took the front wheel off her Raleigh, and with Roger's help loaded the bicycle and the wheel into the police car's trunk. The constable said she would see to it that the bicycle and its owner would be reunited following her treatment.

"Damn everything! Things were starting to go our way, and now this!" Eric stood with his bicycle beside the road where Nancy's fortunes changed for the worse an hour earlier. "Why did she have to ride like such a fucking maniac?"

Roger watched the traffic for a moment, thinking about how dangerous streets and highways could be under certain circumstances. "Her style of driving today would have made Cruella DeVil blush." He watched the traffic again. "What do we do now? Nancy won't be guiding us to Aberdeen with a broken collarbone, and whatever else she might have."

Eric shook his head. He thought for a moment. "I'm ready for a change of venue. We've gotten our taste of the northern and central parts of this island. I could take more of this, but we have less than three weeks left to see everything else we're going to see."

"Are you up to three more weeks?"

"I'd be up to three more years here if I had a good bed and peace of mind. We've come up short on both counts lately, but I think I can stay healthy for three more weeks."

"We passed a railroad station not too far from here, I think. We can call the clinic from there." Roger swung a leg over his frame and clicked his shoe into its pedal.

"Let's see how much it would cost us to ride a train back to London, maybe overnight if there is one. We'll do whatever we can to help Nancy get back to Aberdeen, if that's where she wants to go. She needs to go home to recover. She's in no shape to continue riding with us." Eric got on his bicycle and followed Roger into the traffic lane.

They rode toward the city centre of Inverness and followed some signs to the railway station. An evening departure would arrive in London the following morning, with several stops along the way. The price of a coach-class ticket was within their budgets, but they wanted to know Nancy's fate before they made any plans.

Roger used a pay telephone inside the station to call the clinic the constable had mentioned. The receptionist told him Nancy had been admitted, but could not provide much more information. The receptionist could not say whether her injuries were bad enough to require an overnight stay or surgery. Roger left word that he and Eric would be at the railway station, in case Nancy asked for information. More than a little dejected, he and Eric bought their tickets to London, changed clothes in the men's room, and thought about Nancy some more.

They had seen a liquor store and a bakery on their way toward the railroad station. They rode a few blocks back to the store for some refreshment to take aboard the train. They did not want anything that would keep them awake on the train ride. They anticipated eleven sleepless hours between Inverness and London, and a bottle of cheap Beaujolais Villages seemed appropriate for the occasion.

Eric noticed a tartan shop across the street and down the block from the liquor store. "This is our last chance to get a genuine Fraser plaid something for George, and I bet they'll be closing in a few minutes."

"They didn't have anything to our liking in Edinburgh." Roger started riding toward the tartan shop. "Why do you think Inverness will have something that Edinburgh didn't have?"

"They won't have anything different," Eric said. "We'll buy him a T-shirt. If he doesn't like it, too bad! He could've come with us and picked out his own."

"But we already decided he could easily get one on the Internet, and he might already have one."

170

"All very true, but he doesn't have and can't get one that's actually sold by a Scottish tartan merchant."

"No, I suppose he'll never have a shirt in a bag bearing the label of a store in Scotland and a price tag in pounds and pence unless we bring him one," Roger said. "Let's do it."

Eric found a T-shirt bearing the Scottish flag and the words, "established 1314," and arranged for it to be mailed to his home address so he would not have to carry it in his already overcrowded panniers. He bought a MacLane tie for himself, so he would have something with which to remember a girl and a strange sequence of events in Scotland. He mailed his tie home along with the T-shirt for George. Last, he bought two very small, single-serving bottles of Glenlivet scotch for George and himself. The scotch could not be mailed, but he found a niche for it in his luggage.

Back at the station, Roger returned to the telephone he had used to call the hospital. A few minutes later, he had an optimistic smile on his face that Eric had seldom seen since they arrived in Europe.

"You spoke to Marianne and everything's all right?" Eric inferred.

"Not quite that good. I spoke to her answering machine, finally. I said I would call again on Saturday morning, and I specified the time of day she should expect my call. That way, she can arrange to be near the phone when I call next time. It occurred to me that she might have a new cell phone number by now. She mentioned looking for a better deal from some other company."

"That's progress. Just don't forget to call her when you said you would."

"I spoke to Inga, too. Told her what we're doing. She said we're welcome to stay with them tomorrow night if we want."

Roger scratched his head and squinted, indicating a memory lapse. "I'd kind of forgotten about Marianne. I should have called her more than a week ago. First, the hoodlums, then Nancy…we've had too much excitement lately, too many distractions."

Another half hour went by, while Roger and Eric read newspapers and wrote in their journals. They wrote and mailed some postcards bearing pictures of Loch Ness and the Highlands. A young man dressed in medical garb walked into the station pushing a bicycle with a badly bent rear wheel. Another followed, similarly dressed and carrying a pair of panniers. The second man held the door while Nancy limped in slowly. The men leaned her Raleigh against a wall, set her panniers on a bench, said good-bye to her and left. Eric and Roger stood up immediately upon seeing Nancy and walked over to greet her. She managed a weak smile when she saw them coming.

"My collarbone is broken, and everything else hurts, it does. Two chaps from the clinic were done with their shift, and they offered me a ride here."

171

Nancy was now dressed in baggy shorts and an oversize T-shirt. She wore large bandages on her left knee and elbow.

Roger expected that she had no trouble charming the men at the clinic into doing her a favor like that. It was exactly what he would have done for her, he thought, if he had been one of the clinic employees. "We weren't sure if we'd see you again. We decided to return to London by train so that we could continue our tour in southern England."

"That's probably the best thing for you to do now."

Eric was genuinely disappointed to see her this way. Their rivalry had brought out his best cycling thus far. "What are you going to do next? Back home to mum and dad?" He deliberately said *mum* instead of mom.

"I called my mum from the clinic. She said she'll fetch me at the station in Aberdeen this evening. She even paid for my ticket. I'm sorry I can't ride there with you on our bicycles. I'll be wearing this brace for another four weeks or so." She pointed to a padded figure-eight harness between her bra and her T-shirt. "If you came to Aberdeen, I could show you the football pitch where my team won…"

Eric smiled, then spoke very politely. "My dear, how would you like to have your other collarbone broken?"

Nancy stopped in mid-speech, her mouth still open. "You don't mind me talking about football, do you?"

Eric used his best brogue. "You're a fine lass, aye, but you're a wee bit daft sometimes."

Nancy understood, perhaps for the first time in her life. She sat down in the waiting area, and the men joined her. "I've never had a real boyfriend, not for any length of time. I always thought it was because the boys didn't like a girl who was a better footballer than themselves. I was better than most of the boys at volleyball, track, cycling, skiing and even cricket, and I wasn't about to change my ways just to satisfy some lad's fragile ego. I took a liking to you two because you didn't shrink away when I came on strong." Eric and Roger looked at each other silently, both amazed by her candor. "You put me in my place on that ride from Perth to Braemar, and I probably deserved every bit of it." She laughed, even though it hurt to do so.

Eric laughed with her. He liked her humble side almost as much as he had come to like her other sides. "You'd probably put me in my place in most of the other sports."

Roger concurred. "You'd beat both of us in football, if it were just you with your injuries against the two of us." He still felt awkward saying football when he meant soccer, but he knew that Eric understood and probably felt the same way.

"You're a fine lad yourself, Eric, but you looked more than just a wee bit daft the first time I saw you."

"Yes, I suppose I did. It wasn't my finest hour."

"I saw you two going down that hill and I wondered why you were in such a hurry to get to the bottom. The pavement can be really nasty after a rain. You found that out the hard way. We've all learned a few lessons about cycling this week, haven't we?"

They continued reviewing some of the things they had all done together in recent days.

"I'm starting to get hungry again. It's getting close to supper time," Eric said. "Anyone else hungry?"

"I could use something to eat right about now," Roger agreed. "Nancy, what can we get you?"

"I'm not sure I could eat anything. I'm sore all over."

"How about if I bring you back something? You can save it for when you do get hungry."

"All right. Let me give you a few quid."

"Your money's no good here. My treat." Eric smiled at Nancy and drew a smile in return. He rode back to the bakery for a scone and a Cornish pastry for Nancy. He went across the street to a fish bar for fish and chips for Roger and himself. The fish bar had haggis on the menu. He reluctantly decided to give it a try, this being his last chance to do so. He returned to the railway station with two servings of haggis, chips and cole slaw. The fish bar did not offer the traditional neaps and tatties, that is, turnips and mashed potatoes, to go with the haggis.

Roger had a surprised look on his face when he unwrapped the haggis. "What is this? Some kind of fish?"

"That's genuine haggis, amigo. *Bon apetit*! It came from a fish bar, which is why you get chips and cole slaw with it."

"Why'd you bring me this?"

"Because I wasn't about to try it alone." Eric hesitantly took a bite of the haggis. He nodded in approval. It was much tastier than he was expecting. The black pepper and onions gave it a strong but pleasant flavor.

"Not bad," Roger said. "Not nearly as bad as it sounds. Wise decision, Chief."

"I'm proud of you two for trying haggis, even if it wasn't properly boiled. You'll have to come back for neaps and tatties." Nancy explained Scottish cooking to the two Americans. Once she took the first bite of the pastry, she found her appetite.

They continued talking for another hour until the train to Aberdeen began boarding. Roger and Eric carried Nancy's Raleigh and luggage on board the train. They were all genuinely sorry to be parting company, in contrast to their tenuous introduction in rural Borders. The Americans exchanged addresses with Nancy, then wished her a pleasant journey home and a speedy recovery.

"Would you...do you mind if I give you a goodbye kiss?" Eric had trouble finding the courage to ask. Roger was about to kiss her anyway. He did not even consider asking permission.

"No, I don't mind at all. I'd like that!" Nancy was pleased by Eric's sincerity. He touched her good shoulder lightly and kissed her cheek. She puckered her lips, wanting something better than that. He put his arms around her and kissed her again, this time on the lips and much more slowly. She did not exhibit the shyness she did a few days earlier on the hill overlooking Edinburgh.

Roger kissed her on the cheek, and followed Eric out of the rail car. They waved good-bye to her from the platform, and she waved at them before they entered the waiting room. They returned to their seats in silence to read, write and contemplate all the things they had to tell the Evans tomorrow.

The London-bound train departed Inverness shortly after 19:20, with Eric and Roger riding second class in a dining coach that did not have a kitchen. The coach was not crowded, allowing passengers to sleep across two seats if they dared.

An hour after departure, Roger uncorked the wine with his Swiss Army knife, inhaled the bouquet and offered the first drink to Eric. Eric tried to inhale the bouquet, although nothing registered, and poured some wine into his mouth.

"Slightly bitter," Eric commented, "but I guess we can consider it a toast to Scotland. I'm glad we spent some time here."

"Hair of the dog that bit me." Roger took a drink. "We had some of our best days in Scotland, and maybe a prelude to even better times in the southern part of the island."

"I won't miss the slippery vegetation after the rain, but I miss Nancy already. I became rather fond of her once I started getting to know her. I think she felt that way about me, too."

"I won't miss the bleeding insects, but our ride from Edinburgh to Braemar was our best thus far." Roger sipped the wine again. "I think Nancy was that bonnie lass you were seeking. Too bad it took you so long to realize it."

"We might've fallen in love, but it would've taken a few months. There was no magnetic attraction between us, just a huge invisible barrier that we'd just started to overcome. In hindsight, her crash today was largely our fault, because she wanted to impress us. If we hadn't been so motivated to lose her on the way to Braemar, she wouldn't have been riding like a maniac today. Ego trips can be deadly."

"We'll remember that next time." Roger took a sip and passed the bottle back to Eric. "I'm glad we found George his Fraser-clan memento, and we rode all the way to Loch Ness. My mind is at ease now. You're holding out much better than you expected, and I knew you could. I'm sorry I got on your case for crashing. I slid sideways on that road myself, and I damn near bought the farm."

"I still feel like I could have avoided the crash. It awakened me to the risk I put myself in every time we ride. I haven't had a grand mal seizure yet, though. Not yet."

Roger raised the wine bottle in a toast. "To more good days ahead of us. Many more."

"And to your upcoming marriage," Eric added.

"Especially to Marianne, soon to be my bride."

"By the way," Eric said, "do you still have that wallet from Harrogate?"

Roger smiled as he answered. "I removed the driving license and the cash. The £200 will be more than enough to pay for our frame repairs. Left the rest of the wallet somewhere in the Edinburgh city centre. What did you do with the car key?"

"Left it in the lost-and-found box at one of the hostels," Eric said. "I had no more use for it."

Eric and Roger slept uncomfortably and intermittently throughout the night, but they had pleasant recollections of the time they spent in Scotland. They were eager to begin the next section of their tour, in southern England.

Chapter V: *Salad Days in Warwickshire*

27.

Two slightly irritable young Americans emerged from a train in London's Euston Station at 6:00 without a clue as to how to get where they wanted to go. They looked even more unkempt than usual. Neither had slept much on the train, and what little sleep they did get came in brief intervals in uncomfortable positions across adjacent seats.

Roger and Eric made breakfast out of some remaining digestive biscuits. They did not speak while they ate. Both were thinking about how much they needed to bathe, eat a proper meal, and sleep in a comfortable bed. They certainly did not expect to get fat and lazy while on this vacation.

Lost and disoriented, they spent the next three or four hours touring greater London in search of Romford. Heavy traffic and winding streets did not help any. Their weariness inhibited logical thought, and all the time they wasted made them even more irritable. Neither had a pleasant word to say to the other by the time they finally did get to Romford, but both managed a good-natured façade when they greeted Peter, who was mowing his front yard.

They had plenty to do before they could proceed into southern England: their bicycles needed cleaning, their frames needed straightening, and their clothing desperately needed washing. The weight of their clothing had nearly doubled with sweat, mildew and dirt. They could hear their bodies beseeching them for a bath and a comfortable bed. Peter invited them into the house. He was due at work later in the morning, but he was eager to hear about their travels.

"Sorry to arrive on short notice," Eric said. "We've had our share of troubles lately. I managed to put a dent in my frame on a slippery wet highway."

"We've been expecting you two." Peter was in his usual hospitable way. "Didn't know what part of the day you'd be coming, but go inside and make yourselves comfortable."

The door was open, and Inga was inside. "You both look awfully tired, poor dears. Come inside and rest. I was just about to make a pot of tea."

Inside the Evans' house, they told Inga and Peter what they had done and where they had been during the past two weeks. The Evans were amazed that their guests were still enthusiastic after some of the things that had happened to them. Roger, as usual, did most of the talking while Eric added his occasional two cents worth.

"What did I tell you?" Peter seemed amused after Eric and Roger described their mugging-and-brawl series of incidents. "Trouble has a way of finding you two. Still, I'm glad to see you made it back here in one piece."

The two Americans looked at each other in mild embarrassment.

Inga just shook her head as if to scold them. "Good thing you didn't call us from Old Bailey. I would've responded, 'Roger and Eric who?'"

After Peter left for work in central London, Inga returned to her domestic chores, and Eric and Roger bathed themselves and cleaned and partially disassembled their bicycles. Vickie was at soccer practice all morning, perfecting her game. Roger called Henry Smythe and made arrangements with him to have Eric's frame and fork straightened. Eric took his and Roger's dirty clothes to a launderette, where he spent several pounds in coins washing nearly every garment they brought with them.

Eric finished washing by noon, and he took the laundry back to the Evans' house where he hung the still-damp clothes on a clothesline in the backyard. Both his and Roger's moods had improved since the early morning, but underlying tension remained between them. Eric suspected the previous night's lack of sleep was the primary cause of his headaches and mild seizures that morning and consequently, his unpleasant disposition, but he was sure that more was involved than just his epilepsy. He decided to allow himself and Roger a day's rest from each other's company and irritability. Perhaps the Evans' cheerfulness would set them both at ease.

Roger was helping Inga and Vickie prepare lunch and tea when Eric went inside. Roger could change his mood from one extreme to another and back again on a moment's notice, unlike Eric, and he appeared to be in high spirits and quite energetic compared to Eric.

"Fancy a spot of tea, Chief?"

"Please." Eric did not sound too excited about it. Roger poured cups of tea for Vickie, Inga, Eric and himself.

"Were you unable to dry your clothes adequately?" Inga sensed Eric's discomfort, and tried not to agitate him further.

"I spent a king's ransom in the dryers, and everything was still damp," Eric said. "But that's all right. We've survived wrinkled clothing before."

"How much is a king's ransom, anyway?" Vickie asked.

"That depends whether the king is Atahualpa or Czar Nicholas II, I suppose." Eric spoke in an emotionless, monotone voice. Even Vickie's exuberance could barely improve his mood.

"Epilepsy bothering you?" Roger asked.

"Yes, it is!" Eric's tone of voice hinted that he did not want to be interrogated about it.

Roger took the hint. He resumed telling Inga and Vickie about his and Eric's adventures of the previous two weeks. They were captivated by his eloquence. Vickie was especially interested in Nancy MacLane, as they seemed to have much in common. Nancy sounded like her type.

Roger and Eric volunteered to help Inga with her work to make themselves feel useful and prevent themselves from getting bored. She sent them to a neighborhood market for groceries. The short walk gave them an opportunity to talk in private.

"You've been a crotchety bastard lately," Roger said. "What's on your mind?"

"I haven't slept very well for three weeks, my head hurts and my body is spastic." Eric did not hide his sarcasm. "Aside from that, I'm fine. You've been disagreeable yourself lately."

"I have not."

"Do you always have to have the last word?"

"Probably."

"Definitely!"

"You still haven't answered my question. I haven't heard you complain about your epilepsy all that much until now, even though we've been through worse nights than the last one."

"I've been having problems with my epilepsy since we began this journey, and I've said so several times. But maybe, until just recently, I haven't been in the mood to really complain about it."

"So what put you in the mood to complain?"

"It could be that I don't want to stay in Romford any longer," Eric said. "We spent enough time there already. Too much, in fact. I think we're imposing on the Evans, wearing out our welcome."

"I concur with all of that, but we can't leave until your frame is fixed."

"When will that be?"

"Mr. Smythe thought he could have it finished sometime tomorrow or the day after. He has several jobs in the queue right now. As soon as he finishes, we'll reassemble the bicycles and head southward. Savvy?"

"All right, but no more mooching on our part. I think it was Ben Franklin who said, fish and visitors smell after three days, or something like that. There's a lot of truth in that, you know."

"Too bad old Ben died before refrigerators were invented. We could find one of the London hostels if staying with the Evans bothers you."

"I enjoy staying with the Evans very much, because they treat us like family. But even family members can be a burden. I think if we told them we'd be staying elsewhere for the next two nights because we don't want to be a burden to them, they'd think we don't care for their hospitality. The best thing for us to do is stay with them and be as much help as we can, and then leave as soon as we can."

"You're smarter than you look, Chief. Do you think you can continue our journey for the next three weeks?"

"I can. I'm sure of it. Didn't we discuss that the other day?" Eric said. "I'm also disappointed with the way things turned out regarding Nancy."

"Unrequited love?"

"I don't know about that, but I can still see her crashing in my mind. It hurts every time I think about it. I was starting to like her, and then she crashed right in front of me."

"It was disappointing. I was looking forward to visiting Aberdeen with her. It would've been interesting to spend a few days with a Scottish family."

"Now, what about you, as I asked earlier. What's your beef?"

"Downtime," Roger said. "I hate the downtime. I want to be riding to someplace where we haven't been, instead of waiting for someone to straighten your frame. And I don't want Inga and Peter to think we're a pain in the ass, which would be mostly my fault because I had to have a frame custom-built in Europe. I'll see what I can do to make it up to you and them."

They purchased the groceries Inga wanted, and Eric helped her prepare supper when they returned to the house. Eric was in better spirits than he had been, and he made more of an effort to participate in the conversation. Roger and Vickie, meanwhile, took the two frames and the new headset to Henry Smythe's shop via bus. Roger had long since shed any trace of his earlier bad mood, and Vickie knew the way much better than Roger did. Supper that evening was the best they had eaten for several days.

Peter loaded his bicycle into his car after supper and drove the five of them to somewhere northwest of Romford for a time trial, in which he finished first in a field of eight. An inn with outdoor tables along the racecourse provided a nice place to celebrate Friday's eve after the time trial. Peter, Anne, Hans and some other cyclists from Peter's cycling club joined Inga, Vickie, Eric and Roger for a round of beverages.

Savoring a comfortable night's rest, Eric and Roger dragged themselves out of bed later than usual. Eric slogged his way through breakfast in his usual early-morning, semiconscious style, while Roger contemplated what he would do to occupy his time. Waiting for the frame to be fixed made him edgy, and he felt like he was becoming a nuisance to his generous hosts. He would not be happy until he and Eric were ready to ride southwestward. He decided to catch up on his reading, which would occupy his time usefully.

He had not read any newspapers beyond the headlines in two weeks. He also wanted to write a few postcards and e-mail messages to friends and family.

While he and Eric were in familiar company, Roger wanted to have as much time to himself as he could get. That way, they would be over their irritability by the time they were ready to leave Romford. Roger knew their constant companionship was affecting them both adversely, and he sensed that Eric knew it, too. Their vacation was little more than half behind them, and Roger wanted Eric, the Evans and himself to continue enjoying it.

After breakfast, Eric folded the laundry he washed the previous day and put it away, while Roger rode a bus part way and walked the rest of the way to Henry Smythe's shop. Neither of them was in much of a hurry.

Roger's jaunt allowed him ample opportunity for introspection. Some of the passengers on the bus cast inquisitive looks in his direction. He was obviously not a local. Most of the other passengers were on their way to work, and were dressed accordingly. Roger, taking advantage of the warm sunshine, was the only passenger wearing short pants, a T-shirt and ankle-high white socks. He was comfortable, and he did not mind looking out of place. Nonconformity never bothered him. He especially liked having some attractive teenage schoolgirls smile at him when he walked by them after he got off the bus.

Henry Smythe, the frame builder, told Roger that Eric's frame would be ready the next day. Smythe showed Roger the hydraulic press and custom fixtures he used to straighten frames and forks. Roger inspected his new frame and fork, and gave his approval to the paint to be used. Smythe had brazed all the joints together, but had not filed the lugs or tapped any of the holes.

As he walked toward Romford, Roger took a slight detour. He went to a newsagent and read the magazine covers. He purchased a road map of south-central England and began planning a route. An Internet café next door to the newsagent kept him busy for nearly an hour. He left the computers and went into a pub a block away.

One of only a handful of customers in the pub, Roger sat at a table and ordered a mug of lager, which he thought might help ease his irritability. The lager was not as cold as he would have liked, but it tasted good anyway. He thought about Eric and how he pitied Eric for not being able to enjoy wine or beer much, now that he was old enough to drink and buy it legally. But at the same time, he envied Eric for having such a good, original excuse for not imbibing. Roger enjoyed a cool beer on a warm day in a relaxed atmosphere, or a glass of wine with dinner. He had long since outgrown his desire to overindulge in foamy keg beer at fraternity parties, while many of his college friends had not. He much preferred spending his free time with

Marianne, rather than with his friends. The more he thought, the more his thirst diminished, and he left the pub without quite finishing the lager.

Eric spent the morning reading newspapers and writing letters. Roger returned shortly before lunchtime.

"A Spanish team and a Dutch team are vying for the lead in the Tour de France." Eric seemed to be in a good mood. "If it's of any interest."

"How are the Americans doing?"

"He's several minutes behind overall, but he's hanging in there."

"Only one American to keep up our hopes and aspirations? That's pathetic," Roger said.

"There could be more than one, but the paper only mentioned the top twenty places. It's early yet, just flat stages. They haven't gotten to L'Alpe de Huez yet."

"Any baseball scores?" Roger asked, as if he cared.

"The Cardinals won, seven to four."

"Against whom?"

"The Archbishops, in Vatican League action. What about the frame? Or should I say, dude, where's my bike?"

"Mine is on its way to the enamelers. Mr. Smythe doesn't paint his frames. He expects to have yours ready sometime tomorrow. I know that's not exactly what you wanted to hear, but we're not his only clients right now."

"I know, I know," Eric grumbled. "Guess I'll just have to sit tight another day."

"We'll be back on the road as soon as we can. The moment your frame is ready, we'll put your bike back together and then we'll hit the road. Consider it a promise."

Eric and Roger worked together after lunch in the Evans' garden, or backyard to the Americans, to clean and adjust Roger's Trek. Borrowing some paint thinner and an old toothbrush from Peter, they cleaned the dirtier parts, especially the chain. They lubricated and adjusted everything that needed lubricating and adjusting. In less than two hours, they had before them a truly well oiled machine. Roger was pleased, and even Eric managed a brief smile as they both admired the shiny, clean bicycle before them.

"Damnation!" Roger was proud of his bicycle, and it showed. He had bought the Trek on clearance during his junior year in high school. It had been his most reliable and pleasurable transportation ever since. "We're going to paint all of southern England red just as soon as we can!"

The rest of the day was uneventful for them, but they both felt better having one of their bicycles road-worthy again. They were anxious to get Eric's frame back, and they both tried to imagine what they would see in southern England. The wait for Eric's frame was a lengthy one. Eric was sure he would atrophy if his frame was not ready very soon.

On the following afternoon, Eric and Roger rode a bus to an open-air market, a kind of outdoor shopping center. They were reluctant to think of it as a shopping center, just because it was unlike any they had at home. The dense crowd of shoppers affected Eric in such a way that he suffered a mild seizure, although he did not understand why crowded places caused him to react that way. Meanwhile, Roger impatiently waded through the crowds, oblivious to Eric's discomfort. They got their fill of the market, and left in search of the bicycle dealer where they had been a few weeks earlier.

At the bicycle dealer, they purchased some spare cables, inner tubes and spokes. They were well-prepared for another three weeks of riding over varying terrain and through inclement weather, and they felt like they knew what adverse conditions to anticipate better than they did three weeks earlier.

They left the bicycle dealer and rode a bus across Romford to Henry Smythe's garage to fetch Eric's frame. Quite a number of attractive women were outside enjoying the nice weather, and the two Americans saw several riding the bus. They were beginning to have second thoughts about departing greater London so hastily.

Eric's anxiety was finally quelled when Mr. Smythe presented his repaired frame. Smythe was unquestionably an expert frame-builder, and Eric considered the ten-quid labor charge a bargain. He could hardly wait to take his frame back to the Evans' house to reassemble his bicycle. In his enthusiasm, he barely noticed the women riding the bus on the way back.

A red telephone box beckoned Roger at the last bus stop several blocks from the Evans house. He looked at his watch and noticed he would be calling Marianne about ten minutes later than what he told her answering machine. He hastily inserted his telephone card and punched the buttons, as if hurrying now would make up for the ten minutes. One of Marianne's roommates answered in a sleepy voice. She did not know where Marianne was, had not seen her this morning, did not know her new cell phone number, and did not know when she would return. She was not sure if Marianne heard the message he had left for her a few days earlier. Roger, trying to keep the anger out of his voice, told her he would call again, probably on the following Saturday. If Marianne was pregnant, as Eric had suggested, why all the secrecy? They were old enough to deal with it.

"Who was that?" a young woman asked her roommate. They lived in a sorority house a few blocks off University Boulevard in southeast Denver. She had a large cup of steaming espresso in her hands. Still wearing her pajamas, she was in no hurry to greet the day.

"Marianne's boyfriend. Fiancé, I mean. He's tried several times to get in touch with her. I really don't know what to tell him. She asked us not to tell him she's spending the summer in Hawaii." The girl who answered Roger's call had gotten dressed in shorts and a T-shirt, but without a bra. A bra and makeup were optional, as long as she was inside the sorority house. She liked that kind of freedom.

"She'd better do something, if she intends to keep him. If she dumps him, I'm going to give him a try!"

"Would you really? I mean, she'd probably have a fit if you did. I'd go ballistic if someone I knew immediately moved in on my ex-boyfriend."

"Well, maybe, but definitely not here. I wouldn't want anyone here to know about it. I'd be discreet."

"She'd find out eventually, especially if he gave you an engagement ring."

"Engagement! Who said anything about engagement? I'd just go somewhere with him for a weekend. What she doesn't know isn't going to hurt her."

"It's tempting, but I don't think I could do that, even to Marianne."

"She has more beauty, money, personality, smarts and several other assets I can't think of than the rest of us combined. Yet, she'd let Roger slip away because...why? She says her parents wanted her back in Hawaii for the summer. I think she has a bun in the oven. I wish I could attract boyfriends and dump them as easily as she does!"

"You are so envious of her!"

"I probably am. Or maybe not." She let out a sigh and stretched her back. "I suppose one of us should give her a call and tell her what's been happening. She should handle this herself, and not expect us to cover for her."

28.

Peter was competing in a time trial near the North Sea coast when Roger and Eric awoke from an unusually warm night's sleep. They ate breakfast with Inga and Vickie, then packed their panniers and prepared to embark on the next phase of their journey. Their enthusiasm still showed, and the Evans wished them well as they rode toward the nearest Underground station.

Approximately two hours after Roger and Eric boarded the subway, they arrived at Wimbledon, southwest of London. They searched for a store where they might purchase bona fide Wimbledon tennis shirts for Eric's sisters, both avid tennis players. They found such a store, but it was closed

Sundays. Few British small businesses were open on the Sabbath, unlike so many of their American counterparts.

Although the businesses closed for the day, the motorists were on the highways in full force. Eric and Roger rode toward Guildford, Surrey, on the A24 and A246. The warm air was mildly breezy, and they were comfortable in short riding pants and short-sleeve jerseys. Much of the morning was gone by the time they started riding.

The terrain of south-central England was hilly at times, but not especially difficult for the two cyclists. Some of the hills, known as downs, had small chalk cliffs on one side. The downs separated farms and forests. The highways mostly skirted the downs and the other forested, rolling hills.

A Chinese takeout-only restaurant was open in some wide spot along the highway. Not knowing when or where they would get their next meal, they purchased lunch there, and settled in a nearby park to eat. Quite conveniently, they situated themselves near three women who appeared to be waiting for a bus.

Roger made eye contact with the women and turned on his charming smile as he and Eric walked by them on their way to a park bench. Eric followed Roger's initiative, although he felt awkward. He did not think he had Roger's graceful, natural-looking style. Roger tried to think of some offhand way to start a conversation with the women, but one of them beat him to it.

"Do you know when the bus to Southampton comes by here?" one of the women, about the same age as the two Americans, asked in a French accent.

"No, I don't," Roger said. "We don't live around here, either."

"We've been waiting here more than an hour!" Another one of the women also spoke with a strong French accent. The third member of their party studied Roger's and especially Eric's faces but said nothing.

"You should have ridden bicycles, like we did." Roger patted the saddle of his Trek. "We travel slower than the buses, but we don't waste any time waiting." Eric silently admired the way his friend could break the ice so effortlessly.

"That sounds like a very good suggestion," the first woman said, "but we only have one week to see everything."

Eric made an effort to get in on the conversation. "You'd best get moving then, or you'll still be standing here at the end of the week."

"Are you two from America?" the second woman asked.

"Yes, we are." The question brought a smile of admission to Roger's lips. "How can you tell?"

"You do not sound British," the women agreed. "We want to travel to America next year. Are you from California or New York?"

184

"Colorado," Eric corrected them. "Do you intend to visit California if you go to the U.S.?"

"We have heard so much about California," the second one said. "It sounds like an interesting place. New York, too."

Roger hesitantly stuck his fork into the fried rice. He hated to eat in front of the women, but he noticed they were passing a bag of grapes among themselves. "What part of France do you come from? Maybe I should start with, are you from France?"

"We are from Dijon, in the department Côte-d'Or," the first one said. "It's not as big as London or Paris, but we like it that way." She pronounced Paris the French way, *pa-wee*. Both Roger and Eric noticed it, and glanced at each other ever so briefly.

"The heart of the Burgundy region," Eric observed. "Are you sure you want to see California? It has famous wine regions, too, but it also has more people than you can shake a stick at in some places."

"*L'autobus vient!*" the third Frenchwoman said. She evidently did not speak any English.

Just then, a bus approached. The women picked up their suitcases, wished the Americans a safe and pleasant journey, and boarded the bus when it stopped at the waiting area. They bade the women *bon voyage*, and waved them good-bye as the bus departed.

"Talk about bad timing!" Roger feigned disgust.

"Typical of our luck, I'd say," Eric agreed.

"I was just about to ask them to come with us."

"To a youth hostel? And what about a certain commitment you made recently? You're not supposed to have roving eyes."

"You always have to complicate a perfectly good fantasy with petty details, Chief. What's wrong with you, anyway?"

They finished their grub and discarded their rubbish in a trashcan. Eric donned his helmet in preparation to leave, turned abruptly, and banged his head against the corner of a highway sign resoundingly. He was not hurt, but he was reminded once again of the importance of wearing a helmet, even though he was not actually riding. He thanked his lucky stars for his helmet, and mounted his bicycle. The hostel at Hindhead awaited him and Roger.

Traffic was dense throughout the afternoon, but they did not mind at all the chance to see a number of uncommon automobiles. Many of the cars were Japanese or made by European affiliates of the U.S. manufacturers, but a few were of the sleek, European sports car variety that would be considered high status among Americans. These fancy sports cars were often notorious gasoline consumers, but they certainly looked impressive, and they were definitely chick magnets. They diverted a greater-than-usual share of their attention toward the cars.

185

Eric felt good to be pedaling again, and the warm sunshine made it that much better. He noticed Roger was more agreeable, too, while riding. He found a comfortable gear for the flatlands, and settled into it. He led some of the time, and traded places with Roger frequently. They passed a few other cyclists in both directions. Riding was fairly mundane because Eric did so much of it, but it was what kept him alive. It was his *raison d'être*.

Hindhead Youth Hostel lay at the end of a steep, unkempt and generally treacherous road off the A3, sheltered from the highway by dense trees and foliage. They found it in the late afternoon without too much trouble. The building reminded them a little of the Broadmeadows hostel in Scotland, because it was rustic and secluded. They held their lower handlebars tightly as they negotiated the driveway.

A small building designated as a National Trust cottage, the hostel had plenty of unoccupied beds. The other guests were all about the same age as Eric and Roger, and all seemed very friendly. A staircase leading to the dormitory was steep and narrow, and the log joists in the dining room ceiling were dangerously low. Roger was just short enough to walk safely beneath all the joists, but taller Eric hit his head against one, this time without the protection of his helmet. He was not seriously injured, but from then on he was much more cautious in the dining room.

They registered for the night, staked their claim to one bed each and deposited their gear. They ventured down Portsmouth Road into the town of Hindhead. The town lay in a geographical area known as The Devil's Punchbowl, faintly reminiscent of the verdant rolling hills of rural Appalachia.

Hindhead, Surrey, with all its citizens, looked like any of a hundred other British towns they had already seen. Small towns in the U.K., like those in the U.S. and probably everywhere else in the world, all seemed terribly conventional to them. They did not expect any future prime ministers, football heroes or youth idols to emerge from Hindhead. Big-city life had become the norm for both of them, and they knew they had become prejudiced toward small towns.

"Do you feel any better now that we're back on the road?"

They had just returned to the hostel after an evening meal in the town.

"You know how I think. Ride to live, and live to ride!" Eric once thought it very original, until he read it on the back of a motorcyclist's T-shirt. He liked the phrase regardless. "It's great to be on the road again. I just wish we could have found a hostel with higher ceilings."

"Have you considered walking on your knees in here?" Roger teased. "I suppose everyone would understand and even empathize if you wore your helmet inside. It saved you once today. That's what helmets are for."

"Damn short people! The little bastards who built this place probably thought they were the only ones who'd be using it. I'm not unusually tall. I'm only slightly taller than the average adult male in the U.S."

"We're not in the U.S.," Roger said. "Get a crewcut and walk barefoot. Every little bit helps."

"Put a lid on it, will you?" Eric ended the discussion.

They drank tea with some other guests in the common room. Roger studied a road map while Eric wrote in his journal. Eric remarked in his writing about how happy he was to be on the move after three days of stagnation, and that he and Roger were on better terms with each other than they had been since Scotland.

"Where do you want to go tomorrow, Squire?"

Roger noted Eric's now-cheerful tone. "How does Salisbury, Wiltshire, sound? We can visit Stonehenge on the way there."

"Stonehenge? I've been wanting to see that," Eric said. "We'll do a little sun-worshipping tomorrow, if it's all the same to you."

"It's all the same to me. Isn't that what cyclists do everyday?"

"Maybe we'll meet some sun worshipers there."

"Maybe, but what if they ask what our signs are?" Roger asked. "How do you make conversation with someone who believes in astrology?"

"Maybe the sun worshipers know what eternal truth is, and we're the ones who believe in a lot of nonsense," Eric said.

"No sun worshipers were there today, and it is an interesting place to see," a dark-haired woman said with a German-sounding accent. She was sitting nearby and had been reading a paperback book. They had not really noticed her until she spoke to them, and they assumed she had registered at the hostel while they were in the town. She had that flower-girl appearance, sort of a latter-day hippie. She was not unlike Eric and Roger themselves, in some ways.

"We're being facetious about the sun worshipers," Roger said. "But we do intend to visit Stonehenge tomorrow. You sound like you recommend it."

"Yes, I do," the woman said, "but it defies description. You have to see it for yourself."

"I'm looking forward to it. Was it crowded?"

"Yes, but don't let that stop you. I was able to see everything I wanted to see. The crowd was not that bad. I did not have to wait in a queue."

"Are you from Germany, or Austria?" Eric asked. "You don't sound very Irish or Australian."

She smiled at the suggestion. "I hope I sound Swiss. I'm from Bern, the capital of Switzerland. Are you Americans? You don't sound very Irish or Australian, either."

"Both from Colorado, in the southwestern United States, but Eric goes to college in the Northwest."

"Is this your first time in Europe?"

"First time in Europe," Roger said.

"First time anywhere out of North America," Eric added.

"It must be very exciting for you then. I hope you enjoy your stay here. I've heard of Colorado."

Eric and Roger wound down the evening discussing Europe with the Swiss woman and managed to get into their beds without any further injuries to Eric. They were both in good spirits, and eager to get to Salisbury Plain in Wiltshire County.

"I'll let you sleep on the bottom bunk tonight," Roger said, "in case you fall out of bed."

"Thanks, you're a pal."

"Then again, you'd better sleep in the top bunk, in case you sit up suddenly in the dark."

"I can't win! I'll just have to take my chances, or else sleep with my helmet on." Eric slept without his helmet, and he survived the night.

29.

A svelte young woman looked up from the book she was reading, and gazed upon the Pacific Ocean. She had missed the tree-covered volcanoes rising out of the tropical sea, the open-air Lanai porches and the always casually dressed people of her island homeland, after three years of college on the mainland. Marianne was spending the weekend with a high school friend at a resort on the southern coast of Maui, one of the Hawaiian Islands. Jenny, her best friend since kindergarten, had gone for some refreshments. Marianne looked relaxed, sprawled in a chaise longue under a shady parasol, but she was very tense inside.

Marianne looked fabulous in her yellow bikini, and many heads turned in her presence. The traditional flower that she wore above her right ear accentuated her long, straight black hair. She stayed out of the midday sun, even though she tanned easily. She did not want her skin to age prematurely, like so many of the islanders who worked outdoors. She had always lived a privileged life, and had never considered it a disadvantage, until perhaps now.

Roger Schmidt, her fiancé, was very much on her mind. Was getting engaged to him the right thing to do? She thought so, but not everyone around her did. His head was squarely on his shoulders, she was sure of that. He was not the best-looking boy she had ever dated, nor was he the most stylish, the most charming, the most athletic or the most ambitious. He was certainly not the wealthiest. He had elements of all those qualities, certainly enough of each and not too much of any of them. He had no glaring weaknesses or shortcomings she could think of. He had more self-confidence than anyone she had ever known. Most important, he seemed sincere, without any airs. She was aware of his reputation as a ladies' man and his lust for adventure, but she had found no skeletons in his closet. With Roger, what she saw was what she got. Her immediate family members had hinted of disapproval, regardless of his many fine qualities.

Jenny returned with a mai tai in each hand. She handed one of the tall glasses to Marianne, who immediately removed the silly little paper umbrella that adorned the cocktail. Jenny parked herself in the chaise longue next to Marianne's. The large parasol was between them so that it shaded both chairs.

"Cheers," offered Jenny. She raised her glass, then took a sip. "I'm delighted to have you back home. I've missed you. It's not the same around here without you."

Marianne raised her glass and smiled at her best friend. She wondered why, as she sipped the mai tai, the bartenders at the resorts were so cheap with the rum and flavorings. The cocktail was mostly ice. "I've missed you, too. I've missed a lot of things these past three years."

"Don't be sad. You'll graduate in a year or two, and things will work out with Roger." Jenny used the umbrella to swirl the drink. "I've been looking forward to this outing for nearly a year. I didn't think I'd see you at all when you said you'd be working in Denver during the summer."

"I'm not sad to be here, but I am sorry that I ever introduced my sister-in-law to Roger. I don't know what she told my brother and my parents about him, but I'm sure she had an opinion. She always knows what's best for me."

"I thought you said she liked him. She does, doesn't she?"

"She liked him, but that doesn't mean she thinks I should get married to him. I think she told my family that he's too...I don't know...too cerebral, too conservative, too practical, too opinionated, something."

"Too earthy?"

"Probably. Engineering majors all tend to be rough around the edges, and Roger's no exception. He does have better social graces than most of them. He showed me a photo from his high school prom. Even in a tuxedo, he's handsome but hardly elegant."

"What did his date look like?"

"A gorgeous blonde cheerleader, with fancy hair and fingernails. He says he hasn't had any contact with her since he started college. It's a good thing, too, because I'd hate to have to compete with someone who looks that good. How did he put it? She's built like a brick shithouse. I have to wonder how he describes me to his friends."

"Maybe your brother's wife was put off by his colorful descriptions of prom dates."

"No, because she can be pretty crude herself, although never in front of my parents. She made a big deal of the fact that he doesn't play golf, he's never tasted sushi, doesn't carry an iPhone, or any cell phone for that matter, and he's never been on a cruise."

"How can he live without a cell phone? I'd feel completely naked without mine!"

"Me, too. He said he could afford a cell phone or a trip to Europe, but not both. He's trying to make it through college without getting into debt, and as far as I know, he's succeeding."

"Even with a trip to Europe? That can't be cheap."

"He and his friend Eric found the cheapest flights, and they're traveling by bicycle with camping equipment. I could never do something like that, but Roger lives for it. He says Eric does, too. They've done bicycle tours like this before."

"So Roger's squarely middle-class! Does she really have a big problem with that? She can't be that shallow!"

"Mostly, she's still mad that I don't want anything to do with her cousin."

"Whatever happened with him?"

"I found out he's a father! He got some girl pregnant, then dumped her shortly before she gave birth. He's a party animal, and he tries to live up to that reputation. He gives her a few bucks when he's sober and has some spare change, but he couldn't care less about her or the baby. He sheepishly admitted it after I found out about her, but he wasn't even sure of his son's name! I've outgrown people like that. Roger has his wild side, but he would never be that irresponsible."

"What do your parents think about him?"

"They won't say exactly. They seem to think I'm too young, too immature. I'm still their little girl. I quit the bank in Denver when they insisted I come home and discuss my future with them. In a way, I wanted to come home, but I don't need them to tell me when I'm ready for marriage." Marianne sipped her cocktail. The slush and the alcohol eased her tension, if only momentarily. "I have to wonder, though, how well Roger would fit in here. He's his own man. He wouldn't stand for my parents telling him how he should live his life."

"So quit giving Roger the run-around, girl! Either marry him and stay on the mainland, or give him his freedom. He sounds like a pretty good catch to me."

Marianne let that remark sink in a moment before she responded. "He is a pretty good catch, but I'm not sure I want to stay on the mainland. My best friends are here. I belong in a tropical climate, especially in the wintertime. Maybe I am still their little girl. Or maybe not."

The cell phone in Marianne's handbag rang, but it was within Jenny's reach and she answered it. She muted the mouthpiece before she handed the phone to Marianne. "It's one of your roommates. She sounds like she's nursing one hell of a hangover."

"*Mahalo*," Marianne said to Jenny. Her roommates would not call her unless it was something critical. She spoke for a few minutes while Jenny went for beverage refills.

"Roger's been trying to call me from Europe. My sorority sister pretended she didn't know where I am, but he didn't seem to buy it. He knows something is wrong."

"What are you going to do?"

"The shit is really going to hit the fan when we get back to Honolulu tomorrow. Either I tell my parents I got engaged, or else I let Roger know I'm having second thoughts."

30.

The night treated Eric gently, but he awoke with a headache anyway. Even breakfast with the Swiss woman could not alleviate his discomfort, but it helped. She seemed to know a lot about Stonehenge, European history and some other subjects that were of interest to the two Americans. Eric was impressed by how easily she engaged him in conversation, even though English was not even her mother tongue. They checked out of the hostel after breakfast, booked beds at the Salisbury Youth Hostel, and rode down the A3 toward Grayshot.

Eric and Roger inhaled their second breakfast of the day, pastries from a bakery in Grayshot. The excitement of the ride, and the proper medicament, made Eric forget his headache. The pastries and warm weather helped, too. They took the B3002 and B3004 toward Alton. They encountered some gently rolling hills, but nothing like the moors in Yorkshire and Scotland.

In Alton, Hampshire, Roger noticed an Aston-Martin car dealership. It prompted a closer examination on his and Eric's part. Aston-Martins were rare automobiles in North America, and not at all abundant in the U.K. The price tags, in only a few words, clearly explained why these cars were rare. They had also read that Aston-Martins, their sporty appearance aside, were not known to make the most of a tank of precious gasoline.

Eric peered through the showroom window. "Do you think the salesman would laugh at us if we asked for a test drive?"

"I can't imagine a dealer letting anyone test drive these babies. Still, it might be worth a try."

"I bet some women would notice us if we cruised around town in one of those cars. Maybe we can find a sympathetic salesman who'd let us borrow it for a few hours."

"I've never asked for a Lexus or even a BMW," Roger mused. "Is an Aston-Martin too much to wish for?"

"Someday you can trade your Chevy up for an Aston," Eric said.

"Let's forget about Aston-Martins and discuss something we can afford."

"That'll be a very brief discussion."

They rode from Alton along the A31 to Winchester, the seat of Hampshire County. With 89,000 citizens calling it home, Winchester was famous for many things, but mostly for its cathedral. They both noted that they had been in York and Hampshire, but never in New York or New Hampshire.

To Roger and Eric, Winchester Cathedral looked very much like Saint Paul's Cathedral and York Minster, although Winchester was older than the other two. Regardless of its familiarity, the old church was not uninteresting, and they admired it on its own merits. They paid homage to the tomb of King William II, son of William the Conqueror, who was killed in a hunting mishap and succeeded by his younger brother Henry in A.D. 1100.

The afternoon was warm and sunny as they left Winchester for Stockbridge on the B3049. They stopped in Stockbridge long enough for a banana and a bottle of apple juice. West of Stockbridge, they turned northwest onto the B3084 and bypassed a town with the unlikely name of Middle Wallop. Near the county line, they entered the busy A303 and rode west toward Amesbury. They rode shirtless into Wiltshire County, and traversed the Salisbury Plain in the late afternoon in their higher gears. The plain consisted mostly of rolling hills covered by short grass. Trees were remarkably sparse, even though the English Channel and Avon River were not far away. Only one thing on the prairie was conspicuous.

When they reached the crest of one particular hill, they could see an ominous edifice a few kilometers across the plain. As they approached the edifice, they accelerated until they were standing in their pedals and their panniers were swinging wildly with each pedal stroke. The crowd of tourists gawking at the monument became obvious. The portentous structure was none other than Stonehenge.

Throughout its approximately 4000-year history, Stonehenge had been many things to many different people. It was one of England's oldest and most popular tourist attractions, and possibly the world's most famous sundial. To the ancients who built it, known as the Wessex People and the Beaker People, it was probably a temple for sun worshipers, as it was for the modern-day Druids. To British conservationists, it was a rapidly deteriorating monument that needed preservation, if the fence around it meant anything.

They slowed their sprint when they came to the visitors' parking lot at 17:00, and parked their bicycles there. They donned walking shoes, paid their admission, and walked through the tunnel beneath the highway to see the megaliths.

A scale model of Stonehenge lay on an outdoor display before the genuine article. Fences prevented visitors from wearing down the shallow, concentric circular trenches around the stones and the stones themselves. The purpose of the trenches was a mystery, but not nearly as mysterious as how the huge stones were transported from a quarry to their present site on the plain by people who did not have cranes, trains, dump trucks or even forklifts.

Eric was preparing to take some photographs. "If you believe any of that speculation about ancient astronauts, this might be a good place to launch an investigation."

"I suppose that could be one explanation of how the rocks got here, and why they're here." Roger pulled out his own camera. "Then again, it's possible that people put a little more elbow grease into their labor back then than we do now."

They walked around Stonehenge, taking pictures at various angles and trying to imagine what the ancients did while practicing whatever rituals they practiced. A smaller version would have made an excellent playground for children of any era, but the builders of Stonehenge apparently had never considered the idea.

Eric took a picture of Roger in front of the monument with Roger's camera. "There's a replica of this in south-central Washington, overlooking the Columbia River. I stopped there once on my way to Seattle."

"Are the stones knocked down?"

"No, everything's intact. You can climb on it, too. But it's not quite as awesome as the real thing. Already, I'm picking up vibes from outer space. That didn't happen to me at the other Stonehenge."

"Me, too. I can feel the love!"

As Eric and Roger went back toward the visitor center to purchase some literature, they were approached by some women who identified themselves as representatives of the Ministry of the Environment, or some such government agency. The women requested their opinions of the fences around the monument. Several other tourists were being interviewed by other members of the agency. Eric and Roger were more than happy to cooperate. The interviews lasted about five minutes. The women thanked them for their cooperation, and moved on to query some other tourists. The two Americans were proud of themselves for having their opinions sought by the British government.

They rode back toward Amesbury, passing some other cyclists in the opposite direction, and turned south toward Salisbury via the A345. Having seen a number of hikers and other cyclists throughout the day, they expected the hostel in Salisbury to be crowded. The other adventurers must have been destined elsewhere, as it turned out, for a few beds were still available at the 200-year-old Salisbury Youth Hostel on Milford Hill.

Having secured their beds in the hostel, they unloaded their gear and rode into the city for groceries. They bought peaches, macaroni and marinara sauce for their evening meal, and yogurt, Weetabix and oranges for breakfast. Back at the hostel, they locked their bicycles in the bicycle garage for the night. They ate the peaches as an appetizer, and they were famished by the time the noodles and sauce were ready.

"We should've made Salisbury steak tonight," Roger said while he stirred the macaroni and boiling water on the stove. "I assume that's the specialty in this town."

"I forgot to bring the recipé. Not that I'd want to make it even if I did have the recipé."

Another guest in the kitchen was standing at the stove between the two Americans, cooking his meal. "Actually, Salisbury steak was named for a nineteenth-century physician from your country, if I'm not mistaken. You wouldn't necessarily find it on the menu at any of the local restaurants."

"You learn something every day here."

"The good doctor considered his creation an early version of health food, so they say. I think it's just ground beef with onions and gravy."

"Steak as health food? Imagine that!"

After supper, they gave themselves a walking tour of the Salisbury city centre, even though most of the stores were closed. The town of 36,000 people was clean and attractive, but its lack of after-hours activities did not surprise them. They stopped at the one store that was still open, a liquor store, and purchased nightcaps and chocolate bars for themselves. They drank the ale as they walked back to the hostel.

"I liked Stonehenge," Roger said. "Our Swiss friend was right. It was well worth our time. What did she say her name is?"

"She didn't say, or else I didn't catch it. I don't think I introduced myself, either."

"We'll have to plan on spending some time in Switzerland next time we're in Europe. She made it sound interesting, although I already knew that."

"Next time, Squire, could be when we're senior citizens on a chartered bus tour."

"I hope we meet more people like her."

31.

Eric pulled on his shirt shortly after 7:00. "You look haggard this fine morning." He stood next to Roger, who was sitting on his bunk.

Roger put on his socks and shoes. He always wore white cotton sox, except when he was wearing a coat and tie, which was rare. "You look like hell yourself. But then, you usually do first thing in the morning."

"That guy snored most of the night." Eric pointed to an empty bunk next to theirs. "He was the first one dressed and out of here this morning. I shook him once during the night, but he fired up the sawmill just five or ten minutes later."

"Somebody has to uphold the hostel tradition of nocturnal dissonance."

"I saw the lumberjack when I was brushing my teeth last night before bed, and I said to myself, that man will snore. He was even louder than I'd anticipated."

On their way out of Salisbury, they stopped at a small museum. They found and purchased some additional literature concerning Stonehenge and related archaeological findings in the Wiltshire area at the museum.

Eric skimmed through a pamphlet on Stonehenge. "If Wessex is named for the western Saxons, Essex for the eastern Saxons, Middlesex for the central Saxons and Sussex for the southern Saxons, does that mean the northern Saxons lived in a county called No-sex?"

"That's where all the monasteries were."

Roger and Eric had decided the previous evening, upon scrutinizing their map and the youth hostel guidebook, their next destination would be Bath, Avon. The guidebook described the hostel there as superior grade, whatever that meant. The guidebook also mentioned a wealth of Roman ruins in Bath, well worth visiting. They booked beds in Bath before they left Salisbury.

Following the A36 and the Wylye River northwestward, they stopped in Warminster for lunch after a few hours of riding at a moderate pace. The highway and weather were both quite agreeable to the cyclists. Roger rubbed his sore right knee during lunch. That knee had been bothering him since they left London, but it was nothing serious. The strength of his grip in both hands was diminished, too, but he expected that from leaning on his handlebars for hours at a time, day after day. Eric had also mentioned the loss of grip strength and how it affected his ability to hold and use a pencil.

They arrived in Bath in the early afternoon, in Somerset County. The city of 84,000 residents appeared to be in the center and on the sides of a large basin. All the roads they could see went down steep hills into the city toward the Avon River. They zoomed down one such road to a picturesque covered bridge across the river.

Several small stores lined the roadway over the gray stone bridge. They changed into their pedestrian shoes, and walked their bicycles across the bridge amid numerous pedestrians. They browsed through a few of the stores, then continued on to the other side of the river. They had never seen a bridge like this one.

A park enclosed by a fence awaited them on the opposite riverbank. They paid the nominal admission, entered the park and settled into some lawn chairs next to the concrete retainer wall and wrought iron fence along the river. A number of other people were relaxing in lawn chairs about the park doing essentially the same thing Roger and Eric were doing—watching people and conversing about nothing in particular.

Roger took out his camera and snapped some photographs of the park, the people, the river, the stone bridges and the gray stone buildings that seemed to be so characteristic of the United Kingdom. While focusing his lens on Eric's not-too-photogenic smile, he noticed Eric's and his appearances had declined in just four weeks, and how little either one cared anymore. Their beards were no longer neatly trimmed, hair not combed, clothes wrinkled. Life away from the conveniences of their modern American homes was showing its effects on them, but they did not feel like they were really suffering any.

Eric noticed a young mother with a small child on a blanket nearby. The shapely woman wore a mini skirt and a tight knit tank top. "Now that's what I'd call a Somerset mom!" He made a subtle gesture in her direction.

"She's the razor's edge of human bummage. Did I say bummage? I meant bondage."

They left the park in search of the hostel. They found the street of the hostel's address, but the hostel was near the top of a long hill that stood before them. Roger told Eric to ride ahead of him, while Roger rode more slowly up Bathwick Hill on account of his sore knee.

When Roger arrived at the hostel a few minutes after Eric, Eric had already registered the two of them and claimed a bunk. The hostel, an Italianate mansion, was quite a popular place in Bath, and most of its space had been reserved. They were glad to be there on a Tuesday rather than a weekend. They stowed their gear on their bunks in a men's dormitory and locked their bicycles away for the day. They were starved, but they also wanted to see the Roman bath ruins for which the town was named.

They were walking down the front sidewalk of the hostel when they encountered a familiar face. The Swiss woman they had spoken to at the Hindhead hostel two days earlier was on her way into the hostel, carrying a backpack.

"Hello, Americans!" The woman flashed an alluring smile that Roger had not noticed before, and a forthright manner that impressed Eric.

Roger was pleased to see her. "We were talking about you last night, but we didn't expect to see you again. We liked Stonehenge. It's quite a monument, or sundial, or whatever it is."

The Swiss woman grinned, seemingly flattered that they remembered her so well. "I have been reading a book about Stonehenge. A British archeologist wrote her dissertation about it, and the book is based on her research. Quite fascinating!"

"I'll bet it is." Roger already liked her for her scholarly ways.

"I think the hostel is full already, unless you booked a bed." Eric hoped she did have a reservation.

"I do. I'd been told the Bath hostel would probably be crowded."

"We're on our way into the town for some supper," Roger said. "Would you care to join us, if you don't have any plans?"

"We'll probably find a fish bar, just for the halibut."

She inspected them carefully for a moment, sizing them up. "If you can allow me a few minutes to register and find a bed, I would be delighted to join you."

They sat on the lawn, wearing jeans and T-shirts, while they waited for her. She returned some five minutes later. They noticed that she wore little makeup, and she did not carry a purse, only a small leather satchel hanging from her neck.

"My name is Schmidt, Roger Schmidt."

"Eric Fernandez." The three started walking down the hill toward the business district.

"I'm Yvette Hoffman. Call me Yvette."

"Yvette is a lovely name. Fits her perfectly, don't you think, Chief?"

"Yes it does. A French-sounding first name, a German surname, and you're from Bern. Is Bern in the French- or German-speaking region of Switzerland?"

"Bern is in the German region. My mother is of French extraction, from Geneva, and my father, German. That's why my name is as it is. We are an unusual family, in that the French and German speakers in Switzerland live in harmony but don't mix too much. You both have English-sounding first names, but a German and a Spanish surname."

"I never thought of it that way," Roger said. "I always thought we had American first and last names."

197

"Some of my great-grandparents were born in New Mexico territory, before it became a state," Eric said. "My clan became Americans by annexation. Not that I'm complaining."

"My great-greats became Americans by virtue of sea sickness, indentured servitude, tuberculosis, the Franco-Prussian War and stuff like that," Roger said. "I'm not complaining, either."

"Tell me more about your travels." Yvette walked between the two Americans. "I want to know how Europe looks to Americans."

Eric and Roger had plenty of adventures and misadventures to tell Yvette. She was surprised that they could get as lost and disoriented as they had at times in another English-speaking country. They stopped at a fish bar for supper, something to which Yvette had also become quite accustomed. Roger and Eric were low on cash, and the cashier would not accept a traveler's cheque. They had offered to treat Yvette, but she ended up lending them enough cash to pay for the meal.

"I knew there had to be some reason fate brought us together." Roger wanted to divert the embarrassment. "It would be nice if some of these merchants would realize that our traveler's cheques are worth just as much as cash. I really hate to borrow money."

"We Swiss are famous for our banks, you know. It's only natural for us to lend."

They carried their supper to a bench on the sidewalk outside the fish bar and sat down to eat. Yvette thought Eric peculiar for wanting to put steak sauce on fried fish, in addition to the usual malt vinegar. It was the sort of thing only an American would do.

"Tell us about your journey so far," Eric said.

"I've been traveling around Europe most of this summer, and I've even been in northern Africa. I recently graduated from university in Zurich, and I'm celebrating by taking an extended holiday."

"Almost sounds like what we're doing," Eric said, "except we haven't graduated yet."

"What subject did you study?" Roger asked.

"Pharmacy and chemistry. I will return to Switzerland at the end of this summer to begin work, but it's such a small country. There's a very big world out there, and I've seen so little of it. I'm trying to take in all I can in just three months."

"We're trying to absorb as much as we can in only six weeks." Roger also poured HP sauce on his fish. "We're concentrating on Great Britain, because we have friends in London who invited us here. He was going to ride with us, but he had to change his plans on short notice."

"We might cross the channel before we return home," Eric added, "but most of the rest of Europe will have to wait until some other time for us."

"I've been in England for about a week now," Yvette said. "I will be meeting someone in Oxford on Friday, and then we will travel more in England and Wales. Where are you going from here?"

"We haven't decided that yet. I haven't, anyway. Have you given any thought to it yet, Chief?"

"You know I never make plans that far in advance, Squire. Just like Rick in *Casablanca*. Let's look at a map when we get back to the hostel."

They finished their fish and chips and wandered around the business district for a while. They were in no hurry to go anywhere, just enjoying each other's company. At a pub, they sat down at an outdoor table for a round of cocktails.

"What may I bring you this evening?" a waiter asked.

"How about a round of pine floats?"

"Sir?"

"Never mind," Eric said. "Yvette, what would you like?"

"Gin and tonic for me. I'm told this nation is famous for its gin."

"Ale for me," Eric said. "I'm not worried about catching malaria here."

"Lager, please," Roger said. "He can't hold his pine floats very well."

"Just what is a pine float?" Yvette asked after the waiter had gone. "Is that some kind of American cocktail?"

"Could be." Eric smiled. "A pine float is a glass of water with a toothpick in it. You could say it's a cocktail for teetotalers."

"Or cheapskates."

The waiter returned a few minutes later with three beverages. Yvette paid him, and he left. "Cheers." She lifted her glass. She added something in German that was unfamiliar to Roger or Eric.

"*Slainte mhath.* I learned that from a Scottish friend." Roger was proud of himself for remembering it.

"*Salud,*" Eric said. He had no idea what Roger had just said.

They finished their beverages and left the pub, still deep in conversation. They decided to investigate the city's eponym, the Roman bathhouse ruins. The museum that enclosed the excavated ruins was several blocks away, but they had plenty to discuss along the way.

The Roman bath museum proved to be an early forerunner of the modern-day country club. Nude Romans undoubtedly had a grand time frolicking in the heated stone pool. The place looked like an ideal setting for an afternoon orgy. They tasted the mineral water from a fountain that had supplied the baths for centuries. The salty flavor of the spring water made them appreciate municipal water, and especially bottled water, that much more. They spent an hour or more looking at the baths and other Roman artifacts in the museum, then walked back to the hostel.

The town was pleasantly quiet and the sky dimly illuminated by twilight when they returned to the hostel. As the evening turned into night, they still had plenty to talk and laugh about, even as they grew tired from a long day. They drank tea in the common room at the hostel, and planned the following day's schedule.

"Minehead looks good to me." Roger concluded a discussion of where he and Eric were destined in the morning. "Where are you going tomorrow, Yvette, or are you staying here another night?"

"Wherever my rail pass and my hitchhiking thumb take me. Perhaps I will see you again, if you're staying in a hostel somewhere."

"You're certainly welcome to join us in Minehead."

Yvette had become quite attractive to both Roger and Eric, but neither said anything to that effect to the other. They both fell asleep thinking about her, and she about them.

32.

Eric slept better and felt better in his head than he had for ages, and he arose from his bed more easily than usual. Roger must have had the same impulse, because he still managed to get dressed and be ready for breakfast before Eric. Roger and Yvette were drinking tea in the common room and conversing when Eric arrived. They had a cup of tea waiting for him.

"Did you sleep well?" Yvette asked Eric.

"Yes, quite well." Eric had a satisfied look. A pleasant voice like hers was just what he needed to hear so early in the morning. "Possibly the best I've ever slept in a sheet sleeping bag."

"Won't you be using one when you get back home?" Yvette teased.

Eric sipped his tea. "I'd be more comfortable sleeping in a gunny sack, I think."

They made toast from some wheat bread and marmalade that another guest donated to them, which they washed down with a second cup of tea. They threw their sheet sleeping bags in the laundry bin, packed their gear, and prepared for departure.

"Meet us at the hostel in Minehead, if you get a wild hare," Roger said to Yvette in the front yard of the hostel.

Yvette did not respond verbally to the invitation, but she was considering it. "Have a safe and pleasant journey." She studied Eric intently as she spoke.

"You, too." Eric looked at her for a long moment. "Goodbye."

Roger and Eric got on their bicycles and climbed slowly out of the steep-sided valley where Bath lay. They dropped into their lowest gears to get to the top, where they followed the A367 and B3139 to Glastonbury. Gray clouds threatened them all day, but no precipitation fell. Cool winds blew in every direction except the one in which they rode. The slightly inclement weather, combined with a late start, put them in Glastonbury, Somerset, in time for a delayed lunch.

They devoured a large lunch of various items they purchased at a grocery store in Glastonbury, with plenty of carbohydrates to replenish their internal supply. A low-carb meal was simply out of the question for them. Their pace had been slow and relaxed, but they intended to be in Minehead before 17:00, when the hostel was due to open.

From Glastonbury, they rode the A39 through Bridgwater toward Bridgwater Bay. As Minehead was on the coast, they expected to ride downhill more than uphill, although the wind made them feel as if they had been climbing all day. They seldom used their higher gears, and their bodies were kinked from being in climbing position much of the day. They mostly rode with their hands on the horizontal crossbar, rather than on the brake hoods or the drops. Roger's knee was still sore, but he was not especially concerned about it.

A glimpse of the Bristol Channel just prior to the hostel set the mood for them that evening. Instantly, they liked the setting of the hostel and the town. The surprisingly strenuous ride from Bath was easily justified by what lay at the end of it.

The hostel was as isolated in the forest and as difficult to get to as the hostels of Hindhead and Selkirk. Roger and Eric were there by 18:00, a little later than they expected, but the hostel had plenty of unoccupied beds. Bunks in the men's dormitory were separated by partitions, and each man got his own bunk.

Famished as usual, they rode down Brook Street into town in search of an evening meal, expecting to find a fish bar somewhere. Minehead, Somerset, and its 8300 residents were situated on the edge of Exmoor National Park. Dunkery Beacon, one of several significant hills on the peninsula, lay just south of the town. They had overindulged in fish and chips, but they doubted they would find any alternatives in this coastal town.

After repaying Yvette and buying supper, they were low on cash again. They pondered the idea briefly while eating the usual, then turned their attentions toward the natural splendor surrounding Minehead. They were considering staying another night.

"I feel like I've gained a stone since we left home," Eric said. "Do I look heavier?"

"Not really. It's probably just an erection. Give it time. It'll go away."

"I don't believe that."

"I read it in *Engineers' Day*. Honest! It's a technical journal for engineering students."

"I don't believe that, either." Eric changed the subject. "Too bad we don't have enough time to ride out to Land's End. I'd like to see some of the more isolated places."

"What about the Isles of Scilly, or the Channel Islands? You can't get much more isolated that that."

"Probably costs a small fortune to get to those islands from here. We weren't too far from the Isle of Wight a few days ago. That shouldn't be too expensive, and it's big enough to accommodate our bicycles."

"If we had about a year and several thousand pounds to spend we could see just about everything. But we don't, so forget it."

"Would you get all bent out of shape if I suggested that we pass through Wales on our way back to London?" Eric asked.

"Not likely," Roger said. "Try me."

"How about it then?"

"Fine, just great. But Cornwall is out of the question. Besides, I don't even like Cornish hens."

"Might be a nice change from fish and chips. Then again, there might not even be any Cornish hens there."

"Are there any whales in Wales?"

"I don't know. Let's go there and find out."

They finished their supper and wandered around the town until they came upon a pub, where they each drank a glass of lager for dessert.

"Do you think Yvette will be waiting for us back at the hostel?" Eric's interest was genuine. He missed Nancy in a way, but Yvette was a world apart from Nancy.

"You're really falling for her, aren't you?" Roger knew more than he was telling.

"I don't know," Eric shrugged. "I liked her company, and I think she enjoyed ours."

"I certainly liked having her around, but I haven't figured her out. She's a little vague when she talks about her plans."

"She said she's going to meet someone in Oxford later this week. Friend? Boyfriend? Fiancé? She didn't say. Maybe we'll find out if we see her this evening."

"I guess we didn't tell her all that much about ourselves, either," Roger said, "so why should she tell us anything? If I were her, I probably wouldn't be too quick to divulge that kind of information to two acquaintances."

"Why do you say that?" Eric asked. "We aren't that suspicious-looking, are we? I've always thought of us as WYSIWYG types."

Roger stroked his bearded chin. He did that often, usually without even realizing it. "A few years ago, I think it was when we were sophomores in high school, I had a thing about Mandy Perez, and she had a thing about me, or so I thought at the time."

"I remember her. Good looking girl. Gorgeous, even. Very bright, too."

"Yes, she was all that. Anyway, I must have had the silly idea that I would be more appealing to her if I revealed my inner self, my softer side. Spilling your guts was in vogue at the time, so I told her a lot of things about me that I later wished I'd kept to myself. She told me some intimate things about herself, too."

"I don't remember you going steady with her."

"No, I didn't, and that's my point." Roger gestured with his beer glass, as if to punctuate his words. "Our romance never got off the ground, and I felt like a fool for telling her everything about me. I never repeated anything she told me and, thankfully, she apparently kept everything I told her to herself. I didn't incriminate myself, I just said some things that I wouldn't want repeated."

"I see what you mean."

"Nowadays, I try to be very cautious when I tell someone my life story. My fears, shortcomings, weaknesses, anything that can be used against me, is nobody's business but mine."

"You don't want to get nominated for Wimp of the Year," Eric said. "Maybe Yvette feels that same way. I'm still unsure of her interest in us."

"I'm not going to dwell on the subject," Roger said. "I like her, but you shouldn't assume you're in love with her and then be disappointed. Life's entirely too short for that. I've been there a few times, like with Mandy. You probably have, too."

"Too many times. I've often thought, if your heart hasn't been broken at least five times before you finish high school, you've led a very sheltered life and you need to get out more."

"Mine was broken five times before the end of our freshman year! To be fair, we've probably broken a few hearts ourselves. Like that girl in our calculus class, Sonya Ivanovich-hyphen-something. You certainly broke her heart."

She was strange, kind of flaky. She made a big deal about being an activist for every cause under the sun. Her parents were radicals in the 1970s, and she was a chip off the old block. That's why she had two last names. I liked her hair. Blonde, curly and thick, and almost to her waist. But I wasn't much into politics back then."

"A bit extreme, I admit, but she wasn't bad looking. Especially that hair. Smart, too. Why did you give her the brush-off?"

"I could take the frequent conscience-raising sermons, but she crossed the line when she declared herself a militant ethnic activist of a certain stripe. She thought I should be one too, but she misread me. I didn't mince words when I told her I didn't want any part of it. She was hurt, but you can't say I gave her the run-around."

With that, Roger silently recalled something he had long admired in Eric. Eric was very patient, very tolerant, very thick-skinned in the presence of quarrelsome people, much more than Roger or any of their mutual friends. But even Eric had his limits, and whenever someone exceeded those limits, Eric made his displeasure abundantly clear. The water-closet melee in Harrogate was a stark example of what Eric could do when someone jerked his chain too hard.

"Actually, two of my worst enemies were members of that organization. I wouldn't have joined it even if I did agree with their dogma. Sonya only saw the idealism, not the underlying ugliness, the bullying. She fell out of favor herself, I heard later. Maybe she did see past the rhetoric, finally."

"She gave me grief once when I disagreed with her ultra-feminist viewpoint on some discussion in an English class," Roger recalled. "I jokingly told her she was suffering from penis envy. Poor choice of words! She wouldn't even make eye contact with me for a month after that. I guess we were both on her shit-list."

Eric added, "I did dance with her once, at one of the school dances. That was the only time I ever got to touch her hair. It felt as good as it looked."

They returned to the hostel in the dense, hardwood forest, and put their bicycles in a storage shed for the night. They went outside and sat in a grassy area behind the hostel where some other hostel guests had gathered to socialize. A large, black and white border collie lying in the grass caught their attention. The tag on her collar indicated her name was Vodka.

The dog, a permanent resident of the hostel, enjoyed all the attention everyone gave her. She used her paws to indicate that she wanted to continue to be rubbed. The two Americans were happy to accommodate her. She reminded them of how much they missed their own dogs.

"My friend Vodka," Eric said. "That'll be the title of my novel. But is it a story about a boy growing up with his dog, or the confessions of a lush?"

Yvette did not show up at the hostel, but Eric could not get her out of his mind. Her blue eyes, thick brown hair and smooth, fair skin stood out in his mind, even though she mostly eschewed cosmetic enhancement of her delicate features. Her lithe, slender figure suggested fitness, stamina and strength. He knew she was strong and durable to carry a backpack around Europe all summer long. He fell asleep thinking about her, just as he did the previous night, only more so. He expected she would be on his mind for many nights yet to come.

33.

A restful sleep did Roger and Eric well, but they did not sleep late enough to miss another fried breakfast. They were surprised that no one snored during the night. They were still thinking about Yvette during breakfast. They sat with a British family, among other hostel guests, and chose the continental breakfast.

"Spot of tea or cup-a-joe?" Eric offered Roger.

A girl of eight or so years sitting next to Roger observed. She sipped her tea very properly and held her fork with the convex side up.

"Pour me some java, just to be different," Roger said. "I've had enough tea to last me the next ten or fifteen minutes." Eric filled his and Roger's cups with coffee.

"That's not java," the girl said in a cockney accent. "It's called coffee."

Neither Eric nor Roger quite knew how to deal with inquisitive children. They looked at each other in surprise before they looked at the girl. The girl's family seemed oblivious to her.

"What makes you the big expert on coffee nomenclature?" Eric asked the girl.

"It's coffee. I know it is." The girl was very insistent.

"We're not from around here, little sister." Eric spoke to the girl in a very serious tone. "We don't speak the queen's English, but we do have more than one name for coffee. *¿Lo comprendes, señorita?*"

"You talk strangely," the girl said.

They were amused, but they maintained their serious expressions.

"Did you hear that, Lem?" Roger used a mock hayseed accent.

"I sure did, Seth. Can you imagine anyone sayin' somethin' like that about us?"

"This here, I say, this here younger generation thinks it knows everything about everything. Know what I mean?" Roger poked the table with his index finger for emphasis while he spoke.

"Yup. Truer words ain't never been said."

"I suppose you're from the big city somewhere, missy," Roger said to the girl.

"I'm from London," the girl said proudly.

"London? Hhmmmm." Eric feigned great confusion.

Roger said, "Hhmmmm," in unison with Eric, and stroked his beard as if deep in concentration.

"Where's London, Seth?"

"I think we passed through it awhile back, Lem. You know, that place with the funny buses that drive on the wrong side of the street."

Eric gave the girl a stern look. "Can you say, 'Hey, Heidi! Who has Hubert Humphrey's hula-hoop?'"

"You're most peculiar," said she.

"Let me try it. 'ey, 'oidi! 'oo 'as 'ubert 'umphrey's 'ula 'oop?" Roger volunteered. "'erbert 'oover, or 'erman's 'ermits?"

The conversation continued throughout breakfast. They wondered what kind of misconceptions the girl would have of American people, if she took them to be representative of the norm.

After breakfast, Eric and Roger registered for another night at the hostel, collected the items from their gear they would need for the day, and rode into Minehead. Their immediate goal was the nearest bank.

At the bank, Roger and Eric each cashed a fifty-pound traveler's cheque. The bank, like all the previous British banks they had been in, looked well fortified compared to American banks, with steel bars separating the tellers from the customers. The teller hardly glanced at their passports before handing them the cash, thus casting some doubt on the need for and authenticity of the security features. They felt a tinge of relief, finally having some real money in their wallets.

From Minehead, they rode west on the A39 to Porlock, where they turned southeast up a forested valley to Luccombe. At Luccombe, they turned south up a narrow, steep road toward Dunkery Beacon, the high point in Exmoor National Park. The climbing was taxing, but much easier without their full complement of touring gear. They worked up a good sweat on the climb. Atop the ridge, they left their bicycles at the parking area near Dunkery Gate and hiked to the barren 519-meter summit. They caught a glimpse of the sea between the clouds, and a trio of red deer on a distant moor.

Eric gazed at the sea and took in the view. "So this is what Lorna Doone saw, according to the literature at the hostel." He gestured toward Doone Valley to the northwest.

"That name showed up in the Sunday crossword puzzle I was doing on our flight, but I've never read the book. Haven't seen any of the movie versions, either. I'll have to add R.D. Blackmore to my reading list. Someday."

"We've seen the stomping grounds of several notable authors on this trek. Makes me wish I had more time to read just for pleasure."

"I wonder if Miss Doone liked shortbread cookies, or is that just another urban legend?"

The two Americans hiked back down to the bicycles. They resumed riding over the ridge to Wheddon Cross, where they had a fast descent down the A396 back to Minehead. They rode and walked around the town, looking in store windows and discussing nothing in particular. They were in the mood to watch people, but they saw few passersby. It did not surprise them. They bought some fruit and juice at a small market for a late lunch.

"Eric! Roger!" A voice called their names from more than half a block away.

They did not really expect to see Yvette again, but she found them. She looked very comely in tight jeans, showing just a hint of her shapely midriff.

"I was afraid I wouldn't find you again." Yvette was out of breath. "I saw you from a few blocks away when you came out of the fruiterer, and I ran to catch up with you. You don't mind my being here, do you?"

"Not at all!" Eric was delighted to see her again. "We were just talking about you."

"Since you didn't come here yesterday, we didn't expect to see you again," Roger said. "You must've gotten that wild hare."

"I camped last night on the Lyme Bay coast of Dorset County. An English family on holiday there invited me to share their campsite."

"What brought you here?" Eric asked.

"I thought about you two last night, about how you invited me to join you in Minehead. I wanted to see you again."

"I kind of missed you, too. Didn't we, Squire?"

Roger nodded in agreement. "How did you find us in the town centre?"

"I went to the hostel first in hopes you hadn't left yet. The warden said you had, but that you'd registered for another night. He thought you might be in the town somewhere. I registered for the night, left my backpack, and here I am."

"I'm glad we decided to stay another night. Otherwise, you probably wouldn't have found us and we wouldn't have known you were looking," Roger said. "We don't have any real plans for the rest of the day."

"We had a good ride up the Exmoor this morning. Now, we just want to relax and enjoy the seashore," Eric said. "Will you join us?"

"I'd love to!" Yvette gave Eric that look that made his knees weak. The lingering doubts she had about pursuing the two Americans evaporated instantly once she made eye contact with Eric. She knew it was the right thing to do now. She touched Eric's elbow, and he responded with an arm around her shoulders in a friendly embrace.

On their way through town, they passed a liquor store, where they purchased a bottle of cheap claret, *appellation Bordeaux controlee*. They took their wine to the waterfront, which was not a beach in any sense of the word. The tide was low, and very little sand lay at the water's edge. A cold, westward wind made the area all the less inviting, but they were not deterred.

Isolated from the rest of civilization, they could imbibe in peace and talk about most anything.

Eric took a drink from the bottle. "Do you remember, sometime back, when I mentioned something about writing a song?"

"Come up with something, have you?" Roger said.

"Sort of, maybe. I can easily put together a few lines, but never a complete song. I was thinking of something retro."

"Military march? Big band? Ragtime?"

"Not that retro!"

"Disco? Funk?"

"A little older than that. You know, your name is perfect for a doo-wop song, Yvette."

"Well, what is it?" Roger took the bottle in hand.

"I need another drink of wine. My inhibitions about these things dissolve easily in ethanol." Eric swallowed a mouthful of wine, which gagged him momentarily.

"Does that help?" Yvette teased Eric while he coughed.

Eric regained his voice. "OK, this is it." He strummed an imaginary guitar.

> "I met Yvette in England
> and now she's got me singin'
> I thought she was out of my reach
> Until I saw her on the beach
> Shoo-bop sh'bop sh'bop…"

"Is that all?" Roger asked. "You at least need some 'ooooo' in the background."

"Like I said, it's just a few lines. I can't think of any more yet. And I'm not ready to give up my day job. You don't really need words for that kind of song, just some nonsensical syllables."

"It's a good start, but you need some more vocal rhythm in there. Try this as a background vocal,

> Diddly wop bop ba-da-da
> Diddly wop bop ba-da-da
> Who shoo wa-wa whoooo."

"What language is that?" Yvette sipped the wine, much more gracefully than Eric did.

"It's English, sort of," Eric said. "Call it poetic license."

"I thought of some lyrics for a 1950s melody that someone else wrote. I call it *At the Pub*," Roger said.

> "You can quaff it
> You can drink it
> You can vomit in the sink
> At the pub.
> Where the whiskey is the smoothest
> And the porter is the coolest
> At the pub.
> All the blokes and chaps
> Can get their schnapps
> At the pub.
> Let's go to the pub.
> Let's go to the pub.
> Aye, matey
> Let's go to the pub…"

"Not bad, but I had in mind something completely original." Eric took another drink of the wine, this time without choking on it.

"Don't like my song? Try this," Roger said,

> "I've discovered some of the trails
> That will lead me into Wales
> Now I've heard some very tall tales
> Of the way they brew their ales.
> Everybody now, la-la-la."

"Not bad, except maybe the la-la-la refrain," Eric said.

"All right," Roger said. "How about a shoo-be-do-wa refrain?"

"That might work. I haven't heard a good song with that in it for a long time. Even the oldies stations don't play that stuff very often."

"Hell, I haven't even heard a bad song with that in it for a long time." Roger lifted the bottle to his lips. "We could start a new trend by recycling that stuff."

"Another song I've been working on is in the style of the late, great Richie Valens. He was killed in a plane crash back when my parents were still in diapers. Only seventeen at the time, but he was already a pop sensation."

"Let's hear your song."

"It's in Spanish, naturally.

¿Como te llama, señorita?
Ésta chica es muy bonita
Su familia tiene mucho dinero
¡Mi novia, te quiero!"

"Translation?"

"What's your name, miss? This girl is very pretty. Her family has lots of money. My girlfriend, I love you."

"It sounds much better in Spanish than English. But do you love her for her money or her beauty?" Yvette said.

"Everything! What more could a boy want from a girl?" Eric said. He considered a moment what he was saying to Yvette. He did not want to make the wrong impression on her. "I know it sounds very shallow, but my Spanish isn't that good, especially in verse. Don't take my lyrics too seriously."

"Not bad. Actually, though, the type of song I've been thinking about is something of the surfing ilk," Roger said.

"Surfing?" Eric said. "Even if these waves were big enough for surfing, and I doubt they're even close, the water's way too cold. You'd freeze your buns."

"When did you get appointed high lama of surfing?" Roger asked. "You've never been on a surfboard. You don't know diddlysquat about surfing!"

"I saw some people surfing on television once," Eric said. "That's almost like doing it myself. What makes you think anyone could surf here, or would want to?"

Roger swallowed another sip. "This is an ocean, and a beach, if you use your imagination. To me, that constitutes the premise of a surfing tune."

Yvette watched silently while they debated surfing music. She took a drink of wine when Roger handed her the bottle. These two were not quite what she had imagined Americans to be.

"Yes, quite," Eric reluctantly agreed. "Hang ten, dude."

"Bitchin'! We're going to walk the nose here, Moondawg."

"Let's start with a guitar solo intro, then:

The Prince of Wales threw his board in the Woody
And he boogied on down to the shore
Where the manatees swim
through the coral and kelp
And the seagulls soar."

210

"You're getting the hang of it, old boy," Roger said. "Let's see, what can we add to that?

> The Union Jack was unfurled
> Her majesty was shooting the curl
> They were hanging ten
> From the top of Big Ben
> All the way to Ed-in-bur-ro!"

"Your iambic pentameter is a little out of whack there," Eric said.
Roger squinted. "What's wrong with my...damn Bic pen ammeter?"
"Never mind. Carry on."
"I'm on a roll. Don't break my train of thought. How's this for a refrain?

> From Devon to Gwent
> From Calais to Kent
> We'll be surfing the isles
> From Christmas to Lent."

"We could be onto something here," Eric said. "Top-forty hit, maybe?

> Throughout the year
> When we're surfing the channel
> The water's so damn cold
> We'll line our wet suits with flannel."

"*Surfing the Channel*," Yvette said, "I like that title.

> If we surf the isles
> All the rest of our lives
> We'll see the Firth of Forth
> And the Bay of Saint Ives."

"*Surfing the Isles* might be a better title," Eric said. "Sort of, surfing meets the British Invasion. John & Dean, as it were. Or maybe Mick & Dick."
"I was going to call it *Symphonia Britannia in D Flat Major*," Roger said.
"First movement or second?"
"Now how would I know something technical like that?"

211

"Anyway, I think we have the foundation for a respectable song. Too bad the market's not ripe for surfing songs. Or more British boy-bands."

"We're a few decades too late, even for Switzerland," Yvette said. "But it does have a nice beat and you can dance to it."

"How did you know that?" Eric asked. "You've been watching American television, haven't you?"

"Planet Earth is smaller than you think," Yvette said.

"We could rework it into a hip-hop song," Roger said. "That'll get our foot in the door of the recording business. We just have to figure out some dance steps, and make it into a music video."

"Are we the next Gilbert and Sullivan, or what?" Eric said.

"We're definintely *what*," Roger agreed. "I was thinking we might be the next Zager & Evans."

"The next Strawberry Alarm Clock," Eric argued. "Maybe even the next Cowsills, or the next Association."

"The next Edison Lighthouse," Roger insisted.

"Hold it! Hold everything," Eric said sternly. "There'll never be but one Edison Lighthouse! Got that?"

"Sorry, terribly sorry," Roger capitulated. "How dare I compare us, or anyone, to Edison Lighthouse!"

"Who is Edison Lighthouse?" Yvette interrupted.

The men immediately broke into a verse and the refrain of *Love Grows Where My Rosemary Goes* in unison, almost as if they had rehearsed it just for this occasion. They had grown up with it, having heard it on oldies radio stations many, many times. It had been one of Roger's mother's favorite songs when she was in her pre-teens. They had performed it once in a high school assembly, to promote and embarrass a candidate for student body president named Rosemary.

Yvette reluctantly admitted the song sounded familiar. "Not bad! You were almost on key, even."

They frittered away the next few hours drinking wine and creating doggerel set to nearly every pop music style they knew, from the 1950s to the present. By the late afternoon, they were pleasantly numb and they thought they had enough original songs for an entire compact disc and maybe a concert tour. They liked having the waterfront all to themselves, but they left it in search of a grocery store in the town. Yvette felt very comfortable with Eric and Roger, as if she had known them for a long, long time. They felt the same way about her.

They walked back into the town for some ice cream, then walked along the beach again. On their way back toward the hostel, they negotiated a dense, jungle-like forest, and came out of it a kilometer or two east of the hostel. Roger could see how much Yvette and Eric were enjoying each other's company, and at times, he felt like he was in their way. He felt uncomfortable, and envied Eric to a small degree, but he would not interfere in what appeared to be a budding romance. It was exactly what he hoped Eric would find.

They ate supper at the hostel with thirteen other people, including the family they had met at breakfast. The two men and Yvette agreed to meet later in the common room, then went to their separate dormitories immediately after supper.

"What are you going to do next?" Roger looked at Eric, who was sitting on his bunk looking at a map.

"Depending on what Yvette wants to do tomorrow, let's ride along the Bristol Channel coast to the first bridge across the Severn River." Eric was still studying his map. "That will put us in Monmouthshire County, Wales. There's not a hostel in southeastern Wales, but we can find some place to stay. We'll have to ride through the Bristol metropolitan area, but we can manage it."

"I meant tonight, with Yvette."

Eric set the map aside. "I'm in a sticky situation, Squire." He looked down at the floor with his elbows resting on his knees. He clasped his hands and rubbed them together in frustration. "I'm crazy about her, and I'm starting to think she feels that way about me. Why else would she have gone to so much trouble to find us today?"

"She's definitely interested in you. She must be, or else she wouldn't laugh at your silly jokes."

"That's a good sign, I guess. You know, I'd been hoping that we'd meet some women who are traveling together, like we are, but..."

"I know what you're thinking, and I appreciate your concern for me. Don't push Yvette aside just because I'm all alone. Go have fun with her. I'll be mad at you if you don't. I do have someone waiting for me back home, remember, and I'm about to write a letter to her."

"Are you sure?"

"Damn sure!" Roger said. "If I were you, and you were I, I'd say to hell with you—I'm going to have some fun with Yvette. See you at the airport in about two weeks."

"You're a pal. One thing still bothers me, though. We still don't know whom she's meeting in Oxford, or why. I have to know."

"Then ask her. Invite her to take a walk with you this evening. I'll stay here and write some things in my journal. Find out what her plans are for the next few days, and see where you fit into them."

"How do I look?"

Roger squinted while he looked at Eric from the left side and then the right. "Manly, very manly. You're practically bursting with masculinity."

"Manlier than Truman Capote?"

"Manlier than Michael Jackson, Truman Capote and Boy George put together!"

"I've been hoping something like this would happen." Eric mentioned Nancy, and how nothing truly romantic happened with her. "Yet I feel so unprepared. I keep asking myself what Yvette would see in a stiff like me. I mean…"

"I'm sure you have lots of love to give," Roger insisted. "Just be yourself. Start the conversation by asking her about herself. Everything will work out just fine, unless you don't seize the opportunity. Nothing ventured, nothing gained. Forget about Nancy. Yvette isn't at all like Nancy. Know what I mean?"

Eric took Roger's advice when they met Yvette in the common room. They invited Roger to take a walk with them, but he declined as he told Eric he would. Yvette and Eric walked around the hostel grounds and the surrounding area in the cool twilight. Conversation did not come to Eric so easily when Roger was not there to lead it, but he was determined to do his best.

"What do you want to do tomorrow?" Eric asked.

"I told you a few days ago I would be meeting someone in Oxford on the weekend, and you said you wanted to go to Wales for a night." Yvette's accent was music to his ears. "I was planning to go to Oxford tomorrow night, but that can wait a day. Can we meet in Wales tomorrow and Stratford on Saturday?"

"Sounds good to me, and I'm sure Roger won't mind. You never have told me whom you're meeting in Oxford."

"My secret, but you won't be disappointed. I promise!"

"The suspense is overwhelming!"

"Do you trust me? I won't let you down!"

"Of course I trust you! Roger and I have discussed it. We thought you might be engaged or married or something, even though you don't have a ring."

"I'm not engaged or married. Let me show you."

They were facing each other and standing very close together as they spoke. Far from the hostel buildings and any other people, they were comfortably isolated in the forest. They held each other's hands, gazed into each other's eyes momentarily, then kissed fleetingly. They wrapped their arms around each other and began a much longer, more passionate kiss.

Yvette and Eric returned to the hostel just minutes before lights-out time. Roger was already in bed and nearly asleep when Eric lay down on his bunk one partition away.

"What are we doing tomorrow?" Roger used a low voice so as not to disturb anyone else in the room.

"We'll be meeting Yvette tomorrow in Wales, and on Saturday in Stratford." Eric whispered, but his excitement was unmistakable. "I'll tell you all about it tomorrow."

34.

Eric slept well until the early morning, when he dreamed he was suffering a seizure and had fallen out of his bed. He awoke in the darkness, amazed to find the dream was not quite as real as it seemed, and he was still on top of his mattress. He untangled himself from his sheet bag, searched through his gear for a bottle of acetaminophen tablets, and stumbled into the washroom for a drink of water. He wondered if he really did have a seizure during his dream.

Yvette joined Eric and Roger in the dining room for breakfast. "Good morning."

"*Guten morgen.*" Roger hoped his mediocre German was intelligible to her. Her smile indicated that it was—that phrase, anyway.

"Top o' the morning." Eric managed a smile in spite of himself, and he poured a cup of tea for her. "Have some extra-crisp toast. It's a nutritious part of this complete breakfast!" He meant to sound just like the voice-over on television cereal advertisements.

Yvette was a little concerned about Eric's headache and distressed appearance, but he assured her it was normal for him and not any fault of hers for keeping him out late. They confirmed their plan to meet in the town centre of Chepstow, Wales, at 17:00. Eric had Yvette's cell phone number, in case they had trouble finding one another. Roger was pleased to see them sharing a passionate goodbye kiss. The state of his own love life was questionable at the moment, but he felt some satisfaction for having encouraged Eric to take a chance with Yvette.

Roger and Eric departed Minehead via the A39 at 9:30 and made good time riding near the Bristol Channel coast. They both felt exuberant, and a mild tailwind pushed them northeastward. They returned to Bridgwater, where they turned north on the A38, parallel to the M5. They left the A38 at a roundabout in East Brent, and took the A370 north toward Bristol. The day was ideal for cycling, and they rode into North Somerset in the late morning. Eric felt especially inspired, and he set the pace most of the way. Yvette used public transportation to get herself to Wales.

By noon, Eric and Roger were in Weston-super-Mare, a coastal tourist town. An amusement park sat at the end of one pier they could see from the

215

highway. A nice-looking beach virtually invited them to eat lunch on it. They strayed a few blocks from the highway, where they found a fish bar and a grocery store. They purchased their victuals and returned to the beach.

Before climbing down onto the beach, they put on their sneakers and walked their bicycles. Quite a number of tourists and locals had more or less the same idea they had, among them two teenage girls. The girls were sitting against the long retainer wall that separated the beach from the rest of civilization. One was wearing shorts and a T-shirt, and the other had on a black skirt. Both were attractive, and both sat with their knees up and their arms folded across their knees. Roger and Eric walked by slowly, as if savoring the moment which, in fact, they were. The girls noticed them, too, and held them in admirable, flirtatious gaze for a long moment.

Eric and Roger sat down against the wall some twenty-five meters away from the girls, in the first unoccupied space they could find. They removed their shirts before starting to eat their lunch.

"Lovely legs that blonde one has." Roger had the usual sinister smile on his face.

"A sight for sore eyes!" Eric sounded unusually enthusiastic. "If we were planning to spend a little more time here, I'd suggest we go make small talk with them."

Roger sank his incisors into a fresh currant bun. "Unfortunately, there'll probably be nothing like that in Chepstow. Except Yvette, for you."

"Damn! Once again, you're forced to choose between what you know you should do, and what you'd certainly like to try. Why does our better judgment always seem to win?" Eric bit into a steaming fish filet.

"I was delighted to hear you took my advice last night and it paid off for you," Roger said. "It's amazing what a little self-confidence can do for you."

"I'm the happiest I've been in a long time," Eric said. "I'd been thinking about how nice it will be to get home, but now I'm dreading it. I don't want to say goodbye to Yvette, but our time together is limited."

"You'll just have to make the most of what's left."

"I hope we're not making you miss Marianne too much."

"You are, but don't feel too bad about it. I'm mature. I can handle it. I don't feel sorry for me and I don't expect anyone else to, either. I can't get too lonely when you're having such a good time."

"Remember when we argued about getting out of Romford last week, and you said you'd make it up to the Evans and me?" Eric said. "I can't speak for them, but you've made it up to me many times over."

"See? I'm good for my word."

While they were finishing their lunch, the two girls arose and walked along the beach, once again smiling seductively at Roger and Eric as they passed. The girls disappeared among the many people on the beach before the two Americans decided to take a stroll in that same direction after lunch.

As they walked their bicycles along the beach, they did some intense people-watching. Weston-super-Mare proved to be a good place for that activity. They hated to leave, but they still had some distance between themselves and Chepstow. Eric could hardly wait to see Yvette again, even though he was not sure they would find any romantic places to rendezvous in southeastern Wales.

Farther up the coast, they navigated through some residential and industrial areas on the outskirts of Bristol, one of the nation's larger cities. Eric tried to make a U-turn on a very narrow street, but fell over before he could loosen either foot from its pedal. Roger used his camera to take full advantage of the opportunity.

The M4 bridge over the Severn River was not quite as large as the bridge over the Firth of Forth near Edinburgh, but impressive to them nonetheless. They stopped at the crest of the bridge to spit over the railing. Once over the bridge, they made use of their drop handlebars to increase their speed. Already exhausted by trying to avoid Bristol proper and the motorways, they were further drained by the gradual climb away from the coast into Wales. They arrived in the town centre of Chepstow in the late afternoon, where Yvette was sitting on a park bench. She had already selected a B&B, and led them to it.

For the most part, southern Wales looked like the region of England they had just left. The most immediately noticeable difference was that many of the place names were almost impossible to pronounce as spelled. They would have liked to spend more time in Wales, but their remaining vacation days were dwindling and they had other interests in mind. Wales, with all its natural splendor and friendly people, was an infrequent destination of most American tourists they had met. They both made a mental note to add Wales to their list of places to visit on their next trip to Europe.

They walked back to the town centre for an evening meal. Afterward, they used the time to shower and update their journals. Yvette was not keeping a journal, but helped Eric with his daily entry. She massaged his neck and shoulders while he wrote. It felt so good that he had trouble concentrating on what he wanted to write. He gave her a chair massage, too, after he closed his journal. Chepstow was just barely inside Wales, and they did not expect to see anything they had not already seen in numerous other English towns of comparable size. Yvette had been in England once before, but it was also her first time in Wales.

Roger was ready to retire shortly after Yvette went to the shower. With Yvette's telephone, he tried to book beds at the hostel in Stratford-upon-

Avon, but it was full. They would have to try again when they arrived, as they did in Edwinstowe, or else find other accommodations.

"Great theatrics on that U-turn today, Chief. I'll give you a copy of the picture, and you can show it to everyone and tell them you were doing the Bristol stomp. How about it?"

"A pox on both your houses! And a bad case of hemorrhoids, too!" Eric wrote a few more lines in his journal before he spoke again. "Yvette told me we'll not be diappointed when we meet her in Stratford tomorrow. I assume we'll find out who her mystery companion is."

"It's probably her old man, and he'll insist on escorting her the whole time you're with her. That should make your day."

35.

"Morning has broken," Eric observed as he arose. He wanted to say that, now that he was in Wales. He had learned to play the song of that title on his guitar some years earlier.

Roger's throat was sore and his sinuses congested, but neither was bad enough to prevent him from doing anything other than swallowing and breathing. He was not surprised to find that European allergens bothered him just as much as the North American variety.

Yvette, Eric, Roger and the few other guests who were eating at the inn were allowed ample time to eat their food and drain the tea pitchers before the table was cleared. Everyone leisurely enjoyed more than the usual amount of tea and bread.

"If this toast were Tempranillo wine," Eric said, "it would be superior grade. I'm talking Grand Cru here."

"No wine could be that dry," Roger said. "On the other hand, I'm sure the toast could put silica gel out of the desiccant business."

"Bring your wine expertise to the hostel in Stratford before five o'clock," Yvette said. "I will be waiting there for you both. I'll see if I can book some beds there."

They checked out of the B&B and prepared to ride to Stratford-upon-Avon, Warwickshire. Yvette walked and hitchhiked to the nearest railway station. Eric was especially excited as he anticipated Yvette and her mystery companion, whom they would meet at the hostel in Stratford. As they left the inn at 9:45, the only noticeable thing about it was the old, dead tree in the yard and the decaying logs beneath it. The barren tree, void of any chlorophyll, looked way out of place in the densely forested, verdant coastal lands.

Roger and Eric clicked into their pedals as they mounted their unevenly loaded bicycles. They rode eastward a short distance on the A48 until they were back in England. Their stay in Wales was brief, but their encounter with the Welsh language left them puzzled. They wondered how they should pronounce the names of towns such as Ebbw Vale and Cwmbran.

Over the 48 kilometers between Chepstow and Gloucester, Gloucestershire, they encountered steep hills and dark forests. All the while, a tailwind helped propel them. They had difficulty navigating some roads. They hated to stand in their pedals to climb the steeper hills because of the awkwardness of their fully loaded bicycles, but they often had no choice. They were largely unaware of the strength of their tailwind until they noticed how fast they were moving compared to a stream by the roadside that was flowing in the opposite direction.

A bakery in Gloucester proved to be a good source of lunch. They enjoyed the brown bread and Cheshire cheese, and they also treated themselves to bread pudding. Both the brown bread and pudding had been baked fresh that morning, just the sort of thing necessary to keep cyclists healthy and content. They felt tempted to stay for supper, but the superior-grade hostel at Stratford and a few other things beckoned them.

They debated whether to use the B4632 or the A429 to get to Stratford. The distance appeared to be about the same either way. They rode through the rolling Cotswold Hills and forests of Gloucestershire and Warwickshire after lunch. The thought occurred to them that they might have a better chance of getting unclaimed beds at the Stratford hostel if they got in line as early as possible. Roger's left knee was just sore enough to deter him from hurrying, so Eric rode ahead to try to get in line at the hostel as early as possible. They only had one map of the area between them, which Eric took with him. Eric sprinted away just beyond Stow on the Wold and made use of the A429 from there.

Eric hoped to find Yvette and her companion waiting for him at the hostel so they could all plan their evening immediately. He was eager to be with her again, and he wanted to spend as much time with her as possible. He did not intend to exclude Roger, regardless of Roger's advice to do so. The undisclosed identity of Yvette's companion and the uncertainty of how much private time he would have with her left Eric mystified. He vowed to himself he would not show his disappointment if things turned out in an unfavorable way.

Roger took a drink from his water bottle, returned it to its cage on the downtube of his frame, and rode away in the same direction Eric was going. Roger did not attempt to catch Eric, but watched him gradually disappear in the distance. Eric felt strong, riding in higher gears at high cadence all the way to Stratford. The sweat on Eric's brow that was dripping into his eyes gave him a feeling of satisfaction along with the sting. He imagined himself leading a pursuit team into Stratford, and his pulse and respiratory rate were very high all the way there.

When Eric came upon the edge of Stratford, he stopped to check his maps. He located the hostel on the map, then sped through Stratford to the B4086 shortly before 17:00. When he found the hostel near Wellesbourne Road, his watch indicated 16:59, and already a queue had formed outside the building. He leaned his bicycle against a wall and stood patiently at the back of the queue.

Roger was a few minutes behind, but he was lost shortly after he entered Stratford. He had no maps to guide him, only the YHA signs. At a red public telephone booth along the highway into the city, he stopped for a few minutes to make another call. He spoke to a different roommate this time. She reluctantly told him that Marianne had gone home to Hawaii a month earlier, and was probably still there. Unsure what to think of this most recent development, he got back on his bicycle and followed the infrequent signs as best as he could. He got off course a few times, but eventually found the hostel. Like Eric, he was not sure what to expect upon arrival.

Eric was waiting in front of the hostel with Yvette and another woman who looked and dressed somewhat like Yvette and also carried a backpack. Roger stopped where they were standing and dismounted. Eric looked very satisfied being in such desirable company. Roger liked what he saw, and quickly forgot his telephone conversation of a few minutes earlier.

"Roger, I want you to meet my sister, Desiree." Yvette put her hand on the bespectacled woman's shoulder. Desiree made eye contact with Roger, smiled and extended her hand. The women did not look at all like twins, but they were unmistakably sisters. Desiree had a lighter hair color than Yvette, and she used more makeup, but she wore similar jeans and a sweatshirt. Roger was immediately pleased to make her acquaintance.

"How do you do?" Roger clasped Desiree's hand. "Are you the mysterious companion Yvette didn't tell us much about?"

"Yes, I am. She's told me quite a lot about you, though."

"Nothing bad, I hope." Roger wasted no time turning on the charming smile and glint in his eye.

"Not in the least. I've been looking forward to meeting you and Eric."

"Did you get us a private room in the hostel, Chief?"

"No, they didn't have a room for just the four of us. We'll have to find some other place to stay the night, or else take beds in separate dorms."

Desiree and Yvette looked at each other. "Let's see if we can find a B&B," Desiree said.

"Yes, let's find a B&B with two rooms in it," Yvette said. "Shall we?" She smiled at Eric as she spoke. She was excited, almost to the point of giddiness.

Roger and Eric walked their bicycles alongside Yvette and Desiree into the town in search of a B&B. The women were carrying fully loaded backpacks. The first B&B they saw had only one room available, and the next two were full. They turned down a side street several blocks from the hostel and found a large Victorian home with two attic rooms, its last vacancies. The men parked their bicycles in a garage behind the house, and carried the women's backpacks and their own panniers up the narrow staircase to the quiet attic. Yvette called the hostel on her cell phone to cancel their reservations.

"This is a lovely place." Yvette looked at Eric. "I'm glad we couldn't get into the hostel. This is much nicer."

"We'll have a little more privacy here than at the hostel," Eric added.

The men replaced their cycling attire with jeans and T-shirts while the women asked the innkeeper to suggest a nearby restaurant. The four walked to a fish bar and a green grocer for supper, and settled in the outdoor seating of a pub afterward.

After supper, they roamed the city of Stratford-upon-Avon, population 21,000, in search of some of its landmarks. Stratford was famous as the birthplace and hometown of William Shakespeare, and they expected to find at least one monument of some sort in his honor.

One Shakespeare landmark was a large theater that they did not enter, as a performance was in progress. Another was a statue of the bard himself, surrounded by Sir John Falstaff, Prince Hal, Hamlet and Lady MacBeth. Prince Hal debuted in *Henry IV, Part 1*, and ascended to the throne as the title character in *Henry V*. Falstaff provided comic relief for the prince in the Boars Head Tavern. The four foreigners studied the statue and its inscriptions and took some pictures of it.

"How many calzones did you eat at the Colosseum today, Caesar?" Roger asked.

"*Et tu, Bruté*," Eric replied.

"Only Americans would make a joke like that," Yvette said.

"Do you suppose the locals here ever get tired of Shakespeare festivals and that sort of thing?" Desiree asked.

"Probably not, else they'd move out," Roger said. "If I lived here, I'd be selling souvenirs bearing his name and likeness. I doubt I'm the first American to think of that."

"Think of all the T-shirts you could sell bearing slogans like, 'Alas! Poor Yorick. I knew him, Horatio,'" Eric said. "Imagine statements like that being in vogue with teenagers, television characters and advertising copywriters."

"That day, Chief, will never happen. Still, it is an interesting concept."

Eric looked around the statue for a moment. "I just had a strange thought."

"What's that?" Yvette was holding his hand.

"He noticed that Hamlet doesn't look as much like Sir Laurence Olivier as he was expecting," Roger said.

"No, I was just thinking of a line from *Antony and Cleopatra* that describes Roger and me well, while we're here at the source. In the first act, Cleopatra says to her attendants something to the effect of:

> My salad days,
> When I was green in judgment,
> Blah, blah, blah
> Yadda, yadda, yadda!

I can't remember the rest of it, but here we are in Stratford-upon-Avon, Warwickshire, in the twilight of our own salad days and still very green in judgment. I usually don't think Shakespeare's prose has much to do with my own view of reality, but maybe it does. What do you think of that?"

"Salad days in Warwickshire," Roger said. "Fancy that! Is it any surprise that Shakespeare's works are so long-lived? Much of what he wrote still applies to this day, if you can translate it into modern English."

"You should try translating it into modern German or French," Desiree said. "I'm with you, Eric, except that I might be a little beyond my salad days by now. My favorite Shakespearean quote is from Hamlet, where Polonius advises his son Laertes, 'To thine own self be true.' I try to live by that."

"Everyone likes that line," Eric agreed. "Even if we don't always practice it."

"We're still in our salad days, big sister," Yvette said, "just a little further along, I think."

"Perhaps we are. You, especially."

They took in some more of the town, then ambled back toward the B&B. As usual, they were in no hurry to get anywhere. They took the time to discuss the influence Shakespeare had on modern English, among other things. They wondered if anyone they knew would still be famous nearly four centuries after his or her death.

"Is your knee still bothering you?" Eric asked.

"It's all right now," Roger said. "Bothers me most when I'm on my bike."

"Have you checked the cleat? You might have turned it a little at that ski area in Scotland."

"That's possible, but I think I would've noticed it."

"Give it a look," Eric said. "You might be surprised what you find."

"Might be worth a try." Roger's sore knee was not a big concern at the moment. He was thinking about a possible shift in his and Eric's vacation plans, now that Yvette and Desiree had entered the picture. "We have ten or eleven days of vacation left. How are we going to spend that time?"

"Yvette and I have been talking about France," Eric said.

"Desiree and I would love to show you some of our favorite spots," Yvette said. "We could agree on a place to meet, like we've been doing, and you would ride your bicycles there and we would ride trains or buses, or hitchhike."

Roger thought about the possibilities before responding. He knew Yvette and Eric wanted to be together as much as possible, but he was engaged and he did not want to create any problematic situations for Desiree and himself. Desiree did not appear to have any objections to the plan, if the pleasant smile on her pretty face meant anything. "I'm game. That's a lot of ground to cover in that short amount of time, but while we're this close, let's take in all we can.

"I'm sure you two would like some time to yourselves for a while," Desiree said to Yvette and Eric. "Walk with me, Roger. I want to know you better."

"Meet you at the B&B in an hour or two." Roger and Desiree left the other two and walked toward the Avon River.

"I'm very much in the dark as to where you fit in Yvette's travel plans," Roger said when they were a block away from Yvette and Eric. "What's going on?"

"Sorry for being so mysterious about everything. I've been attending a business seminar at Oxford all week. My company sent me. I made arrangements with Yvette to meet me there and we would do some traveling and camping after the seminar. We did something similar to this last year in Germany, except that she was still in college rather than celebrating her graduation."

"Why didn't she tell us that when she met us?"

"She's not usually swept off her feet, but she was taken by Eric almost from the moment she saw him, or so she told me." Desiree's English, like Yvette's, was flawless. "That would have been the end of it, except that she met you again entirely by coincidence in Bath. She was very attracted to him by then, but she wasn't sure if he felt that way about her."

"She should have asked me. He definitely noticed her. I made a point of telling her where we'd be, in hopes that she'd find us again."

223

"You are very clever, just as I thought. She talked to me by telephone after that, and said that you'd be in..." Desiree could not think of their next destination.

"Minehead?"

"Yes, Minehead. I told her to trust her judgment, to look for you two there because you invited her."

"She almost missed us. Eric was bummed out for a while there, and so was I, in a way. We thought, maybe she wasn't all that keen on him. We were so glad to be wrong that time."

"She was, too. She had such a good time with you on the waterfront in Minehead. Her doubts disappeared from that time on. She couldn't wait to see him again."

"She still didn't tell us about you, even after that. I think she just told him that we wouldn't be disappointed, and I'm not, of course. Why the secrecy?"

"She knows I don't like her to be the matchmaker for me. I was married briefly, but we went our separate ways more than a year ago. I don't socialize much. I've been fully occupied by my work ever since, and I like it that way."

"Why did you let Yvette talk you into meeting us here in Stratford?"

"I was very hesitant to meet you. Two factors overcame my unwillingness. One was that Yvette was so infatuated with Eric." Desiree paused, as if she did not want to say any more.

"And the other?"

"She told me about the songs you wrote in Minehead. It was the most outrageous thing I could imagine anyone doing. I wish I'd been there!"

"It's normal for Eric and me, however silly. Why did that make such an impression on you?"

"When I was at university, I was in a choir, a chorale group. We performed in two or three stage musicals. We sang some American songs from the 1950s and sixties and Broadway at a club near the campus, if you can imagine that."

"Not easily." Roger smiled at the idea. The lyrics of many of his favorite oldies were hardly in English.

"We sang several songs from the girl groups of the 1960s, especially Motown, and some other songs in English." The enthusiasm in Desiree's expression was sincere. "We had a wonderful time. Do you know any of those songs?"

"Classics all," Roger said. "I didn't think Motown was all that big in Europe. It was very popular in the United States, but long before my time."

"So what made you a fan of the British Invasion, and surfing music?"

"When Eric and I were in high school a few years ago, we performed a medley of songs at an assembly with two of our friends. It was a 1950s and '60s revue, Oldies Day. The band teacher talked us into putting together a combo. We dressed the part, and slicked our hair back. Eric is pretty good with a guitar. I played a string bass, sort of. George Fraser, who almost came to Europe with us, played his saxophone, and Antonio Gonzales sang lead and played the piano. We called him Speedy Gonzales, like the cartoon rat, because he was the district champion in the 1500 meters. He was also first tenor in the all-state choir our senior year. We wanted to call ourselves the Four Nicators, but the assistant principal went ballistic when she found out. She gave us a long, boring lecture about setting a good example for the underclassmen. We changed our name to Edsel & the Studebakers, which might explain why we didn't last very long." Roger realized he was rambling, but it was one of his fondest memories of high school. He did not want to bore her with his reminiscences. "Had a great time, good harmony, and we've been hooked on oldies ever since. We came by it honestly, though. My dad listens to oldies on the radio all the time. He actually grew up with that stuff. So did my mom and Eric's parents. We pretty much knew the songs already. It is sort of a guilty pleasure for Eric and me."

"Guilty pleasure?"

"That means things we like that are intended for people way above or below our age group. I like rock and roll from my parents' generation and earlier. I still like comic books, too, and movies based on comics. Those are my guilty pleasures."

"I see. I don't think we have a term for that in German or French. My guilty pleasures are stage musicals, and maybe ballroom dancing. I still have a stuffed animal on my bed that I had when I was a little girl."

"The stuffed animal is definitely a guilty pleasure. Are you much of a musician?"

"I once considered a career as a concert pianist or an actress in stage musicals," Desiree said. "I was good, but not good enough to make a career of it. Swiss entertainers are not likely to succeed anywhere outside of Switzerland, and the Swiss market for entertainment is very small. I still wonder sometimes what might have been had I given it a try. I suspect that you and Eric are a little like I am in that regard."

"We imagine ourselves as pop stars all the time, but we aren't really very talented. We both know it's not our calling."

"I admire your honesty with yourselves, and your mettle. I knew you were being yourselves when she told me about it. You seemed like my kind of people."

"Have you had any big singing and acting roles?"

"*Die Fledermaus* is one of my favorites. I once played Laurie in an amateur production of *Oklahoma*! Musical theatre is your country's greatest contribution to the arts, I think."

"That, superheroes and mountain bikes. I like *Oklahoma*!, too, and I bet you made a great Laurie. Did you know that Eric was a Shark and I was a Jet in *West Side Story* when we were in high school? His sister, only 15 years old at the time, landed the lead role as Maria. She's a fabulous singer. Dances and acts pretty well, too."

They continued walking slowly through residential neighborhoods until they were within a few blocks of the B&B. Roger kept his hands in his pockets, even though he felt tempted to take Desiree in his arms and kiss her passionately. He was engaged to someone else and he did not want to ruin it. He had not mentioned his engagement to either Yvette or Desiree, and something inside him kept him from doing so. The moment did not seem quite right for that yet, he thought.

"Yvette said you met another cyclist in Scotland, who broke her collarbone in a crash."

"We might still be with her in Scotland, but she had to abandon the ride. She went home to Aberdeen to recuperate, and we rode an overnight train back to London. We wanted to see southern England."

"Did you really get in a fight with someone in Yorkshire who attacked you?"

"Yes, we did. It was one of the stupidest things we've ever done. I hope you don't think we're barbarians."

"You wouldn't sound so apologetic about it if you were a barbarian. Did you get hurt?"

"Not nearly as much as our enemies did." Roger did not want to talk about the altercation, so he quickly changed the subject to something more pleasant. "What do you have in mind for us in France?"

"My sister told me you and Eric have not had any specific itinerary, that you stay overnight wherever you feel like stopping. The Continent has many youth hostels, too. I would like to travel that way in France, if you like. We'll get you back to London in time for your flight."

"Sounds very agreeable. I wish I'd met you a long time ago. Too bad our time together will be so brief."

"I wish we had more time together, too, but it's probably a good thing that we don't. Yvette and I are likely to have our travel plans shortened, I've learned."

"Why is that?"

"My mother has been in contact with me by telephone in recent days. Our grandmother, her mother, appears to be on her deathbed. She suffered a major stroke two days ago. She was diagnosed with cancer several months ago."

"I'm sorry to hear that."

"She lives in a retirement home in Geneva. She's in her eighties now, a widow for several years. When she dies, she'll be cremated. Relatives and friends of the family will be gathering at our parents' house, and Mother will need us to provide for everyone."

"Do Yvette and Eric know this?"

"I told Yvette our grandmother is sick, but I didn't say how sick. I didn't want to spoil her fun."

"I hope everything works out for all of us," Roger said. "Tonight is the best evening I've had on this vacation, and we've had some good ones. I want all of us to spend a few more evenings like this one together."

"Roger, do you object at all to being with me tonight?" Desiree asked. "You didn't know what you were going to get when you came into Stratford, and you didn't get a chance to disapprove. Are you sure you don't mind?"

Roger had been considering the answer to her question long before she asked, since the moment he saw her, really. He still did not have an answer that was quite satisfactory to him. He did not want to burden her by telling her about how he was engaged to Marianne but still harbored some misgivings about it. The phone call he had made earlier in the day just muddied the water that much more. He was not going to be dishonest with her, either. "You're very considerate to ask. But with you, I don't mind at all. You didn't know what you were getting, either, really. Any objections?"

"I knew more about you than you knew about me," Desiree said. "I have no objections. This has been my best evening here, too."

Yvette and Eric were sprawled on a public lawn they found. They held hands, and they discussed romantic ideas. She stroked his hair with her free hand, and they kissed frequently. They were oblivious to everything but each other.

"I'm already thinking about how I'm going to travel to the United States to see you someday," Yvette said. "Do you want me to come?"

"Only if you promise to stay a long time," Eric said. "I could show you lots of things in Washington or Colorado, or wherever I am when you come."

"I want you to spend your first paycheck on airfare to Zurich, or wherever I am then," Yvette said. "Say you will!"

"I won't get any vacation time that soon on a job," Eric said. "How about after I've worked for six months?"

"I can't wait that long!"

When Yvette and Eric returned to the B&B, they encountered Roger emerging from the bathtub room. Eric motioned Yvette into the first sleeping room where Desiree was reviewing some papers from her business seminar, her hair still damp from having been washed very recently. Eric noticed that Desiree and Roger had arranged their gear in one bedroom, and Yvette and Eric's gear in the other room.

"I'm sorry if I got you into a sticky situation," Eric said to Roger in private. "Are you going to be all right? What did you tell Desiree?"

"Carry on! Don't worry about a thing." Roger was surprisingly nonchalant. "It's all happening according to the prophecies."

Eric was puzzled. "Did you call Marianne again?"

"I spoke to one of Marianne's roommates on my way into Stratford. Marianne's still in Hawaii, but I don't know any details. Her roommate didn't know much, or wasn't telling."

Eric hesitated. "Are you sure this will work? Don't feel like you have to…"

"I want you and Yvette to share a room, without me this time. I'm sure that's what she wants," Roger interrupted. "Don't mind us. I mean that. I know what I'm doing. Desiree and I plotted all this. We'll see you in the morning. Give Yvette something to yodel about!" He emphasized that last remark with a wink and a sly smile.

Yvette entered the room where Eric was. Roger rejoined Desiree in the adjoining attic bedroom and closed the door.

"I was worried that they might not get along so well." Eric was deliberately euphemistic as he peeled off his shirt. "They're doing all right, I think."

"No need to lose any sleep over them." Yvette wrapped her arms around him. "They don't look at all disappointed with each other."

"I'm not disappointed either," Eric pulled her tight against his chest and kissed her tenderly. "Not at all disappointed."

"Make love to me tonight!" Yvette said softly, her eyes brimming with passion.

Chapter VI: *Field Duty in Bavaria*

36.

Eric awoke shortly before 7:00 to the pleasant sensation of Yvette snuggled next to him. He looked out the lone window into the dreaded rain that had soaked the town during the night. He dressed in the semidarkness, and he could hear Roger or Desiree getting out of bed in the adjoining room. Yvette looked beautiful even as she slept, her hair swept over her pillow.

They all packed their gear and were out of their rooms before breakfast. They went down to the dining room by 7:30 for breakfast and to discuss their plans for the day. Yvette stood up and walked in front of Eric with a bulge under the lower part of her sweater.

"I'm pregnant, Eric. Now you have to marry me!"

Eric gagged on his tea and his droopy eyes opened wide very suddenly. "How did that happen?"

Yvette wrapped her arms around him and kissed him on the cheek. "It's a joke." She pulled a folded sweatshirt from under her sweater. "You need a little shock therapy to get you going in the morning."

"You're cruel! You know that? I was minding my own business, and then you start messing with my brain! Have a cup of tea."

Desiree looked across her teacup at Roger and Eric. "How far do you want to ride today?"

"All things considered, London seems far enough away." Roger savored his tea.

"I'll reserve four beds for us at one of the hostels in London," Desiree said. "You two can suffer one night in separate sleeping rooms, no?"

"Try to get us a private room!" Yvette protested.

"Let's not keep them apart too long," Roger said. "They'll whine if we do."

"Let's not keep us apart too long, either, *Liebhaber*." Desiree spoke in a sensual tone of voice that Roger liked to hear. Marianne often spoke to him that way. Eric was puzzled by the comment, but he let it pass.

"I hope you girls can get to London without getting as soaked and miserable as we will be," Eric said.

"You boys ride safely and take care of yourselves," Yvette said. "Consider our way of traveling next time you come to Europe."

"Not a chance!"

Desiree booked a private room at the Earl's Court Youth Hostel in southwestern London. The City of London and Oxford Street hostels she tried first only had a few beds left in different rooms. She and Yvette put on rain ponchos before they left the B&B. They walked and hitchhiked to a train station, where they rode a train into London.

London did not seem as close to Stratford as it did the previous day when Roger and Eric were looking at maps. The only thing they loathed more than talking about weather was admitting to themselves how important it was to the success of their vacation. They swapped their jeans and heavy shirts for their woolen cycling attire. Outside, they put their rain suits over their woolens and loaded their gear onto their bicycles. Their cold, wet, slightly numb fingers had minor difficulty hooking their panniers onto their rear racks. Roger checked his cleat before they left Stratford. It did appear to be slightly out of its original position. He adjusted the cleat with a hex key, and his left knee started to improve almost immediately.

"My knee is bending only in the plane of my leg now, instead of rotating in a horizontal plane with each pedal stroke," Roger commented. "It feels right. I should have noticed that earlier."

"Good advice you gave him, Eric, old boy." Eric talked as if he were addressing someone else. "You should consider a career as a physiologist, Eric."

Hills and a stiff headwind thwarted them all the way to Banbury, Oxfordshire, which seemed much farther from Stratford than it actually is due to the slow pace. Traffic splashing along the A422 helped keep their skin, clothing and spirits damp. Condensation of perspiration inside their rain suits made the rain suits virtually useless. Their rear brakes and the backsides of their downtubes and forks were blackened with road grime within minutes of their departure from Stratford, and water leaked through the zippers and seams of their panniers.

Only one restaurant in Banbury was open on Sundays, and it did little to brighten their day. One table was available, and they sat down to eat while keeping their complaints to themselves. At least they were out of the rain.

Thirty minutes after they entered the restaurant, they were ready for more punishment, even though their hands and beards were still as wet as when they stepped out of the rain. The air was too humid to dry anything. They got back on their bicycles and plodded on down the A422 to Buckingham, where they turned onto the A413.

"Snail approaching, wants to pass." Eric shouted it, although he was barely audible to Roger just a few meters ahead. They still had not reached Winslow.

"Move aside then," Roger shouted back. "I thought I saw something flashing its brights at us."

Quite some time later, they arrived in another hamlet they suspected of being Whitchurch, although the town they were in displayed no signs identifying it thus. They were delighted as well as surprised to find a petrol station open on a Sunday, where they purchased some chocolate bars with hazelnuts and raisins. They took shelter in a deserted bus stop, ate the chocolate and watched the rain fall. The rain eased a little, and they pushed on to Aylesbury.

They stopped at a loo in Aylesbury. Standing under a shelter, they studied their map. Two others were also under the shelter, waiting out the rain.

"Let's find out where the nearest Underground station is," Eric suggested. "We should be able to ride the Tube from somewhere in the northwest."

"Pardon me, but you can catch the Tube in Chesham or Amersham," a bystander informed them. "They're not far from here." She pointed out the two towns on their map. "They're the west ends of the Metropolitan Line."

Eric and Roger thanked her and departed. They felt modestly inspired, now that they knew where they were going. They rode the A41 southeastward past Tring, then south through Cholesbury on a little-used highway. The rain slackened to a light but steady drizzle, and they suffered all the way to Chesham. They were still a ways out of London, but by mid-afternoon, they found their Underground station.

They spent the next two hours getting to the Earl's Court station in London. Holding their bicycles in front of them, they sat in the last car of each train, with only a few other people in the car at any time. A light rain was falling in London, too, and they absorbed more of it on their way to the hostel a few blocks from the station. Two reserved beds in a private room awaited them when they finally arrived, soaked to the bone, in the late afternoon. Yvette and Desiree were also waiting for them, and brought smiles to their tired faces. The two Americans secured their bicycles in a shed and stowed their panniers under their bunk before they showered off the day's road grime. They probably would have been in foul moods if not for the women, but instead they were quite cheerful even after the miserable journey back to London.

Sightseeing was out of the question, due to the rain, and none of the four were much in the mood for it anyway. The hostel was in a lively neighborhood, with plenty of eateries and small stores nearby. Yvette and Eric purchased some bread, cheese and fruit at a market a few blocks from the hostel after the rain subsided, while Desiree and Roger pooled everyone's dirty clothes and washed two loads in the hostel's laundry room. They congregated in the self-catering kitchen in the basement of the hostel, after their grocery and laundry chores. One door of the kitchen opened into a courtyard, and they kept the door open for ventilation.

Eric began peeling a banana for the second course of his supper. "Yvette and I had an idea. Tell me what you think, Squire. What if we call Inga and

Peter and ask if we can park our bikes in their garage for a few days. That way, we can hitchhike or ride trains with Yvette and Desiree into France."

"We'd cover a lot of ground in short order that way, and we wouldn't get separated from you. Sounds like a winner."

Yvette watched Eric carefully peel the banana, then took one for herself. "Give your friends a call as soon as we're done eating. You can ride to their house in the morning, and meet us at the Hovercraft docks in Dover, yes?"

"Whatever you say." Eric leaned over and kissed Yvette just below the corner of her jaw.

The Evans were entertaining some friends and Inga's parents when Eric called. Peter wanted to hear about their adventures and misadventures.

"Sorry to interrupt like this," Eric apologized. "We seem to have a knack for it."

"On the contrary," Peter said, "we were hoping to hear from you at some point."

Inga joined in from a second telephone. "I bet you have some stories to tell!"

"We made friends with two Swiss sisters, but I'll tell you more about them later." Eric asked if he and Roger could leave their bicycles. Peter and Inga had no objections.

Inga returned to her guests, while Peter mentioned that he had finished a 161-kilometer time trial in less than five hours that morning. The French and British once again had failed to get a spot on the winners' podium in the Tour de France earlier in the day. Eric provided a few details regarding his burgeoning romance with Yvette, and their plans to spend a week in France with the Hoffmann sisters. Peter was delighted to hear of the romance, and he encouraged Eric to wholeheartedly continue pursuing it.

Roger wrote a few lines in his journal after he said goodnight to the ladies and Eric. He mentioned his bewilderment regarding Marianne and her extended stay in Hawaii. It all seemed so fishy, yet he could think of any number of reasons she might leave her summer job in Denver. Why did the first roommate not tell him the truth? Why was the second so reluctant to tell him anything?

37.

Like clockwork, Roger awakened everyone at 7:00. Desiree and Yvette provided tea, toast, bananas and digestives for breakfast. Still tired from the previous day's journey, they all would have liked staying in bed until 8:00 or later. A marginally sunny day awaited them outside, and they wondered why they did not wait another day to leave Stratford.

"We could have watched a matinee double feature of *A Comedy of Errors* and *Love's Labour's Lost*," Eric said, "if we'd have stayed another day."

"Was that showing at the Globe?" Yvette asked.

"Hell if I know! We'd have a dry ride today."

Eric and Roger loaded their bikes and checked out of the hostel. They had little trouble finding the Evans' house in Romford this time, and their ride through greater London was pleasant and uneventful. Their hurried pace reflected their eagerness to get back to their Swiss friends. Yvette and Desiree spent the day in the city centre of London before traveling to Dover.

Roger called Henry Smythe from the Evans' house to inquire about the progress on his frame. Smythe still had some work yet to do, and he thought it might take another week. The frame repairs he had done for Roger and Eric delayed Roger's new frame and several other jobs that Smythe was doing concurrently. Roger hoped the new frame would be done in time for him to take it home with him, instead of Smythe having to ship it without Roger's final approval, and at extra cost to Roger.

After lunch, the Evans gave them a ride out to the intersection of the A127 and A128, and wished them the best of luck at hitchhiking. They promised to bring back a bottle of genuine Champagne. They carried only one pair of panniers, two handlebar bags and two sleeping bags between them. Already, they wished they had rucksacks for carrying their gear instead of bicycle luggage.

Ride number one came only a few minutes after the Evans left. A man on his way home from work took them to Gravesend on the south bank of the River Thames. A second man, who spoke with an Irish accent and said he had been to California but not Colorado or Washington, took them on to Chatham, on the A2. The third wait was longer than the first two, but a bohemian couple in a clunker they said they had bought recently for about fifty pounds gave them a ride to Canterbury, where their pitiful car decided to call it a day.

In Canterbury, Kent, they waited an hour before a man with a Japanese accent driving to his home in Spain gave them a ride all the way to the ferry docks below the cliffs of Dover. The driver was also on his way through Calais, but he let them out at the dock at about 20:00 before he drove his car on board the ferryboat.

"There they are." Eric pointed toward Yvette and Desiree after he and Roger had searched the dock area briefly. "Hope we haven't kept them waiting long."

"We've been wandering around here for about an hour," Yvette said when the men caught up with her and her sister. "It's not surprising that you

233

had several delays and needed several rides to cover the distance from London to Dover."

"Do we get to cross the channel in a Hovercraft?" The prospect of riding in a Hovercraft for the first time excited Roger.

"Not this time," Yvette said.

"Hovercrafts are not used after dark," Desiree said. "The woman selling tickets told us that."

"The fare seems a bit steep," Eric said. "What do you think?"

"It is, but we are crossing national borders," Desiree said.

"There's a tax for leaving England, a tax for entering France, and an additional tax for entering France from England," Roger explained. "And a surcharge for people who are neither English nor French." They all boarded a ferryboat and walked to the passenger deck where they reserved a table for themselves.

The ferryboat departed Dover at 21:30, and the men still had not eaten any supper by that time. Eric's hunger was giving him a headache and blurred vision, but he did not want any junk food from the snack bar. The boat did not offer much of anything nutritious like fresh fruit. Desiree and Roger went for a round of lager.

"You're in luck," Yvette said. "We stopped at a grocery in Dover and bought some fruit and scones." She pulled a sack of bananas and oranges out of her backpack.

"Fruit! Just what the doctor ordered!"

They all drank lager liberally to wash down the food. Eric wondered when their next real meal would be, while Yvette soothingly stroked his head and neck. When he felt better, he returned the favor.

After the meal, Roger and Desiree played a slot machine while Eric wrote in his journal with Yvette's help. Desiree and Roger lost two pounds worth of coins in the one-armed bandit without winning anything. They got frustrated, and decided to take a tour of the boat. They walked out of the cabin and onto the outdoor observation deck where a comfortable breeze blew across the dark, choppy water. They talked about swimming across the channel, even though the water did not look the least bit inviting at the moment.

Desiree and Roger went below the deck to where the cars were parked, where they could get a closer look at the water. He had ridden on a ferryboat many years earlier, but the experience still felt new to him, and he was always fascinated by boats and oceans.

"Do some folks get seasick, even on short journeys?" Roger asked.

"You must've noticed the large basins in the water closets," Desiree replied. "I hope you're not getting sick."

"No, I feel fine. But I've never seen sinks like they have on board here."

They walked slowly together in the moonlight for a few minutes, discussing nothing in particular, then returned to their table inside. Desiree suggested to Yvette and Eric that they inspect the deck and the water.

"We're alone again, finally." Yvette led Eric outside. "Isn't this romantic in a strange way? A deserted deck on a large boat, in moderately rough water after dark. Too bad it's such a short passage."

Eric embraced her. "I could enjoy this all night long. I'm very happy right now. I know this is going to end all too soon."

"Let's not talk about it, then." Yvette drew him into a passionate kiss. They held each other more tightly as the cool evening breeze blew around them.

The ferry docked at Calais, Pas-de-Calais, France, at 22:30, about an hour after leaving Dover. They went through customs without any delays, even a spot inspection. Roger and Eric's passports were not stamped, either, much to their disappointment. Their passports had been endorsed at Heathrow Airport with a message that they had been granted leave to stay in the United Kingdom for six months, but the French authorities refused to recognize their presence in France.

Walking in the darkness on the pier toward the city lights, they had no idea where they were going. Calais, a city of some 70,000 people, was probably more foreign to Eric and Roger than any place they had ever been. Few pedestrians or motorists were about, but the city did have some nightlife. They heard American and British pop music coming out of several pubs, but that was the only form of English language they could find among billboards, graffiti and loud conversations.

"Isn't that song from *Grease*?" Yvette asked as they passed one particularly loud pub.

"No, I think it's from Italy," Eric deadpanned.

She slapped him playfully on the shoulder. "Stop trying to be funny all the time!"

"Hey! You're the one who told me your dad was an officer in the Swiss navy, and for about one second, I actually believed you!"

"People who've never been in Switzerland usually do believe me when I say that."

"I once bred a male shore bird with a female sheep, if you can believe that."

"Probably not. What did you get?"

"I made a ewe tern."

"I definitely don't believe that!"

They continued walking through the business district, away from the nightlife. They did not see any overnight accommodations anywhere.

"So France and the U.K. built a tunnel between Dover and Calais, I understand," Roger said. "Could be a job for some engineers to maintain it. Maybe if I swim across the channel now, they'll consider me for a position."

Desiree walked close to him. "Is that one of the job requirements?"

"Not likely, but it could be useful, in case of disaster. It would look impressive on my résumé, anyway."

"If you'll spend a few months in Switzerland with us," Desiree said, "We'll teach you to speak French. That would look impressive on your résumé, if you want to work in Europe."

"Do you speak French as well as you speak English?" Eric asked.

"Probably better," Desiree said. "What do you think, sister?"

"I think English is our third language, after German and French," Yvette said. "Our parents both speak all three languages, so we've been learning them all our lives. We understand some Italian, Romansch and Dutch, too, but we're not fluent in any of them."

"I'm impressed," Roger said.

"I'm starting to feel at home again," Eric said as an automobile passed. "People are driving on the side of the street where they should be."

"Where are we going, by the way?" Yvette asked.

"I don't know," Eric said. "I'm following you."

"At least we'll get a nice after-hours tour of the waterfront and downtown," Roger said. "That is, if this is downtown Calais."

"Looks like downtown to me," Eric said. "I can't help but wonder where we'll end up between now and morning."

"We'll know it when we get there, as usual," Roger said. "I just hope it's soon. My body doesn't like carrying our luggage this way."

"I don't envy you two carrying your equipment like that," Desiree said, "but I'm glad you left your bicycles with your friends in London. It's so much more fun to travel with you."

Eric switched the panniers to his right arm and the sleeping bag to his left. "We hated to leave the bikes, but we do want to ride trains with you two. We'll cover a lot of territory this week, more than we would have on our bikes."

Roger was as uncomfortable carrying the equipment as Eric. "Bicycles are a great way to see the country, but not a great way to move quickly when you don't care what's in between stopping points. I don't expect we'll see much of France between railway stations."

They continued aimlessly through the streets of Calais, the men with their handlebar bags over one shoulder and their sleeping bags in the other arm. They took turns carrying the panniers. They had been warned by Inga to beware of swindlers and pickpockets, so they watched carefully what little activity was happening around them. The women were quite comfortable carrying all their own gear in their backpacks.

By 23:30 London time, they found a well-illuminated park. They were in a different time zone, though, and local time was 00:30 Tuesday, to add to their disorientation. One light was out near a cluster of trees and a grassy area, and that was where they chose to camp for the night. The park was clean and otherwise deserted. They all felt reasonably safe and obscured from public view.

"Like Brigham Young allegedly once said, 'This *is* the place!'" Roger said. "See? I told you we'd know it."

"Young was quoted out of context, you know," Eric said. "What he really said was, '*This* is the place?'"

"That may be true, but this is the presidential suite, as far as we're concerned."

Eric set his gear on the grass and shook some sensation back into his tired arms. "Too bad our bags don't zip together, Yvette."

"We might have to make other arrangements. Good night, Desiree and Roger."

"How is your knee holding out?" Eric pulled his sleeping bag out of its stuff sack. "Did my suggestion help?"

"Must be better." Roger arched his back in a stretch after he set his gear down. "I'd already forgotten about it."

Eric was proud of himself. "Amazing how those minor adjustments can make the difference between agony and ecstasy."

"You should have considered a health profession, like your old man. You have some aptitude."

"Not really, but I could argue that subject all night long. Some other time, maybe."

"We've had some interesting experiences sleeping in European parks so far." Roger secured his luggage for the night and climbed into his sleeping bag next to Desiree in her sleeping bag. "Some hoodlums almost murdered us, a dog almost...never mind."

"We've slept in a few parks like this one, haven't we, big sister?"

"We might sleep in a few more before this holiday is over." Desiree snuggled close to Roger.

A dapper man in a worsted wool suit and silk tie drove his Range Rover up to Henry Smythe's shop in the late afternoon. He carried his briefcase with him into the garage. "Hello, Smythe. You're looking well today!"

Smythe turned and pushed his spectacles up his nose, not immediately recognizing the man. "Oh, hello, Mr. Whitcombe. What can I do for you?"

Geoff Whitcombe was a bicycle racing promoter and, more recently, the manager of a semi-professional team. He was also an executive at the industrial supply company founded by his grandfather. Smythe had built frames for his team on numerous occasions over the years.

"I'm in a bit of a bind, you see. I hope you can help me. I recruited this Italian chap from Milan earlier this year. He's been moving up the European rankings very quickly, and I was lucky to get him to sign a contract with our team. I expect he'll be our team leader next year, unless someone else offers him a better contract. I don't want to lose him to another team. He ruined his favorite bike in a crash last week, and he needs a new one as soon as possible."

"Don't you have several spares on hand for him to use? Most teams do."

"Yes, of course, but he wants a custom, and I immediately thought of you. In fact, he requested one of yours as his primary bike. We have several frame suppliers, but all of them are booked through the end of the racing season. What's more, I don't think theirs are quite as good as yours. I'm willing to pay a 20% premium on top of your usual fee. Can you do it? I have the specifications from his last frame right here in my briefcase."

"Well, I do have some customers in the queue who need their frames in short order. I can't let them down."

"Tell you what, old boy. I'll pay double if you make this job your top priority. What do you say?"

Smythe thought about the offer for a moment. His daughter's wedding was coming up soon, and he could certainly use the extra money. He hated to keep his other customers waiting. That young American, in particular, would be going back home in early August and would be very disappointed if his frame was not ready on time. Whitcombe had been a very good customer in the past, and he always paid handsomely for Smythe's work, even if he was a bit of a stuffed shirt.

"I'll see what I can do. Leave the papers on my desk, and I'll call you with a quote in the morning."

"Splendid then! I knew I could count on you, Henry."

Henry Smythe returned to the frame he was working on for Roger, after Whitcombe left. He pondered how he was going to meet all his deadlines.

38.

Eric passed Peter, then Roger, and prepared to sprint to the finish line. Sweat was practically gushing down his face, and he was sucking in all the air he could. He came up even with Rob, poured on a little more speed, and passed him too. The finish line was just ahead, and no one else was in front of him. A car appeared out of nowhere and made a sudden turn right in Eric's path. Eric desperately reached for his brakes and then...

Eric jerked upright in his sleeping bag. He was panting, just like he was in his dream, and all his muscles were tense. The race and the car evaporated instantly. He felt leg cramps coming on, then subsiding after he shook his legs. The sun was up, and he had a sore spot in his back. He turned and slid his hand beneath his sleeping bag.

Yvette rubbed her eyes and yawned as she awoke. "Did you sleep well?"

"Someone must have had an attack of pancreatitis here." Eric had a pebble in his hand. He had been sleeping on top of it.

"How would you know that?" Roger was awake, too.

He held up the pebble for all to see. "I found a Gaul stone."

A beautiful French morning and a dormant, deserted park greeted four weary but content campers as they arose. Yvette, Eric, Desiree and Roger noticed as they stuffed their sleeping bags that the whole town of Calais seemed rather subdued so early in the morning. They carried their gear into the business district in search of breakfast, where they found a café. They were served the strongest coffee Roger and Eric had ever tasted, along with some pastries.

"Did you read this?" Roger pointed to his coffee cup. "It says, 'In case of accidental swallowing, do not induce vomiting. Dilute with milk or water or dry red wine. Call physician immediately.'"

"You can't say they didn't warn you, Squire. Mine says, 'Avoid contact with skin. Flush affected area with cold water for twenty minutes.' Has it in four, count 'em, four languages!"

"I can tell you two haven't been in France before," Yvette said.

"What are we going to do today?" Roger wondered aloud.

"Would you like to go to Paris?"

"I'd Louvre to see Paris," Eric said.

"Might as well," Roger agreed. "I'm sure we can get an Eiffel of something interesting in Paris, if we have enough Monet. Maybe a Rubens sandwich."

"Your puns are driving me in Seine!"

"How are we going to get there? Hitchhike or train?"

"You don't want to hitchhike in France. They don't give rides to Americans."

"How would they know we're Americans?"

"They just know. Trust me on this. The train is the best way to get there."

"Do you know of a place to stay overnight, or should we take our chances on a hotel?"

"Let's find an Internet café when we're done here. We can book beds at one of the hostels."

"Sounds like a plan. Let's do it then."

They found an Internet café just down the street from where they ate breakfast. Desiree booked a private room for them at the Clichy Youth Hostel in a northwestern suburb of Paris. A big hostel, it had nearly twice the capacity of the Eglinton or Earl's Court hostels. The web site described it as near the Arc de Triomphe and the Louvre. While Desiree made the arrangements, Eric looked on with an incredible feeling of euphoria. Fate had finally delivered him to the right place at the right time. He was happier than an unknown on the winners' podium at the end of a grueling stage race.

The railway station was several blocks away from the Internet café. The city of Calais was starting to show some signs of life. They stopped at a public restroom to freshen up, as they were unable to do the previous night once they got off the ferry from Dover. They had nearly an hour to kill while they waited for the next train to Paris. Desiree and Roger stayed in the railway station with everyone's luggage while Yvette and Eric went back to a bookstore they had passed earlier. Eric wanted to buy a French-English dictionary and a postcard to send to his family.

The three-hour train ride to Paris included a few stops along the way. The scenery was mostly ordinary to the two Americans, and entirely mundane to the Swiss sisters. Nonetheless, it was the first real view of France for Eric and Roger. They looked out the window and asked many questions. The ride ended at the gigantic Gare Saint-Lazare railway station in northwest Paris. The women seemed to know where they were going. The men followed and tried their best to avoid looking like clueless foreign tourists.

A ride on Line 13 of Le Metro, the Paris subway system, took them northwest to Clichy in the department of Hauts de Seine. The hostel was just a short distance from the banks of the meandering Seine River, on rue Martre. As before, the women led the way and did all the talking at the hostel registration desk. They were assigned to a room on the third floor with four bunk beds. They carried their gear to their room and let out a collective sigh the moment they were able to set it on the floor.

"I'm starved and I need a shower in the worst way," Eric said. He was soaked with sweat from the stifling summer heat, as they all were.

"Forget about the shower until later," Yvette said. "We have things to do. You'll just get sweaty again."

On their way back to the Metro station, they stopped at a bakery for a croissant and a green grocer in the same block for some fruit for a late lunch. Eric and Roger both noticed France's most famous landmark towering over the city. Travel was so much easier without the cumbersome panniers and sleeping bags.

"Where are we going?"

"Don't worry! You'll know it when we get there."

"Just like last night?"

"Not quite. But you won't be disappointed."

"You've used that line on me before! And I'm falling for it once again."

They got off the train, left the Cité station and walked a few blocks amid heavy traffic and crowds of pedestrians. The gothic church they were approaching did not register at first in the minds of the two Americans. It took them a few moments to recognize the Cathédrale de Notre-Dame.

"Are you familiar with this church?"

"It rings a bell."

"I had a hunch back there you'd say something like that."

They walked around the outside of the twelfth-century cathedral and took plenty of photographs. Much like central London, it was crawling with tourists from around the world. They decided not to go inside for a tour. The sisters had seen it some years earlier, and the Americans had seen enough old churches. The admission fee was steep enough to discourage them. They stopped at a bank where the Americans each exchanged a traveler's check for euros. They got back on the Metro with their all-day passes and rode to another stop after they had their fill of Notre-Dame.

"We thought you two cyclists would want to see this street," Yvette said as they came to another busy street.

Eric looked up at the street sign to confirm what he was thinking. "Avenue des Champs-Èlysées? So this is where the peloton enters the city center."

Roger pointed to a traffic circle a few blocks away. "That must be L'Arc de Triomphe."

"You have watched the Tour de France on television, I can see. You know some of the landmarks," Desiree said.

"Every July! Can we get a closer look at the Arc?"

"We can go inside to the upper wall, if you like."

"I'd like!"

They walked down the Champs-Èlysées to the Arc. Roger and Eric expected to see plenty of Tour de France souvenirs in the stores, but they were disappointed. The clothing stores had more soccer and tennis apparel than cycling garments. The World Cup and the French Open appeared to be more popular than Le Tour.

"When a Frenchman wins the Tour, you will see more cycling items in the stores," Desiree explained.

"Hasn't happened since 1985," Eric said. "It's been a long drought."

"They haven't even had much in the way of serious contenders any time recently," Roger added. "Just a lot of polka-dot jerseys for the best mountain climber."

They took a tunnel under the busy street to the Place de Charles de Gaulle, and waited in line to enter the Arc. Desiree and Yvette explained the significance of some of the details of the friezes, and pointed out the landmarks they could see from the top. Paris seemed to go on forever in every direction.

"Is it too late in the day for the Eiffel Tower?" Roger asked. He looked south toward the tower and tried to estimate its distance.

"No, it is open after dark. We will go there tomorrow, early," Desiree said.

"Would you like to see the Louvre, too? I think we can do both in one day," Yvette said.

"Whatever you want to do is fine with me," Eric said. "Everything here is new and different to us." He stood behind Yvette and wrapped his arms around her waist. "I'm happy just to be with you. Life doesn't get any better than this."

Yvette put her hands on his and pressed her back against him. She was also as happy as she had ever been. "I've always wanted to be in Paris with my lover. And here we are!"

The afternoon turned to early evening, and they stopped at a restaurant on the Champs-Èlysées with outdoor seating. The traffic decreased, and the sun was low enough that their sidewalk table was in the shade. They dined on a four-course meal: salad with raspberry vinaigrette dressing, white cheese called *fromage*, a seafood platter called *fruit de mer* and creme caramel for dessert, accompanied by the house Chardonnay. Roger seemed preoccupied, but only to Eric. Desiree and Yvette did not notice the subtleties. Was he imagining himself racing past the Arc in the final stage of the Tour de France, or reconsidering his engagement?

"Do you want to see anything else today?" Yvette asked as they left the restaurant. "There are so many things to do."

"Where do you get so much energy? I'm about ready for bed," Eric said. He took Yvette by the hand. They walked slowly toward the Metro station a few blocks away.

"It has been a long day," Roger said. "A very good day, but a long one. That was a good meal. French restaurants are not very common in the U.S. Not rare, really, but not very common either. It hit the spot."

"We should get to bed, because we have a big day tomorrow," Desiree said.

They rode the Metro back to Clichy and found the hostel in the twilight. Desiree and Roger went inside immediately and headed for the showers.

Yvette and Eric kept on walking until they came to the river. They kissed passionately as darkness fell. What would his high school classmates think if they could see him now? The shyest boy in their class was romancing his European sweetheart on the banks of the Seine on a warm summer evening. Maybe the City of Lights was not as overrated as Eric had once thought.

39.

A shower and a good night's sleep put Yvette, Desiree, Eric and Roger back in good spirits. They had a breakfast of croissants, yogurt, fruit and tea in the hostel. They registered for another night at the hostel before they made their way to the Metro station. Two train changes kept them alert. Desiree and Yvette arose when the subway arrived at the Trocadéro station, and the two Americans followed. They walked past the Palais de Chaillot, the buskers and the dancing waters of the Trocadéro fountains. A bridge over the Seine took them to the Parc du Champs-de-Mars at the base of the Eiffel Tower.

A sizable crowd, just a few of the six million annual visitors, had already gathered at the tower before they arrived. The Americans were awed by Gustave Eiffel's iron masterpiece, built for the Paris Exhibition in 1889. The base of the tower had an entire square block as its footprint. The queue in front of the elevator was long and slow-moving. The walk-up route was less expensive and much less crowded. Roger and Eric needed some physical activity after two days of riding in motor vehicles. They all took the stairs to the first level at 58 meters. They spent nearly an hour, taking in the view in every direction and browsing in the retail kiosks.

The view from the second level, at 116 meters, was even better than the first. Eric and Roger bought postcards and had them stamped by the cashier, certifying the postcards had actually been purchased at and mailed from Le Tour Eiffel. They read all the historical displays and plaques that described the construction of the tower.

"Is that domed building down there where the Senat meets?" Eric was looking to the east. A building several blocks away had a slight resemblance to the U.S. Capitol.

"No, that is Les Invalides. I think it was once a home for wounded soldiers established by Louis XIV," Yvette said. "Napoléon is buried there."

Eric noted the absence of any real skyscrapers, unlike Manhattan and the downtown area of most of the big cities in North America. The Parisians seemed to like their hotels, banks and corporate headquarters in smaller buildings away from the center of the city. The land consisted of gently rolling hills, once covered by lush forests. Modern Paris was still very green, especially the Bois de Boulogne recreation area to the west. The vast metropolitan area once known as Île de France was an impressive sight from Europe's most recognizable structure.

The only public route to the third level, at 276 meters, was the elevator, and the queue was as long and sluggish on the second level as it was at the ground level. Eric and his three companions took lots of photographs with panoramic views of Paris in the background. They decided not to go up to the third level, not wanting to wait in line. They had a snack instead, bought some key-chain souvenirs for family members back home, and walked down the stairs. Two hours in the tower seemed long enough, and they still wanted to see the Louvre.

"Ready to move on?"

"I could stay here all day, but we should get going. What's next?"

From the Trocadéro station, they rode Line 9 to where it crossed Line 1. Line 1 took them east to the Musée du Louvre, the greatest art museum in France if not the entire world. The building itself was a museum piece, and once served as the royal palace. Louis XIII resided there in the early 1600s, as mentioned by Alexandre Dumas in his novel *The Three Musketeers*. They walked around the perimeter until they found an entrance to the courtyard. The famous glass pyramid caught the Americans' attention and drew them toward the entrance to the art exhibits.

They made a point of finding the *Mona Lisa* first, in the Denon Wing. Leonardo Da Vinci's most familiar work was surrounded by a thick crowd of admirers. The protective glass made photography of the painting difficult at best. A well-dressed Japanese tour group moved into the viewing zone next to Desiree and her entourage. The tour group leader, probably a professor of art, was obviously passionate about the painting. His audience paid close attention to every word in his lecture. The Swiss and Americans could not understand any of it, but they paid attention to him, too. They would have liked to hear a description of the masterpiece from an expert.

"I expected it to be bigger for some reason," Roger said. "It's not even life size."

"Yet much bigger than life, in many ways!"

Desiree, Yvette, Eric and Roger looked at the other European Renaissance paintings from Da Vinci, David, Rembrandt, Vermeer, Rubens, Delacroix and others on the first floor. They took a break for lunch in a cafeteria beneath the glass pyramid.

Roger set his tray down on a table where the other three were already seated. "No reuben sandwiches, no Rubens sandwiches. Don't these people recognize a good marketing opportunity?"

"I got Manets on the side with my sandwich," Eric said. "They're catching on, slowly."

"I've only met a few Americans, but you all seem to have marketing in your blood," Desiree said. "You're thinking about business even when you are making lame jokes. Why is that?"

"It might be that we're exposed to advertising and sales promotions from day one," Roger said.

"Commerce is at the heart of our culture, I suppose," Eric added. "Good or bad, that's the way we are."

"Surprisingly, maybe, some of our neighboring countries are almost the opposite."

"Is it a bad thing?" Eric asked.

"No, not wrong in any way. I would call it a distinguishing feature of Americans."

After lunch, they toured the sculptures on the ground floor. The Code of Hammurabi in the Richelieu Wing and Michelangelo's *The Dying Slave* were interesting, but Venus de Milo in the Sully Wing was the main attraction. The statue of Aphrodite, carved by an unknown Greek artist in the second century B.C., was discovered on the island of Milo in 1820.

"I'm waiting for an Aphrodite joke," Yvette reminded Eric.

"OK then, she's very disarming," Eric said. "How's that for a start?"

"We'll have to come up with something more original than that! Something about the arms race, maybe?"

"That's not very original either. Do you suppose her favorite Hemingway novel is what I think it is?"

They spent the rest of the afternoon looking at art and antiquities. When they had their fill, they rode the Metro back to Clichy. Seats on the train felt good after several hours of standing and walking. A dearth of drinking fountains in the Louvre and elsewhere forced them to buy bottled beverages more than once. The Americans were pleased that they had seen so many things they were not expecting to see on this journey. The Swiss sisters were satisfied sharing the cultural treasures of Europe with someone special.

Eric was about to suggest they buy groceries and prepare their supper in the self-catering kitchen at the hostel, when they all noticed several enticing restaurants just off the path from the station to the hostel.

"Why cook when you can have creme brulée and sorbet and fresh bread?" Yvette said to Eric.

"OK, you talked me into it. Do we have a consensus?"

"Sure. We can cook tomorrow if we must."

They found a cozy bistro next door to a hardware store that sold Peugeot power tools. Roger and Eric were familiar with Peugeot cars and bicycles, but not aware of the company's many other products, things not exported to America. They looked in the window of the hardware store for a moment, then went into the bistro. The hostess greeted them with a smile, some rapidly spoken small talk not understood by the Americans, and a set of menus. She showed them to a table comfortably separate from the handful of other diners.

"Are you brave enough to try escargot?" Desiree asked the two Americans. Escargot was one of the entrées on the menu.

Eric and Roger looked at each other, each silently daring the other. They both noted how *entrée* had a different meaning in French, one that made more sense than the English use of that word.

"I know it's snails, but how is it served?"

"Like clam soup," Yvette said, searching for the correct word. "What do you call clam soup?"

"Clam chowder? Is that what you mean?"

"Yes, clam chowder. It is like clam chowder."

"I will if you all will," Eric said.

"Same here," Roger added.

They all ordered escargot to start. The escargot was served in a white broth, heavy on the butter and garlic, but quite tasty. They followed that with *le fromage*. All the cheese selections were white and, like the soup, very appetizing. Yvette explained that orange cheese, such as cheddar, is very rare in France. The women ordered quiche for the main course, Eric had bouillabaisse, and Roger had *poulet au jambon*, a chicken breast stuffed with ham, cheese and spinach and topped with a tangy sauce. A carafe of pinot blanc helped wash the food down. For dessert, they shared a chocolate mousse, profiterole, cannelé and creme brulée.

"I'm impressed by how much you two seem to like French food," Desiree said. "Yesterday morning, I was afraid you would complain about the food and not want to eat anything."

"Not much chance of that," Eric said. "I've liked just about everything we've tried here. Some of the desserts are to die for." He refilled everyone's wine glass to finish off the carafe.

"So much good food, so little time," Roger said. "When we're with you, everything tastes good."

"I've got to propose a toast before we leave," Eric said. He looked at Yvette, and she smiled back at him with a look of deep satisfaction.

"What do you want to drink to?"

"To the four of us." Eric raised his wineglass. "May the good times never end!"

40.

A café and *boulangerie* across the street from the previous evening's restaurant looked too tempting to pass up for breakfast. It did not disappoint Yvette, Desiree, Roger and Eric. A fresh eclair and a cup of *café au lait* was a great way to start the day.

"Do you want to see more of Paris, or should we move on?" Yvette asked the two Americans.

"What else here would be worth visiting?"

"The Rodin museum is near Les Invalides, if you like sculpture, La Place de la Bastille, Le Sacré Cœur, L'Opéra…"

"I'm sure they all have their charm, but I'm ready for something else."

"How far is Chamonix from here, and is it expensive to stay there?"

Desiree's cell phone interrupted the discussion. She looked at the display before she pressed the button to answer the call. "It's our mother. She probably has some news about our grandmother." She answered the phone in French, then spoke to her three companions. "Excuse me for a few minutes, please." She stood up and left the café.

"This is both the best and worst holiday I've ever had. Neither Desiree nor I really want to know how our grandmother is right now. She'll only get worse, I'm sure."

"Some day, fifty or sixty years from now, maybe, our descendants will be mulling over our sick, worn out bodies, waiting for us to die," Eric said. "Dreadful thought, isn't it?"

"I'm sure she is ready for the end. Her health has been declining for such a long time. We'll miss her, but no one will say she did not live a full life."

Yvette, Eric and Roger waxed philosophical over the meaning of life, aging and related matters for a few minutes until Desiree returned with a sad expression.

"She died very peacefully in her sleep last night," Desiree said. "Mother is overwhelmed by visitors already. Father is on his way back from a conference in Berlin."

"Did she ask us to come immediately?" Yvette knew the answer already.

"Yes, she needs our help," Desiree said. "I was afraid this might happen before you two return to America."

"Would you mind very much if we went back to Bern for a few days?" Yvette asked Eric. She searched her mind for some way to mitigate the situation. "You could even meet us there at the end of the week."

"We don't mind at all. It has to be that way." Eric was dejected, and it showed. "Take care of your mother. She needs you right now even more than we do." His words rang very hollow in his own mind.

"The funeral is scheduled for Saturday, and our relatives will be leaving soon afterward," Desiree said. "Telephone us at our parents' house or our cell phones on Saturday afternoon, and we'll make arrangements to pick you up at the railway station in Bern, or else we can meet somewhere in France or Germany if you like. Say you will!"

"You can even stay with us in Bern," Yvette said, "if...if your hair gets wild."

"We will." Roger resisted the temptation to correct her use of that expression. "We want to spend every moment we can with you. Right, Chief?"

"Absolutely! I also want to extend our deepest condolences to your family. We'll call you on Saturday."

"Where will we be on Saturday?" Roger wondered aloud. "Where do we go between now and then?"

"We can check out France on our own. We'll be all right."

"I'm sorry we have to leave you," Yvette said. "I hate to let you get lost in France. The French people don't speak other languages as well as the Swiss, the Dutch and the Germans. You'll have to learn some French very quickly."

"We'll manage," Roger assured her. "We're prepared for most anything."

"I'll miss you," Yvette said as she hugged Eric. She sounded just as dejected as Eric, and she choked back tears as she spoke.

"I'll miss you, too, but we'll be back together soon."

The four checked out of the hostel and walked to the Metro station. They rode back to La Gare Saint-Lazare, where the women boarded a train that would eventually take them to Bern, with several stops in between Paris and Bern. All were sad to be parting company, but all had high hopes of meeting again on the weekend, and they were discussing plans accordingly until the train departed. The men waved the women off, and carried their burdensome gear back to the ticket area.

"We need some provisions before we pursue our trek any farther," Roger said. "A bookstore or newsagent would probably have maps. Still have that pocket-size French dictionary with you?"

"Side pocket of the left pannier. We'll be able to ask someone for directions to a place to eat and sleep." Eric had a strong urge to ask Roger what had transpired between him and Desiree, but he resisted. He knew Roger would say something when he was ready. "We've been here too long already."

They followed their instincts, and found a bookstore a few blocks from the station. The city was beginning to show some signs of life. The warmth of the morning sunshine was gradually overcoming the locals' activation

248

energy barrier. Except for the titles of the books, the store could have passed for any American neighborhood bookstore. They purchased a map of Western Europe.

"Now for the big decision." Just outside the bookstore, Eric opened the map. "Where do we go first?"

"I've been thinking, as I've had some idle time here. Remember our old friend Danny Sanchez?"

"He's in the army, somewhere in Germany. That's where he was last I heard. What about him?"

"Why don't we see if we can locate him? That should keep us busy until Saturday. He told us last time we saw him that we have a standing invitation. Said he knows a great bordello where he's stationed."

"Germany's a big country. Where would we start looking?"

"He was stationed somewhere in Bavaria at that time. Let's hitch a ride to Munich and start with the first U.S. Army base we come across. I bet any base will have a directory for all personnel in Germany. It's worth a try."

By midmorning, they were standing and sweating near a freeway entrance ramp. With their thumbs extended, they watched car after car pass, but no one offered them a ride. Several drivers looked at them with an expression that said, "*Oubliez lui, étrangers!*" In other words, forget about it, foreigners. For two frustrating hours, one rested while the other stood with thumb in position. No one waved at them, no one threw rubbish at them, few acknowledged their presence with a glance, and no one stopped.

"Bloody hell! It's time, I think, to execute Plan B," Roger said. "Plan A is definitely not working."

"What is Plan B? Take a train to Munich?"

"Unless you can think of a better way to get there."

"Let's go, then," Eric conceded. "The train is going to be expensive, though."

"We're not exactly saving money by standing here, going nowhere. I am slightly tempted to go back to Romford for our bicycles. Let's get tickets to Munich before that urge overcomes me."

Though not moving in the direction they wanted, they felt reassured to be going somewhere, anywhere. The train schedule was not so easy for them to translate. They checked the words on the train schedule in their new dictionary, and decided that a train leaving for Munich via Strasbourg was what they wanted to ride.

With time to waste before the train's departure, they found a *crêperie* near the railway station. The *crêperie* was nicely decorated and comfortably furnished. They almost felt like the place was too respectable for anyone who looked the way they did. An older waitress showed them to a table, and said something in French.

"*Le menu, s'il vous plait.*" Eric felt a little daft for having to ask.

The waitress handed each of them a menu and disappeared. They were able to pick out the key words so they knew what they were getting. The waitress returned a few minutes later to take their order.

"*M'sieu?*"

"*Deux crêpes avec fromage.*" Eric hoped his crude French pronunciation would suffice. He gestured to indicate one of crêpe for Roger and one for himself.

"*Et deux jus du pomme.*" Roger held up two fingers to emphasize two beverages.

"*Tres bien.*" The waitress nodded, wrote their order on her pad and went into the kitchen.

"You surprised me there," Eric said. "I didn't think you were going to try to say anything in French. That's why I ordered a crêpe for you."

"I gathered that. You should know that I have learned a few things in college besides shear and moment diagrams."

While they waited for their food, they inspected the eatery's other clientele, which included some business-lunch types and some attractive women. One such woman, who also fit the business-lunch description, made eye contact with Eric and smiled at him in a way that he could not help but interpret as seductive. He was sure his imagination was wandering.

A few minutes later, the waitress returned with two cold glasses of lightly fermented apple cider and two steaming hot crêpes filled with melted white cheese. They paid her, and quickly devoured their lunch. They kept a close but subtle watch on two or three women, especially the one who had smiled at Eric. She occasionally glanced at them, each time with her come-hither look.

"I kind of like it here," Roger said. "The *crêperie*, that is. I hope we can find more like this one."

"Seems like the sort of place where wild adventures might begin." Eric took the last bite of his crêpe, which he assumed was the French version of a quesadilla or a grilled cheese sandwich. "You know what? A crêpe filled with raspberries and ice cream would hit the spot right now."

"Damn, that does sound good." Roger looked at his watch. They still had two hours to kill while waiting for their train. "Was that on the menu?"

"What part of *crêpe framboise* don't you understand?" Eric gestured to get the waitress's attention. "*Garçonne?*" He ordered two more crêpes with raspberries and another round of cider. The dessert crêpes were served cold.

Before they finished lunch, they saw their lady friend's female companion, whose back was toward them, get up and leave. As she left the table, she kissed the woman with the seductive smile in a way the two young Americans found mildly arousing. They looked at each other with incredulity. As Americans, they would have shaken hands or just waved goodbye to each other. Once again, Eric felt as if he needed Yvette there to explain European customs to him.

They walked back to the railway station after their late lunch. On the platform alongside the tracks where passengers await their train, they spotted someone who looked very interesting to both of them. Their train was due in less than ten minutes, and she appeared to be awaiting the same train.

Roger and Eric were brainstorming silently, trying to think of a clever, unobtrusive way to start a conversation with this woman, but they did not even know if she understood English. She could have been from most anywhere in Europe, they thought, but they could not see anything about her that gave away her nationality. She was holding a book in one hand, but her forearm covered the title.

Changing to a more comfortable stance, the woman looked up and ever so briefly made eye contact with Roger. She cast her glance downward again and put the book in her other hand. Both Roger and Eric, who were standing within two meters of her, looked at the book, but only Roger was in a good position to see it. The title was in English, something about a guide to hitchhiking in Europe. He could not have asked for a better book—that subject was on his and Eric's minds. He knew exactly how to start the conversation.

"Have you had any luck hitchhiking in France?" Roger boldly said to the woman. She looked at him again, pleasantly surprised.

"Some places have been better than others." The woman had an accent that did not quite sound European to them.

"We tried to hitch a ride through France," Roger said. "You can see how that turned out."

The woman opened her book to a passage she showed to them. The passage mentioned something to the effect that a woman hitchhiker should be well armed with contraceptives, as male drivers are likely to expect favors in return for transportation.

"That may be one of the reasons I'm riding the train today." The woman had a twinkle in her eye and a smirk on her lips. "I'm not as easy as this book says I should be."

The conversation continued for several minutes until the train arrived. The two Americans introduced themselves to Christina, age 25, from Australia. The train was crowded. Eric, Roger and Christina climbed aboard one car, but the only available seats were singles, so they decided to stand at one end of the coach until some adjacent seats became available after a stop.

Christina had plenty to say, in a lovely voice at that, about her travels through Eastern Europe since May. She wore a blue, knee-length skirt, high-heeled sandals and a short-sleeve blue blouse. Her wavy, dark brown hair was shoulder-length, her makeup conservative and her tan just the right color to nicely complement everything else about her. She was quite a bit shorter than the men, and very shapely. Unlike them, she looked very prim, and not at all like the seasoned world traveler she really was.

The train ride to Châlons-en-Champagne was entirely too short and too fast. The three had so much to discuss and so many common interests. Christina was on her way to Reims to meet a relative, to visit the wineries, and to explore some historical sites. She explained to them the Battle of Châlons in A.D. 450, when the Huns and their allies led by Attila engaged the Visigoths led by Theodoric and the Romans led by Aetius. When the train came to a stop, Roger and Eric carried Christina's luggage off the train for her.

"Have a pleasant journey in Reims," Roger said. "Too bad our ride here was so brief."

"I've enjoyed your company," Christina said. "I wish we had more time to talk. There's so much I want to know about your country."

"Come to the U.S. someday," Eric said. "It's a good country, and quite unlike Europe in many ways."

"Come to Australia sometime. It's a good country, too, and also quite unlike Europe. I hope you find your friend in Germany, and your girlfriends in Switzerland."

"We'll have fun searching Germany, even if we don't find him," Eric said. "Switzerland will be interesting, too."

"*Au revoir.*" Christina waved to them from the platform.

"Enjoy the Champagne," Eric said through the open window, "and the crêpes, too."

"G'day, mate," Roger said. "Isn't that what they say in your country?"

"Only in the movies. I never say that." The train began to move, and they waved to her as she left. She turned and waved at someone in the station who came to receive her.

"Seems like we're always seeing women off at the train station." Eric picked up his gear once again and carried it toward an empty seat. "That was the third time."

"You appear to have doubts about us seeing the Hoffmann sisters again."

"It's a long shot, really. Even if we do see them again, we won't have much time with them, and we won't have much money left. In spite of all that, my hopes are still high."

"We'll be thrifty in Germany, so we'll have enough to get us to Bern and then back to London. It'll be worth every shilling we have to see them again. You know it will."

"We should probably plan to stay with them in Bern. That'll save us the cost of lodging. If we play our cards right, everything will work out."

They arrived in Strasbourg, Bas-Rhin, in the evening. Their train to Munich was not due to leave for another two hours, and would be an all-night journey. The city on the west bank of the Rhine River was a strategic site during the Franco-Prussian War in 1870 and again in the Great War, when Bas-Rhin was known as Alsace. It seemed serene and ordinary to the two Americans, some nine decades later. They carried their burdensome luggage out of the railway station, into the city center. The spire of another Cathedral of Notre Dame was the highlight of the Strasbourg skyline.

Hungry again, or perhaps still, they purchased two baguettes, two eclairs and a bottle of red table wine at a bakery, and some bananas at a green grocer. They continued their walk through the business district, stopping to eat fresh French bread by the loaf and drinking Provençal wine, like two transients. Although conspicuous with their sleeping bags, panniers and handlebar bags in hand, they did not attract much attention to themselves. Most of the businesses were closed for the day, and most of the people were at home.

After eating, walking and looking at the few French people who were out and about, they sauntered back to the railroad station. All the cars on their train were divided into compartments containing opposing bench seats. They sat in an empty compartment, but were soon joined by a woman and her three small children. The children fell asleep soon after the train left Strasbourg. The woman paid no attention to Roger and Eric's conversation. They guessed that she was a native who did not understand English.

"I'm glad we're getting the hell out of France," Roger said. "We're moving again, finally. I feel uncomfortable in a nation where they don't pick up hitchhikers."

"Maybe we're the clowns who brought the hell into France," Eric said. "As for hitchhiking, I'm not sure I'd offer a ride to someone who looks like us."

"It would take us a long time to get bored by familiarity here. We could find plenty of adventure in France, with only a little effort."

"I'd like to come back some day, with about ten thousand euros worth of someone else's money and a few weeks to spend. We could have a good time getting lost and not being able to communicate."

"I think I figured out what's wrong with France."

"What's that?"

"They have a glut of culinary talent, but a shortage of lead-free solder."

"Why is that so bad?"

"Too many chefs and not enough indium."

"Ugh! Don't give up your day job just yet!"

"It needs a little polish before I use it in my stand-up routine."

The train made several stops on its way southeast. Each time, a conductor examined everyone's ticket. When night fell, they had trouble sleeping. They envied the children, who were small enough to get comfortable on the seats and had someone else to hold their tickets. They were able to catch a small amount of sleep in between interruptions by the conductors. Their time in France was interesting and educational, but they looked forward to Germany.

41.

At 6:30, English and Bavarian time, a train rolled into Munich with two very weary Americans on board. Eric looked like he was about to have a seizure or some other calamity, but he and Roger collected themselves from their berth and carried their gear to the nearest exit.

In front of the train station, they just stood for a moment and gaped at the huge city surrounding them. *München*, as it is known to the Germans, more than 1.3 million residents strong, struck them as the sort of place where they were likely to get lost. They had no map of the city, no clue where they were, and no idea where they wanted to go.

"Lead the way," Roger said.

Eric returned a facial expression that was too dull for words. "I know this is starting to sound a bit hackneyed, but let's discuss our immediate future over breakfast. There must be an eatery somewhere near here."

"I was about to suggest we buy a municipal map, but that might not be much use to us if we can't read it. I bet we can find something to do around here."

"We've gotten this far without any real planning."

A feeling of déjà vu swept them when they entered a café a block or two from the train station. The café and its food were very similar to the one where they had eaten breakfast three days earlier in Calais. A waiter who spoke no English served them each a cup of industrial-strength coffee and a large Danish pastry.

"Are there any U.S. Army installations here?" Roger asked. "That would be a good place to start."

"I doubt it, and I doubt we could find it even if there is one," Eric said, "but there's no penalty for asking. There's probably a U.S. consulate here. We could look for that, too."

"Might as well give it a try."

"A city the size of this one ought to have some sort of public transportation, if we can't hitchhike. Maybe we can find a place to spend the night near there. I bet Munich has a youth hostel."

The previous night's lack of sleep had no effect on Roger, and surprisingly little on Eric, now that they had a plan. They were unsure of what they would be doing once they arrived at an army base, but they were determined to get to one anyway. They started with an Internet café, but the sites they looked up did not give an address or directions to the U.S. consulate in Munich, or any army bases. They did find addresses for two youth hostels. They already had a subway map from the station where they arrived, and they downloaded a map of the city with what little detail would fit on one page.

They tried to ask several passersby for directions, starting with, "*Sprechen Sie Englisch?*" to which the usual reply was, "*Nein.*" Nearly everyone they asked, even those who did not speak any English, was very polite. Eventually, they collected enough information from those who did understand some English to figure out how to get to what they thought was a consulate or U.S. Army base. They utilized a combination of the MVV railway system, walking and hitchhiking to get to the north side of town. Their last ride let them out, but not at an army base as they were expecting. The driver assured them, in his best English, that this was where they wanted to be. They thanked the driver for the lift, but they were not sure why he brought them to the Olympiapark München of all places. They had no trouble translating that phrase.

"So, where's the army base? Or the consulate?"

"Either the driver misunderstood what we wanted, or the map meant something other than what we thought it meant."

"Let's check it out as long as we're here. I've never been to an Olympic site."

"Me neither. Looks like quite the tourist draw. We'll find something interesting here."

They could not have chosen a better day to be there. Plenty of people, both tourists and locals, were enjoying the numerous facilities and the warm summer sunshine. They opened a bottle of Kabinett wine from the Mosel Valley and ate some apples they purchased at a market near the park. They updated their journals while sitting on a grassy hillside, enjoying their pre-lunch appetizer.

From where they were sitting, they could see many of the products of post-war reconstruction and other examples of modern German architecture. A wide highway, the B2R Georg-Brauchle Ring, formed one border of the park. The Bavarian Motor Works headquarters stood on the opposite side of the freeway from the park. The BMW complex included a shiny tower consisting of four connected circular cylinders and a museum shaped like a gigantic teacup bearing the familiar logo on its roof. The park itself contained several spectacular structures, one of which was the Olympic Tower, not unlike Seattle's Space Needle.

The 291-meter tower caught their attention, and they decided without hesitation to ascend it. An elevator carried them and their burdensome luggage to the observation deck at 190 meters, quite high above Munich but well below the antennas atop the area where the public was allowed. From the observation deck, they looked out across Munich and the broad plains of Bavaria. They could see the transparent domes over the stadium and swimming pool, a lake and canal, the vast Munich skyline, and the many people in summer attire who were also admiring the view. They took out their cameras and put them to use.

The swimming pool looked appealing to them from the viewing tower. Covered by a glass canopy, the huge pool lay next to one of the lakes and a sunbathing area enclosed by a fence. They rode the elevator down to the base of the tower, walked over to the fence surrounding the sunbathing area, and set their gear down on the grassy hillside. They sat on the grass, removed their T-shirts, and discreetly noticed the multitude of sunbathers and swimmers.

"That swimming pool beckons," Eric said, "but I do like just sitting here watching."

"We haven't swum since we left Colorado," Roger said, "and for that matter, I haven't swum all summer yet. We have all day. Want to?"

"You talked me into it."

They walked down the hill to the entrance of the pool. They paid their admission fee, bought rubber swimming caps as required to keep hair out of the pool, and went into what they correctly guessed to be the locker room, a very big locker room at that.

Roger started to remove his pants. "Why is there only one locker room? You can't say they couldn't afford a second one."

"I think we're supposed to use these dressing booths." Eric pointed to a series of doors between rows of lockers. "Get in there before you moon somebody!"

"That's what I meant to do! This is a novel idea as far as I'm concerned, one locker room for both sexes. I'm starting to feel at home here, even though this isn't at all like home." Roger went into a booth and closed the door.

"This is the first time I've ever worn a rubber cap for swimming," Eric said after changing. "I hope the ladies like my swim suit."

"It makes your hips look big."

"I knew I should've bought the one with vertical stripes!"

"Put your stuff in the locker, and let's hit the pool."

The huge pool contained a myriad of people speaking a myriad of languages, but they found plenty of room to get wet. The diving tower overlooking the separate diving pool was closed, but the springboards were open. Although swimming was something they could do at home, they had access to few Olympic-sized pools and no genuine Olympic pools. It was the best way they could imagine to mingle with the people of Europe. The North Sea and the English Channel were too cold or too rough for swimming when they were there, and they had no desire to look at museums or art galleries when they could be in a place like this. They were as content as they had been at any time during their tour, just swimming.

After an hour or two of swimming and diving, they dried off and went out to the sunbathing area, where they admired and were admired by a number of women. Roger found an abandoned Frisbee, and he and Eric captured some attention as the only Frisbee throwers on the lawn.

Having had enough sport, they returned to the locker room in the late afternoon and made liberal use of the showers, something they had been unable to do since leaving Paris. They dried off again, dressed in shorts and T-shirts, and left the pool building. They walked across the park until they came upon a stone walkway, a cast statue of a gymnast, and the velodrome.

They had seen only one or two real bicycle racing tracks before the Munich velodrome, none of which was as elaborate as this one. They went inside and sat in the bleachers, where they watched and photographed several future Olympians in training, some of whom were cruising around the steep-banked, wooden track on tandems. The grandstands had seating capacity for a few thousand, and four tennis courts were in the center of the track. They conducted themselves on a thorough tour through the facilities, took more photographs, and left the velodrome.

"Where to next?"

"How about the stadium, as if we've never seen a stadium."

The stadium grandstands were covered, like the velodrome bleachers and the swimming pool, by the distinctive glass canopy, but the athletic field was uncovered. A religious organization's worldwide convention was in progress, but its members occupied only a small fraction of the available seats when Eric and Roger were there, so they were not interrupting anything.

"There's something odd about that field," Roger said. "It doesn't look right."

"The lack of football goal posts or a baseball diamond, maybe?"

"Could be. You never see a stadium in the U.S. without one or the other."

As suppertime approached, the crowd of tourists dissipated, except for the religious group. The two Americans walked through the park in search of a restaurant. They dined on some regional specialties, including red cabbage, and had apple strudel with whipped cream for dessert.

The sun had set by the time Eric and Roger finished their supper, and a light rain had started. They still had no plans for where they would spend the night, so they walked through the park discussing the possibilities. The rain quickly became torrential, driving them to the nearest shelter, which was the edge of the swimming pool canopy. Deafening thunder made them take notice, and the most spectacular lightning they had ever seen illuminated the night sky like a giant flash bulb. They abandoned any hope of finding a B&B or hotel. A youth hostel was not far from the park to the southwest, but getting there on foot in the rain and darkness was out of the question.

"We should've found the hostel earlier, when we had the chance."

"Should have, but we were having a good time. What fun is searching for a hostel when you can swim with the sweet young things?"

"I think this is what they call *donner und blitzen*."

"What do Santa's reindeer have to do with it?"

"The reindeers' names are German for thunder and lightning. I learned that in a German class. One of the few things I remember from it," Roger said. He observed the electrical storm for a moment. "Looks like we're stuck right here, Chief."

"What are we going to do now?"

42.

"You got engaged?" Marianne's mother was flabbergasted. She had big plans for her daughter, but this scenario was not quite what she had envisioned. She suspected Marianne was being less than candid.

"This comes as quite a surprise," her father began, in one of his usual paternal lectures that always got under her skin. "You've mentioned Roger a few times, but we had no idea you were considering anything like this! We haven't even met him yet."

Marianne was trying her best to keep her cool. She had waited until her older brother and his wife left for California before telling her parents about her engagement to Roger. Two against one was less of a mismatch than four against one. "You can meet him in September. He's on vacation in Europe right now."

"We'd like to get to know him before you make such a big commitment. You have to think about how you are going to meet your own expectations, where you're going to live and work, things like that. It's not something to be taken lightly." Mrs. Murakami was hinting that Marianne had not really given much thought to any of these things.

Marianne had always been a high-maintenance girl, and that had not changed much even as she was becoming an adult. "Mom, I know what I'm doing! Roger's not some beach bum, like the kind Leslie's always trying to line me up with. You should be glad I told her cousin to take a hike. He's such a loser!"

She has a point there, Mr. Murakami thought. He had a very high opinion of his daughter-in-law and her immediate family, but some of her relatives were questionable. "You are an adult now, sweetheart, and you have to make these kinds of decisions for yourself. I understand that. We just want to help you see the big picture, and know where you fit into it. We've been there ourselves. Your brother made some very wise decisions when he and Leslie got married, and we want you to do that, too."

"Roger's family isn't as well off as we are, but I don't see anything wrong with that. If I limit my choices to the sons of your friends at the country club, I won't have much to choose from. Besides, he has a whole lot going for him. He's not from the ghetto, and he's an engineering student."

Mrs. Murakami had some thoughts about that, but she would discuss them in private with her husband first. She certainly did not want Marianne marrying some gold-digger, nor did she want this Roger Schmidt character to underestimate what he was getting. The engagement ring Roger had given Marianne was lovely, but it was, at best, comparable to the costume jewelry worn by her more affluent friends. Roger attended a public university in his home state, where he would be paying in-state tuition. At least he lived within his means, apparently. She admired that, although she wondered what sort of European vacation he could afford. "I'm sure Roger is a very nice young man, but I insist on meeting him before we give our blessing. It would be nice to meet his parents, too. That will give you some time to think this through."

"Mom!"

"Your mother's right, Mari. We have to meet him. What little we know about him hasn't exactly won me over."

"I can manage my own life, thank you very much!"

"He's different from you in so many ways...religion, race, social standing and a whole lot of other things. He's a mainlander and you grew up next to the ocean. These things might not seem like much now, but they will be a big deal after you've been married for a year."

"Stop treating me like I'm still in high school!"

"The time to think these things over carefully is now, not after you tie the knot!"

43.

Eric and Roger unrolled their sleeping bags directly on the hard brick walkway, without benefit of any cushioning other than their bags. The ground beneath them was dry, but the incessant rain had formed a shallow river of drainage water less than two meters away from where they lay.

The rain diminished but continued throughout the night, as did the steady stream of conventioneers walking past their campsite. The conventioneers were courteous and hardly disturbed them, and they slept surprisingly well in spite of the adverse conditions.

A testy policeman awakened them with a few terse words that neither understood at 5:30, shortly after dawn. His uniform, tone of voice and facial expression told them that he was a police officer, he was ordering them to leave, and they should not be sleeping where they were.

"Verstehen Sie es?" the policeman demanded.

Roger said something to the effect of, *"Ja, ja, Ich verstehe Sie,"* and the policeman left them alone.

"What was that all about?" Eric was still half asleep.

"I'm not sure, but I think he told us, in so many words, to get the hell out of here," Roger said. "I think I said, 'Yes, I understand.' I lied, though. I didn't understand any of what he said."

They dressed, packed their gear, and walked over to the stadium. The grass was still damp but the sidewalks were dry, and the sky had few clouds in it. Very little remained to remind anyone of the fury unleashed in the stratosphere the previous night.

At the stadium, the religious convention was already underway, although Eric and Roger doubted it had shut down completely during the night. They sat in the grandstands to discuss their plans for the day. Neither was in the habit of rising at 5:30, especially since they had been on vacation. The world looked and felt slightly different to them so early in the day.

As far south and east as they felt they should go in their search for their friend, they decided to travel north and west, toward either Stuttgart, Frankfurt or Nuremberg. They wanted to be back in London by mid-Thursday, which would give them only about two days with the Hoffmann sisters, but they also wanted to find an American military installation somewhere along the way.

They carried their gear to the edge of the Olympic Park, where a delivery van driver offered them a ride across town.

"Sprechen Sie Englisch?" Roger queried.

"No," the driver replied in the only English he knew.

"Get in," Roger said to Eric. "He knows we need a ride."

He drove them to the northwest side of Munich and left them on a city street near the highway to Stuttgart. The situation looked promising until they noticed they were standing on the same street corner as twenty or so other hitchhikers.

"This looks hopeless," Eric said. "Let's find another corner where the competition isn't so stiff."

"Wait, I just noticed something." Roger turned his head suddenly and stood on his tiptoes to look over several other people.

"What is it?"

A Ford van with California license plates turned the corner, past the other hitchhikers. Roger instinctively shouted, "Hey, California," at the driver, who stopped at the curbing upon hearing it. Roger ran to the passenger window of the van, exchanged a few words with the driver, and motioned to Eric to carry their gear over to the van. They climbed in the van, while some twenty hitchhikers looked on in amazement. Two newcomers had just hitched a ride in front of people who had been waiting for an hour or more. Eric had no idea how Roger did it, but he was not about to debate the fairness of it with the other hitchhikers. Roger was both proud of himself and astonished by his luck.

The driver was a man in his mid-thirties, a professional sports photographer from Luxembourg who spoke fluent English and had been in California recently, where he purchased the van. He was on his way back to Luxembourg, but would be crossing the Rhine River near Mannheim. He knew of some U.S. military bases in that area, and also recommended Heidelberg as a tourist attraction. He told them he would not have stopped had Roger not caught his attention.

The van was luxuriously carpeted and had a table and refrigerator installed. Roger rode in the passenger seat and Eric sank into a bean bag chair in the back. Roger discussed Europe and California with the driver, while Eric added an occasional comment but mostly watched the German countryside go silently by him.

Eric tried to identify towns and other landmarks from the signs along the highway. Augsburg was easy for him to identify, and he looked carefully at the Danube River—*Donau*, on his German map—to see if it really is blue. In Stuttgart, the capital and largest city in Baden-Württemberg, he saw the Mercedes-Benz factory and, in the distance, an airborne dirigible. He had never seen a dirigible except on television.

From Stuttgart northward, the driver followed the Neckar River to the northern border of Baden-Württemberg. The *Schwartzwald*, or Black Forest, was somewhat a misnomer. All the trees Eric could see were undeniably green, and he saw plenty of tall trees. The driver let them out in Heidelberg

261

in the mid-afternoon, beyond the Black Forest but still very much in some forest.

In downtown Heidelberg, they bought some groceries, ate, and rode a bus to the outskirts of town. There they came upon an army housing facility, a community of military families known as Samuel Adams Village. As they walked into the grounds, they saw some boys throwing a football, the ellipsoidal type used in the American version of that game.

They walked into the lobby of a guesthouse in the village to inquire the whereabouts of their friend, Danny Sanchez. A no-vacancy sign was in the window. The manager of the guesthouse wore a military-style nametag identifying him as Alexander. He greeted them as soon as they entered.

"What can I do for you gentlemen today?"

Eric wanted to say, "I'd like German Comedians for $200 please, Alex," but he resisted the urge. Instead he explained his and Roger's search for their friend.

The manager let them use his telephone and gave them some numbers to call for information.

"How may I help you?" a disembodied voice asked.

"I'm trying to locate a soldier named Sanchez, Daniel E. Sanchez, from Pueblo, Colorado," Eric said.

"May I put you on hold?" The woman put him on hold before he could say no. He waited for what seemed like forever and a day until another voice acknowledged him.

"Have you been helped?" the second voice said.

"I'm trying to locate..." Eric started his spiel again.

"Let me transfer you to Personnel Records." The second voice put him on hold again for another long stretch.

Eric was transferred and put on hold several times, until finally, an operator told him that her records indicated a Sergeant D.E. Sanchez was stationed in Aschaffenburg, Bavaria. That small bit of information took them nearly half an hour to obtain, but it was all they needed for the moment. The manager showed them Aschaffenburg on a map beneath the glass on the counter. They were not far from Aschaffenburg, and that would be their next day's destination.

The lawns of the village were well kept, so they cast their burdens on the grass outside the guesthouse and thought about their next move. They exchanged greetings with many of the bored-looking teenagers passing their way. They thought about going back into Heidelberg to look for the hostel and some nightlife, until three teenage boys stopped to talk.

The boys, out of school for the summer and looking like they would sacrifice anything to get back to the United States, wondered why two American hitchhikers had landed in Samuel Adams Village, of all places.

They explained their search for their army friend and their method of traveling without an itinerary. The boys expressed envy, and discussed how they felt trapped in the tiny world that was Samuel Adams Village, unable to feel at home, even though their German counterparts were friendly to them.

In time, more teenagers arrived where Roger and Eric had parked themselves, including some girls who caught their attention. Some of the teenagers left to see a double feature at the village cinema about a block away. Flirting and uneasy attempts at romance between the boys and the girls were apparent. One of the boys briefed them on the subject of which girls were available and which ones were not.

After the movie started, the seven teenagers remaining suggested a pub near the village. With nothing better to do, Eric and Roger decided to join the teenagers for some elbow exercise. The three girls in the group were attractive, and one showed more than just a little interest in Eric. The teenagers led them through some fields, toward the city, to a building with some cars parked around it.

Roger, Eric and their younger friends sat at a table in the pub and ordered a round of locally brewed beer in bottles. The girl who looked interested in Eric sat next to him and introduced herself as LaTonya. Shortly after the beer was served, two of the boys and one of the girls excused themselves to see what some of their friends were doing and saying on the other side of the room. The bar had a dance floor in the center and a karaoke stage at the opposite end. Most of the other customers appeared to be German locals. Eric and Roger did not notice anyone in military garb.

"Are you kids old enough to be served here? Legally, that is," Roger asked.

"You have to be sixteen in Germany." One of the two remaining boys introduced himself as Tim. "Most of us are old enough now, some still aren't."

"Nobody checks cards here, though," the other boy added. "The Germans don't enforce that law very much, I guess."

"That's probably good for us," Eric said. "I'd hate to be arrested for contributing to the delinquency of minors. We've already had one brush with the law today."

"Everyone lives close, and none of us drove," Roger said. "I think we'll be all right, as long as nobody starts a fight or passes out."

The teenagers told them more about life on a military base in Germany, as well as how to buy marijuana in Heidelberg from German citizens. They did more listening than talking, but put in a few words edgewise regarding their search for their friend Sanchez, and how they thought they had located him in Aschaffenburg. None of the teenagers had been in Aschaffenburg. It was just another army base to them.

As the sun set and the evening became nighttime, Roger wandered onto the dance floor and, in time, danced with most of the girls who came with him and Eric and several German women as well. LaTonya motioned to Eric to follow her outside, which he did. Tim and the other boys left the table to mingle with the crowd.

Leaving the noise behind them, Eric followed LaTonya outside to a dark, grassy patch of ground beside the pub. He left his gear at the table with Roger, hoping that Roger would not get too distracted from it.

"I had to get out of there," LaTonya said, "but I didn't want to leave you by yourself. I can tell your friend is having a good time."

"He did look that way." Eric sat down on the grass and made himself comfortable. LaTonya sat down, too, but not intimately close. He at first expected her to put the moves on him, until he realized that was not her intention at all.

"The real reason I wanted to come out here is that Tim has been bothering me to go out with him."

"And you don't want to?"

"He's a friend, that's all. I don't want to get involved with him. I had a boyfriend in the States, but I haven't heard from him since Christmas. He's probably dating someone else now, and I don't blame him. I'd probably do the same thing."

"So why don't you? There are bigger fish in the ocean."

LaTonya's sorrow was genuine, but she was not really seeking sympathy from Eric. She just needed someone to whom she could vent her emotions without fear of fueling the rumor mill. "I'll get over it, but I'd get over it sooner in the United States. Tim will leave me alone as long as I'm with you, but you won't be here tomorrow."

"In a way, I envy you for being here."

"What's enviable about living here?"

"You have some opportunities that most Americans never get," Eric said. "If I lived here, I'd learn all I could about Germany. The people, their language, the history, the geography, the wine, everything. I probably sound like your teachers or, worse yet, your parents, but I guarantee you'll never regret having worldly knowledge. Make something of your time here. Otherwise, you'll be sorry when you can't go back and rectify old mistakes."

"I'm from Earth! What planet are you from?"

"Let me rephrase that. It didn't come out quite right."

"You don't sound at all like my teachers or my parents. They all want to get back home as much as I do."

"Yes, I see. Forget I mentioned it." Eric laughed inwardly at his naïve optimism. He knew he sounded like a fool for what he had just said.

"No, you have the right attitude," LaTonya admitted. She patted him on the shoulder and smiled at him in a condescending sort of way. "You wouldn't have that attitude if you were an army brat like me, but it is the right attitude. I'm not sure I can convince any of my friends of that. Some of them would do anything to escape from Germany. The truth is, I have learned a whole lot about Germany. I'll be the expert on Germany in my class when I get home."

"My situation is almost the opposite of yours." Eric explained his newfound romance with Yvette. "When I'm back in Colorado, and then in Seattle, I'll be thinking about how and when I can return to Europe to be with my girlfriend. Maybe I should join the army."

"There's a house next to ours that'll be vacant soon," LaTonya joked. "You could be our neighbor."

"It was just wishful thinking. I really want to finish college before I make any big plans to move somewhere. But I'll keep the offer in mind."

"You must really be in love! It's been a long time since I've heard anyone sound so dreamy about Europe. I hope I feel that way about someone someday soon."

LaTonya and Eric talked for another half hour or so, discussing Heidelberg, Nashville, Pueblo and Seattle, among other things. She was about four years younger than he, but she seemed delighted to be talking, for a change, to another American who was new to the area and had no military connections. She told him she considered Nashville home, even though she had never lived anywhere for very long. Both of her parents had grown up in central Tennessee, and she still had many relatives there. She knew she had less than one year to go in Germany, and she was already making arrangements to attend Tennessee State University.

Back inside the pub, Roger was still swing-dancing with LaTonya's friend Keisha, enjoying every minute of it. LaTonya and Eric took to the dance floor for one song, then sat down long enough to collect their things and prepare to go back to the village. The four left the pub and walked back through the fields in the darkness to the military village. Keisha held Roger's hand as she led him through the field.

"We placed third in a karaoke contest," Roger said.

"Both of you?" Eric asked.

"We sang a duet," Keisha said. "We won ten euros. Good thing both of us know that song."

"At first, I suggested *Tequila* or *Let's Go*, but she didn't know the words to either one."

"He didn't know any recent Top 40 songs very well, but we found one where he knew the refrain and the melody, and sight-read the rest."

"It pays to listen to the radio once in a while. We spent our prize money almost as soon as we earned it on another round of beers."

Roger and Keisha clearly had a good time at the bar. They ended the evening with a tongue kiss. Eric harbored a strong suspicion that Roger's engagement problems were due to his own seeming lack of commitment, as much as to Marianne's strange behavior.

They parted company near the spot where they had met a few hours earlier. After a brief hesitation, LaTonya and Eric shared a brief kiss, their only one of the evening. LaTonya pulled Keisha away from Roger, and the two girls went home. Roger and Eric carried their gear in the opposite direction, toward an expanse of flat grass near the fence bordering the village.

They unstuffed their rain ponchos and sleeping bags on the grass, some 200 meters from the nearest dwelling and comfortably far from any streetlights or thoroughfares. Their campsite was secluded from everything except mosquitoes, which forced them to cover all exposed skin in spite of the warm summer air and humidity around them.

Knowing they were in for a rough night of insects, sweat and other forms of misery, they tried to make the best of it, and hoped the following night would be better.

44.

At the conclusion of yet another mostly sleepless night, Eric and Roger arose sometime around 6:00. The village was still asleep, so they were able to change clothes and break camp unnoticed by anyone. Eric's brain ached, and he could not conceal his discomfort.

"I wonder how many more nights like the last one I can tolerate," Eric said.

Roger compressed his sleeping bag into its stuff sack. "You aren't the only one. What I'd give for a comfortable bed, with air conditioning and mosquito nets!"

They cleaned up their campsite and carried their gear to Speyerer Strasse, the highway in front of the village. The shoulder seams on their T-shirts were getting frayed by the shoulder straps on their luggage. They both remarked for the umpteenth time how they wished they had their backpacks. They waited briefly at roadside until a bus stopped and took them into Heidelberg.

Breakfast consisted of some pastries and tea in a bakery in downtown Heidelberg. The city and most of its 130,000 residents were located in the fertile Neckar River valley. The river was several hundred meters wide where it flowed through Heidelberg, quite impressive to the two Americans but nothing unusual in Europe. Most of the buildings were tall and constructed of red brick and stone, and the yards were small but well tended. Steep roofs and attic living space were common to many of the houses and small businesses.

After breakfast and a bit of meandering, they rode a bus to a hillside section of town called Altstadt, "Old City", where they walked up a road behind some other tourists toward the ruins of a magnificent castle. The castle was by far the largest and most impressive they had seen so far. Its walls abutted residential yards in some places, towering five stories or more above neighboring houses.

They paid a nominal admission fee and went inside the castle, where they were met by a number of medieval trappings, including a large wooden door with ornamental iron hinges and handle. The view of the city and the river from the highest existing floor was quite spectacular, and deserving of several photographs. A colossus lay in the center of a water fountain in one part of the castle grounds. They took plenty of time exploring the numerous passages and walls of the castle, and they captured as much as they could on photographs.

Coincidentally, a group of American soldiers on leave from Frankfurt was also touring the castle and admiring the tall evergreens.

"You wouldn't happen to be from Aschaffenburg, would you?" Roger asked a soldier.

"No, Frankfurt," the soldier answered. "You know somebody there?"

"Yes, and we've been trying to locate him. A friend of ours from high school. Sgt. Danny Sanchez is his name."

"Don't know him, but we're going back to Frankfurt at about four o'clock this afternoon. We've got a few empty seats on the bus, and you're welcome to ride with us to Frankfurt if you want."

"We'd appreciate that, if your commanding officer doesn't mind."

"Even if he knew, he wouldn't mind," the soldier scoffed. "Be here at a quarter to four, and we'll get you to Frankfurt."

"Thanks, and we'll see you then."

Eric and Roger left Altstadt at lunchtime and rode a bus back into the business district. They purchased some groceries at a store that very much resembled most American supermarkets, but on a smaller scale. The choice of groceries was also very similar to what they would expect to find at home. Although they could not read but a few key words on product labels, they had no trouble choosing what they wanted. They carried a loaf of dense wheat bread, a block of cheese, some fruit and some bottled water to a park bench near the store, and made their lunch.

They updated their journals over lunch and discussed their plans for how they might get back to London by Thursday. They walked over to a nearby hotel of what appeared to be a major German hotel chain, and went into the spacious lobby. Acting like guests of the hotel, they used the men's room to wash their faces and brush their teeth. The room was clean and luxurious, and no one else came in while they were using it. They felt slightly guilty for taking advantage of the nice facility, but justified in that no one else used it much. They left the room as clean as they found it. They would have liked to thank the hotelier for the use of it.

Squandering the afternoon in downtown Heidelberg, Roger and Eric returned to Altstadt by 15:45, where the soldiers were boarding their bus. They found some empty seats and immediately started a conversation about the people and geography of southwestern Germany with the soldiers. The soldiers were all friendly and helpful, and seemed happy to have civilian countrymen among them for a change.

The bus left Heidelberg promptly at 16:00 and followed highways along the Neckar, Rhine and Main Rivers to Frankfurt, the largest city in Hesse. Downtown Frankfurt had the luster of a new city with its modern buildings and electric commuter trains. They suspected that much of what they were seeing had been renovated or completely rebuilt as a result of Allied bombing in the 1940s. They bought some fruit to eat later from a sidewalk vendor, then boarded a train to Aschaffenberg.

A railway employee who spoke English gave them directions to a U.S. Army base that was several kilometers across town from the train station, on a street named Sälzer Weg. They hoisted their luggage to their shoulders and took a stroll through the city as the sun approached the horizon. Aschaffenberg, Bavaria, a city of 55,000 people, was located in a region where four states, Rhineland Palatinate to the west, Hesse to the north, Bavaria to the east and south, and Baden-Würtemberg to the south, bordered each other or were very close together. They were back in Bavaria, but not any closer to Munich than they had been in Heidelberg.

At the guardhouse outside McCready Barracks, they inquired about their friend Danny Sanchez. The guard made some telephone calls and returned to announce that Sgt. Sanchez was out somewhere on field duty with his unit until mid-August. While they were talking to the guard, a local woman of about their age stopped her car at the gate. She was recognized by the guard, and drove into the base. The guard explained that she was delivering fried chicken from a nearby takeout but was also the girlfriend of one of the soldiers. They left a written message for Sanchez with the guard, then set their gear down across the street from the gate. They sat down on the curbing to discuss what they would do now that their plans had changed.

"Bloody hell!" Eric's voice was weak, barely louder than a whisper. "We weren't prepared for this! I was planning to spend the night in a real bed somewhere that Danny would know of, but all I have now is massive brain ache. If I don't get a good sleep soon, I'm going to have a massive seizure!" He rubbed his temples with one hand. "What was it that Richard the Third said in his dying breath? 'A whore! A whore! My condom for a whore!'"

"I don't think that's quite how he put it."

"Maybe not, but that's what he meant. What now?"

"We saved ourselves some money and the chance of getting arrested, but at least we might've had real beds to sleep in." Roger alluded to Sanchez's bordello offer. "I was planning on a shower tonight to wash off last night's sweat. How bad is your headache right now, anyway? Are you going to ralph?"

"I'm a little woozy, but my headache is bad enough that I don't much feel like moving." The dazed look on Eric's face confirmed his words. "Before we got here, I felt it coming, but it's gotten much worse in the last half hour or so. Notice the way I keep squinting and contorting my face."

"You look miserable, all right. The best whore in Aschaffenburg would have trouble bringing a smile to that face."

"Got any ideas?"

"You take some drugs and watch our gear. I'm going to take a walk to see if there are any hotels or B&Bs available. There might even be a youth hostel somewhere. I'll be back within an hour."

"Make damn sure you don't get lost or mugged, savvy? I won't come looking for you."

The twilight had diminished to darkness as Roger walked along the busy street toward the central business district. He did not expect to get lost if he stayed close to Sälzer Weg. He found a modern-looking hotel about two kilometers from the base, but the concierge told him the hotel had no vacancies. Roger wondered if that was the truth, or if he had been denied a room because he looked somewhat derelict. He spent another hour or more looking for lodging, but he found nothing. He did not even see a park that looked like a good place to camp, and he was concerned about the possibility of Eric having a grand mal seizure. Their situation was getting worse by the minute, and all Roger could do was go back to the base empty-handed.

Roger found the street again that led to the base, and began his return. He tried to think of a tactful way to tell Eric that his search was fruitless. The evening air was warm and pleasant and the sky was clear—desirable conditions for camping, if they had a place to camp.

A car approaching from behind Roger slowed and then stopped beside him. He was expecting someone to ask for directions in German or something else that he could not answer. He looked at the driver and saw that she was the woman who had delivered fried chicken to the base earlier. She seemed to recognize him.

"Going to army," the woman said, in very broken English. "Give you ride?"

"*Ja*, I mean yes!" Roger felt hopelessly inept at any language other than English, and perhaps even that. He knew his German was even worse than her English, but he felt relieved to be offered something. "We need a place to stay the night, a youth hostel." He got into her car. Her expression indicated she was not quite certain what he meant. "*Wo ist ein Hotel, bitte?*" He tried to recall what little he remembered from his middle school German class. He did not know the German phrase for youth hostel. He extracted his IYH card from his wallet and showed it to her. She nodded in acknowledgment.

Back at the base, Eric had made himself comfortable by leaning back against his stuffed sleeping bag, but he still looked dazed. The woman stopped where he sat, and she and Roger got out of the car. Eric was surprised to see Roger emerging from a car.

"I couldn't find anything," Roger said, "but she says she might know of a place. Get in."

"Sounds good to me." Eric got in the back seat while Roger loaded their gear into the trunk. The three drove to another place where the woman had to deliver chicken. She spoke to a taxi driver stopped next to them at an intersection. Acting on the taxi driver's advice, she drove several kilometers across town to a dark building in a residential neighborhood.

One window in the building was illuminated, and the woman rang the doorbell. An older woman in her bathrobe answered, and the two women spoke to each other in German for a minute or two. The older woman inspected the two young men for a moment, then hesitantly opened the door to them.

"She has room for you." The younger woman smiled, proud of herself for being able to help. She went with Roger and Eric back to her car to unload their gear.

"We're very grateful to you." Eric wished he knew some German. He felt so relieved to have a real bed to sleep in, and he did not even care to ask the price.

"*Danke schön*," Roger said. Eric repeated it to the woman after he heard Roger pronounce it.

"*Nichts zu danken*." The woman drove away to resume her deliveries.

They followed the innkeeper to a room at the end of the upstairs hallway. The building was quiet, and no light emanated from under any doors, so they tried to be as quiet as they could. They thanked her in German, to which she nodded acknowledgment and then returned to her quarters on the lower floor.

The room was small but comfortably furnished with a chair, a table, two single beds, a sink and a shower. The toilet was in the adjacent room on the hallway. They unpacked their luggage and sleeping bags to allow everything to dry, as their gear was still damp from the previous night. They each showered until all the "scud"—a combination of scum and crud—was gone, then settled into real beds for the first time since they left Paris.

Yvette had been very busy since her return to Bern a few days earlier, but she missed Eric terribly. Her heart ached in a way that she had scarcely even imagined. She had not been looking for love in southern England, it just found her. Eric was very shy, and not a great conversationalist, but he had really grown on her in a very short time. She liked what was on the surface, and she liked what she had found underneath. Her life had taken a dramatic turn within the last two weeks, and now her good fortune was evaporating as quickly as it began. She felt powerless to do anything about it.

"Supper will be ready in about half an hour," Yvette said in the Swiss dialect of French to her teenage cousin Giséle. Giséle had been raised near Lausanne, and spoke French primarily. Giséle was looking bored, so she added, "Set the table for us, please. That will give you something to do."

Desiree had been on the telephone all week with her business contacts to handle some sort of crisis, and their parents were receiving visitors in anticipation of her grandmother's funeral the following day. Yvette was left with the sizable task of entertaining her mother's sister's and brother's families. In a way, Yvette was glad Eric was not there, because it would have been difficult to compete with Giséle for his attention. Seventeen-year-old Giséle was very fashionable, and quite popular with the boys in her school. She was tall and curvaceous, with long blonde hair in braids. She cared little for sports or scholastics, but she was big in the social scene, and her parents doted on her constantly. Eric and Roger would notice her, Yvette thought. How could they not notice her?

Yvette continued slicing celery and onions to add to a potato dish she was fixing. Her parents' house was spacious by Swiss standards, and very comfortably furnished. Her parents were both professionals and enjoyed an above-average income. The house felt small with several overnight guests in it, but no one suffered for lack of any amenities. She would have liked a little more privacy in this time of sorrow, but she knew she would get it soon enough.

"Grandma told me for years she was going to take me to Paris someday," Giséle confided to Yvette in the kitchen. No one else was in the room. "Did she ever tell you that?"

Yvette smiled. "Paris, Berlin, Vienna, London, Rome and several other places, when Desiree and I were little girls. The big plans faded as I grew up. She couldn't see or walk well enough for the last five years to take you anywhere. She was nearly blind, and very feeble."

"I know, but I liked to hear her talk about living in Paris during the War. She always made it sound very romantic and exciting. I'm going to miss that."

Yvette was a little surprised to hear Giséle sounding so sentimental. It seemed way out of character for her. Maybe she was not as self-absorbed as she always seemed to be. "I'll miss her, too."

Yvette and Giséle held each other for a moment, each shedding a tear in silence. They had never been especially close, until now. For Yvette, it was the happiest and saddest time of her life. She looked forward to seeing Eric again soon. The way her luck was going, she wondered if she would ever see him again.

45.

A deep, restful sleep was just what the doctor ordered for Roger and especially Eric. Eric could feel his bed spinning, or so it seemed, and dreamed of having seizures, but his headache was gone when he awoke. They were both ready and eager to go to Bern, but not before breakfast.

They shook the remaining dried grass from their sleeping bags, then stuffed the bags and loaded their other things into the panniers. They used some tissues to sweep up the grass they had shed all over the floor, then left the room and went downstairs. They paid the innkeeper on their way out the door. The reasonable price nicely complemented their refreshing sleep.

"When do you want to call Yvette?"

"They're probably at the funeral now, or they soon will be. Let's go back to Frankfurt, and I'll call from there. We'll probably have to go through Frankfurt anyway to catch a train to Bern. You might want to do some calling yourself."

"I probably should."

Walking through Aschaffenburg like two transients, they bought breakfast at a bakery. They continued until they came to the highway to Frankfurt, the A5, where they waited a few minutes with thumbs extended. Two rides later, they were in Frankfurt. Clad in summer attire, they walked and sweated in that large city for an hour, until late morning. Eric found a pay telephone while Roger entered a nearby Internet café.

Roger deleted a whole page of spam that had eluded his keyword filters before he read a short note from Marianne. Her missive said everything was fine, but that she needed to spend one last summer with friends and family in Hawaii before graduation and marriage. He could easily understand that. Her roommates could have told him that, instead of giving him the run-around.

"This is Eric. We're in Frankfurt. What's happening there?"

Yvette answered the telephone at her parents' house. "Eric, I've been so anxious for you to call. I could hardly wait to hear your voice again. Why are you in Frankfurt? I thought you'd be near Chamonix, or somewhere in France."

"We rode a train to Munich. We were looking for an old friend who's in the army. We found his base near here, but he was out on some assignment, and now we're here in Frankfurt." He continued with a detailed explanation of how and why they were in Germany, and what they had been doing the past few days. He had no trouble at all making conversation with her.

Yvette had plenty to say about her week. She told him in great detail about her extended family. "I have bad news. Desiree has had trouble at work all week, and she's there now. Her department had some sort of crisis, and they needed her to return immediately."

"I see." Eric sounded disappointed. "I guess that means..."

"She asked me to tell you to give Roger her love, and she misses him. She was so disappointed that she won't be able to see him."

"Tell her that he sends his love to her, too, and he misses her," Eric said, even though Roger had not actually said that. He wondered what sort of thing Roger really would say, in light of his engagement, if he still considered himself engaged. "He'll be very disappointed, too."

"I hope everything works out for Roger. Anyway, my mother asked me to go with her to Geneva tomorrow to pack some of the things our grandmother left for us, and to settle her estate. I know she needs me but I still want to be with you."

"Your mother wins again. You'd better go with her."

"I'm sorry it turned out this way." Yvette sniffed, and Eric could tell she was crying even though she tried to be phlegmatic. "My mother did say if I go with her tomorrow, she'll buy me round-trip airfare to Colorado next year. Not Seattle, she said, but Colorado."

"She doesn't fully trust me yet. Still, it sounds like a good deal. Take her up on it."

They continued talking for nearly an hour, neither wanting to end the conversation. They tried to describe to each other everything they had done since they parted the previous Thursday.

"I love you, Eric," Yvette said in a very sweet, sincere tone of voice to end the conversation.

Eric paused a moment as if to absorb what she had just said before he responded. "I love you, too, Yvette. Goodbye."

Roger knew the situation from Eric's downcast expression even before Eric said anything. Eric gave Roger a summary of what he and Yvette said, save for some intimate details. Roger was disappointed, too, although not overly surprised.

"I have to wonder if I'll ever see her again," Eric said. "The best thing that's ever happened to me has slipped out of my grasp already."

"She said she'd come see you in the U.S. next year. That's a long time to wait, but it'll be here before you know it."

"A lot could happen between now and then. People change with time. What if one of us loses interest?"

"What if the Cubs win the Series? You'll just have to send plenty of e-mail and a few gifts, but don't give up too easily. You haven't lost her yet."

"Why am I listening to your advice? You're the one who's been sowing wild oats in Europe, not I! What about your engagement, and Desiree?"

Roger took a deep breath to collect his thoughts. "I told Desiree about my engagement, and all the miscommunications I've had lately. She felt bad for me, but we agreed to do whatever was necessary to accommodate you and Yvette. She didn't want to come between Marianne and me, and she didn't, really. Her divorce was final about a year ago, she told me. Yvette was trying to be the matchmaker, bring Desiree out of her doldrums. Desiree's husband quit his job a few months after they were married, and stayed home to play video games and surf the Internet. She was about to give him an ultimatum when he announced he was leaving her for someone he had met in a chat room. They divorced, and her ex-husband's new lover left him a few months later for someone else she met in a chat room. Meanwhile, Desiree found refuge in her career, and she's been very successful at it."

"So I've heard. Yvette told me about Desiree's divorce, and how her life consists mostly of work. Her ex got what he deserved."

"Anyway, she cautioned me to think long and hard before I commit to something I'm so unsure about, because she's been there and regretted it. She advised me to meet my in-laws and get to know them before I marry into the family, because the bride or groom is always part of a package deal."

"I'm not sure I understand what all that means, but you still have time to save your engagement. What happened in Europe is a secret Marianne will never know unless you tell her."

"Not much did happen in Europe. I didn't make love to Desiree, if that's what you're insinuating. I was tempted to, I really wanted to, but I just...couldn't. It wouldn't have been right. We talked in bed for a long time. She understands me better than I understand myself."

"At the time, I couldn't imagine two people who needed each other less than you and Desiree, but the two of you appeared to be having a good time together."

"We had a great time together," Roger clarified. "Wouldn't trade it for anything."

"I never thought I'd see the day when Roger Schmidt would admit he couldn't make love to an attractive girl in bed next to him." Eric's tone was getting lighter already. "Who the hell are you, and where are you holding the real Roger Schmidt hostage?"

"I'm the real McCoy! She was eating digestive crackers. I *had* to throw her out of bed! Need I say more? I hate this growing-up stuff—I'm getting an ethical streak in me."

"All the better reason to call Marianne again."

"Why bother? We'll be in Colorado again in less than a week. Plus, I think it's the middle of the night in Hawaii right now."

"It might be the best time to catch her at home."

"She sent me an e-mail, finally. Sounds like everything is all right with her." Roger told Eric what Marianne had told him in the e-mail. "No need to roust her out of bed over nothing."

"Call her anyway. Tell her you've been thinking about her and you miss her. She'll eat that up."

Roger reluctantly agreed, and inserted his card into the telephone. He did miss her, and he had been thinking about her. He just needed to hear her tell him everything was all right. He first had to call a roommate in Boulder, Colorado, to look up Marianne's unpublished number in Hawaii in an address book in Roger's desk drawer. The roommate was barely awake, but he found the address book and read the number to Roger. Roger gave a moment's thought to how big his next telephone bill would be.

Eric sat down on the bench, took out his Swiss army knife, and tried to trim off a hangnail that had been bothering him since he awoke. He winced when the blade slipped down into the groove between fingernail and skin, but he drew no blood. The hangnail shaved off, he closed the knife and put it back in his pocket. Roger was on the telephone longer than on any of his previous attempts to call Marianne from Europe. Eric assumed he must have reached her finally.

Roger hung up the telephone and walked toward Eric with the kind of expression that suggested something tragic, like a death in the family. "Her old man answered. Like he'd been expecting me." He paused.

"And?"

"Dirty bastard offered me ten thousand dollars to break the engagement!"

"Ten thousand dollars!"

"Ten grand! Said he didn't have anything against me personally, but the missus, Marianne's mama, doesn't think it's a very good idea for us to get married right now, and he supports her decision. That's how he put it."

"*Caramba*!" Eric shook his head. "Big slap in the face! Did you tell him to fuck off?"

"No, I told him to mail me the cheque."

46.

"What? You let him buy you? I thought I knew you, Schmidt!" Eric was almost shouting.

"Don't get discombobulated, Eric! Chill! I didn't say I was going to cash the cheque. I just want to know whether he's bluffing. He's a big executive, you know. To him, it was about the same as handing a low-level employee a pink slip and a paltry severance payment. My response was just an impulse on my part. I wasn't expecting that, so I really didn't know what to say. I didn't have time to think about what I should say to something like that."

"What did Marianne have to say about it?" Eric was a little calmer now.

"He wouldn't even let me talk to her, but it hardly matters now. I can read the writing on the wall. The big question is, what do we do now? Back to London?"

"Might as well. We're done here," Eric said. "But we have a few days yet, so let's not hurry. No need to ride an overnight train back to Calais. I'm sorry things worked out for you the way they did. You didn't deserve that."

"Shit happens." Roger felt that same empathy for Eric, but he was in no mood to say any more about it.

They walked in the summer heat until they found what looked like a good spot to hitch a ride. A man driving a BMW sedan stopped about twenty minutes later when Eric caught his attention. The man, in his mid-thirties, was on his way to Cologne, had plenty of room in his car, and wanted someone to talk to during what he considered a mundane journey. They loaded their luggage into the trunk, and Eric sat in the front passenger seat while Roger sat in the back.

The driver was something of an adventurer himself, and talked at length of his own travels and romances associated with them. His accent was strong, but his English very understandable. He drove westward to Rhineland Palatinate, then followed the Rhine Valley northwestward.

Numerous cities and towns lay in the densely populated valley, and the river looked very wide to Eric and Roger. They were not used to seeing ships navigating the rivers back home. The forests were dense and radiated brilliant shades of green between cities. The castles and vineyards, in addition to everything else, left them wondering why the driver was unimpressed with the valley.

When the driver came to a stretch of highway he apparently knew well, he sank his right foot into the throttle and gave them a ride like they had never had. The driver's boredom turned to a show of pride as he pointed out the efficiency of the *autobahn* and how interesting and scenic the valley was at high speed. Eric noticed the speedometer indicating 180 kilometers per hour, twice the speed limit of the two-lane highways in the United States, while Roger watched the other cars on the highway getting passed as if they were standing still.

The trip through Rhineland Palatinate was brief, and soon the three were in North Rhine Westphalia, the most populous state in Germany. They passed through Bonn, the capital of West Germany before it was reunited with East Germany and the capital moved back to Berlin. It was much too fast for them to have appreciated being in another national capital. To them, Beethoven's birthplace looked like just another urban area with a freeway through it.

About forty kilometers downriver from Bonn was Cologne, the largest city in North Rhine Westphalia with more than one million residents, plus suburbs. The driver let them out near a huge cathedral in the city known to the Germans as *Köln*. They set their luggage and their bodies down on a bench in the plaza in front of the cathedral and discussed their next move. A wide variety of Germans and foreigners stood in or walked through the plaza. They wondered how long they could sit on the bench before being asked to make a small donation to a vagrant, but then they realized that they, too, resembled vagrants.

Thinking about an evening meal and a place to sleep, they found a public restroom near the plaza. They walked back across the plaza in the late afternoon, and sat down again. An older man, probably homeless, pointed at their panniers and said something in German, which they interpreted as an offer to search through their gear for something to eat or wear.

"*Nein!*" Roger said resoundingly. The man backed away, with a sad look on his face, then made the same offer to some people sitting on another bench, who also refused him.

"Hell of a way to eke out a living," Eric commented after the beggar left.

"True, but as we brought just the bare necessities of clothing with us, and we're looking for something to eat ourselves, I didn't think it was a very good idea to let him take whatever he wanted. What do you think?"

"He's in no danger of freezing to death here and now, even in that ragged coat he's wearing."

"Probably not. So what is the panhandler to do?"

"What are we to do for a place to sleep? Find a park?"

"I don't have any better suggestions right now, unless we can find an Internet café. A good start would be to find a restaurant or pub. Shall we?"

A few blocks from the plaza, they dined on fish and chips and beer in an eatery. The meal was filling, if nothing else. Afterward, they wandered back toward the familiar plaza. The one Internet café they came across was closed for the day. The sun was on the west horizon, and noticeably fewer people were in the plaza. They took their journals from their panniers and tried to catch up to the present, as they had been a day behind for several days.

An older, slightly built man, casually dressed in a white shirt, white slacks and white shoes, had been observing people in the plaza, then turned his attention to Roger and Eric. He was obviously not a beggar, nor was he a wealthy industrialist. He approached them and, with a friendly smile, greeted them in a language that sounded Italian to Eric and Greek to Roger, whose knowledge of Romance languages was far worse than Eric's.

Eric responded with the Spanish greeting, *"Hola,"* and Roger just nodded. The man said some more things that Eric did not recognize. The man spoke more slowly and made some pantomime-like gestures. He had something he wanted to tell them, other than just making idle conversation, but they were not sure what it was. He continued talking, pointing at their sleeping bags, and waving them to follow him. He wanted to take them to a place to sleep, they reasoned.

At first, they were suspicious of the man. Why was this stranger, who did not even speak their language, so concerned for their welfare, they asked themselves. They were hesitant to follow him, but he was persistent. He offered to help carry their luggage, but they refused, still suspicious of his motives. They followed him, cautiously.

For nearly twenty blocks they followed this mysterious man, while he chattered away in Italian. He spoke at length about the Catholic Church, but all they could gather was that he was a devout Catholic, or something similar. He seemed to know his way around the streets and high-rise apartment buildings of Cologne in the dark. They were still unsure if they were being led to a B&B, hotel, Salvation Army shelter for the homeless, or a convenient place for a mugging. Somehow, their curiosity kept them in tow.

The man motioned that he had brought them to their destination for the night, a building of several stories with numerous lights on inside. They could not identify the building until they saw the International Youth Hostel logo on a sign on the front of the building. Eric and Roger looked at each other in silence and bewilderment, overwhelmed by their pleasant surprise. They immediately dropped their guard and did all they could to make the man feel like a trusted friend, which he was.

They registered for the night in the hostel, and let the man carry their handlebar bags up to their dormitory. Once they saw him in the light of the hallway, they could see that their benefactor was a Catholic priest—Eric could, anyway. They set their gear on their bunks, and then the priest blessed them before leaving. They thanked him with a simple *grazie*, which he understood. He left, perhaps to help some other beleaguered travelers find shelter. The two other hostel guests in the room spoke just enough English to say they were from Japan.

"We keep getting assistance from unexpected sources, like American soldiers, German women and Italian priests. Makes me wonder who is watching over us."

"Some really weird things have happened to us lately. Not that I'm complaining, mind you."

"I'm glad that guy found us, and resisted our efforts to resist his efforts to help us. I really didn't want to sleep in another park in a city the size of this one. Cologne is so bloody foreign to us, and we just arrived here."

"Luck has a way of finding us once in a while. Bad luck, usually, but not this time."

"We deserve a little solace. We've both had it rough lately."

They spent the remainder of the evening writing in their journals. In the plaza, they had thought they were through writing for the day, but now they had something to add that was well worth mentioning. Some simple acts of kindness they received from strangers in recent days had made quite an impression on them.

47.

A second consecutive restful night for Roger and Eric struck them as unusual, but they were not complaining when they arose from their bunks. They still wondered how the Italian priest found them and knew what they needed, and they were still glad he did. Roger's anxiety had been replaced by a feeling of loss. He showed no emotion, but he was also uncharacteristically quiet and sullen.

The hostel breakfast of tea and two slices of rye bread with cream cheese and cherry jam was most appetizing but hardly filling. They sat with their two Japanese roommates, both sides attempting to make some understandable conversation. They gathered their gear, checked out of the hostel, and took a westbound street in search of a ride.

Traffic was light, which did not surprise them on a Sunday morning. The street where they were standing led to the highway to Aachen, a city near the Belgian and Dutch borders, according to their map. They wanted to get closer than Aachen to Calais, but they chose that as a good direction to start. They expected to spend the night in any one of three nations: Netherlands, Belgium or France, a choice that was entirely new to them.

Eric and Roger alternated curb duty for about half an hour. An employee came out of a nearby office and started a conversation, even though he spoke no English and quickly learned that his audience did not understand German significantly. A jolly man, he was amused by their thus-far unsuccessful attempt to hitch a ride. His word for the practice was "autothumbing," which they clearly understood. He wished them luck and went back into his office.

A police car stopped a block down the road from where they were standing. The police stayed in their car, but their presence meant trouble to the two Americans, who were about to look for a different place to hitchhike when two cyclists approached them.

"You're not likely to get any rides with them waiting there," one of the cyclists said in a British accent. "They've been known to harass hitchhikers."

"We know, all too well," Eric said. "We're about to find another place to stand. No one would be crazy enough to pick us up here."

The conversation continued for a few minutes, with no particular topic. The cyclists continued on their way and, soon, the police got bored and also left after Eric and Roger walked around a corner, out of sight, and then returned to their spot after the police had gone.

More than an hour after they began "autothumbing," a Belgian couple stopped and offered them a ride to Antwerp. The Belgians were a young couple, perhaps in their early thirties, and dressed as if they had attended some formal occasion. Eric and Roger set their gear in the trunk of the small car and sat in the back seat with the couple's poodle, who was named for an all-too-familiar American beagle caricature. The Belgians spoke English as well as their native tongue, Walloon French, and said they were on their way home to the city of Antwerp in the province of the same name. The two Americans knew little about Antwerp, and all the rest of Belgium for that matter, but the kindness of the first Belgians they met left them with a favorable outlook.

The Belgians conversed easily with them as the man drove westward toward the Dutch border. A radio report in French announced, as interpreted by the woman, that flights out of London were being delayed by a strike. The news was definitely not what the Americans wanted to hear. The woman changed the subject of conversation and soon they were back in good spirits.

Crossing the border from North Rhine-Westfalia, Germany, into Limburg, Netherlands, was a new experience for Eric and Roger and old hat for the Belgians. Several uniformed men approached the car and glanced inside through the windows. Looking unconcerned, one of the guards wished the four occupants of the car a pleasant journey through the Netherlands, and the man continued driving. Roger and Eric were disappointed again that no one stamped their passports. The journey through the southern tip of the Netherlands was brief and uneventful. The scenery was bright green but mostly flat, even though it was considered the highlands of Holland.

Another border crossing, from Limburg, Netherlands, into Limburg, Belgium, was similar to the previous one. Again, no passports were inspected or stamped. The provinces of Limburg and Antwerp were also mostly low-lying flatland, but the vegetation flourished everywhere. Eric and Roger regretted not being on their bicycles. They were unable to appreciate any of the places they passed through in automobiles. They made mental notes of all the things they saw from car windows that they wanted to come back and see from their bicycles.

The Belgians let them out somewhere in Antwerp, the second largest city in Belgium, with a population of some 480,000 people, plus many more in the suburbs. To the Belgians, it was *Antwerpen*. Once again, the Americans wondered why their own language had a different name for a European city than what the locals called it. They were in another big foreign city without a clue as to where exactly they were or how to get anywhere.

Knowing that a youth hostel stood somewhere among the thousands of gray buildings surrounding them, they gathered their gear in their arms and launched their trek. They had not eaten lunch, and they anticipated a long walk between their present location and the hostel, so their top priority was to find something to eat.

A sidewalk vendor sold them some sandwiches and French fries, which they carried over to the base of a statue to eat. They sat on stone blocks that formed the foundation of a statue of four cast figures, two climbing and two chiseling stones, with the Flemish inscription "*Aan Bovmeester Appelmans*" on the backdrop. The whole scene stood against the gray brick wall of a building. A policeman saw them sitting on the base of the statue, walked up to them, and said something that they did not understand.

"I think he wants us to find another place to sit," Eric said to Roger.

"No, no," the policeman said, in plain English. "Please be sure to discard your rubbish in a proper receptacle."

"Yes, of course," Roger said. The policeman's command of English took him by surprise.

The policeman thanked them and left.

"The police certainly seem to find us easily."

"We probably look like a couple of dweebs. If you were a policeman, you wouldn't want any dweebs causing trouble on your beat, either."

"Probably not."

The policeman must have been doing his job well, for they could not see rubbish strewn anywhere around them. They were impressed by the overall cleanliness of Antwerp. It was one place where they would have liked to spend more time. A tower with a large clock resembling Big Ben stood not far away. The scaffolding surrounding it was an indication that the Belgians wanted to keep their city clean and attractive.

A man with a monkey and an organ mounted on a cart parked his cart near the statue. He cranked the organ while the monkey carried the cup around to the gathering crowd of spectators. Roger dropped a coin in the cup and took some photographs. The monkey got a bit testy with some children who tried to pet him, and the organ grinder had to restrain his pet.

When the excitement subsided, they began the long walk to the hostel. They had its address from a booklet they picked up at the Cologne hostel, but they were still disoriented and some five to ten kilometers away from it. Meanwhile, the sun disappeared behind ever-darkening clouds and then reappeared, repetitiously. To them, most of the buildings looked the same, and they suspected they were taking the long way to get there. About halfway there, they encountered a trio of Germans on single-speed bicycles who were also destined for the hostel. The Germans, who spoke English very well, rode slowly and led them to the hostel.

The *Vlaamse Jeugdherberger Op Sinjoorke* of Antwerp was quite modern and, like the rest of the city, beautifully maintained. A bit tired from the long walk while carrying their gear in their arms, they opted to eat supper at the hostel for a small surcharge. The menu consisted of soup, rye bread and tea, but enough of everything was available that they were satisfied. Only a handful of other people were registered for the night, so they had a choice of bunks.

With several hours of daylight still, Eric and Roger left the hostel after supper to tour a ship museum within a castle on the banks of what they thought to be the Scheldt River. The city lay near the navigable mouth of a short river formed by the confluences of several other rivers, including the Scheldt, Lys, Senne, Demer, Nethe and others. The Scheldt estuary looked like an ideal place for shipbuilding and related industries, sheltered from the North Sea by the Beveland Islands of the Dutch province of Zeeland.

They saw some things in the ship museum they had not seen previously. Roger the engineering student was interested in the structures of earlier whaling vessels. The nautical artifacts contrasted sharply with the military museums of England and Scotland.

A fierce but brief thundershower struck as they left the museum. They waited out the rain beneath an archway attached to the castle. When the rain diminished to a trickle, they walked back to the hostel but again had difficulty finding it.

Back at the hostel, they showered their daily sweat off, then joined some of the hostel guests in the common room for tea. Some other people had registered in the hostel while they were out, including an Indian woman, a graduate student from Bangalore. They conversed with the woman and drank more tea. They wrote in their journals while one guest, a young man who spoke English with a strong German accent, produced a guitar and accompanied himself. A few others, including the three Germans who had led Eric and Roger to the hostel, harmonized with him. By bedtime, the hostel was as lively as it was comfortably modern.

"May I?" Eric extended his hands when the man offered his guitar. "Any ideas, Squire?"

"How about the theme from *The Brady Bunch*?"

"I was considering the theme from *Gilligan's Island*."

"Great minds think alike, almost!"

Cable television had poisoned their minds. Eric began playing the guitar. He sang lead while Roger added harmonies to *Rendezvous with Rhonda Sue*, a song they had composed and last performed together at a high school assembly, about three and a half years earlier. Eric had added a verse and embellished the guitar part in the interim, but Roger hardly missed a note of the modified version.

"Edsel & the Studebakers' reunion tour," Eric noted at the end of the song. "One night only! In Belgium, no less. Or are we the Two Nicators?"

Roger could not suppress a broad grin. "It's good to be back!"

They took a bow as the other hostelers applauded, then Eric handed the guitar back to its owner. They sat in for more songs led by the German, who sang in French and Dutch as well as his own language.

"Our tour is winding down quickly, Chief," Roger lamented as he and Eric took to their respective bunks. "I hope we've accomplished all we intended."

"I guess we have, Squire. We never did get inside the Tower of London, we missed Sanchez, and most important, we didn't get to go to Bern to be with Yvette and Desiree, but we'll just have to live without those things this time." Eric thought about Roger's very unexpected offer from Marianne's father, but decided to say nothing about it. Roger would bring it up if he wanted to talk about it.

"We didn't get to the Alps, and we missed some of the neighboring nations around here, but we can always come back for more."

"We got knocked up by a good-looking hotel clerk in England, but it wasn't nearly as much fun as I was expecting."

"Kind of a letdown, wasn't it? Getting knocked up is way over-rated."

"Are you already planning another tour?" Eric asked.

"I've been thinking about it. This part of the world looks so small on a map compared to North America, yet it's so much more diverse per square kilometer. Every time we come back here, we'll want to come again to see something we missed. That alone should give you plenty of incentive to pursue your romance with Yvette."

Roger and Eric had two days to get back to London, and it was a long way to hitchhike from Antwerp.

Yvette and her mother were loading their luggage into their car, in preparation for the drive to Geneva. Their relatives had gone home after the funeral, and everything was getting back to normal. Yvette had talked at length to her parents and relatives about Eric and Roger. She was feeling the letdown from all the excitement and turmoil of the last two weeks.

"Are you sure you're all right, dear?" Mrs. Hoffman asked. Her daughter's melancholy was as plain as day. "You're taking your grandmother's death very hard. She always wanted her children and grandchildren to be happy. She said that many times. It was very important to her."

"It's not so much that, although I do miss her. I'm still thinking about how disappointed Eric was when I talked to him yesterday. He was as hurt as I was. I wish he were here!"

Mrs. Hoffman was about to get in the car when she had an idea. "Why don't you call Eric's friends in London before we leave. Ask them to have him give you a call before he returns to America."

"That's not much consolation."

"No, but it's better than nothing. You don't want him going home on such a sad note. You should never part that way. Make sure he takes home fond memories of your time together."

Yvette smiled at her mother. She had just turned fifty, and was still an incurable romantic. Yvette went in the house and called the Evans at the number Eric had given her. Her confidence and mood were rising already.

48.

Classical guitar music broadcast through the public address system awakened all the hostel guests at 6:30. The night had been warm, and Eric and Roger slept comfortably without any blankets. The guitar music was soothing and irritating at the same time.

Breakfast was essentially the same as that served the previous day in Cologne—bread with jam and tea or coffee. Belgian waffles were not on the menu. They sat with their Indian and German friends and discussed where they expected to be by the end of the day. They wanted to stay in Belgium all the way to Adinkerke, West Flanders, if they could. After breakfast, they packed their luggage, checked out of the hostel, and cast themselves at the mercy of Belgian motorists.

Cold, intermittent rain made hitchhiking a dismal prospect, but they wanted to try it before resorting to other means of transportation. They started on an entrance ramp to a motorway, westbound, and got a ride toward Ghent, East Flanders. A woman and her daughter gave them a ride to a truck stop on the outskirts of Ghent, locally spelled *Gent*. The woman explained that she could not take them into Belgium's third largest city because she feared the police there might give her a ticket for transporting hitchhikers. They soon regretted accepting the ride when they had to walk through nearly a kilometer of tall, wet grass to get into Ghent. No one promised hitchhiking would be all fun and no work.

In Ghent, they supplemented their hostel breakfast with victuals they purchased at a small grocery store near the highway. They stood with thumbs pleading to motorists for an hour, until someone stopped and gave them a short ride out of Ghent. Some walking, another brief ride, and some more walking got them to Oostende, a coastal town in West Flanders, by mid-afternoon.

They walked along the beach at Oostende, which was closed to swimmers due to wind, waves and rain. They talked about how they would have enjoyed spending some time on the Mediterranean coast of Spain, France or Italy, where swimming conditions probably would have been more desirable than the North Sea. That idea became part of their plan for their next European jaunt, whenever that would be. They spent most of their remaining euros on a late lunch and train ride to Dunkirk, Nord, in France.

Passing through Adinkerke as planned, they again found nothing eventful about crossing the French border. In Dunkirk, they saw a small marker denoting the site of the famous escape by French and British troops from the Germans in May 1940. Other than that, the scenic seaside town exemplified tranquillity. There were no other obvious remnants of war.

The afternoon turned to evening, and they had only a few euros between them. They tried hitchhiking, but not surprisingly, without success. A bus stop was nearby, and when the westbound bus finally came, they decided to give it a try. They did not expect to find any currency exchange offices open that late in the small towns, and they assumed they would be spending the night beneath a bridge somewhere in Dunkirk if they did not have enough money for the bus fare.

As the last passengers to board the bus, they looked at the sign inside the bus that told them the fares. They pooled their money and, somehow, came up with just enough to pay for two tickets to Calais. They were left with less than one euro between them, but they were assured of getting to Calais without having to wait a day.

"It's been nearly twelve hours since we left Antwerp," Eric said when they were ready to board a ferryboat in Calais in the evening.

"I was rather hoping we'd spend the night in Romford with the Evans," Roger said. "Slim chance of that."

"We're still several hours away from Romford, at best."

They boarded a ferry after dark and arrived in Dover about an hour later. They used their time on the boat to write in their journals and buy a bottle of Champagne for the Evans as they had promised. Eric picked the cheapest bottle with the name of the city of Reims on it. All the Mumms and Piper-Heidsieck Champagnes cost a bit more than he could afford. The on-board liquor store accepted his travelers cheque. They were both getting tired, but they were not ready to sleep yet.

In Dover at approximately 23:00, Eric wearily stood roadside for a few minutes until a motorist gave him and Roger a ride to Canterbury. They were just a bit surprised to get a ride that late at night, but they were prepared to unstuff their sleeping bags and sleep wherever necessary. At least Canterbury was dry. The rain had not followed them across the channel.

Still clad in short pants and a T-shirt, Roger ducked into a dark doorway to change into jeans and a rugby shirt while Eric held out his thumb. Eric then changed while Roger thumbed. Traffic was light and Canterbury was lifeless around midnight, but they maintained their efforts to secure a ride. A few motorists passed, and all of them ignored the two hitchhikers.

"They're all giving me that sneer. We can't really expect anyone to offer us a ride at this time of night, can we?"

"Let's give it another half hour. Right here is as good a place to sleep as any, if we have to."

By 1:00, Roger and Eric could barely keep their eyes open and were ready to make camp in downtown Canterbury, when a man in his thirties, driving a Volkswagen van, offered them a ride to London. They accepted without hesitation, and were finally on their way again. The van was comfortably equipped, and its driver said he had been driving across northern Africa for two years and was on his way home to London.

Eric sat in the front passenger seat and talked to the driver. Roger slumped onto a bench seat in the rear and fell asleep. Eric was usually the more tired of the two, but he had a little more energy in him than usual, and he did not want Roger to have to bear the burden all the time of being pleasant company to the driver when they were hitchhiking. He felt like he owed it to Roger after Roger's brilliant maneuvers—or was it just luck?—in Munich and Aschaffenburg.

The driver stopped at an all-night restaurant somewhere near the southeastern edge of greater London. He and Eric went into the restaurant for tea, while Roger dozed in the back seat. The driver let them out at Paddington Station in London at 4:30, where they had thirty-five minutes to wait for the first train of the day.

"How strange it is that I had a good time on the Continent even though we didn't accomplish anything we wanted to do. No Yvette and Desiree, no Danny Sanchez, no Bern, your engagement disaster. Our only real success is that we got back to London on time, I think. What day is this?"

"Seems like we left Antwerp a long, long time ago." Roger's eyes were barely open. "It doesn't look that far from London on a map."

"When we get back to Colorado, I think I'm going to sleep in my dear old bed for about a week." Eric paid no attention to what either he or Roger said. "I like it here, but I'm ready to go back to the U.S. Are you?"

"I'm ready for just about anything."

The two sat on a bench in the deserted train station, trying to stay awake and thinking about all the things they would have to say to their families and friends. The thought of another sleepless night, the airplane ride, had not yet occurred to them.

Chapter VII: *Epilogue*

49.

Eric and Roger were among the very few passengers on the first train through Paddington Station on that pleasant Tuesday morning in early August. They were barely able to stand or walk by the time they arrived at the Evans' house at 7:30. Inga and Peter were not surprised to see them so early, having suspected that they traveled all night.

"Breakfast is delicious, Inga." Roger managed to find a trace of energy within himself. A cup of strong tea helped.

Eric added an affirmative grunting sound that indicated his agreement.

"Yvette called for you, Eric. She wants to speak to you one more time before you return home," Peter said. "Sounds like you've found yourself a very nice girl, that one."

Eric smiled at the comment. "Yes, I certainly have!"

"And Marianne called here for you, from Hawaii," Inga said. "Asked for you to return her call as soon as possible. Anytime, day or night, she said. She sounded rather urgent. I hope that's a good sign for you. I told her I didn't know when you'd return, but that I thought it would be just a day or two before your flight back home. She said she has a new cell phone, and that's the number she gave me."

"Why bother now? I'll talk to her when I get home, maybe. I finally got through to her house in Hawaii, but her dad intercepted the call. Her parents want us to break the engagement. Even offered me ten thousand dollars to break it. I never did speak to Marianne." Roger's response, delivered without much inflection, left them stunned.

Peter broke the silence. "Your intuition was true, then. Wish we had something encouraging to say."

"It ain't over 'til it's over, as they say in baseball," Eric said. "Give her a chance to speak for herself. The cell phone number should get you directly to her."

"Aye, let her have her say," Peter agreed.

Roger looked at Inga for a moment, silently soliciting her opinion before proceeding. She hesitantly nodded in approval. Everyone continued eating in silence for a few minutes, no one making eye contact with anyone else. Even Vickie, normally very opinionated, said nothing.

"All right, I'll call her this afternoon. I might as well hear it directly from her."

More silence followed.

"I didn't do so well, either, during the last week." Eric described their unexpectedly early parting with Yvette and Desiree, and their unsuccessful attempt to locate Danny Sanchez.

"Have some more tea, dear."

Inga was a little nervous, and it showed. Roger's announcement certainly caught her off guard. She and Peter listened intently while Eric talked about France, Germany and Belgium. The Evans had been to some of the places where they had been, and had similar impressions of those places.

After breakfast, they took a short ride with Peter. The ride rejuvenated them. They took their bicycles apart, cleaned them superficially, and packed them in their crates. By noon, the bicycles were ready to be loaded on an airplane. They missed their bicycles during their week on the Continent, but knew they would not have covered as much ground as they did in so little time on their bicycles. Perhaps in a few years, they thought, they could come back and tour Spain, France, Italy, Switzerland, the Benelux countries or Germany by bicycle for six weeks.

Noontime dinner, again prepared by Inga, was the best meal Roger and Eric had eaten for quite some time. Peter returned from his morning errands, and the four ate roast lamb, potatoes, rolls and gravy. They washed the food down with the Champagne Eric brought from France.

"Peter and I are going over to Mr. Smythe's shop this afternoon to get my frame. Care to join us?" Talking about the frame seemed to uplift Roger's mood just a little. He had called Mr. Smythe in the morning. Smythe gave him the only good news Roger had heard recently—his frame was ready.

"No thanks. I promised my sisters some tennis paraphernalia from Wimbledon, so I'm going to ride the Tube there to get something."

"Tennis is such a preposterous game. How could anyone..."

"You and I know that, but my dear sisters don't. They'd never forgive me if I didn't."

"That store we saw a few weeks ago ought to be open today." Roger handed Eric a twenty-pound note. "Get them something extra, and it'll be from me."

"What's the occasion?" Eric asked.

"Marcia's always good to me, and Mimi's still my favorite virgin."

"And you think she'll stay that way forevermore if you bring her something nice from Europe?"

"Probably not, but it's a nice thought. I'll see you here around suppertime, if not later. Don't get lost."

Roger and Peter went to Henry Smythe's shop to inspect Roger's new frame. Mr. Smythe had rejected its first paint job, and sent it back to the enamelers. The new paint job, as Roger and Peter knew the moment they saw it, was fabulous. Mr. Smythe had pressed Roger's new headset cups into the head tube, and attached the fork to the frame. Roger brought his camera along and, like a proud father with his newborn child, had Peter photograph him holding his handsome frame alongside Mr. Smythe in front of Smythe's garage.

The frame had a brilliant metallic, aquamarine finish, decorated with a few decals bearing Mr. Smythe's distinctive yet modest logo. Cut-away lugs, filed with painstaking precision, held Reynolds' best double-butted tubes and stays together at optimum angles. All the necessary details graced the frame: plenty of brazed-on bosses, a sloping fork crown, and drop-forged fork tips and dropouts. The frame was nothing less than a work of art.

Roger tried to suppress an ear-to-ear grin. "Let us pray that I don't crash on it before I wear it out."

"It came back from the enamelers just in the nick of time, yesterday in fact," Mr. Smythe said. He had bags under his eyes from the fourteen-hour workdays of the past two weeks, but he was satisfied. "I had strict deadlines with you and some other customers, and I'm pleased to say I met them all." He gestured at a racing frame in a work stand he had begun to assemble with a Campagnolo Record gruppo.

"You look like you've been working hard," Peter commented. "Somebody's going to be very pleased with this one." He took a moment to admire the frame in the work stand, and read the custom label on the down tube. "Whitcombe Lenoir? It's a beauty!"

"Yes, I think their new racer will be very pleased with it. I've put in long hours on that one." Mr. Smythe was as tired as he looked, but he knew he would have enough money to pay for his daughter's wedding without going into debt. His young American customer was also very satisfied, and that made him proud of his work. He would never become a millionaire building frames, but he felt like one sometimes.

While Roger and Peter were out patronizing the arts, Inga took the liberty of washing Eric's and Roger's laundry, and Eric took a bath. Eric had intended to wash the dirty clothes himself, but he was not surprised to find Inga had already done it when he finished bathing. The Evans treated Roger and him too well, he thought.

Eric walked to the Dagenham East station, boarded a train, and arrived in Wimbledon about two and a half hours and two trains later. He was relieved to be able to travel somewhere without a sleeping bag in one hand and his panniers in the other. He felt a little uneasy, not having slept the previous night, but he was determined to accomplish his journey to Wimbledon. He had forgotten to take his epilepsy medicine since the ferryboat ride across the channel the previous evening, and that also affected him.

A clever idea, based on an unlikely possibility, struck Eric as he was walking from the train to the station exit. He saw a red telephone booth and made several calls with the help of a plastic card. He spoke to Yvette for nearly an hour, and they were both in much better spirits than they had been when he called from Frankfurt. The calls completed, he left the station smiling and feeling lucky once again. Not in any hurry, he stopped in a salon for a haircut and shave. Forty minutes later, his hair looked and smelled great, and he hardly noticed the discomfort in his head.

The sporting goods store they had seen previously in Wimbledon was open this time, and Eric went inside and bought several polo shirts for several people. He chose one shirt for himself. He also bought a shirt for Roger, knowing that Roger would probably want one, too.

Eric had plenty of things on his mind when he left the store, especially thoughts about what he was planning to do as a result of the telephone calls he had made. He was about to cross the main thoroughfare between the store and the train station, and he looked to his left out of habit to see if any cars were coming. None were, so he started across the street. Out of the corner of his right eye, he saw a dark green, older-model Citröen coming toward him very fast, and only a few meters away.

"Jesus!" Eric realized too late which direction cars would approach from, and he jumped back toward the curb as the car swerved to avoid him. He lay in the street, his sack of shirts and tennis items dumped behind him, and he could hear a string of epithets from the driver directed at him.

The driver, a young man about Eric's age, cursed at him and continued driving away from the scene without any concern for Eric. The voice faded into the distance as the car got farther away, but Eric did not need any more verbal abuse.

Dazed but not seriously injured, Eric collected himself and his purchases, and thought about how much that car looked like the one in North Yorkshire with which he and Roger had some fateful encounters. The driver was different this time, but almost as hateful as the previous one.

"Are you all right?" A pedestrian who had witnessed the incident from the other side of the street ran across to help Eric get back on his feet.

"I will be, in a few days." Eric was grateful for her concern. His hands were shaking.

"You could've been killed!"

She continued to politely lecture him on traffic safety, but Eric did not really hear any of it, his mind wandering off to another time and place. They finished picking up his purchases, and she wished him well and reaffirmed her warning as she left.

Eric walked uneasily to the Underground station, his knees weak and his fingers groping for change in his pocket to buy a train ticket. He was furious at the driver's apathy and rudeness, even though he knew he was legally but inadvertently at fault. He would not treat a Briton in the United States like that if the Briton looked the wrong way before crossing a street. His brain felt like it was pounding inside his skull, and his skin was tense, as if it had shrunk a few sizes. His lips quivered and he detected a foul odor, even though his sense of smell was all but destroyed by his brain injury. He knew the odor was entirely in his imagination, the aura preceding a grand mal seizure. He pressed his back against a wall in the passenger waiting area, breathing rapidly and deeply, fighting the major seizure that was trying to engulf him. Several long minutes passed before the train arrived. He slowly pushed himself away from the wall and boarded the train, his respiration gradually slowing to normal.

Sitting alone and deliberately avoiding other passengers, Eric contemplated the scenario of having a seizure on the train and losing consciousness. Would anyone come to his aid, he wondered. Would someone steal his wallet or his polo shirts? Or, would everyone just ignore him, assuming him to be a drunk? In any case, no one would know whom to notify.

At the next station, a girl of about seventeen years boarded the train and sat down next to Eric. Dressed in a leather miniskirt, black fishnet hosiery, a tight sweater, stiletto heals and some outrageous jewelry and makeup, she studied Eric for a moment.

"Pissed to the gills so early in the day?"

"No, I'm about to have a s...s...seizure." Eric stuttered in a voice that was barely more than a whisper. Trying to focus on something, he found himself counting the number of places her face had been pierced for jewelry.

"You really are pissed, aren't you?"

"No, honest, I'm knock drunt! I'm drock... I mean, I'm...not...drunk!" Eric winced and clasped his mouth with his hand after a jaw spasm caused him to bite his lip.

"The conductor will throw you out if you vomit in here." She still did not believe Eric was anything other than inebriated. "He could have you arrested for public drunkenness." She discreetly sniffed him, but he did not reek of alcohol. He smelled more like fragrant soap. His collar and forehead were decorated with minute hair clippings. She nudged a little closer to him and detected the aroma of a hair salon.

"Listen to me! I'm not pissed and I'm not going to vomit. I'm an epileptic and I'm having a seizure. That's why I bit my lip just now."

"Epileptic? How did you catch that?" she asked, as if he had leprosy.

"It's not a disease, just a symptom of a head injury."

"You're not from around here, are you?" She studied him some more before speaking again. "Are you lost?"

He shook his head. "I'm a foreigner, but I don't think I'm lost. Yet."

The conversation helped Eric regain his composure to some degree. He somehow managed to get back to Romford without further ado after the girl reminded him to get off the train when it stopped at the station he told her he wanted. She squeezed his hand momentarily as he was about to leave the subway, and wished him well. Once again, he was grateful for the kindness of strangers in this faraway land. His natural color was replacing the paleness that had been his face for nearly two hours.

When Eric returned to the Evans' house, they were preparing a light supper, and Roger was showing his new frame to Melanie in the garden. Roger was so eager to show it to Eric and explain its intricate detail that he hardly noticed Eric's distraught countenance. The frame was indeed a masterpiece in every aspect, and Eric began to wish he had ordered one for himself.

"How's your romance with Rory going?" Eric expected to hear a dreamy description of how Rory was everything that Eric himself was not.

Melanie seemed mildly insulted by the suggestion. "Who? Rory? Haven't seen or heard from him in, what? Two, three weeks now?"

Eric was surprised, and he waited for an explanation. He was also surprised at how easily he was making conversation with her, without any prompting from Roger.

"All he wanted to do was drink Guinness with his friends and talk about football. And cricket. And auto racing. Sports, beer and all that rubbish. Boring, it was!"

"I'm sorry it didn't work out for you." Eric was not at all sorry in reality, but he had to be polite.

"Bollocks! Nothing to be sorry about, that!"

Melanie asked about Eric's shopping excursion, and continued talking to him for another half hour. "Well, I'd best be going. Mum's preparing jerk chicken for supper, my favorite! Wouldn't want to be late for that, now would we?"

Inga peered out the back door before Melanie left. "Join us for evening tea, won't you, dear? Roger and Eric have lots to tell us about their travels on the Continent. About seven?"

"Yes, thank you, Mrs. Evans. I'd love to. Seven it is." Melanie flashed that irresistible bright smile at the two Americans on her way out the gate.

Inga summoned everyone inside to prepare for supper. Vickie set the table while Peter began carrying food into the dining area.

"I wired a bouquet of forget-me-nots from a florist here in Romford. Took a bit of finagling, but I'm glad I did it." Roger's sorrowful mood and weariness were nowhere to be found.

"Wired a bouquet of forget-me-nots to whom?"

"I can't recall."

"Yvette and Desiree, maybe?"

Roger snapped his fingers. "Must have been." The flowers were actually roses and both he and Eric knew very well where Roger sent them.

"Good work, Squire. Why didn't I think of that?"

"We each got an e-mail from a certain Sgt. Sanchez in Bavaria," Roger added.

"What did he say?"

"'Sorry I missed you. Will see you in Colorado at Christmas,'" Roger quoted. "It's been quite a day. I also called Marianne from a pay phone. She was asleep when I called, but she answered quickly, before anyone else could, this time. Actually, I called her new cell phone, so I suppose no one else would have answered it."

"And?"

"A senator from Hawaii has a son, a few years older than we are, who just graduated from Harvard law school." Roger was emotionally empty, like someone who had just been released after a long stretch in solitary confinement. "She didn't say if he's a state senator or a U.S. senator, but it doesn't matter. Her parents want her to consider marrying this senator's lawyer son. The connection would be a good one for both families, she says. You know, big business and politics."

"So she's dumping you for some Ivy League bigshot? I can't believe it!"

"No, it's nothing like that. She wants to elope. With me." Roger let the idea linger a moment before he continued. "She begged me not to accept the ten grand. I said we'd discuss it when we both return to Colorado. She admitted she hadn't told her parents we were engaged, until a few days ago. Her sister-in-law told her parents I was too low-brow for her, in so many words. She was very upset, of course. I was a fool for doubting her love for me, but she could have been more forthcoming about things."

"Why didn't someone tell you that when you called a few weeks ago?"

"She'd hoped to have it all ironed out with her parents before I returned from Europe, so that I wouldn't be in the middle of her family squabble. Her roommates knew a little about what was going on, but they weren't sure what to say when I called, so they just ignored me and hoped I wouldn't call back."

"What are you going to do?"

"I want to think long and hard about it. At this point, I don't know what to do. When I get home, I'm going to get on my mountain bike, go for a ride, and think about it some more. The saddle of a bicycle on a lonely road is the best place to be when you need to think."

"We're so sorry for him," Inga said, "and for her, too, I'm sure."

"If not for bad luck, you wouldn't have any luck at all," Eric said. "I wish things had turned out better for you."

Inga and Peter nodded in agreement.

"I do, too." Thoughts of Marianne were too much for Roger to bear at the moment, so he changed the subject. "Has your day been as exciting as mine?"

"Has it ever! Let me tell you about how I almost became somebody's hood ornament. I was this close," Eric indicated a distance of about one centimeter with his thumb and index finger, "to having a grand mal seizure after that car almost hit me. It was another Citröen, just like the one in Harrogate!"

"Dreadful," Inga said. "You've certainly had your share of disasters this holiday, or near-disasters."

"Citröen makes fine cars," Peter added, "but lucky for you there aren't many in America."

"Did you find what you were looking for in Wimbledon?" Inga asked.

"Yes I did, and more," Eric said. "There is some good news in all of this. I called our airline from the Underground station near Wimbledon to find out about delaying my flight back to Denver by a week. Then I called Yvette and asked if she could meet me at the airport in Geneva. Actually, I spoke to her dad in Bern, and he told me she was in Geneva. So, I called her cell phone."

"I'm beginning to get the picture," Roger said. "I guess I'll be flying back to Denver alone tomorrow, and you're flying to Geneva for a week."

"That's the long and short of it," Eric said. "I hope you don't mind. This is really important to me. My flight to Geneva also leaves Heathrow tomorrow afternoon."

"I know it's important to you." Roger was genuinely impressed by Eric's mettle. "That would explain the haircut, too."

"I asked the hair stylist for a shag, and she slapped me! I settled on a buzz cut instead."

"Did you call your parents?"

"I did." Eric laughed at the thought. "My dad wasn't too keen on the idea, especially when I asked him to wire me some money. I asked him what he would have done, when he was a young buck. He started to see things my way after that."

"What about Yvette?" Roger asked.

"She was delighted with my change of plans," Eric said. "I'm going to help her and her mother ship some things from Geneva back to Bern, and clean out her grandmother's quarters. I think she lived in a retirement home of some sort. We probably won't get much time alone, but I'm looking forward to it. Her dad speaks great English, and he sounded as though he was expecting me. She must have talked about us at length."

Roger was dumbfounded. "He hasn't been this happy since...high school graduation. I still don't know why that was so special."

Eric could not hide a mischievous smile. "I'd rather not say."

"Sounds like he's in love, doesn't he, dear?" Inga said to Peter.

"He does indeed. We'll have to toast it this evening."

Eric had almost forgotten something. "I made one other call, too. Nancy's doing fine, expects to be done with her harness in another week or so. How did she put it? 'Me mum's drivin' me bats, she is. I canna wait to get back on t' road.' I didn't mention anything about Yvette to her. Nancy doesn't need to know that just yet."

"That sounds exactly like Nancy." Mention of Nancy reminded Roger of some of the fondest memories of his vacation. "I'll have to send Nancy a postcard with a picture of Rocky Mountain National Park when I get back on campus."

"I've accomplished a little something myself whilst you were traveling about. You two gave me the push I needed a few weeks ago," Inga said.

"What's that?"

"I'm on the last chapter of *Tom Jones*. I expect I'll finish it in a day or two."

"She's a lady, and much more!"

"I can see it!"

"That's why you should never say no!"

"We could go round and round on this one!"

"Just help yourself to my quips, to my yarns!"

"I can't wait to mow the green, green grass of home when I get there! After I put the new pussycat indoors."

The Evans, Melanie and their American friends drank tea in the parlor and reviewed their journey in Europe. Inga served spotted dick for dessert, which the Americans liked very much, to their pleasant surprise. Eric was still shaken while he talked about his brush with fate. Tomorrow, the Evans would take them to Dagenham East in the morning, and they would board their respective planes for Denver at 13:30 and Geneva at 15:10, tentatively, depending upon the French airport workers' strike.

"There might be some great spiritual, heavenly meaning in your incident today," Roger said after he and Eric were in their beds, "but I'm damned if I know what it is."

"A warning, maybe? A reminder?"

"Maybe. We'll probably never know for sure."

"Do you really believe in that sort of thing, or could it be one of those one-in-a-billion coincidences?"

"I don't know. I probably wouldn't admit it if I did believe in auguries. Maybe it was just a warning to look both ways very carefully before you cross the street, because you can't always be sure the oncoming drivers are driving the way you expect them to be driving, just like we learned in kindergarten."

"That would be the practical interpretation of it all. I guess there's no reason to lie awake thinking about it. See you in the morning, if you can drag yourself out of bed."

"Right." Roger was almost asleep before he finished saying it.

Eric and Roger fell asleep easily, not having been in that state for nearly forty hours. They were glad to be spending their last night in Europe in real beds, although Roger was actually on a cot, instead of in their sleeping bags on grass or cobblestone. Tomorrow night, Roger would be in his own bed back in the real world as he knew it, and Eric would be with his newfound love.

50.

On their last morning in England, Roger and Eric looked and felt just about the same way they did on their first morning in England. Roger's hair was a mess, but he was ready to greet the day. Eric looked like he was suffering from a hangover, even after a restful and much-needed sleep. Roger was excited to be going home, but he knew he would miss Europe, and Eric was certainly excited to be going to Geneva. The last six weeks might well have been the most significant six weeks of their lives. They would not soon forget any of it.

Breakfast with plenty of strong tea helped revive Eric. Peter and Inga would be driving them to the railway station in a few hours. They finished packing their luggage by midmorning and were ready to leave. Satisfied that they had everything that was theirs, they took one last look at the room that had been like home to them for six weeks, and went downstairs.

Outside the Evans' house, Roger snapped some photographs of the other three, then gave his camera to Inga and became one of the subjects of the next photograph. Roger looked unkempt now, compared to six weeks earlier when his haircut and beard trim were less than two weeks old. Eric felt a little strange without his whiskers, but he looked well prepared to meet Yvette and her parents.

With other matters to attend, the Evans saw Roger and Eric onto the train, exchanged handshakes and embraces, and bade their American friends a safe flight home.

"We've enjoyed having you stay with us," Peter said. "Hope you've enjoyed Great Britain."

"The pleasure's been ours!" Eric took the initiative for a change. "We want you to plan to visit us within the next few years."

"And bring Inga and Vickie next time," Roger added. "There are plenty more things we'd like to show you in Colorado."

"I want to see Disneyland, the Grand Canyon and the Statue of Liberty," Vickie said.

"You can see all three from my parents' front porch," Eric said. "But I recommend Pikes Peak and the Royal Gorge if you come to southern Colorado."

"We've been thinking about it, whilst you were riding about the northern part of the country," Inga said. "It's definitely in our plans."

"Splendid, then," Roger said. "Keep us informed, and thanks again for taking such good care of us. We're very grateful."

Eric smiled at Vickie one last time and put an arm around her shoulders. "Catch you in the funny papers."

"Cheerio, lads," Peter said. "All the best!"

The Evans went home and the two Americans boarded the District Line. After the long ride to Heathrow Airport, they ate lunch at one of the airport restaurants and watched the drizzle outside. The rain had greeted them when they arrived, and it had been so prevalent during their vacation that it hardly surprised them. Their flights, they learned, were delayed by two hours, not by the rain, but by the French airport workers' strike. Some weary travelers had been waiting for two days to board their flights.

Eric and Roger endured the indignity of airport security, found some seats on the concourse and spent the next hour reading some paperback books they had brought from home but not yet finished. Eric excused himself for a moment while Roger guarded their carry-on luggage.

Eric returned five minutes later. "Wow! I saw Jimi again in the men's room! Or maybe it was Sid or Jerry or Anna Nicole!"

"What's he doing here again?"

Eric got indignant. "If you must know, he was taking a…"

"No, no, I meant, why is he following us? It's really creepy when entertainment has-beens follow you around. He knows we're onto him."

"Especially when they've allegedly gone to a better place. I bet he has a UFO parked at one of the gates. He'll be out mowing patterns in the wheat fields after we leave."

They returned to reading for another hour or so. Tired of reading, they broke a long silence between them and reviewed their journey. Their experiences in Europe gave them much to think about, in addition to their journals and photographs that documented what they did.

"I'm going to be a zombie when I get to Denver," Roger said. "Your folks'll want to know, in full detail, what we did for six weeks, and I'll be too tired to speak."

"Worse yet, if Mimi is with them, she's going to interrogate you. Third degree. On top of all that, you'll still have a good three or four hours between the time your plane lands and when you're at home in your own bed. Then, your parents will have plenty of questions for you. One week later, I'll get the same treatment."

"Do you think we'll ever get to bed? I can imagine how you'll be when you get there, not having slept for so long. The lack of sleep has been getting to me, too, lately."

"I'll be tense and uneasy, no doubt, but you'll agree that I've survived some tough situations in recent weeks."

"Yes, you have. Never let it be said..." Roger started to say.

"...that you would deny anyone freedom of speech?" Eric interrupted.

"No, that's not what I was going to say. Don't interrupt my oration. Never let anyone say that you aren't now capable of anything you could do before your crash. I mean that, Chief. Six weeks ago, I wasn't sure you were up to this, but as it turned out, you had to drag me along in some places. Now, I have no doubts you're everything, physically, mentally and otherwise, that you've always been, maybe more."

"Thanks for saying that, Squire." Eric was genuinely pleased to hear it. "I might add that I feel a whole lot more assured than I did six weeks ago. I haven't had much self-confidence since that crash. Everything's been downhill, it seems, until just recently."

"I feel stronger, too, in another sense. We got an education that just isn't available in textbooks or classrooms. We both grew up a little."

"Are you ready to face Marianne?"

"Better yet, is she ready to face me? Elopement sounds very appealing to me right now. I have no respect for her parents. I'd disown mine if they offered her a bribe to dump me. I'll have plenty of time on the airplane to think about what I'm going to say to Marianne."

"Be sure your head is out of your arse before you make any big decisions. There's a lot at stake for you, you know."

"It will be, this time. Bet on it."

Trying not to sound maudlin, Eric took a moment to find just the right words to sum up their journey. "We made a good team, Squire."

Roger had no such reservations. "We made a damn good team! A great team! And I'd do it all over again in a heartbeat, even with all the troubles we had."

Eric did not doubt for a moment that he meant it. "Before Yvette and I hung up the phone last Saturday, we said to each other, 'I love you.' Do people really mean that or is it just small talk?"

Roger gave it some thought. "I think you both meant it. You would know better than I would whether either of you meant it."

"I think I know, but it could be some time before I'm really sure of it."

"You played your cards exceedingly well with Yvette. I'm envious."

"A lot of guys are, but, well, you know the drill."

"We've exchanged that gag more than a few times since seventh or eighth grade."

"We'll have to plan on taking our bicycles back to Europe again sometime, or our backpacks, climbing boots and a tent. I want to climb something in the Alps or the Pyrenees."

"I do, too. We have plenty yet to do here."

Eric and Roger continued to discuss what they had done and seen and what they missed in Europe. After six weeks together, they were still in good spirits with each other, and not at each other's throat as they had been a few times. They were talking about where their next bicycle tour would be, when Roger heard his boarding call.

"Would you mind picking me up in Denver in a week? I'll probably have a lot to tell you."

"I'll be anxious to hear it. Should I ask Mimi to come with me?"

"She'd love that, and so would I. See you in a week, and thanks for helping me get together with Yvette. It never would've happened without your help."

"Don't mention it." Roger smiled as they shook hands. "My pleasure."

Roger picked up his handlebar bag and walked toward the gate where a flight attendant was collecting boarding passes. He entered the airplane without looking back. Eric returned to his book without looking up again.

A few hours later, Eric entered the Geneva airport still thinking about how bad he felt seeing Roger off, his friend's life in a state of disarray that was apparent only to Eric and a few others. Just inside the gate a sweet, familiar voice interrupted his thoughts. Yvette looked even better than he remembered her.

"I thought I might never see you again, Chief." Yvette spoke the only English Eric could hear against a background of conversations in French. Her mother was seated in a nearby waiting area.

"I thought that, too." Eric embraced her very tightly. "Glad we were both wrong."

"I have many things planned for us."

"Then let's get started. Time is precious."

Yvette and Eric walked hand in hand through the concourse toward Yvette's mother. Eric's thoughts returned to how a mere bicycle tour had made such a difference in his and Roger's lives, and how much he wanted to do another one in a year.

🚲

About the Author

Bo Edwards (a pseudonym) has been active in bicycle commuting, touring and racing since the 1970s. Born, raised and formally educated in Colorado, he is a metallurgical engineer in his day job. His bicycle-touring experience includes Great Britain, the TransAmerica Trail, and Ride the Rockies in Colorado. He lives with his wife, daughters and grandson in Oregon. *Live to Ride* is his first novel.

The photograph of Bo on the cover was taken at the summit of Swaledale. The setting is mentioned in Subchapter 19.

🚲

www.ingramcontent.com/pod-product-compliance
Lightning Source LLC
Chambersburg PA
CBHW020340180626
46812CB00001B/283